Angels *without* Wings

THE PATH TO SACRIFICE
Book 2 of the Series

Angels without Wings

www.angelswithoutwingsseries.com

www.facebook.com/angelswithoutwingsseries

The Path to Sacrifice is the second book of the © *Angels
without Wings* series by author Chris Smith. The first book in
the series, *Scepter of Faith*, was released on March 5th, 2013.

Published in the United States of America

Fiction / Christian / Fantasy

13.08.15

Matthew 13:41

The Son of Man will send out his angels, and they will weed out of his kingdom everything that causes sin and all who do evil.

For God, we fight!

ANGELS without WINGS

THE PATH TO SACRIFICE
Book 2 of the Series

Acknowledgement

I've given thanks to my wife and my mom with every book I've written. The same holds true for *The Path to Sacrifice*. Their support with the *Angels without Wings* series helps keep the goal in sight. Without their love and encouragement, *Angels without Wings* wouldn't exist.

I'd also like to thank my dad for making the cross on the cover and for establishing in me a drive to succeed through hard work and dedication.

There are several more people who have been a big help. From proof reading to brainstorming on plot and cover design, these people know who they are and how much I appreciate their assistance.

And as always, I couldn't end an acknowledgement without thanking our Lord and Savior Jesus Christ. The *Angels without Wings* series for me has been a voyage of faith. I've never been good at verbally communicating my faith and views, these books have provided a means to express myself.

Note from the author:
The *Angels without Wings* series is a work of fiction. Since it is purely fiction, I didn't feel comfortable including any scriptures from the Bible. While I based the books on messages from the Bible, I didn't feel comfortable including any direct quotes from the Word of God.

Look for Angels without Wings on Facebook. Or visit our website: www.AngelsWithoutWingsSeries.com

Prologue

Emily Young smiled at the thousand foot vertical drop below her feet. Sheer granite cliffs dove to a river fed valley that shined green and blue in the afternoon sun. A soft wind rustled her blonde hair as she leaned out holding onto a small crease in the rock with one hand. She peaked at her climbing partner and her smile grew as big and bright as any sunrise in the Rocky Mountains of Colorado.

"Can you believe that place?" Kyle Downey said with uncontrolled giddiness pouring into each word. "I wonder if anyone has ever found it before?" The tense muscles in his thirteen year old arms flexed as he leaned away from the cliff. The Spirit swirled around him and Emily was almost sure he could let go and not plummet a thousand feet to his death, like any normal climber would.

"I doubt it," she laughed. "It was so beautiful. I like your name for it... God's Grove. It's perfect."

"We're not going to tell anyone else, right?" Kyle asked before springing up fifteen feet and latching onto the tiniest of bulges in the rock for a handhold.

"Not even Brian?" Emily questioned as she looked up at him. His chiseled cheeks tightened for a fraction of a second but a wide grin flourished a split second later.

"If you want, that's fine. What about if we kept it a secret for a week? You know... something between the two of us? You two have kept secrets from me, right? Brian and I have stuff that we don't tell you."

"Like what?" Emily barked with a frown. "Me and Brian tell you everything. We don't keep any secrets."

Kyle chortled with a shake of his head as he moved sideways across the granite shelf. "Just stupid stuff," he said and studied the edge of the cliff. Only one more bend remained before they would be back on the deck of Passover Hill. They'd taken their first tentative steps over the ledge nearly four hours ago, but Brian was the only person who would miss them; and he had left the Hill for the day to pray with his dad, John Decker, before some dangerous demon hunt.

"And anyway," Kyle continued while Emily leapt into a narrow alcove twenty feet to his left. "I know you and Brian have kept some things from me... you've talked about my dad behind my back."

"Only to think about ideas to help," Emily huffed. "We've never kept any real secrets from you. And not telling Brian about God's Grove would be a big secret. He wouldn't be happy if he finds out we kept it from him for more than a day."

"We can talk about it at dinner," Kyle called as he crested the ridge.

Emily nodded but froze as she saw Kyle's fingers slip and he slid ten feet down the sheer drop before catching himself. A scream hung in her throat as Kyle warningly shook his head a fraction sideways.

"Downey!" a giant of a voice boomed from a hundred feet above Emily. She looked up but the bend of the granite ridge kept the person out of view. There was no doubt who it was though. Mr. Stockford – the massive, Spirit filled teacher they had for the archangel Michael's class. "What are you doing? You know no one is allowed over the balcony!"

Emily stared horror struck at Kyle. The whole trip had been her idea. A test of their abilities, she'd said and begged of her friend who had been reluctant to go. And she'd been sure they would find something cool if they dared the cliffs. The fact that they had, didn't matter now. Emily had never been a victim of Stockford's renowned punishments but the terror he produced in the other angels in training was legendary. She could see him smiling as he made them climb miles of ropes in the obstacle courses in his gym. And he would for sure rejoice in calling their parents with his scepter to recount their juvenile delinquency. Or he would for Emily's parents; for Kyle's dad, the domineering angel would have to go in person since Kyle's dad wasn't an angel.

"Kyle," Emily hissed. "I'm so sorry. You told me-"

"Shh," Kyle said and ducked his head. The Spirit glowed from every part of his body in a soft shine. "Your parents will kill you if they find out," he whispered barely moving his lips. "I hid you with the Spirit. He didn't see or feel you. Stay put until he takes me inside. I won't tell-"

"No!" Emily spat. "Your dad. Stockford will take you straight to him. My parents will only ground me. We worked so hard on your dad... don't let something stupid ruin that. It was my idea."

"I'm not going to let you get in trouble," Kyle growled and began climbing the sheer rock. Emily could feel the power of the Spirit radiating from above where Mr. Stockford waited in his wrath. "My dad will be fine," Kyle breathed quietly with the smallest of sideways glances at Emily. A fearful swallow followed his words. "His faith is strong now... Stockford only saw me. There's no reason for your parents to kill you too."

"No, Kyle, stop…" Emily cried. Her own fear rose at the thought of seeing her mom and dad's faces when she next saw them, if Stockford found her. She could see the small features of her mom as they blazed in righteous anger. "I… you can't take the blame. It's my fault."

"Stay there," Kyle hissed but stopped his next demanding plea as a light shined so bright they both shielded their eyes for a heartbeat. When Emily found her friend again, he was wrapped in pure white robes. The second of God's gifts to angels. Innocence and love beckoned from the soft, shimmering material. The unending love of God's grace hung in the mesmerized air.

Emily's eyes found Kyle's and they locked in wonder until he jumped and disappeared behind the crest of the cliff above.

The long, smooth wood reminded Troy of a half foot wide paddle forged of some indestructible tree in heaven. The handle was big enough to grip in both his hands and the smooth blade widened at the far end giving it an almost axe-like quality. He'd pictured himself swinging it thousands of times before but he'd never gotten to hold it until this morning.

His dad stepped from the truck with his sword springing into existence in the sheath on his back as he crouched by the front bumper. In his left hand, a scepter of utter magnificence shined in the dawn light. A flowing palm branch spun down the length of the thin rod.

Troy looked at his own scepter and a stirring of pride beat against his chest. The golden metal didn't hold the same grace as his dad's, but his name, *Troy Decker*, was inscribed by the very hand of God at the top. He'd only had his scepter for a little over six months. And it hadn't been an easy task for him to accomplish.

Ever since that day in a run-down house in his hometown of Mustang, Oklahoma, Troy had finally felt like an angel. Or an angel in training at least. The golden scepter glowed as a beacon of hope every time he set eyes on it. At this same time last year, he'd thought for sure God had made a mistake and forgot to grant him any kind of powers with which to call himself an angel. But everything changed when he saved his best friend in the world, Tyler Henry.

Troy smiled at the thought.

"God, schmod," Tyler had often been heard to say in his brazen voice. "That religious mumbo jumbo was made up by a bunch of people looking to get rich. My parents say it all the time. Just ask them. My mom can give you a hundred of examples of God being a figment of someone's imagination. You and Becky can go on and on about Jesus this and Jesus that, but it won't work on me."

These days a different tune sang from Tyler's mouth. And it was all thanks to Troy and his other friends; Angela Williams, Clark Smith, and of course, Becky Lopez. Helping Tyler find his faith in God had been enough of an accomplishment to make even Troy's dad smile, which was no small feat. All the previous miseries of being an angel in training (who was behind the curve of other angels his age) had vanished just as all the demons in that house had on the fateful day when Tyler was saved.

None of the winged selvo demons survived the blasting power of Troy's Grandma Denise who drained the energy from her body using Gabriel's gift of voxis, the Voice of God. The hair on Troy's arms stood up at the memory of the sheer power.

And the tondeo demon camouflaged as an innocent girl had escaped through a broken window. Of course, that was directly Troy's fault who had let the demon go rather than destroying it in its false form of the girl he'd hoped to save in exchange for being granted a scepter. He hadn't been able to muster the resolve to strike the tondeo down, but in the end, his mercy had been the final stepping stone for Tyler to accept his faith in God.

"You coming?" Troy's dad's voice pulled him from the memories. Troy's shoes crunched on gravel as he scrambled from the truck near an overgrown field separating them from the warehouse. He knelt beside his dad and examined the bright, crimson angel marks on his dad's tanned face. The markings intertwined in a graceful swirl from his temples down his cheeks then behind his ears.

Troy's own angel marks were the dullest green. He frowned every time he saw them in a mirror. Some of his earliest memories were of trouble he'd run into with his mom when he tried to darken them with a permanent green marker. He could still hear her normally soft voice shrill as she yelled, "Stop it!"

"We'll hit the nylla hard and fast," his dad whispered. "Remember that they'll try to swarm around behind us. Use the mace… and your dagger if they get too close; but don't forget to use the archangels' gifts too."

"Michael's and Gabriel's mainly?" Troy questioned with the mace planted on his shoulder.

"Huspos from Seraphim is good as well. It keeps them at bay if too many of them get around you at once."

Troy swallowed and jogged his memory on the use of Seraphim's huspos ability. He remembered Adam and Eve mentioning it in a class at Passover Hill the previous summer but fell back on his practice with Angela for a more concrete application. Angela was an angel in training his own age who went to the Hill; and lived in Mustang only a few streets away from Troy's family. Troy still blushed with each thought of the tall, blonde girl.

"Me and Angela have practiced using it quite a bit," Troy mused. "It was tough without demons to try it out on though."

"The same principles apply whether there is a demon or not. Use the Spirit and maintain your faith." His dad paused for a few seconds and Troy felt the power of the Spirit build and sweep across the gently blowing grass of the field. "There's more of them than I thought," he said after a minute of concentration. "A few hundred at least. You sure you're ready? I know you've wanted to go hunt demons with me and your mom for a while, but it's a little different once you're here."

Troy instantly nodded hoping none of the nervous butterflies fluttering furiously in his stomach were audible to his dad's highly tuned angelic hearing. "Wait until Angela hears about it," he smiled. "She'll be mad she didn't get to go."

"Maybe so. But it's not a competition. Both of you need to spend most of your time concentrating on your studies and on how to get your robes. Demon hunting is important but think of this more as practice. That should make it easier." He paused and then added, "But don't forget that it's dangerous… very dangerous."

Troy held back an angry grimace at the mention of robes; his next step towards becoming a fully-fledged angel. The robes were granted for a showing of sacrifice. To Troy, they were the least important of the five gifts granted by God and also, the most mysterious. How was he supposed to go about looking for something to sacrifice? At least with his scepter it had been a clear goal. Find someone who needed to be saved and brought to faith in God; save them; and a scepter was granted. Simple, and even if it wasn't easy, straightforward.

"What's wrong?" his dad summoned him from the thoughts.

"Just thinking about the robes," Troy said truthfully. "They're not the easiest gift to plan ahead for."

A whisper of a smile creased his dad's mouth. "I thought the same thing when I was trying to get my robes. They may not be as clear cut of a goal as getting your scepter or your wings, but you can still watch for signs."

"How big of a sacrifice do I have to make?"

"That's between you and God. It's different for all angels. For some it's not much of a sacrifice… it wasn't really a big deal for me. For others it's big. It's up to God to decide in the end." He read Troy's face and continued. "It's a personal thing… if someone doesn't volunteer the information, or you don't know why they got their robes, then you shouldn't try to dig it out of them."

Troy sighed at the answer which he'd already heard in one form or another at least a hundred times in the last few months. "You or mom either one will tell me how you got yours," he mumbled. "Not specifics at least. It's tough to know where to look."

"A little more faith would be a start," his dad answered in his calmest but scariest voice.

Troy bit back another retort and adjusted the wooden mace on his shoulder. He was sure his dad's and his mom's sacrifices had something to do with their old friend Kyle Downey but he knew better than to ask. His dad's icy stare would surely show up if he mentioned the leader of the fallen angels, and he didn't want anything to ruin his first official demon hunt. All the news stories the last six months had been filled with horrors and atrocities of the rampaging forces led by Kyle. Ever since the day Troy was granted his scepter, the fallen angel had been ramping up the War for Sins to new heights. Not since Troy's grandpa, John, had defeated a fallen angel named Xavier had the War been as brutal and bloody as it was at the moment.

"Let's pray and then get this over with," his dad said and crossed his hands. Troy followed suit and bowed his head. "Lord grant us strength to do your bidding and the protection of your Spirit. Let us not fall to the beasts of the deceiver and continue forth with your mission of saving those who need to be saved. We praise and worship you as angels you created to protect the world from the struggles of evil. Lord, grant us peace. Amen."

Troy echoed the "Amen" and stood with his dad. They began to march across the overgrown fields with their eyes locked on the broken windows and dented doors of the warehouse. To his left, Troy saw his dad's wings unfurl and his halo beam into life in a perfect, glowing circle above his head. He glanced at them in wonder like he did every time he saw them. It would be so awesome when he had wings and a halo of his own. But he had a long way to go before he got there. Robes first, then a sword.

"We'll go through that office door over by the docks," his dad whispered. "Don't make a sound. And remember; For God, we fight."

"For God, we fight," Troy whispered the incantation in return.

With a blast of light from his dad's scepter, the door burst open at their approach. Not even a breath of noise escaped the rusted door under the power of the Spirit. They slid into a dusty office, empty except for a derelict desk and a few loose phone cords. Troy followed his dad through another door and down a short hallway. Plumes of brown dust swirled with each step they took and Troy held a sneeze in the back of his throat. A cracked picture of the building in its prime hung sideways on the wall.

"Ready?" his dad mouthed.

Troy nodded and tightened his right hand around the mace and his left around his scepter. The sheath and dagger were poised ready at his waist, but he hoped he wouldn't need them.

The door swung open at the slightest touch from his dad and Troy got his first look at a live nylla demon. The picture from Paula Tindall's book was eerily accurate but didn't capture the unnerving whir of their wings or the hissing language they spat at each other. All the colors of an appalling apparition of a rainbow flew through the dusty air. Tiny, sharp fangs shimmered behind drooling mouths of each demon. To Troy, it looked like thousands of them were swarming in a ball at the far end of the long warehouse; or bouncing here and there off the crumbling walls. Rusted drilling machinery wasted away on the concrete floor. Troy swallowed the rolling butterflies in his stomach and followed his dad.

At once a screech went up among the nylla and several of the miniature flying horses raced at the two new comers. Troy noticed the barbed tails rising and pulsing in terrible anticipation behind their backs. His dad sidestepped the first nylla and sliced it neatly in two with one stroke from his sword. Troy lunged forward and with a mighty swing crunched the next buzzing demon. The sound of a homerun, struck by a major league baseball player, cracked across the concrete.

"Huspos," his dad called and a bright, white cloud streamed from his scepter. The scent of a fresh, springtime rain invaded the moldy smell of the long abandoned space and a soft mist drizzled in the morning light coming through the cracked and dirt caked windows. The swarm of nylla danced away from the cloud in a horrible imitation of an in-air ballet. With a yell of sheer and frightened delight, Troy jumped into the fray. Crack after crack echoed through the long room. From behind him, a tiny popping sound (like a beetle getting stepped on) cut over and over again as his dad sliced with his two handed broadsword - now stained with black, smoking blood.

"Swivel your hips more," his dad hollered after a few minutes of the harrowing work. "You're not killing some of the ones you're hitting. Look over by the wall, those two you just hit are getting back up."

Troy grunted an acknowledgement and swung the mace at an approaching trio. All three demons slammed into a haphazard stack of scrap metal a moment later. None got up.

"Sidestep," his dad shouted over the buzz of wings and the nylla's screeching voices. "Cut more angles to get around them. And watch behind you. Use more of the archangel's gifts. Don't rely only on the mace."

"Okay," Troy rolled his eyes in indignant frustration. What was he supposed to do? He'd killed at least fifty of the foul little creatures and only two he'd bashed had survived... big deal. He held back the desire to stick his tongue out at his dad's flashing form and instead spun with his scepter arcing up. Between him and a group of ten nylla, a bright translucent shield popped into existence - Gabriel's Shield forged from the power of the Spirit. It was Troy's favorite archangel ability. He shot it forward with a twitch of his scepter and it charged the panic frenzied demons. Troy was sure he caught a glimpse of fear in one of the demon's red eyes before it was obliterated by the force of the blow.

"Argh!" Troy whipped around and saw his dad fling a nylla from his right hamstring then split it in two with a stab from his sword.

"You okay?" Troy yelled as he swatted away a couple of the pesky beasts who'd dived at him the moment he looked at his dad.

"Fine," his dad murmured and neatly decapitated a small, screaming horse head. "Should have had my robes on. Stupid thing wouldn't have been able to sting me through the cloth." He winced a little as he continued on his way with a slight limp and Troy turned back to the business at hand trying hard to hide the gloating smile spreading across his face.

For twenty more minutes, they worked their way around the warehouse. Stacks of fuming nylla bodies littered the floor. Troy gagged at the sulfuric smell but never halted his attack. Finally, after every nook and cranny and dark corner had been searched, his dad sheathed his sword.

"Pretty good," he said in his calm voice while Troy leaned on the mace laboring for every breath. "But you need to rely more on the Spirit and less on your body. Let it fuel you and you won't burn all your energy." He paused for a few seconds gazing at the blood splattered calm left after the battle. "You handled the mace pretty good. Nice job."

Troy's chest ballooned at his dad's compliment. "You want me to try to use hesdia on your leg?" he asked between breaths.

"No, I'll be fine," his dad said. "It doesn't really work on nylla stings. You never got the hang of using it anyway, did you?"

The momentary balloon popped in Troy's chest and he shook his head negatively.

"Come on," his dad continued with a look around the abandoned warehouse. "Let's clean up and get home." With a flourish he flicked his scepter and two brooms from a far corner zoomed into their hands. Troy set the mace down carefully against the wall and wrinkled his nose as he brushed the disgusting nylla corpses into a pile.

Once they had all of them, his dad poured a whole bottle of holy water onto the bloody mess. Troy watched as the nylla smoked then disintegrated into a small pile of ash.

"Good riddance," his dad said in revulsion. "Let's get out of here."

"How did it go?" Troy looked up at the first words to greet him after he walked through the door into his house in Mustang, Oklahoma. Not even the best rays of sunshine compared to the smile that met his eyes. Every worry he had washed away when his mom, Emily Decker, treated him to the best gift a person could give. Her white angel markings looped gracefully from her temples halfway down her cheeks near her delicate ears. She stepped forward and hugged him bringing a sweet scent of freshly cut flowers.

"It was okay," Troy smiled. "We got rid of them all."

"And you didn't get stung," his mom crooned. "That's impressive on your first nylla hunt. I think I got stung twice the first time I went up against the little monsters."

Troy nodded and looked at his dad who was limping into the spacious, tile floored kitchen from the garage. His mom's eyes followed his and the shortest snorting chuckle escaped before she could stop it with her hand. "So, uh…" she said. "Breakfast? I bet your dad didn't feed you anything this morning."

"I did too," his dad sniffed indignantly. "Didn't I, Troy?"

"Yeah," Troy agreed in an instant.

"Probably a protein bar," his mom sighed after a look at the stubborn guilt on his dad's face and headed back to the stove where a batch of scrambled eggs, bacon, and sausages were simmering. "Big day tomorrow Troy. Your fifteenth birthday. I know all your friends are coming over today for the little get together but you've never told me what you wanted. I've been waiting and waiting to get your present."

Troy glanced at his dad who was carrying his mace towards the hallway leading to the bedrooms of their suburban house. "What about my own mace?" he asked. "Dad's is cool but it would be awesome to have my own. I could take it to the Hill to practice with instead of using one of the beat up ones that we have to use in Butler's class. A lot of the other guys have their own."

His mom's eyebrows rose for a second then she shrugged. "Sounds fine to me," she said as she flipped the bacon with a wave of her hand. Troy watched with interest as he always did when adult angels used the Spirit. He hadn't been able to master the abilities well enough yet to use in everyday life. His parents said it would get second nature but Troy was sure the day would never arrive for him. "I'll talk it over with your dad," his mom continued. "But I imagine he'll be okay with it."

They sat together at the huge mahogany table in the dining room and Troy scarfed down huge mounds of eggs, six pieces of crispy bacon, and four sausage links. His mom had them walk her through their early morning mission to eradicate the nest of nylla; but soon Troy's dad left for some sort of scouting operation in Midwest City.

"I've got some errands to run this morning too," his mom called from her room a few minutes after they'd cleaned up the kitchen. "You want to go?"

"No," Troy responded. "Tyler, Becky, and Clark are going to be here in a little bit. I'll wait around for them."

"Okay."

"Have you heard where Angela is?" Troy asked.

"Uh, no. I haven't talked to Susan today," his mom said referencing Angela's mom. "She isn't coming over?"

"Not from what Tyler said on the phone last night," Troy said.

His mom entered the living room with a knowing look on her angular, pretty face. "I'm sure she'll be around sometime," she purred.

"Yeah... I... you know, wanted to tell her about the nylla hunt this morning," Troy cleared his throat. "She'll be mad she didn't get to go."

"I bet she will," his mom smiled. "I'll be back in a bit."

For the next two hours, Troy poured over his ragged copy of Paul Tindall's *Dangerous and Deadly Demons*. He made notes on the nylla page with his experience from the morning as he had on the other pages with demons he'd encountered. A small broken heart with a rough sketch of the girl with the innocent eyes peered from the page of the tondeo. In his tidy hand writing was written: *Don't let theses deceivers fool you again.*

A little after noon, the doorbell rang. Troy opened the door as he swallowed the last remnants of a peanut butter and jelly sandwich he'd made himself for lunch.

"Bout time," Tyler joked with a punch to Troy's arm. "Thought you were going to make us wait out here all day." Tyler sauntered past Troy into the kitchen and went immediately to the stainless steel refrigerator.

"Where are Clark and Becky?" Troy asked with half his body inside the door and the other half outside.

"Went around back to see if the back door was open," Tyler said while he took out a bag of deli turkey, a tomato, and two slices of American cheese. "Took you so long to answer the door, we thought there might be a trickel demon in here eating you for lunch or something."

"It didn't take me that long," Troy huffed. "I was finishing my sandwich."

"Figures," a smallish voice said from Troy's left. Around the corner of the brick house walked Becky in her leopard-like flowing gait. Directly behind her shoulder, Clark hovered as if he was the biggest Secret Service Agent of all time in protection of a Mexican dignitary. "All you guys do is eat." She smiled and winked at Troy as she brushed past him into the house.

"Hey," Clark murmured as he turned sideways and managed to barely squeeze through the oversized front door.

"You just ate," Becky huffed and rolled her eyes when she saw Tyler setting a plate down with a freshly made turkey sandwich.

"Can't call that a full lunch," Tyler squeezed in around his first bite.

"You had five slices of pepperoni and hamburger pizza," Becky said with a revolted twist on her exotic face. "I would have puked if I'd eaten half that."

"Yeah, but you're tiny," Tyler swallowed a hearty bite and held up an additional sandwich. "Want one Clark?"

"Sure," Clark smiled bringing the fading, acne spots on his dark cheeks into focus. His short, curly black hair was cut neatly on his gigantic head.

Becky sighed and took a seat as Troy made himself a bowl of Cheerios to round off his lunch. "You won't believe what I got to do this morning," he crunched.

"What?" Tyler asked. "It's Saturday morning. I just woke up a little bit ago."

"It's Saturday afternoon now," Becky corrected. "Not all of us sleep til 11:00."

Tyler shrugged as he downed a huge glass of milk.

"I went on a demon hunt with my dad," Troy said and laughed when Tyler spit and spluttered half the milk out of his mouth.

"What kind of demons?" Clark managed before the other two found their voices.

"Nylla," Troy answered with a proud smile. "They're these little horse demons with wings. There were tons of them. A few hundred at least."

"Go get your book and show us," Tyler said excitedly while he wiped milk off his chin.

"Okay, hold on a minute," Troy raced to his bedroom and retrieved *Dangerous and Deadly Demons* from his desk. When he ran back into the kitchen he was met by three expectant and anxiously awaiting sets of eyes. He flipped to the nylla page and Becky grabbed it from his hands.

"Wow," she murmured with uplifted eyebrows as if she was trying to open her eyes as wide as they could go in order to take in every single detail of the demon.

"How'd you kill them?" Tyler asked. His fingers were tracing over the notes Troy had written.

"I used my dad's mace," Troy answered. "It's kind of like a big, wooden paddle. About three feet long. You swing it like a baseball bat. And when I hit the nylla with it, it sounded just like hitting a homerun. My dad used his sword. He sliced them in half so easy… it was cool but kind of gross too. I don't think he ever missed."

"What about if one of those things had stung you?" Becky questioned. Her left hand was cradling the cross necklace that always hung around her neck.

"It would have hurt a little, I guess," Troy replied but withheld the information about his dad getting stung on the leg. He didn't want the perfection that hovered around his dad hindered in his friends' eyes. "As long as it was only a few stings, it's not supposed to cause any lasting injury."

"It still sounds really dangerous," she said. "I'm glad you made it out of there okay. I can't believe your dad and mom let you go."

"It's awesome!" Tyler roared. "A little danger is part of being an angel. Right, Troy?"

"Seems so," Troy said smiling. "It's been that way for the last year or so at least. Ever since I started to really try to get my scepter."

Tyler saluted and his head lifted, "And who do you have to thank for that?"

Troy and Clark laughed but Becky responded with a roll of her eyes. "Whatever," she sighed. "You should be thanking Troy every day for saving your sorry-"

"Speaking of which," Tyler cut her off. "I finally talked my dad into going to church tomorrow."

Troy, Clark, and Becky stared at him in disbelief. Tyler's parents were the most ardent atheists in the whole city of Mustang. Getting them into a church was like Clark managing to fit into a bumper car at the state fair.

"How'd you talk him into going?" Clark asked.

Tyler shrugged and a sheepish smile brightened his handsome face. "Kept pestering him. I knew he'd give in eventually. My mom's a different story though. She's pissed at him for going. And all she does is scowl at me lately."

"What church?" Troy asked.

"Christ Lutheran. Out on Highway 92."

"That's awesome," Becky beamed. "All those years we went out with each other and I tried to get you to go to church with me a thousand times… and now you've talked your dad into going. Pretty impressive. I guess we should have broken up a long time ago. Seems to have done you some good."

Tyler bounced his eyebrows in a nonplussed fashion and got up and washed off his empty plate then stuck it in the dishwasher. "He grew up in a Lutheran church," he offered. "It's the only place he'd even consider. My grandparents are kind of religious. I think it's mainly my mom that's worn him down over the years. She still hates anything to do with the church or when I talk about my faith. You should hear her go on about it."

Right then, the garage door opened and Troy's mom walked in carrying an armful of plastic bags from Homeland grocery store. Both Tyler and Clark instantly scrambled to help her.

"Thanks guys," she said with a gracious, stunning smile. "There's a ton more in the Tahoe."

"We'll get them," Clark said and lumbered into the garage.

"Want me to help you put them up, Mrs. Decker?" Becky asked.

"Sure. And I've told you a million times, Becky. You can call me Emily."

Becky blushed and nodded while she put a bag of chicken and a sleeve of pork chops in the freezer.

"I got steaks for dinner," Troy's mom called to the three boys.

"Great, I'm starving," Tyler said. Becky shook her head.

"Are Angela and her parents coming over?" Troy asked.

His mom put up the last of the groceries then turned into the living room. "They can't make it tonight," she said after slinging a huge sack of charcoals out the back door onto the porch. "I'm not sure exactly what's going on but it's nothing big." She added when she saw the look on Troy's face. "They've had some family issues to take care of. Nothing serious."

Troy's stomach dropped a fraction at the news. What would keep them away from his birthday dinner? He knew it wasn't really his birthday until tomorrow but they'd been planning the evening dinner for a couple of weeks. He studied his mom and wondered for the briefest of seconds if he should take a chance to use Gabriel's gift of auditome on her. It was probably the archangel gift he'd gotten the most proficient at using and would allow him to catch thoughts or feelings his mom might be trying to hide. In the end, he decided against it – mainly because he was sure his mom would catch him.

"There is a surprise for you… kind of," his mom said offhandedly. "Luke Fischer will be joining us for dinner."

Troy's eyebrows knitted in concentration as he tried to put the name with a face from his memory banks.

"You might not remember him," his mom continued. "He's friends with your dad. You've probably only met him a few times and it was years ago. He's a member of the Justice Ministry."

"Wh… really?" Troy stuttered.

"What's the Justice Ministry?" Tyler asked while he lounged in the recliner and flipped through channels on the TV with the remote.

Troy looked from his mom to each of his friends. "Demon hunters," he supplied and watched Clark's eyes grow as big as dinner plates. "Angels who get specific training on demons and know exactly how to kill them. They're the best of the best."

Chapter 2: Tales of a Minister

T-bone steaks, baked potatoes with butter and cheese, corn on the cob, and green beans filled the long table in the dining room that night. Troy and his parents sat with three of his best friends and enjoyed the early evening meal, but Troy's eyes never strayed far from the door. He didn't know whether it was a continued hope of a surprise visit from Angela or the imminent arrival of a Justice Minister.

"Here Troy," Becky said after he blew out the candles on a cake his mom had spent an hour perfecting earlier in the afternoon. On it a gleaming scepter was hovering in front of the gate to heaven. The tall, pointed arch of the gate captivated Troy – even in the cartoonish fashion shown on the cake. He only wished he could see the real thing in the sanctuary at the Cathedral. So far, God had not granted his prayers to catch the smallest glimpse of the brilliant gate.

"What is it?" Troy asked but knew instantly when he grabbed it. He ripped open the package to find a book with a fierce, caricature-looking angel glaring from the cover.

"A book about angels," Tyler said. "One of those expensive research books."

"We thought it would be cool for you to see how humans have portrayed angels throughout history," Becky added with a sweet smile. "It shows different opinions and beliefs from a lot of different religions but the main focus is Christianity."

"Do you like it?" Clark asked.

Troy studied the front cover and read the small summary on the back. "Sure," he nodded. "I can make a project out of it in Noah's class at the Hill. He'd love to see a comparison of this book and the history books in the library there."

"Yeah, get you some extra credit," Tyler laughed. "You're always thinking ahead. I wanted to get you a sword or a stun gun or something sweet like that. But they," he said motioning with his head at Becky and Clark as he munched on a bite of cake, "thought a book would be good. Like you don't have enough of those."

"It's a very good gift," Troy's mom interrupted.

Troy grabbed the ripped wrapping paper and examined the small card attached to the bow. "Is it from Angela too?"

"Oh, uh… no," Becky chewed on her bottom lip. "Just us three."

"Cool…" Troy searched for words to not show his disappointment. He was saved by the slow chimes of the door bell ringing.

"I'll get it," his dad almost jumped from his chair and sped towards the front door. Troy, Tyler, and Clark eyed each other then scrambled to follow in his wake. As the door opened, they peeked over Troy's dad's shoulder. Leaning against the brick walls of the entry way was a tall, blonde haired man who looked to be in his mid thirties.

"Howdy Brian," the man's smile showed crooked but very white teeth. His broad shoulders stretched nearly as wide as Clark's but he tapered down at the waist giving him the v-shape of an amateur body builder. A tight fighting yellow, v-cut shirt hugged his frame over a pair of blue jeans. Wiry chest hairs climbed onto his neck and threatened to creep towards his face.

Troy's attention instantly latched onto his blue-green eyes. Many battles (maybe too many) shined behind the soft color. On his cheeks, striking blue angel marks zig-zagged. Long, golden hair, which hung past his shoulders, curtained from a part in the middle of his massive head. "Long time, no see. For God, we fight."

"For God, we fight," Troy's dad clasped an outstretched hand. "It's been too long Luke. Haven't heard from you in a couple of years. What have you been up to?"

"Oh… a little of this and a little of that," Luke shrugged and followed Troy's dad into the house.

The three boys stumbled over each other to clear a path for the two angels. They trailed behind and made their way into the living room where they scrunched together absent-mindedly on the couch. Troy didn't even wince when his ribs almost got broken by being sandwiched between Tyler and Clark.

"So what brings you to Mustang?" Troy's mom asked rather stiffly while she offered the husky Justice Minister a thin glass of sweet wine.

"Dropped by to talk with Paul Williams," Luke scratched at the stubble on his chin. He took in the surroundings and settled into an end chair which was usually more of a decorative piece than an actual sitting spot. "There's a nasty horde of dawos demons up in Chicago and he has some specialty in the area. Thought he might offer some advice. He slaughtered a whole group of them on his own about five years ago."

"I thought Mr. Williams was an expert on reidlos?" Troy piped in.

Luke looked at him over his glass with a penetrating gaze. "He's an expert on lots of things," he said. "Used to be one of the best of us until Susan settled him down."

"Rightfully so," Troy's mom sniffed.

"Wow," Tyler said in awe. "That's awesome. I didn't know Angela's dad was so cool. He seems kind of like one of the nerdy lawyers at my dad's office."

Luke chuckled and looked from Tyler to Clark then to Becky. "You three seem to know a lot for not being angels," he glanced at Troy's dad.

"It was all by the rules," Troy's dad offered. He pointed at Clark and Becky. "Those two pretty much figured it out on their own. And Troy got his scepter for saving Tyler. That was when Kyle tried to kill them using the tondeo. I'm sure you've heard the story… Anyway, they've all been friends for years."

"Hey, makes no difference to me," Luke held his hands up and snorted. "I just wanted to make sure I'm clear to talk about all manner of subjects; but if they've dealt with a tondeo and Kyle Downey all at the same time, they're good in my books."

"Not everything is open for discussion," Troy's mom warned.

"Fine," Luke smiled. "You tell me to shut up whenever I approach a subject that isn't allowed."

"I will."

"We want to know about the War for Sins," Becky charged into the conversation. Everyone, even Luke, sat back in their seats in stunned acknowledgement of her declaration. She swallowed shyly and tried to smile. "Sorry, Clark and me never get much in when the topic comes up. We get a piece here and there but not the whole story."

"Join the club," Troy grumbled.

"Yeah, well Clark doesn't get a word in at least," Tyler quipped. "When have you ever not gotten a word in when you wanted?"

This time everyone laughed, again even Luke, and the mood settled. Troy watched Luke and could almost feel saliva dripping from his mouth in anticipation. He was sure that this was an angel who could tell them the scariest stories. Plus, he looked the type who wouldn't hold back.

"The War's not going too good at the moment," Luke admitted. "Too many demons and not enough Justice Ministers to go around."

"The rest of us do just as much in the War," Troy's mom said.

"I suppose so," Luke shrugged. "And as you know we're falling further and further behind every day. Downey's got too many fallen out there raising demons left and right. And they're breeding like wildfire."

"Yeah, Troy and his dad took out a nest of those nylla demons this morning," Tyler bragged impressively. "They looked scary in that *Dangerous and Deadly Demons* book."

Luke's eyes came together and he looked to Troy's dad with a wry smile. "See what I mean. Untold horrors abound…" He chuckled to himself for a couple of seconds and took another sip of wine before continuing. "We've been wiping out reidlos and selvo on a daily basis. But like I said, Downey is one step ahead of us wherever we go."

"What's he done now?" Troy's dad heaved a huge sigh.

"The usual," Luke rubbed the back of his hand against his cheeks absently but his eyes were thousands of miles away. "For him at least. Two Justice Ministers were killed last week."

"Yeah, the Angelic Agenda harped on and on about it," Troy's mom almost spat. "Poor Terry and Mykaela... I only met both of them a couple of times but they seemed like great angels. The Agenda barely even mentioned their names. It's all about Kyle. They haven't told a single positive story in almost a year."

"Can't blame them really," Luke sighed.

"Ah, you're one of those," Troy's mom huffed.

"One of what?" the grizzled Justice Minister chortled.

"One of those people who see the final battle with Lucifer around every corner," Troy's mom articulated.

"Oh maybe so," Luke grinned with a lopsided twist to his mouth. "Each soul Lucifer takes makes him that much stronger. And they've always said once he's strong enough and finds the one particular soul he needs; he'll try to rise from the pit and come over the abyss."

"And if he does Jesus will strike him down again," Troy's mom said without pause. "It's the same story once or twice a generation. It won't happen and if it does, it will be the opening needed to send Lucifer to his final judgment. And then all believers will be in paradise. I heard it as a girl. I heard it as a teenager. People screamed about it in Xavier's time. And now I'm hearing it again. I'm not too worried about it. And even if I was, like I said, it would clear a path for Jesus to defeat him once and for all."

Luke cleared his throat and popped his neck with a loud crack. "Yeah, well… our side knows that to be true but the other guys think they can win the War."

For a long time Luke's words sunk into every fabric of the room. Becky's hand was massaging the cross necklace and Troy was sure Clark was saying a silent prayer.

Tyler fidgeted making Troy flinch at the tight confines of the couch. Across the room on the recliner, Troy's dad was studying the Justice Minister as though he was a tedious, yet fulfilling textbook.

Finally Luke continued, "It's getting bad out there. Downey and his fallen are pulling reidlos from hell like they're gnats on a four day old piece of anchovy pizza. I've never seen hordes of them like we've been seeing. We took out a few hundred of them a couple of days ago. Nasty job. They killed three innocent people before we caught up with them... Hopefully their faith was strong before they stood for judgment. I'd hate to think that the devil got three more souls. He could use them to make thousands of demons."

"Don't sound too sad about it," Troy's mom sniffed.

"Emily," his dad's voice was cool and calm but a distinct danger wove into the single word.

Luke chuckled and swallowed the last drop of his wine. "I usually let the Soul Gazers deal with that kind of stuff. We're there to fight. Leave the saving up to them."

"So who cares if a few innocent souls are lost?" Troy's mom asked in a hiss. Troy glanced sideways at Tyler and Clark who were staring at his mom in what looked to be utter fear mixed with bewilderment. And Troy could understand. It was very rare to see his mom in such a testy mood. He didn't envy Luke, who was the target for her rising wrath, and he wasn't totally sure he didn't side with the muscled Justice Minister in any case. Fighting was way cooler than slowing down to lend a helping hand to someone. If there were demons on the loose, wasn't exterminating them more important so they couldn't kill more people?

"I didn't say anything of the sort," Luke replied holding a hand up to stop Troy's dad from interrupting the discussion again. "I've been called for a different purpose than the Soul Gazers. I don't get in their way and I appreciate it when they don't get in mine. They aren't too good at fighting, as you well know."

"They're called Forevers," Troy's mom snapped. "And they're needed just as much as you and the rest of the Justice Ministers when the War is going bad. Y'all barely stop to look around and wonder if someone around you might need the slightest push to find faith in God. You zip right by them and look for the next fight. The Forevers come in your wake to help those who need it."

"I can't say you'll get a lot of argument from me there," Luke conceded. "But I save my share of souls. We know it's our primary purpose and we don't shirk our duties…. We might just have a better eye out for a potential fight then most angels." He winked at Troy, Tyler, and Clark then leaned back in the decorative chair which caused it to squeak in protest.

For a few seconds Troy's mom looked ready to charge into a fight of her own but she clenched her teeth after a look at his dad who was shooting daggers from his calm eyes across the room. Troy took the opportunity to ask a question about a demon that scared him more than anything else in the world. Ever since one was reported almost a year ago as being involved in the death of his grandparents, Troy had wanted to know more about them. "Have you ever fought a trickel?" he nearly swallowed the stream of broken words.

Luke's gaze swiveled to him and he shook his head. "No," he replied with the tiniest of shudders. Troy wasn't sure if it was fright or excitement behind the angel's answer. "I've seen one from a distance though. We never caught up to it. Surrounded by a few hundred reidlos and selvo. That would have been a fun fight… Can't say I would have survived it though. Trickels are tough to kill. There's only been one or two, we think. They hide deep in the ground when they aren't summoned by the fallen. Only thing worse would be a deygon and there hasn't been one of those in a few centuries."

"Don't talk about it," Troy's mom squawked with a genuine shudder rocking her entire body. She rubbed her hands over bare, goose bump covered arms.

"So you haven't heard anything more about Kyle's whereabouts?" Troy's dad steered the conversation.

"Nothing much. Been lots of rumors but nothing solid. We have heard he might be after specific targets. You know Dan Multon? He's been trying to pose as a fallen. Trying to get info from some likely targets but it's a tough business when he can't show the dirty bastards the mark of the beast shining red on his forehead. He's not sure what's true and what isn't… or if any of them are really fallen. It's all a cat and mouse game. He said he definitely heard something about Downey wanting to target a few specific angels though."

"Probably us," Troy's mom offered though still clenched teeth. "He's not exactly fond of our family."

Luke shrugged. "Maybe so. But there's a lot of protection around this place now. Had to jump through hoops just to come over for a drink. You guys should be fine. I doubt he'd try anything after failing a few months ago. He's had a lot of activity over in Europe again. We're not positive he's in the States at the time but he could get back here anytime he wanted, so it doesn't help much anyway."

"What about the Williams?" Troy asked. "Could they be targets Downey is after?"

"Your guess is as good as mine," Luke said with his blonde eyebrows bouncing.

A tingle of terror jolted up Troy's spine at the thought of Angela cowering in the shadow of a trickel demon. Where was she? And what was the deal with his mom offering so little information about her absence from his party? It was too weird to be something simple. Were the Williams' in danger? Was that why Luke was really here? It couldn't be so he could ask a few questions of Paul. They had scepters for that. They could talk anytime.

"How many fallen is Dan saying Kyle has on his side now?" Troy's dad asked drawing him from the foreboding thoughts.

"Somewhere between ten and a thousand," Luke snorted. "We have no clue really. All around the world, I'd venture a guess somewhere around a hundred. It's increasing faster than it did when Xavier was pulling angels onto his side. Don't know how he's tricking them so easy. There have been lots of rumors of fallen angels infiltrating all the Cathedrals in the US. It'd be nice if we had a way to identify them. Then we could take them out like we do the reidlos. Nice and simple assassinations." He smiled showing his crooked teeth.

Troy's mom stood up suddenly from her chair. "You need to take a close look at yourself in the mirror," she fumed. "You talk about angels like they are demons."

"Eh, fallen angels count about the same as demons in my book," Luke croaked with a coughing but subdued laugh.

"They have souls," she barked. "Just like you and me and everyone other person on this planet. They are not demons. Those aren't judge's robes you wear when you're out on the hunt. They are angel robes. You'd do well to remember that. Anyone can be saved. God's highest demand of us is to help people find their faith."

With that she stormed from the room leaving a wake of silent nervousness.

After a solid minute of swallowing and throat clearing, Troy's dad stood and gestured to the hallway. "Luke, let's finish this up in my office."

"Sounds good," Luke chimed with a nonchalant grin as if the fiery argument from a minute before was already forgotten.

"That was intense," Tyler whispered once the friends were left alone in the living room. "What was up with your mom, Troy? She looked like she hated Luke. I've never seen her that mad before."

"You have too," Clark murmured.

"When?" Tyler countered.

"Last year when that selvo came after us," Clark said. "And at the house when we went to save the little girl. She looked ready to tear Kyle's head off."

"It was a tondeo - not a girl," Troy said before he could stop himself. He constantly reminded his friends of the fact every time they brought up the terrible events. The disguise was so good, it seemed as though they almost forgot with each retelling of the story. The reminders helped to solidify the demon's betrayal in his own head and push away the haunting image of the innocent, green eyes that stalked his dreams.

"I probably need to get home," Becky sighed. Her hand was tightly clenched on the crucifix around her neck. Fear shined from her brown eyes, but her lips arched when she looked at them. "Can you three pry yourselves off the couch? You're crammed in there like sardines. I've never seen you move so fast. If all of you move that fast on the football field next year, we're sure to win the state championship. You snuggled up like the sweetest boyfriend and girlfriend couple of all time."

"Shut up," Tyler griped and squirmed his way free.

"Y'all are walking each other home, right?" Troy asked a few minutes later as his friends squeezed out the front door.

"I'll get them home safe," Clark said with a huge hand resting on both their shoulders.

"And that's why he's the best lineman in the state," Tyler grinned. "Always there to protect me." He winked and punched Troy on the arm as they left.

"Bye Troy," Becky called. "And happy birthday!"

"Thanks," Troy waved and shut the door. He meandered slowly to his room with a short pause outside his dad's office. None of the discussion filtered through the closed door so Troy figured his dad had used Raphael's subbia gift which suppressed sound in a small bubble of space. He remembered Noah mentioning it last summer at the Hill but had never gotten good with it.

"Hey Troy," he turned as soon as he entered his room. His mom walked around him and took a seat on his bed. "How was your day today? Was the party okay?"

"It was fine," Troy replied and sat next to her. "What's up between you and Luke?"

She fanned her hand in front of her like she was shooing away an annoying fly.

"Nothing major," she assured. "Luke and the other Justice Ministers are always trying to get your dad to join them. It's been that way for twenty years... ever since your dad got his wings. They've never stopped trying. Grandpa John was a member for a long time so they figured he'd join right up too."

"I didn't know that," Troy said. "I guess it fits though."

"Yeah, it would have been nice if you'd had the chance to get to know him," his mom smiled sadly. "He was a great man. One of the biggest heroes in the last couple of centuries. But in the end, he saw that a lot of the Justice Ministers have their priorities backwards. Grandma Denise eventually talked him into stepping away from them. He hadn't been a member for several years when he faced Xavier."

Troy snorted in disbelief. "That doesn't sound like her. She'd fit right in with them. I figured her and Luke were best friends."

"She has her moments," his mom's face turned into a genuine smile that shined into the room. "Just like your dad... what I really wanted to come in here to talk to you about was the nylla hunt this morning."

"Oh... it was cool," Troy said offhandedly. "It wasn't really that dangerous. I could tell that Luke wasn't very impressed."

"Forget about him," Troy's mom wrinkled her pointy nose. "He doesn't know saving a single soul is more impressive than killing five trickel."

Troy laughed and set into a detailed telling of the morning excursion with his dad. "It was really fun," he said with renewed enthusiasm. "Just glad I didn't get stung. I didn't kill half as many as dad did though."

"Your dad said you did an unbelievable job," she said.

"Yeah, right," Troy snorted. "All he did was tell me what I was doing wrong the whole time."

His mom shook her head but with a wry smile. "Trust me," she laid a hand over his. "He was really proud of you. It was all he could talk about for an hour this afternoon. How good you were with the mace. How you used Gabriel's shield and offered to use hesdia where he got stung. He was impressed. I bet he'll start asking you to go on more hunts in the future."

Troy studied his mom to detect any hint of a white lie behind the words. He couldn't believe that his dad would compliment him – particularly not for a whole hour. All that echoed through his memories of the fight were the barking instructions on how he was doing stuff wrong as he hammered away at the howling horse creatures.

"Trust me," his mom assured again as she read his face. She patted his hand and stood up. "For tomorrow… Grandma Denise is going to come over for worship service in the morning. I know you mentioned earlier about going to church with Tyler since his dad is going, but we made plans to head over to the Cathedral around noon. We can get your present when we get there."

"Okay," Troy agreed absently with his mind still wandering over the short battle from early that morning in an attempt to remember any semblance of positivity from his dad. It was true, he had told Troy that he was suited for the mace, but had then immediately chastised him right afterwards for not being good with the hesdia gift. Troy spent the next couple of hours reading through the illustrated book Becky, Tyler, and Clark had given him for his birthday. Many of the so called angel histories made him laugh but he went to bed with his mom's words ringing in his ears.

"He was really proud of you."

Chapter 3: Revenge of the Fallen

The next morning Troy woke to the smell of coffee and the sight of Grandma Denise smiling at him from the small table in the kitchen.

"Bout time you got up," she said over a simmering cup of coffee. "We've been waiting to get started for a half hour. Oh... and happy birthday," she reeled off. "I must say you are looking your age. Taller than me now, aren't you? You'll be taller than your dad in six months."

"I hope so," Troy quipped somewhat uncomfortably. Grandma Denise was difficult to read on the easiest days so he never knew which way to take a conversation. "But Tyler is still two inches taller than me. And Clark is already six foot four."

"Good boys," she reflected into her coffee. "Clark at least. I'm still waiting on Tyler to come all the way around."

"Well, you shouldn't," Troy's mom jumped into the conversation as she strolled into the kitchen. She went straight to the refrigerator and pulled out a bowl of already soggy Cheerios then set it on the table in front of Troy. "He talked his dad into going to church this morning for the first time in over twenty years. It's a big accomplishment. Happy birthday," she added in a whisper.

"Only because of Troy," Grandma Denise said as she reached for the Holy Herald newspaper that his dad had already read and left. "That boy would still be headed to Lucifer's awaiting arms if Troy hadn't saved him."

"Maybe so," Troy's mom rolled her eyes behind his grandma's back.

They ate breakfast then went to the study for an hour long worship service led by Troy's dad. Troy loved the intimate Sunday services when it was only his small family in the room. It was the only time he truly felt safe in the ballooning tumult of the War for Sins. They prayed for the promise of peace bound in their faith of the Holy Trinity and gave thanks for the overwhelming power and glory God granted in order for them to fulfill their duties as angels. Troy's dad read verses from the Bible and ended with the Lord's Prayer.

Afterwards, they sat in the living room and watched TV. Troy half listened to a story Grandma Denise told of an unsuccessful ambush in California by a small group of fallen on a family of angels. "Lucky to be alive," she finished. "Wouldn't be if it hadn't been for Joe Taylor. He saved them at the last second."

Troy swiveled at the mention of Joe Taylor. "That's Adam's dad, right?"

Grandma Denise's eyes squinted for a second, "Yes, I think that's their son's name. Good family. Even with all the funny business that happened last year."

Troy swallowed the derisive comment that flooded into his throat. It wouldn't have surprised him if the Taylor's were the fallen angels that had created the ambush in the first place. He was still almost one hundred percent sure that they'd set up a reidlos attack last year when Troy and his friends had been lured into Kyle and the tondeo's trap. But he had no proof and his parents had accepted the Taylor's story; so he was stuck with only his assumptions and his deep loathing of their son, Adam, who had dated Angela for a couple of summers at the Hill.

At noon, Troy, his mom and his grandma loaded into the Tahoe and headed for the Cathedral. His dad had left an hour earlier on some sort of secret mission that made his mom scowl. Troy figured it was something to do with Luke and the Justice Ministers; and made a mental note to try to weasel any information he could out of his dad when he got home.

Within five minutes the tall bell towers of the Cathedral popped into view. Troy never tired of seeing the wonderful angel building. He constantly had to stave off requests from his friends to be granted the ability to see the ornate, stone structure.

"It's only allowed in very special circumstances," his mom had explained to the three non-angel friends on numerous occasions.

Along the stone walls of the church, windows of the finest stained glass beckoned with the great stories from all the ages of the angels. His favorite was, of course, the reflective testimony of his Grandpa John's famous victory over the fallen angel, Xavier.

Troy stepped in front of the glass with Grandma Denise beside him. "You look almost exactly like he did when he was around your age," she said with watery eyes locked on the stunning figure who wielded a flaming sword. "Your dad took after me... it's a shame."

"Really?" Troy's head tilted sideways as he looked closely at the depiction of his grandfather's face. The eyes and nose did look familiar a little bit but he thought it looked more like his dad than him. The rippling, muscular arms definitely didn't match the skinny twigs he saw in the mirror every morning.

"Yep," Grandma Denise nodded. "I bet the resemblance will only get stronger as you get older. Grow another half foot and fill out a little bit, I bet they could replace a picture of you with him and no one would be able to tell the difference."

"It would have been awesome if I'd been able to know him," Troy said with his head tilted up. "Lots of people at the Hill ask about him."

"I bet they do," she said. "Probably expect you to be as great as he was. Everyone would like to have another like him. One of the best angels of all time. He was granted his wings at sixteen and went straight into battles most of us will only have nightmares about. Speaking of which… have you been looking to get your robes?"

A soft sigh escaped Troy's mouth and he nodded absently. "Kind of but…"

"It's a tough gift to plan for," she admitted with a low snort. "But you need to get a move on. The War's only getting worse. You need to be a true angel as fast as you can."

"How did you get yours?" Troy questioned and bit his lip remembering the multiple times his dad said it was bad tact to ask how angels had received the mysterious gift.

"Direct question," she said with her arched eyebrows going up into her hairline. "I like it." With that she rolled up her sleeve revealing long, smooth arms that didn't possess the same wrinkles that spider-webbed across her face. Above her elbow, a long scar tore a line from her bicep to her shoulder.

"When I was fourteen, my best friend was being attacked by a pack of selvo," she informed with a wistful look into her memory. "This was back when Charles and his Nightwalkers were growing – way before Xavier took over. I almost lost my arm when I jumped between her and a selvo that was sneaking up to kill her from behind."

She swallowed and paused for a long time with her eyes glued on the stunning stain glass in front of them. "It was a tough time. They got her in the end. Almost ten years later. Xavier killed her when we all thought things were quieting down in the War. Your grandpa and Aaron Russell had driven the fallen in the United States into hiding but… it just goes to show, never let your guard down."

Troy stood in silence for several seconds then watched his grandma closely as she turned and headed for the huge oak doors. He walked behind her past the tall palisades that lined the sacred building. His grandma often told stories as she'd just done. A recurring thought that she must have lived a rough life bounced around in his brain after most conversations with her. Would having his arm cut-off be worth getting his robes? He wasn't sure and shivered a little bit at the thought as he stepped into the arched doorway.

Like every time he'd been to the Cathedral before (which had to have been in the thousands), Troy wished he had a hundred sets of eyes and ears to see and hear everything around him.

As the front door opened, a booming voice met Troy and his grandma. "Welcome! Welcome!" roared the gigantic statue of Samson. Behind his earsplitting voice filtered the sound of harps and the soft voices of angels in the middle of beautiful hymns. "What might you be doing here on this holy day? Worship and prayer? Or have you come to see my magnificence?" He spread his arms wide then curled with an impressive bulging of his biceps.

"None of the above," Troy's mom smiled. "Here for a little shopping. It's Troy's birthday."

"Young man…" Samson's bearded, stone face swiveled to him and he reached forward as though welcoming the dearest of friends. "Out of my way," he roared. "You're blocking my view of the loveliest of angels. Be gone with you," he shoved Troy to the side and turned to his mom. "Dear lady angel, have I ever told you that I once fought a pack of starving jackals for the briefest of views at the fairest maiden in the land. And you are twice as beautiful as her. If a pride of lions stood between me and you, they would stand no chance to withstand my rage."

Troy rolled his eyes and looked up at the splashing mural of the Red Sea parting high above on the ceiling. A wizened angel waved at him between notes on a polished flute. Across the long entryway, the statue of Jacob preached to a group of young children on the virtues of God's undying grace and the wonderful paradise awaiting those who held firm in their faith.

"For angels were granted the power to do his will," Jacob's bronze eyes met Troy's. "And with the strength of the Spirit as your ally, none can stand before you."

"What are they going on about now?" Grandma Denise fumed and drew Troy's attention to the large, projected screen on the far wall between two tall pillars of smooth marble.

"*All the Cathedrals and training camps shown on the map have moved to high alert,*" the regal angel on the screen intoned. A business suit rather than robes covered his rather narrow shoulders but behind his back his wings flexed and above his head a halo shined. "*There are rumors Downey may be forming a group big enough to attack even the most sacred of grounds.*"

"Impossible," Troy's mom complained as she dodged Samson's floundering arms. "I wish they'd give us one positive story instead of all the doom and gloom all the time."

"That's where I trained," Grandma Denise said as she pointed to a star on the map in northern California. "Whispering Trees," she continued with her gaze locked on the small star. "Long time ago."

"So Troy," his mom looked at him. "Want to go pick out your mace?"

"Sure," he almost yelled into the relative hush of the chamber.

"First we have a surprise for you," his mom said with a genuine, magnificent smile.

"What's that?"

Her chin lifted as she indicated something over his right shoulder. He turned and the floor dropped out from beneath his feet. There stood Angela with her parents in tow.

"Hey Troy," she said shining in the soft light of the Cathedral. Her blonde hair bounced and swayed hypnotically at the softest touch of wind from the open door. The angel marks on the edges of her smooth cheeks were perfectly pink. She raced forward and thrust a small box into his hands. "Happy birthday!"

For what seemed like a short eternity, Troy stammered as he tried to catch the breath that had been knocked from his lungs. "I… thanks," he finally managed. "Where have you been the past few days?"

"Open your present first," she said as her parents grinned and waved in greeting. Her mom's blonde hair was a little longer than Angela's but she often kept it bunched at the back of her head instead of fluttering and flowing with every move like Angela's did. Light blue angel markings spun on Susan William's upper cheeks.

Troy fumbled with the wrapped box for a few seconds. After he tugged away the plain, brown paper, he opened a thin box to discover a small statue made of lustrous wood.

"It's Gabriel," Angela said hopefully. "I got it in a little shop at the Cathedral in Brazil. The angel who sold it to me said you'd be the first person to actually touch it. He said it was carved with the Spirit, not by hand. Do you like it?"

Troy licked his lips and cleared a huge frog from his throat. "It's awesome," he said as he rubbed his thumb along the powerful wings attached to Gabriel's back. The archangel stared unmoving in a majestic pose. Troy pulled his eyes away from the figurine of his favorite archangel and looked up at Angela. "What were you doing in Brazil?"

"Not a lot," Paul Williams said as he reached around his daughter and shook hands with Troy. "A little of this and a little of that. Happy birthday." The diminutive angel smiled in his pleasant way. His dark hair and brown angel markings gave the impression that he'd fit right in at an angel accounting firm, but Troy had seen the wrath of the Spirit behind his eyes and knew he wouldn't want to get on his bad side.

"Come on Troy," his mom called with an upraised and inviting arm. "Let's go get something to eat then wait for your dad to get here so we can pick out your mace."

Troy smiled and settled in beside Angela who was busy dodging the flirting bombardment of Samson who'd turned his attention on her. Troy physically had to hold his hand from reaching out like Samson's to get the smallest touch on her skin which was purer than the whitest snowflake. He remembered his lips being within an inch of hers after she'd been granted her scepter the previous year.

He'd been so close but still so far away. Only his imagination fulfilled his ultimate fantasy of sharing even the briefest of kisses with the stunning girl; who'd grabbed his attention at his first visit to Passover Hill several years before. Of course, he hadn't even really talked to her until last year when she moved to Mustang with her family; but he thought everything had been progressing as well as could be expected since then.

"I'm not real hungry," Angela said as they made their way into the hallway that led to the sanctuary. To his right, Troy looked up at a tall cross that bore witness to the ultimate sacrifice in forgiveness of sins. In front of him, lined along the walls, were the wonderful stores which held most any item an angel could ever need or want.

There was Michael's Angel Fixings where he'd soon buy his very own mace. Beside it, Divine Delights beckoned with the sweetest smell of bubbling chocolate. A sign in the window read: *Forbidden Fudge, So tasty it can't be a sin.* Across the hall was Scepters and More where Troy and Angela had been forced to start wearing ferriolas last summer. At that time, the injustice and embarrassment of wearing the bracelet (which could communicate with scepters) had felt like a sledge hammer blow to his stomach. But the small device had saved them from being killed in Kyle's trap. Troy still wore his pulsing bracelet in honor of that fact.

"I'm not really hungry either," he echoed and hoped his rumbling stomach wouldn't betray him as they stopped in front of Spice of Life where burgers were flipping in the air from small bursts of light from the owner's scepter. "Can I go take a look in the sanctuary real quick?"

His mom grinned and nodded with a glance at Angela. "Fine," she purred. "We'll meet you beside the statue of Jacob in an hour. Your dad should be here by then."

And so Troy grabbed Angela's hand and steered her towards the sanctuary. The burning bush stood silent in its patch of sacred dirt at the end of a long hallway but Troy ignored it and rushed through two kissing doors. Rows and rows of pews lined the rough, stone floor. Overhead the tall, oak ceiling echoed their soft footfalls. Troy held his breath and lifted his eyes to the far wall. Nothing but a bare stretch of white stones met his gaze. He turned to Angela and saw her taking in the magnificence of the gate to heaven.

"Still can't see it?" she asked as her eyes darted from side to side at the glory.

"No," he admitted trying not to be too downhearted. What did he need to do in order to qualify to see the gate like most other angels? Like he had his whole life, he tried to take a quick peek out of the corners of his eyes in a futile hope to catch a glimpse of the gate.

"Maybe next time," Angela breathed as though she was savoring, even, the smell and taste of the gate. They turned and made their way slowly back to the store lined hallway. "Want to grab a bite to eat? I heard your stomach growling when we were in the sanctuary."

Troy chuckled with a sheepish shrug. "Sure. I can wait though if you've already eaten or something."

"No, a burger sounds good," Angela replied and pushed her hair behind her ear. "I only said I wasn't hungry so we could ditch the parents." Another rumble lurched in Troy's stomach but this one had nothing to do with food. He closed his mouth from where it had fallen open and ran a hand across his face to make sure no drool was escaping.

They stepped into Spice of Life a few seconds later. "Hurry up," Angela urged with a hand pressing into the small of Troy's back.

"What's wrong?" he asked.

"Ben Lewis and Justin Baker are coming," Angela hissed and ducked into a booth with Troy dragged along behind her. He peeked over his shoulder into the hallway and saw the two boys walk by. "They'd talk our ears off," Angela continued. "At least Justin would. He's got to be the biggest gossiper at the Hill. I'm not looking forward to all the questions he'll bombard us with this summer."

"Yeah, he caught me here a couple of months ago," Troy laughed. "Said he'd heard I'd been killed by a pack of selvo and you'd been kidnapped by Kyle Downey to ransom for my parent's lives. He seemed kind of disappointed when I told him what really happened."

"Not quite as cool," Angela giggled. Her arm shook with the laughter and for the first time Troy recognized that he'd been pulled into the booth on the same side of the table as her. He froze not knowing if it had been intentional on Angela's part or happened on accident in the mad scramble to stay out of Ben and Justin's view. He eyed the booth across the table and wondered if he should move, but before he could make up his mind, a plump angel woman flitted to their table.

"What can I get you two?" she asked with a gracious smile.

"Burger and tea for me," Angela replied with her eyes coming off the menu.

"Same for me," Troy said. "With cheese and pickles."

"It'll be right out," the woman said and trundled away.

"Did Tyler, Clark, and Becky give you that book?" Angela said drawing his attention. Troy couldn't stop himself from noticing how their shoulders rubbed together and the sweet smell of fresh linen poured at him from her direction. His stomach clenched and unclenched with each breath and he called on the Spirit to calm his racing heart.

"Yeah," he answered trying to sound like he really cared about the book when all he could think about at the moment was the slight touch of her arm against his. "It was pretty cool. I looked over it last night. Had some funny stories about angels in it." He stopped without knowing what else to say. Angela was absently twirling a packet of sugar in her hands as she listened to him. "So, what were y'all doing in Brazil?"

"Oh, nothing really," she informed. "My dad was giving some advice on a horde of reidlos. The usual… kind of boring for me and mom. We didn't get to see much of anything but the Cathedral there. We even spent the night in a visitor's room back behind the sanctuary. My parents never left me alone for a single second. One would go somewhere and the other would pop into their place like some type of weird magic trick. I mean, all the way to Brazil and I didn't get to see anything."

"It's been that way ever since Kyle almost killed us, hasn't it?" Troy said more as a statement than a question.

"I suppose, it's getting old though."

"We had a Justice Minister come by our house last night," Troy added. "Said he was wanting to talk to your dad."

"Who was it?"

"Guy named Luke Fischer."

"Oh man," Angela said with a serious look around. "Don't say anything about him around my mom. Her head will explode. She can't stand most of the Justice Ministers but Luke is always calling my dad and trying to get him to join them again. I'm not sure if my mom hates anyone but if she did… he might be up there as my first guess."

Troy smiled remembering his mom's attitude towards the Minister. "My mom wasn't very nice to him either. What was it like when your dad was a Justice Minister?"

"I don't remember really," Angela sighed. "He was gone a lot and my mom always seemed worried. They argued about it quite a bit but she finally got him to quit."

"So… did you hear what I got to do yesterday?" Troy asked.

"Yes and you suck," Angela fumed but with a sweet smile. "My parents would never take me on a demon hunt. I couldn't believe it when my mom told me."

"It was just nylla," Troy said.

"Still, it had to be cool. What were they like?"

Troy spent the next ten minutes describing the screaming horse demons and each step of the fight. They ate their burgers and talked about all the news on the War for Sins they'd heard the past few days.

"Luke said some stuff about Kyle last night," Troy started but stopped as his mom almost flew into the shop. Her robes had appeared; as had her halo and wings which were locked in a rigid stance.

"Come on," she said with a searching look around the restaurant.

"What's up?" Troy asked.

"I'm not sure," his mom replied and swept them from the store as she dropped money on the table. "I got a call from your dad a minute ago and he said something terrible has happened. He didn't say much more than that but we're supposed to meet him in the sanctuary in ten minutes. We have time to get your mace real quick."

They rushed down the hallway and stomped into Michael's Angel Fixings. Angela waited outside with her parents who both had their scepters in hand. A clean-shaven angel with orange marks smiled at them. "Hey Emily," he said. "For God, we fight. Can I help you with something?"

"It's Troy's birthday," his mom pulled him forward. The ever present smell of spring flowers filled his nose as she draped an arm over his shoulders. "And he wants a mace of his own. Doesn't think Brian's is cool enough."

"I see," the store clerk said with a nod that made his halo twinkle. "Right back here. We have one of the best selections around." He eyed Troy for a brief second then grabbed a mace from a rack where the weapons were lined beside a row of steel shields. "How about this one? It's kind of on the big side. A little heavier than most but you're going to be a big guy. It'll be something you can grow into." He handed the paddle-like weapon to Troy who accepted it with wonder on his face.

The feel of the wooden handle was perfect in his hands. Every twitch of his arms brought the wonderful weapon to life. The balance never faltered. Troy knew he didn't need to try another one. "It's perfect," he stammered as he studied the smooth, almost marble looking, wood. The fat end looked primed and ready to smack nylla at any drop of a hat.

"Very good," the clerk said. "I'll throw in this shoulder strap for free. It won't come and go like your sword and sheath will when you get them, but it's a cool way to carry around a mace."

Troy accepted the strap and slung it over his arms. The mace slide in without a single bump and automatically closed snug around it. "Michael's doing," the clerk winked. "He blessed it so it wouldn't slide around."

While his mom paid, Troy drew the mace in and out of the strap and relished the feeling of the fabric grabbing and releasing the weapon.

"Sweet," Angela voiced in awe as he exited the shop. "Tyler is going to be so jealous. You should make him beg before you let him swing it." She nudged him playfully with her elbow but before Troy could agree his dad charged down the hallway from the direction of the sanctuary.

"Where's your mom?" he barked at Troy.

"Right here," she answered from the doorway of Michael's Angel Fixings. "What's wrong?"

"Come on," his dad snagged her arm and began dragging her towards Samson's chamber. Troy followed close behind with Angela and her parents following on his heels. "Jessica Randell was killed this morning," his dad explained in a whisper that Troy noticed made several angels in close proximity jerk their ears upright in attention. "Luke took me to Little Rock where she was living. The Justice Ministers had a fight at her house last night with some reidlos... but they're sure it was Kyle who killed her."

Troy's mom blanched and her face went pale white. "Why would he kill Jessica? He's left her alone all these years. She was sure he'd never bother her. Are you sure it was him and not the reidlos?"

From his pocket, Troy's dad drew out a silver necklace. On it dangled three precious gems. A sparkling white opal hung in the middle with a green amethyst on one side and a blue sapphire on the other. Troy's mom covered her mouth and choked. "I haven't seen that..." she started but stopped in a sob.

"Since Kyle asked you to give it back to him," Troy's dad finished. "He gave it to Jessica afterwards when they were dating... It was tied on the wall over her body."

Tears fell down his mom's cheeks as angels all around stopped what they were doing to watch the mad dash out the front doors. Samson barely got a thundering word out before the doors slammed behind them. Troy's parents and grandma hustled him and the Williams to the Tahoe. His dad's words bounced around his head as the tires squealed out of the parking lot. What was going on? What did the necklace mean? And why did his mom look like she might die of a heart attack at any moment?

Angela's bewildered gaze met Troy's and he could see the same questions swirling behind her startled eyes. Something awful was lurking behind the horrid murder of one of his parent's old friends. Troy prayed it stopped there but knew deep in his heart that the storm was only building.

Chapter 4: Guardian Angels

"So your parents wouldn't say anything else about it?" Tyler whispered over their cafeteria pizza at lunch the next day.

"Not a word," Troy answered as he picked off a round, rubbery slice of pepperoni and popped it in his mouth. "I heard them arguing about it but then one of them used subbia."

Tyler's face twisted in confusion. "It suppresses sound in a small area," Angela explained. "Our parents use it all the time to keep us from eavesdropping."

"I know my mom cried quite a bit about Jessica," Troy confessed. "I heard her ask, *why now,* several times before they sealed out the sound. I think they were all friends back when they were students at the Hill. They went to the funeral this morning."

Angela stared into space for several seconds while she crunched on a crouton from a leafy salad. "Seems like Downey's really starting to go after everyone your parents have ever known," she mused.

"That's scary," Becky said with her teeth chattering from her spot directly to Troy's right. "He was so terrible at that house. I don't know how anyone can stand up to him."

All the friends stewed on Becky's words while they finished up lunch. Finally, Tyler broke the subdued silence.

"I'm ready to show the coaches what's up at the 7 on 7 drills this afternoon," he boasted. "You better be on your game today, Troy. We need to secure the starting spots for the fall and that all starts right now. Especially since you'll be gone all summer. Even if you'll be doing all the cool stuff in Michael's classes with that Butler guy you talk about all the time, you need to practice with a football. Just toss it up and down to keep your hands fresh, at least."

"What?" Troy asked shaking away the thought of his mom crying. He never liked seeing his mom sad. Part of it was because he knew it had to do with Kyle most of the time; which meant a shadow of danger lurked in the background. But mostly because none of her wonderful smiles beamed rays of sunshine when tears were brimming in her eyes.

"7 on 7, this afternoon," Tyler enlightened in a slow voice as though he was talking to someone who didn't understand English. "The coaches will be watching us to see how we stand up to Blake and the other guys who'll be seniors next season."

Troy blinked and pushed away an image of the sparkling necklace his dad had returned with from the grisly murder in Little Rock. "Oh, yeah," he said. "I'll be ready."

"Troy probably doesn't care about football much right now," Becky jumped in as though she read his exact thoughts. "There's a lot more important stuff going on that kind of trumps football, you know."

Tyler chortled and shook his head. "You won't ever understand guys," he laughed. "Football trumps everything, including angel stuff."

Becky rolled her eyes as they stood for the afternoon bell signaling them back to class. "See you in sixth hour," Clark waved and led Tyler and Becky down the hallway of the west wing of the Mustang 9th Grade Center.

"Later," Troy called and headed to geometry with Angela. At the fork leading to the basketball gym, Troy did a double take at two mopping janitors. Yellow angel marks dotted one face and red swirled on the other. Both men nodded as Troy and Angela walked by. "There's more of them than there used to be," he whispered after they took their seats in class with a few minutes to spare before the tardy bell. "Everywhere I go there are angels keeping an eye on me."

"It's getting like that for all of us," Angela shrugged. "Everyone is on high alert these days. They know Downey's history and that he's most likely after you. He said as much in that house last year. Your parents are just worried. And rightfully so."

"Gets old," Troy fumed. "Everywhere I turn there's another angel hovering over my shoulder. They should be out killing demons or catching fallen angels, not stuck here babysitting us."

Angela nodded a little as she opened her textbook and withdrew the homework they'd been assigned on the previous Friday. "With the War getting so bad I think a lot of parents are worried that fallen angels might try to kidnap their kids from school. It won't be as bad when we get to the Hill. The fallen can't get any demons in there with them... or not easily at least."

"Have you heard your parents say much about the War lately?" Troy questioned as he looked over his own homework to discover he'd forgotten to finish the last answer when he'd started studying *Justice and the Spirit* the previous night. He quickly diagrammed the remaining lines and angles of the polygon and filled in the proper formulas as Mr. Purcell entered the class with his briefcase in tow.

"Not really," Angela whispered. "Nothing more than we talked about yesterday."

The rest of the afternoon spilled away with fresh assurances from the teachers that the end of the year exams would be the most difficult they'd ever faced. Troy made notes but found himself daydreaming about the fight with the nylla more often than not. Becky had to nudge him in the back when Mrs. Kingfisher asked him a question in sixth hour English.

"Man, Troy," Clark murmured on the way to the varsity boys' locker room after the class. "You're going to start getting in trouble if you don't pay attention. Mrs. Kingfisher wasn't very happy with your answer."

Troy shrugged with a sheepish smile. "Lots of people mix-up Shakespeare stories," he offered.

"Yeah, but not many can blend Hamlet, Macbeth, Romeo and Juliet, and Henry V into one answer," Tyler laughed with a slap on Troy's back in mock celebration. "That was a brilliant answer. I never knew Macbeth hated Juliet so much. Makes sense, I guess."

Clark guffawed as they entered the locker room to change for football practice. All around them the players poured into the sweat smelling confines. "Look at him," Tyler hissed under his breath. "He thinks he so cool."

Troy followed his gaze to find Blake Mitchell changing into a blue target jersey indicating he was a quarterback and off-limits to being demolished by a blitzing linebacker. Behind him, the two angel janitors were pretending to exam an overhead light. "He's not bad," Troy sighed. "He's always been nice to me. Some of the other senior guys can be jerks."

"It's all an act," Tyler hissed some more. "He knows he's supposed to be a *leader*." He stressed leader with a vehement twist. "But I think he's egging on Darrell and the other lineman to not block as good for me."

"I doubt it," Clark assured as he tucked his enormous helmet under his beefy arm. "I think he wants what's best for the team."

"Yeah, you keep thinking that," Tyler jeered. "He's got everyone believing it."

"You don't like him because he's probably going to be the starting quarterback next year," Clark said.

Tyler glared at their big friend for a fraction of a second before donning his own quarterback jersey. "Whatever," he grumbled. "Just remember who your friend is when we get out there. And block a little better for me."

Practice lasted almost two hours in the hot and windy afternoon. Troy found himself having to pull his concentration away from thoughts of necklaces, fallen angels, and demons before every new play. He still managed to grab two touchdown passes from Tyler to the loud whoops of his fellow players and the coaches.

"That was awesome!" Tyler roared as the trio made their way to his dad's Cadillac Escalade. "There's no way we won't beat out those seniors."

"Not many sophomores get to start," Clark warned as they piled onto the leather seats of the SUV.

"Hey guys," Mr. Henry, Tyler's dad, hummed from the front seat. A Rolex watch flashed in the sunlight as he drove forward. Tyler's wavy, blonde hair matched his dad's almost down to the single lock. "You all look in good moods," he said as smooth as silk.

"That's cause we whooped up on the older guys," Tyler boomed. "They don't stand a chance."

"Well good," Mr. Henry smiled a million dollar smile.

Tyler settled into his seat with a deep, satisfied breath. "I threw four touchdown passes," he boasted. "Two of them to Troy. Blake only threw two touchdowns and he threw a couple of interceptions too."

"Fantastic," Mr. Henry beamed. "Good for you guys. Sounds like the varsity spots will be all yours. Clark already has his lined up from what you've told me and now it looks like you and Troy are set as well. I knew they wouldn't be able to break the three of you up. You've been playing together since Little League."

Tyler nodded in utter satisfaction but Troy's attention was drawn to a pair of faces in a car driving beside them on highway 152. Sparkling angel marks reflected at him through the tinted windows. A man and a pleasant looking woman looked away in a hurry when they noticed his gaze. Troy heaved a sigh and tried to melt into the plush leather.

"How am I supposed to know if they're good angels or fallen?" Troy griped to Angela later that evening. They were lounging in his bedroom practicing subbia.

"What?" Angela mouthed. Troy shook his head and released the power of the Spirit. "You got it to work really good that time," she praised. "I didn't hear anything at all. I just saw your mouth move."

"I was saying, how are we supposed to know if all these angels following us around everywhere are good or bad?" Troy repeated. "It would be an easy way for Kyle to follow me around too. Stick one of his people on me to pretend like he's there to help and he'd know where I am all the time. It'd be like that Raymond guy all over again," Troy said referencing a blue marked fallen angel who had tailed him for Kyle the previous year.

"At least we'll know there are angels within reach if we need immediate help," Angela said. "I heard my parents say there might be Justice Ministers stationed at the Hill this summer. They seem worried there might be an attack there."

"Surely not," Troy sputtered. "They can't send demons onto sacred ground without breaching the rules of the War. And the fallen would be idiots to attack by themselves. In fact… I wish they would. Then we could round them all up in one sweep."

"I don't know," Angela's eyebrows knitted giving her a cute puppy dog pucker. "Everyone's really stressed out with all the killings that have happened in the last few months. Think about it, Jessica Randell's son goes to the Hill. He's a year younger than us."

"I forgot about that," Troy admitted as he searched his memory for the boy's face. "Can't believe I didn't think about him. His name's Billy. They came over to our house a few years ago. Only for a couple of hours. That's the only time I ever met Jessica. I think my parents tried to keep their distance from people in their past."

"Makes sense," Angela agreed. "It's so sad to think about him losing his mom. At least he knows she's in heaven… I heard she was a Healer. That's what I want to be when I get my wings."

Troy nodded in agreement to both statements. He couldn't imagine having either of his parents killed in the War and with how things were going, more and more dangers lurked around every corner. And Angela, of course, would be a Healer under Raphael when she was gifted her wings.

"A Reader for me," he said. "Like both my parents. Maybe one of Michael's Soldiers but I've always been more drawn to Gabriel than any of the other archangels." He glanced at the small wooden statue Angela had given him for his birthday. The archangel stared proudly in all his glory from the desk beside Troy's laptop.

"And you're so good with auditome and with the shield," Angela said. "I bet you're right."

"Have to get all the gifts first," Troy let out a resigned breath and tried subbia in a space that enveloped his entire room. The Spirit briefly brightened from his scepter and the transparent bubble shimmered for a split second.

"It worked good that time," Angela grinned in acknowledgement. "I bet we could scream at the top of our lungs and our parents wouldn't hear us."

Troy laughed but shook his head and waved his hands as she drew in a deep breath to let out an earsplitting holler. "Have your parents told you how they got their robes?" he asked with a chuckle when her cheeks deflated comically.

"Nope," she frowned. "It's all so secret and *we're not supposed to ask*." She said the last part in a falsely deep voice that Troy guessed was an imitation of her dad.

"My grandma told me and showed me how she got hers," Troy contemplated and saw Angela's interest peak. "She jumped between an attacking selvo and one of her friends. About got her arm chopped off."

Angela grimaced and massaged her own arm. "That doesn't sound like fun," she said with a twist to her perfect lips. "I guess we'll have to be on the lookout for demons to jump in front of. We can send Tyler out as bait."

Troy chuckled and read another passage in *Touching Grace* by Demetra Davenport. A diagram of a young male angel in full concentration illustrated Raphael's ability of azaria which helped angels sharpen memories. Troy flipped the page quickly with a sigh. He couldn't wait until all the abilities became second nature to him like they were for his parents. For now, he heard his dad's voice ring in his head, "*Study hard. And have faith.*"

The week of school rolled by in a cascade of homework and a flood of touchdown passes from Tyler to Troy during football practice. On Friday, Troy sat in the gym bleachers at 3:00 in the afternoon waiting for the end of the day bell. Coach Lokey, the head varsity football coach, had attended an offensive schemes seminar at the University of Oklahoma in Norman so the football players had been given a free hour.

"Glad your mom can give us a ride," Tyler quipped at Troy. "I'd hate to have to walk home."

"Hey," Angela called from the big double doors leading to the hallway. "Let's go." Becky stood by her side waiting for the three boys as they descended the steps of the bleachers.

"Having fun?" Becky teased. "Must be nice to have a free hour."

"Eh, I'd rather be showing up Blake again," Tyler said and draped his arms around both girls' shoulders to turn them around. Becky rolled her eyes and shrugged from his grasp but Angela only smiled and let Tyler lead her into the school hallway. Troy hurried to get in front of them and racked his brain for an excuse to pull Angela into a conversation. But before he managed the smallest of brain waves; tiny, inaudible words filtered into his ears.

"Oh God. Please, not again," the soft voice cried.

Troy stopped midstride and held his breath.

"What's up?" Clark asked as the gigantic lineman nimbly sidestepped him avoiding what would have been a potentially lethal collision for Troy.

"I heard something," Troy explained. "With auditome."

"Gabriel's gift of reading minds?" Becky whispered with her hazel eyes going wide.

"Is it a fallen angel?" Tyler squawked. "Or a demon?"

Troy squinted and waved away their frenzied suggestions. He shook his head to concentrate. The Spirit flowed and streamed down the hallway leading to the cafeteria. Around a bend, Troy caught the subtle textures of a mind. A frightened, scared girl stood just out of sight.

"Go the other way," the voice begged. *"Not this way. Go the other way. Please God, make them go the other way. Oh no!"*

"Hey Alex, look!" hollered a boy's voice from the adjoining hallway. "It's fatty Patty!"

Troy and all his friends looked at each other then headed down the hallway towards the commotion. The Spirit pulsed and a vision of a short, somewhat round shouldered girl flashed before Troy's eyes. In front of her, three taunting boys laughed and poked. Troy pushed the vision away and sped faster down the hallway.

"Hey fatty Patty," a new voice cackled. "Have any Twinkies you can spare?"

"What are you talking about?" the first voice jeered. "Even if she brought a whole box this morning, she wouldn't have any left by now."

From around the corner, Patty Lovelace, scurried in a desperate attempt to create space from the taunting voices. Thick glasses adorned a rather pug-like nose and extended over chubby cheeks to her ears. Troy worried the glasses might slip and fall to the floor since her eyes were glued to her shuffling feet. He had history in third hour with the shy girl who sat in the back of the class rarely saying a word.

Five seconds later, two teenage boys scrambled around the same corner behind Patty. Wide smiles spread across their faces but they stumbled to a halt when Troy and his friends came into view.

"What are you guys doing?" Troy growled while Clark flexed his considerable muscles.

"W-w-what?" Gavin Robison faltered. "Nothing man… we, uh, h-h-how's it going?"

"What were you just saying to Patty?" Tyler barked using his quarterback's cadence to recoil the two boys.

"What?" Alex Gibson gritted his teeth. Long, black and unkempt hair dangled down his head and obstructed half his face. A baggy, grungy t-shirt hung over sagging jeans. A faded skull leered from the black cloth. "Don't know what you're talking about, man."

"We heard you," Angela pressed and stepped next to Patty who had slouched over to the wall with a look like she'd love nothing more than to magically absorb her way through it. "Don't try to say you didn't do anything wrong."

"Whatever," Alex griped. "Just cause the cool kids say we did something doesn't mean it's true."

"How about we ask Patty?" Becky asked with a not so innocent (or nice) grin directed at the now back peddling boys.

"C-c-come on Alex," Gavin sputtered and turned.

With a flash of light from the Spirit, Troy caught a long but rapid series of snapshots. Each vision was of Gavin cowering beneath the hands of an older version of himself. With every blow, Gavin diminished behind a wall of shame. Years and years of not brutal, but continuous, beatings lay in the boy's past.

"Gavin," Troy called at the bullies' hasty retreat. The boy turned halfway around as Alex pushed him down the hallway. "God loves you… and so does your brother. Don't let him tear you down. Hurting other people won't make the pain stop. Have faith and God will show you the way."

Gavin froze and Troy thought he saw a shimmer of tears at the corner of his eyes before Alex yanked him around the corner.

"Thanks," Patty murmured barely more audible than the words Troy had heard in his head with auditome.

"You okay?" Becky leaned down and looked up into the girl's gaze which was still locked on her sneakers.

"Yeah," Patty sniffed and looked up. "It's not too bad."

"They shouldn't be doing it," Clark rumbled and for a second Troy thought he was going to charge down the hallway in pursuit of the two boys. His ham-sized fists looked ready to rain down knockout blows.

"It's okay," Patty wiped the back of her hand across her nose. She began to trundle towards the doors.

"Are you sure?" Angela asked. "Do you need a ride or anything?"

"No thanks. I ride the bus."

"We'd be happy to take you home," Troy offered. "My mom is picking us up. We'll have plenty of room."

"That's okay," Patty continued forward awkwardly.

"Come on," Tyler said. "It's not a problem."

At his words Patty stopped and peeked over her shoulder at Tyler. "I'll be fine," she produced the smallest of smiles. "I saw you at church last week."

"Oh, yeah," Tyler cleared his throat. "I remember seeing you too."

Troy gritted his teeth and managed to keep a scowl from crossing his face at the obvious lie.

"Tell your dad it's not polite to text during the sermon," Patty said as a dimple creased her cheeks. She glanced at Tyler with an accusatory, but hopeful twinkle on her face then headed for the door with somewhat of a small bounce in her step. "And, it was really nice what you said to Gavin about God," she called over her shoulder now looking at Troy. "Not many people will talk about stuff like that at school." With that she pushed her way out the glass doors.

"Why do people act like that?" Angela snapped with her eyes going from Patty then glaring down the hallway where Alex and Gavin had fled. "It's so stupid."

Troy swallowed to make sure the smallest hint of a smile didn't lift his lips. Not even the absolute anger on her face could hide the natural beauty. He tried his best not to stare at her.

"What were you saying to Gavin about his brother?" Becky asked pulling Troy's attention away from Angela as they followed Patty outside. A brilliant blue sky met them along with a wash of hot, dry air.

"I got a vision of his brother beating him up," Troy explained. "It's been happening for years. Ever since they were little kids."

"That doesn't give him the right to pick on other people," Angela said.

"No, it doesn't," Troy agreed as he watched Patty board a yellow bus with a friendly but shy greeting at the driver.

"There's your mom," Tyler pointed into the parking lot. "Let's go before my shoes melt to the concrete. Has it ever been this hot in May? If we'd been in full pads yesterday, I probably would have passed out from heat exhaustion."

"Moses said the increased demon activity causes some of it," Angela said as she shielded the sun from her eyes with her right hand. Troy remembered their teacher from the Hill railing on the subject the previous summer. He smiled at the picture of the tall wooden sculpture twisting and jabbing during the discussion.

"I forgot about that," he recollected with a chuckle. "I definitely need to go on some more demon hunts... It's getting unbearable." He glanced at Patty's bus and noticed the two janitor angels now disguised as police officers directing traffic out of the parking lot. They waved and smiled at Troy's mom when she drove past. His smile immediately vanished and he didn't participate in the joking conversations on the short drive home.

"Do I have to have angels following me wherever I go?" Troy asked his mom after Angela jumped nimbly from the Tahoe and waved her thanks for the ride. All Troy's other friends were already dropped of safely at home as well.

"You've noticed?" his mom asked innocently.

"Uh, yeah," Troy snorted. "It's pretty obvious."

"It's just added precautions," she shrugged and turned onto their street. "With Kyle targeting so many people we know and with everything that happened last year... we think it's a good idea to have some extra security."

Troy brooded on the facts as they pulled into the three car garage of their spacious, suburban home. "What does Kyle want with me so bad?" he asked.

"Probably the same thing he wants with everyone else we've ever known," his mom sighed. "To hurt me and your dad by killing you. I think he's trying to kill everyone we've ever talked to."

"He didn't say he wanted to kill me," Troy cleared his throat. "He said he wanted to watch me fall… like he did."

His mom shivered as she walked through the door into the kitchen. "Don't believe anything he said in that house last year," she said matter of factly. "He's one of Lucifer's followers now. I imagine he has all sorts of twisted reasons for doing all the terrible stuff he's done. It's all lies." She slid her purse onto the counter and turned with a beaming smile. "You want something to eat? I could whip up some brownies real quick."

"Just some cereal or something is fine," Troy flopped into a chair at the kitchen table. "It just feels weird having all these angels following me around. I don't even know if they're good or if they might be fallen spying on me. What if you give me a picture of all the angels watching me? Then I'd maybe be able to spot a fallen angel if there is a spy. Or maybe you could introduce them?"

"You know… that's a pretty good idea," his mom poured milk on top of a full bowl of Cheerios. "Want peanut butter in it? That's how your dad eats it."

"No thanks," Troy laughed and accepted the glass bowl. "Is he out on another demon hunt?"

"Not today," his mom sat down beside him with a glass of water. She stared into it for a long time while Troy munched on his snack. "We thought about moving," she said quietly.

"What! No way," Troy gagged on a mouthful of cereal. "I'm not leaving my friends. They might be targets for Kyle now too. He saw all of them at that house. He knows who they are. He has to know where they live and everything." His brain sparked with pictures of all his friends flashing. Angela's soft grin held before his eyes as he looked intently at his mom. "We can't move."

"I know," his mom said with a flustered wave of her delicate hand. "It was just something we thought about for a while. We knew it wouldn't be for the best in the end. God didn't grant us all the gifts to hide... but with Jessica getting killed, it's something we might have to think about again. She was a powerful angel. It shouldn't have been easy to kill her but your dad said it looked like a quick fight."

Troy watched her in silence until he finished his cereal. She didn't say anything as she continued staring at her glass of untouched water. Then he stomped to his room and pulled a picture off his desk of all his friends. Loads of smiles and laughter echoed from the photograph of all of them standing in front of the Christmas tree last December. Troy's forefinger ran over the image of Angela and he swore to himself that he'd never leave her side.

Chapter 5: Demons on the Rise

Tests, homework, and football consumed the next three weeks for Troy and his friends. A small scrapbook with pictures of all the guardian angels resided in Troy's backpack and he found himself studying his protectors every chance he got.

"Do you remember any angels following you that aren't in there?" Becky asked on the last day of school. They were sitting in the shade of an oak tree on a table outside the east entrance. Heat simmered in the air above the parking lot and sweat was running freely down Troy's back.

"Nope," he sighed not letting the broiling frustration fill his words. He'd been sure a spy would be unmasked when he knew the identities of the security detail. But unless a fallen angel had infiltrated the deepest corners of his parent's protection, his theory had been dashed.

"That's good then," Becky smiled and signed his yearbook with her big, loopy letters. "It's going to suck when you and Angela leave for the summer. Everything can still feel a little weird between me and Tyler when y'all aren't around."

"Really?" Troy asked looking closely at her. He couldn't see any signs of stress in her smooth, olive face. "I figured you were both over that. It's been quite a while since you broke up."

She shrugged and finished her note in his yearbook with a quick but wonderful sketch of a pair of angel wings.

"We went out for a long time," she said working her mouth around in small circles as though her nose itched and she couldn't scratch it with her hand. "My mom still calls him my boyfriend whenever she sees him… which is funny since she never really liked him."

"She probably would more now," Troy laughed. "Since he's going to church."

"Yeah, he's coming with us this Sunday," she admitted. "He said his dad doesn't want to push his luck too much with his mom. And he's gone to church for three straight Sunday's so he's worried about lightning bolts burning him down from her eyes. Here he comes."

Troy turned and saw Tyler directing Angela through a doorway with his arm draped over her shoulder. For a brief second, an angry monster jumped into Troy's chest but he forced it down with an amused smile as Tyler tromped forward and threw his other arm over Becky's shoulder. She started to shrug away but instead settled against the handsome quarterback with a resigned sigh.

"School's done," Tyler crooned. "Time for a whole summer of fun!"

"You guys are going to have to be careful," Angela warned. "Downey knows who you are. He could come after you."

"Oh please," Tyler scoffed. "Y'all worry too much. Besides, we'll probably have ten of those people from Troy's scrapbook guarding us all the time."

"Hopefully," Troy said wiping a trickle of sweat from his cheek.

"What are you talking about?" Tyler half shouted. "All you do is gripe about them."

"Yeah, when they're following me," Troy joked. "But y'all need the extra protection."

Becky punched him in the ribs playfully. "And you don't?" she asked stubbornly. "You're Kyle's main target… and all you do is get grumpy about a few angels hanging around. I think it's pretty cool."

"It's not like they don't have other stuff to do," Angela smirked in agreement with Becky.

"And that's my point," Troy said with the start of a scowl.

"Whatever," Angela said but she winked at him. "Hey, there's Clark. We still need to sign his yearbook and have him sign ours." She grabbed Becky's hand and they swayed in their hypnotic gaits towards the hulking boy who had exited from the north entrance of the L-shaped school.

Troy watched them go and noticed Tyler doing the same. "Do you still feel weird around Becky at all?" Troy asked as the girls bounded up next to Clark looking like oversized dolls beside the humungous lineman.

"What?" Tyler shook his head and pulled his gaze to Troy. "No. Not really. Why should I? She broke up with me. It's not like I was the one who ended it. I'm on to greener pastures…"

"With who?" Troy laughed as he looked back where Angela and Becky were forcing Clark to sign their yearbooks.

Tyler glanced around as though there might be secret agents listening in conspiratorially on the conversation. "You might not know her… she's a sophomore this year but she's on the varsity cheerleading squad. Lacey Blackwell."

"What?" Troy gaped in shock. "But… I thought she was going out with Blake?"

"Eh, not really," Tyler shrugged and cleared his throat. Troy studied his best friend and didn't need auditome to see a certain guilt budding behind his eyes.

"You're not going after her just to mess with Blake, are you?" he asked. "Cause that wouldn't be very cool."

"No, of course not," Tyler fumed a little too hard. "I… you know. She's hot."

"Come on man," Troy scolded. "You can't be doing stuff like that. People of faith are expected to live up to certain standards. I mean, I… well, do you really like her? Or are you doing it to mess with Blake?"

"Yeah, I really like her," Tyler fidgeted. "Kind of." He looked at Troy and rolled his eyes. "Fine. I won't-"

But his next words were cut off by the squeal of tires. They both whipped around to see Angela's parents tearing across the parking lot in her mom's Dodge Charger.

"What in the world?" Troy bellowed and began jogging towards Angela, Becky, and Clark. Tyler stayed right behind his shoulder.

When the car skidded to a halt, Angela's dad immediately jumped out and placed his arm protectively over his daughter. "Come on," he said. The power of the Spirit simmered in the air around him like a divine cocoon.

"What happened?" Angela squeaked.

"Let's go," her mom called from the driver's seat.

"Tell me what happened," Angela repeated with her voice growing stronger.

"They got Joseph Tennison," her dad spat.

"Oh God, no," Angela cried. "When?"

Her dad ushered her into the backseat. "This morning," he said and slammed the door then turned to Troy. "Your mom should be here… yes, here she comes." All of them turned to see Troy's mom's Tahoe flying around the corner of the neighborhood that surrounded the school. "She'll take the rest of you home."

With that, Angela and her parents raced from the parking lot. Troy's mom pulled into the spot they vacated less than ten seconds later. "Another angel killed?" Troy questioned already knowing the answer.

His mom nodded sadly. "Get in," she called. "All of you. I'll run you home. We have to hurry. Your dad and me have to get up to the old Hyatt hotel by the Cowboy Hall of Fame."

"What's going on?" Troy said as he jumped into the front passenger seat. Tyler, Becky, and Clark scrambled into the back.

"Your dad found a big reidlos horde hiding in the basement," his mom informed as she wiped away a tear. "I have to go help them deal with it. There's a pretty big team going."

"Can I go?" Troy asked eagerly.

"No."

"I can help," Troy said pulling his scepter, and the sheath which hid his dagger, from his backpack. "I have my scepter now. I'm supposed to be helping with stuff like this."

"Not with reidlos," his mom answered with a tightness to her jaw that made any further objections stick in Troy's throat. "Not until you get older and have all your gifts from God. They're too dangerous."

"Where are Angela and her parents going?" Becky's shaky voice asked.

"A funeral," Troy's mom sniffed. He saw Becky stiffen and stifle tears in his peripheral vision. "Joseph was one of Paul's best friends. He was a Justice Minister." She paused in silence before continuing with more matter-of-factness to her voice. "Becky, your mom already called so I'm going to drop you off at your house. Tyler, your dad said you two had plans tonight. He's waiting for you at home."

"It's not something that can't be cancelled," Tyler said in a rush of words. "I'd rather stay with Troy. We should all stay together."

"Not tonight," Troy's mom countered. "Clark will have to stay at our house for a while because his dad is out on a call at a hospital but we think it would be safer for the rest of you to keep your distance. The last reidlos horde was a trap for... well, you know, we don't want to put you guys in danger. Troy and Clark, y'all will stay inside at our house. And I stress, inside. Grandma Denise will stay with you. There will be angels guarding all of you."

Troy's head spun and spun as his mom reeled off the plans. There'd been so many deaths in the last six months. When would it stop? He looked over his shoulder at his three friends and saw the same question reflecting on their faces. "Did Kyle kill this Joseph guy?" he asked tentatively.

For several seconds his mom chewed on her lower lip. Finally, with an angry burst of air she answered. "Not directly. It was some type of demon. We haven't heard all the news yet. But in the end... it all starts with Kyle. Either him or one of his fallen angels raised the demon, so it falls on their heads."

No more words were said as she drove first to Becky's house then to Tyler's. "Later," Tyler raised his head in farewell. "Call me."

"Okay," Troy returned the wave and they made the short drive down the street to his house. Grandma Denise sat in the recliner waiting for them. On the TV, the Angelic Agenda was blaring with a sad montage of a striking, dark headed angel who looked to be in his early thirties.

"*Joseph Tennison,*" the news anchor intoned. A somber suit and tie mourned under his gently flapping wings and shining halo. "*Was an angel that many of us should strive to be. A Justice Minister and a family man who saved countless souls. His death is another tragic turn in the War for Sins. Nobody can describe-*"

"I can't stand listening to them anymore," Troy's mom spat. "Turn that off, please." Grandma Denise complied without a word. "I have to go meet Brian. Keep a close watch Denise. Frank, Julia, and Linda will be outside." With that, her wings popped behind her back and her halo shined over her head. She strode forward and gave Troy a hug as her robes flowed slowly into view. The sweet, flowery smell persisted for several seconds after she departed out the front door in a gust of wind behind her wings.

"So what am I supposed to do with you two?" Grandma Denise chided. "Play checkers or something? They leave me stuck on babysitting duty more often than not anymore. I guess they don't think I can handle the dangers in my old age."

"I'd rather be going too," Troy said and slumped onto the couch. He tapped his scepter against his leg and let the soft light wash over him like a relaxing massage. "I never get to do anything cool."

"You're not a fully qualified angel yet," his grandma countered with a piercing look that told Troy he better watch his words carefully with her at the moment. "I, on the other hand, am. But they still stick me here babysitting instead of going out to fight."

"I would have taken you with me if I was them," Clark fidgeted in the recliner on the far side of the room. "I almost pass out every time I think about what you did in that house last year. It was so… awesome. Like God was standing right there beside us."

Grandma Denise contemplated the large boy for some time before breaking into a wrinkled smile. "It's nice being around people like you Clark," she offered and let out a slow breath. "I needed someone to cheer me up. I'm getting crankier with each new wrinkle. I didn't used to be this way." At this Troy stifled a laugh with a small cough. When had Grandma Denise ever not been cranky? His dad's stories of his own strict upbringing, under her stern watch, were legendary around the dinner table. She eyed Troy with a scrunched, lined forehead but turned to Clark. "So back to… what do you two want to do with the evening?"

"Could you tell us about the War for Sins?" Clark questioned before Troy could even think about opening his mouth. "Troy and Angela tell us what they know but they always say there's a lot more to it than they hear."

Grandma Denise sat back and looked slowly from Troy to Clark. Troy was sure he could see her thoughts twirling behind her bright eyes. "I wouldn't normally even consider it in front of someone who isn't an angel," she finally said. "But you, and Becky too, are as close as I've ever seen to a human being an angel. If Tyler was here, I'd have to decline… what do you want to know?"

"Everything," Clark said in awe which made Troy and Grandma Denise laugh.

"Troy can let you read his history books if he wants," Grandma Denise chuckled. "I don't think it's his favorite subject."

"It's because of how they teach history at the Hill," Troy said quickly. His scepter flashed in annoyance at his outburst. "If they concentrated on the battles and stuff, it would be a lot more interesting. Besides we want to know-"

"That's only a small part of the story though," Grandma Denise argued cutting him off. "And it doesn't show you the problems that led to the battles in the first place. Learning about the stuff between the battles might help us prevent the same problems from happening in the future."

"What about recent history?" Clark asked. "Like about Troy's grandpa and Xavier."

Grandma Denise looked long at Troy. He was sure a proud appreciation shined from her bright eyes. "I'm glad he's told you something about his Grandpa John," she said. "He was a great man. At the age of sixteen he was already one of the strongest angels around. The first time I saw him, I knew I would marry him. It was at an angel tournament. Xavier was there too. I was only twelve at the time and thought I was the luckiest girl in the world. John and Xavier were the same age but went to different angel academies. They were big rivals. That was the first time John beat Xavier… but not the last." She breathed deeply as her eyes fixed on the ceiling that Troy knew she wasn't seeing. "Nobody is for sure, but everyone believes Xavier was already a member of the Night Walkers at that time. They were only a handful of fallen angels that were trying to gain power. They eventually grew into a big problem. John always said he wished he'd noticed the darkness in Xavier then. He told me on a few occasions that he had dreams about going back in the past to tell his younger self to watch for the pain and anger that led Xavier down his dark path. It was one of the few regrets he ever mentioned… And it's why history is important. Always pay attention to those around you. You never know when they might need the smallest bit of help that will help mold their whole future."

"What about Kyle?" Troy asked quietly.

Grandma Denise harrumphed and a frown creased her face. "That's a story for your parents to tell. I remember him as a sweet boy with a polite smile and the best of manners. His mom was a great angel. She died tragically when he was eight or nine. His dad wasn't an angel and didn't cope well with her death. I think that was the start of Kyle's problems. Rumors are that Xavier came into his life then. And that definitely didn't help his situation. But I didn't notice much of a change. He even stayed with us quite a bit. Him and your dad were so close. Inseparable in those days."

"What happened to make them hate each other so much?"

"Your dad doesn't hate Kyle," Grandma Denise informed and her eyes came to rest on him. "You really are looking more and more like your grandpa."

"Come on," Troy grouched. "Don't change the subject."

"And acting more like him too," she tittered. "It's not a story for me to tell. Only your parents know what happened. They've always kept it a secret and may not know the whole story anyway. You won't find the reason in any history book either. Probably never will. Something snapped inside of him… I think it had to do with some lingering pain from his mom's death. Or maybe how his dad… it doesn't matter. All that matters now is that he's one of the worst fallen angels in the last two hundred years."

"He's scary," Clark mumbled and Troy could tell the big boy was holding away a shiver. "His sword was terrible."

"That's not his original sword," Grandma Denise informed. "The sword granted to him by God was magnificent. Not that monstrosity he got from Lucifer."

"He got his sword from the devil?" Clark choked.

"A lot of fallen angels discard the gifts they receive from God when they embrace evil," she said.

"But they still have their original wings and halo and stuff, right?" Clark asked.

"Some may. But most of God's gifts are abandoned. In some cases - the worst ones - God renounces the gifts altogether."

"I wish he'd take away the gifts as soon as an angel joins Lucifer," Troy said as he watched his scepter and hoped for a call from his parents or Angela.

"What about all the fallen angels who have repented in the end and embraced their faith in God?" Grandma Denise asked with one, penciled eyebrow lifting into her white hair.

Troy shrugged. "Doesn't seem like it happens very often. It would really help us if they didn't have their original gifts to use to spy on us."

"Faith and forgiveness," she warned in a very close resemblance to Troy's dad. "You need more of both."

For the next hour, Troy sat in silence and listened as his grandma told Clark stories out of the angel history books that had collected dust in his room. Fifteen minutes to 6:00pm, the doorbell rang.

"That will be your dad, Clark," Grandma Denise flitted from the room and answered the front door.

A few seconds later, the burly preacher stepped into the room with his normal, huge smile shining. He was dressed in his Sunday best. A short beard speckled with white covered his dark face. "Here are the fine young gentlemen we're looking for," he boomed. "What are you guys doing inside on such a glorious day? It's cooled off enough for you to go out riding around on your bikes like you do so often."

"Just talking to Troy's grandma," Clark said shyly.

"We had a wonderful conversation about faith," Grandma Denise smiled at Clark and his dad. "And the power of the Lord."

"Well, I guess that's as good an excuse as any," the preacher said as he held an inviting arm out for Clark to follow. "We'll head out and leave you fine folks to your evening."

"I was going to make some pork chops for dinner," Grandma Denise said. "You're welcome to stay."

"Oh, no," Mr. Smith shook his gigantic hands. "We're having supper at a Bible study over at Mr. and Mrs. Powell's house. Thanks for asking though."

"Bye Clark," Troy called.

"Bye," Clark waved.

"And God bless you," his dad added as he closed the door.

"That's the type of a friend an angel should have," Grandma Denise nodded and made her way into the kitchen. With a few flashes from her scepter the refrigerator door opened and all the ingredients she'd need to make pork chops and mashed potatoes spun through the air and onto the counter. "You want to help me?"

"Sure," Troy said with a look at his own scepter. He'd been praying non-stop for the last half hour to get a call. "You think my parents will be okay? My mom said it was a lot of reidlos they're going after?"

"They'll all be okay," Grandma Denise consoled softly. "Brian is a great angel. Almost as strong as John. And your mom isn't too shabby in a fight either."

"I wish they would have let me go," Troy complained as he started unwrapping the thawed chops.

"Only fully qualified angels should fight reidlos. They're tenacious fighters and hard as hell to kill." She chuckled and waved her scepter. Batter poured into the bowl in front of her followed by two eggs that cracked and split of their own accord in mid-air. "You should worry more about getting your robes."

Troy did his best to hold a frustrated sigh and saluted with a fork. "Watching for sacrifices at every turn," he breathed.

He turned to Grandma Denise who was staring at him. At once, a twist of nerves the size of the Empire State building clenched his stomach. But before he started to utter an apology, she smiled. "Getting more and more like your grandpa every day," she said. They spent the next hour preparing a meal for what Troy thought had to be an army.

"The angels guarding us outside would probably like to eat as well," Grandma Denise said when he asked how they were going to eat all the food.

Just as she finished the doorbell rang. "Stay here," she said with her scepter appearing in her right hand. With graceful steps she crossed the tiled kitchen and peeked through the peephole in the front door. "It's Angela and her dad," she breathed and opened the door.

Angela walked in with red, puffy eyes. "I can't stay," Paul said halfway in the doorway. "We're going to investigate more around the area where Joseph was killed."

"You want something to eat for the road?" Grandma Denise asked. "We made plenty."

"No thanks," Paul said. "I better get back."

"You two hungry?" Grandma Denise asked after she shut the door. Angela shook her head softly in denial. The sadness etched on her face made Troy's stomach twist. He wished he was brave enough to wrap his arms around her but with his grandma in the room, he wouldn't dare.

"I could eat," he mumbled. His grandma nodded and fixed him a plate then five others.

"I'm going to take this to our guards," she said while balancing the plates with her arms and the Spirit's help. "I'll be back in a few minutes."

"We really need to practice," Angela choked once the front door clicked closed.

"Do what?" Troy asked hastily swallowing a mouthful of mashed potatoes and almost making himself gag.

"With our angel abilities," Angela explained. "There's so much happening right now. I don't want to get caught off guard."

"We can practice more. We already do quite a bit though."

"I need to concentrate more on the fighting abilities," she frowned not seeming to fully hear his response. "It was awful being at that funeral. Joseph's wife and his daughters were there. They're just one and three. I couldn't stand it. Even though they know he's in heaven, I could tell they were completely devastated. I'm not going to let something like that happen to me."

"My mom said it was a demon," Troy cleared his throat. "Was it a reidlos or something?"

Angela stared at the table for several seconds. Troy thought he saw a mixture of anger and pure terror in her brilliant, brown eyes. "It was a sinna," she said in almost a whisper. "And my dad said there might have been a trickel too."

Troy's brain scrambled to the page in Paula Tindall's *Dangerous and Deadly Demons*:

Half lion and half human, the sinna demon is a brutish force. From its tail pour poison quills that inflict the hatred and malice of Lucifer's fire. Small pricks from a single quill will put a victim to sleep. A direct hit will kill within a couple of minutes. Take care around these assassins of evil. Humans see them as one of their own but feel the wrath of Satan hovering around them. The terrible claws on the beasts' hands are death and destruction. Wage war against a sinna with the utmost care. The tail is its weakness but also its most dangerous weapon.

"Sinna," Troy repeated in a hushed breath. "I remember Butler talking about them last summer. He said they were tough to fight because they attack from hiding most of the time. And another trickel..." he added with an arc of hatred and fear rising into his throat.

"That's why we need to practice," Angela said with a little more authority in her voice.

"Sounds good to me," Troy agreed. "You know that all of these angels that have been getting killed lately knew more than us though, right? The fallen are raising terrible demons... and they're even more deadly themselves."

"More reason for us to practice," she huffed as the front door opened and Grandma Denise strolled into the kitchen.

Troy nodded and concentrated on his pork chops and sweet kernel corn. He kept watch on Angela out of the corner of his eyes and wished for the millionth time that he could do some great heroic deed right in front of her. He was sure she only needed to the slightest push to view their relationship like he did. If only he could get a brainwave on how to get his robes...

Chapter 6: Shopping for Reidlos

"So your parents didn't say anything about the fight with the reidlos?" Tyler questioned around a mouthful of rocky road ice cream.

"Not much," Troy answered. "Just that nobody got hurt and the reidlos had been destroyed."

"I thought they were like some type of mega monsters," Becky joined the conversation from the living room. "Your parents are always going on about how dangerous they are."

"They're supposed to be," Troy nodded in agreement. "But I guess if you know how to handle them; they aren't that tough. I don't know. All the books make them sound pretty bad."

Clark shuffled in the kitchen chair he was sitting in. A loud creak made Troy worry that the strong, wooden chair might not be up to the task of supporting his gigantic friend. "The pictures of them in that book are scary," Clark mumbled. "I wouldn't want to fight one."

"And now both your parents and Angela's parents and your grandma are at some secret meeting?" Tyler said jumping back into the lead of the discussion. "Is something big going down?"

"Your guess is as good as mine," Troy conceded because he knew it was the truth. His parents had returned the same night they'd gone on the hunt for the reidlos horde. But as much as he'd pestered them for details, they'd offered very little. Then they'd kept their distance yesterday and told him this morning that they had a meeting with the archangels at the Dome of Windows.

"Your friends can come over," his mom had warned.

"But stay out of trouble," his dad had finished with a searching look. "We'll be gone most of the day. We don't expect anything bad to happen but you never know with everything that has been going on lately. Barbara Lassitar and Thomas Carr will be on watch today. Only talk to them if there is an emergency."

Troy's friends had arrived at his house less than a half hour after his parents had left. So far they'd played the X-box then watched Troy and Angela pass a small ball back and forth across the living room with the Spirit.

"So it's something do with Kyle then?" Tyler concluded with his last scoop of ice cream.

Troy smiled and saw Angela peek over the top of *Justice and the Spirit* which she had been studying a lot the last couple of days. "Probably so," Troy said. "Who else?"

"And there's only two guardian angels on duty today?" Tyler asked.

"That's what my parents said," Troy answered not liking the sparkle that had appeared on his best friend's face. "My dad told me to stay out of trouble."

"Whatever," Tyler snorted. "You've been wanting to get away from the Secret Service angels more than any of the rest of us."

"It doesn't mean I would," Troy argued.

"Come on man," Tyler countered. "You and Angela are leaving Friday. We only have three more days together."

"And I'd rather not be grounded for those three days. And then for all the next school year when I get back."

"I'm not talking about anything big," Tyler's voice dropped to a whisper. "More like a test."

"A test of what?" Angela asked with her face scrunched in suspicion.

"You and Troy's angel skills," Tyler said matter-of-factly. "See if you can sneak the five of us over to my house."

"What would be the point?" Becky crossed her arms and leaned against the oak doorframe. Her right foot tapped impatiently as she stared acidly at her former boyfriend.

"A test," Tyler repeated. "For fun... and like I said, to let them practice their angel espionage skills."

Troy chortled but Becky was the first to reply. "You have no idea about their angel skills," she said looking like a tiger ready to pounce on a mid-morning snack. "You haven't looked at any of their angel books except for *Dangerous and Deadly Demons*."

"So what," Tyler waved as though he was shooing an annoying fly. "That doesn't mean I don't listen. And Angela has really been wanting some practical training the last couple of weeks. What better way to do that in a non-threatening environment?"

"You're always looking to get us into trouble," Becky stormed.

"We won't get into trouble," Tyler said but slid further into his chair away from Becky. "It's just for a little fun. It's not like we're trying to break into Fort Knox or anything. Its two houses down and across the street. Surely there isn't a rampaging horde of demons waiting for us to step a single toe outside. We're in Mustang, Oklahoma. What could go wrong?" He paused for the briefest of moments but charged forward as Troy and Becky both opened their mouths to remind him of the house less than a mile away where they'd almost been killed last year. "The test is doing it without the angel guards noticing. If they catch us, they'll scold us and send us back inside. No big deal. There aren't any demons between here and my house. Your parents killed all the demons in Oklahoma in that fight. Right?"

"I don't think so," Troy laughed and looked at Angela. A strange reluctant, passion simmered in a red glow on her cheeks.

"I kind of like the idea," she said in a rush of words. "It won't be dangerous and Tyler is right that it will let us have some practical experience with angel abilities we haven't gotten to use in a real situation."

"Are you kidding?" Becky said with her mouth falling wide open. "Tyler always has the worst plans. Remember the pool last year?"

"That was a fluke thing," Tyler shook his head as he leaned towards Angela. "It won't happen again. We'll be outside for all of thirty seconds. There are two fully qualified angels right outside. They'd know if there were any demons around."

"Troy," Becky said with an oncoming whimper. "You don't think it's a good idea, do you?"

"I, uh, I don't know," he stuttered with a glance at Angela. "It doesn't sound too dangerous, I guess. I'm okay with giving it a try. I doubt we'll make it anyway and we can play it off when they do catch us."

"Oh God," Becky looked at the ceiling. "Why do I even try?"

For the next fifteen minutes, Troy and Angela took turns using auditome to try to locate Barbara and Thomas. Troy found both of them first.

"So you've got a solid feel for both of them?" Tyler asked as he diagrammed their locations on the make-shift map he'd drawn on the back of a leftover pizza box. "Perfect. We can go out the back door, then through the fence on the west side of the house," he explained with excitement dripping from every word. "Then sneak over to the Johnson's house and cut through their backyard."

"What about their dog?" Troy asked pointing at the roughly drawn house in question.

"I'd bet a million dollars they left Buttons inside," Tyler said while he chewed on his bottom lip in concentration. "It's going to be over a hundred degrees today and Mrs. Johnson treats the dog better than she does her real kids."

"That's true," Becky agreed in a low breath. She'd refused to join in on the plans at the start but had reluctantly conceded to the group's will. "Ever since Jennifer moved out last year after she graduated, I think Buttons has been pretty spoiled."

"Exactly," Tyler continued. "That will get us out of sight of Barbara and Thomas. Mr. Johnson has that line of bushes all the way down the side of his front yard. We can crawl behind them then make a dash across the street."

"I don't know if the bushes will hide me or not," Clark said as he looked over all of them at the map as if it was a mysterious artifact from a treasure island.

"It will be good enough," Tyler said dismissively. "Do you think it would be better to go across the street altogether, in pairs, or one at a time?"

"I'd say one at a time," Angela said. "Me and Troy can keep an eye on Barbara and Thomas with auditome. If we stick close together, I can use subbia to hide any sounds we make. And Troy, you've gotten pretty good with Uriel's strates gift."

"What's that do?" Tyler asked.

"Makes someone hear a sound from the opposite direction," Troy said. "Kind of a distraction."

"Awesome," Tyler grinned.

"And Angela is good enough with tibota to walk across the street without them ever seeing her," Troy added quickly. Tyler and Clark looked dumbfounded at him. "It lets her make herself invisible or to change her appearance."

"Are you joking?" Tyler boomed and turned to Angela. "I didn't know you could do that!"

"I only started getting the hang of it when me and Troy were practicing last night," she said in a low voice but a smile was creeping behind the words. "It takes a lot of concentration. I'd never be able to do it if I was real nervous or in a fight."

"I have to see that," Tyler and Becky called out in unison which made everyone laugh.

"Okay, hold on a sec," Angela breathed deeply. Then with a shimmer, she popped out of view. Troy reached with the Spirit and at once she became visible to him again.

"Sweet!" Tyler hollered while Becky and Clark shifted this way and that way trying to get a view of their invisible friend.

"You can see me, can't you Troy?" Angela asked.

He nodded as their eyes met. "But only because I knew you were there," he offered. "If I didn't know you'd used tibota, I don't think I would have noticed you."

"That's so weird Angela," Becky whispered. "Your voice almost sounds different when I can't see you. I guess since it's coming out of thin air or something. I don't know. Just weird." They all laughed as Angela winked back into sight.

"Well, I suppose we're all set then?" Tyler said with a mad, excited shine pouring from his entire body. He turned to Troy. "You still have a good connection on the two of them?"

"As good as I'm going to get," Troy said hoping the upticking beat of his heart wasn't audible to anyone in the room. "I don't want to let the contact get much stronger or they might notice. I'm only feeling for their most basic emotions and what they're concentrating on."

"And it's not on us?"

Troy reached with the Spirit with the tiniest more strength. He got an image of Barbara perched in the shade beside a chimney two houses to the east. Her scepter sounded with a whispered voice and Troy got the feeling she was being updated on what was happening in the meeting at the Dome. Thomas was lounging between two trees with his eyes on Troy's front door.

"Not that I can tell," Troy offered. "They definitely don't seem worried or anything at least."

"Let's get this party started then," Tyler whooped and headed to the back door.

It didn't end up being as bad as Troy thought. He kept a subtle touch on both the angel protectors with auditome as their group duck walked, or crawled, from one hiding place to another. The only section Troy's stomach truly clenched was when they snuck one at a time across the blazing hot street.

"It's got to be a hundred and twenty out here," Becky complained in a hissing whisper as she dashed beside Troy to wait for Clark's crossing. At a sign from Troy, the big boy lumbered over the residential street in six giant strides.

"Give Angela the sign and let's get inside," Tyler said. A minute later they stormed through Tyler's back door with a burst of successful laughter. "I told you it would be a piece of cake," Tyler roared as he went through his living room stuffed with expensive, flashy art and into a luxurious kitchen. He grabbed five Gatorades and tossed one to everyone. "Congratulations," he held up his own in a salute and downed half the bottle in two swallows.

"You and Angela are lucky you're going to the mountains in a few days," Becky said wiping sweat from her forehead. "I bet it will be above a hundred degrees here all summer long."

"Demons," Angela said as a continued smile made the smallest of dimples crease both her cheeks. The pink angel marks that swirled on her temples mesmerized Troy for a couple of seconds before he remembered it wasn't polite to stare or drool. "When the fallen angels raise demons," she went on. "They bring some of the fires of hell with them. The whole world gets hotter when the War for Sins is raging."

"No more doom and gloom for the day," Tyler interrupted with a nod at the seventy inch TV positioned on the wall between two carved pillars of cherry mahogany. "Let's play some games."

Every time Troy sat on the plush couch in Tyler's living room, he thought for sure it had to be the same feeling as floating on a cloud. With the X-box controller in his hands, he couldn't help but smile as his friends joked and ate the multitude of snacks Tyler's parents always kept available. For almost two hours Troy, Tyler, and Clark worked their way through a separate set of military missions on the humungous screen. Loud bursts of gunfire and continuous reanimations of downed characters filled the once peaceful living room.

"Clark, just around the corner is the last bad guy," Tyler prodded. "Get him, get him! Oh, yeah. And that's that. About the twentieth time I've beaten this game."

"Maybe you shouldn't play so much," Becky teased as she sat with her legs tucked under her in a recliner. Tyler's notebook computer shined on her lap. Her favorite website with daily devotions and scriptures seemed to almost smile at Troy from the screen. "You could spend more of that time studying..."

"Whatever," Tyler griped but a wide grin spread across his face. "I've never gotten anything below an A on a report card. Why study when you have natural smarts? And speaking of which..."

He sprang from the couch, ran towards the hallway that led to his room and returned a few seconds later holding a small card. "My parents gave me a $100 gift card to Gamestop for my grades."

"Awesome," Troy shouted. "I wish my parents gave me anything at all for my grades. I get straight A's too."

"My mom is trying to bribe me to stop going to church," Tyler explained with a bounce of his eyebrows. "Still wish I could get her to believe…"

"She'll come around," Angela said with a surety ringing in her voice Troy couldn't find room to believe. He was sure Angela hadn't been around Mrs. Henry enough. She was one of the most adamant atheists Troy had ever seen. To say she hated anything to do with Christianity, or any religion, was a gigantic understatement. The truth of it reflected on Tyler's now conflicted face.

"Maybe," he breathed. "Anyway… now that we've beaten the game again. I need the new one. It just came out last week."

"Uh oh," Troy said not liking the building excitement within his friend. He was sure for a fraction of a second he could see a tiny devil standing on Tyler's shoulder and whispering in his ear.

"Don't stop me before I get started on a brilliant plan," Tyler countered. "The one earlier went off without a hitch, right?"

"What are you up to now?" Becky pulled her attention away from the computer screen.

"Nothing really," Tyler squawked. "You know… we only have three days left with Troy and Angela. I thought a little bit of fun would be good for us."

"That's what we've been doing today," Clark said as he looked at Tyler out of the corner of his deep, brown eyes.

Troy saw the fear of getting into trouble - but not being able to stop himself from following his reckless friend - brewing behind Clark's thoughtful expression.

"We play video games all the time," Tyler griped. "And since we've beaten all of them we need some new ones, right? So, how about we go get some." He flipped the Gamestop card into the air and caught it.

"That's like a mile and a half away," Troy said. "I'd never be able to keep an eye on Barbara and Thomas from that far away. It would take us forever to get there and back."

"Not if we drive," Tyler offered with a dangerous grin.

"What do you mean?" Angela asked. She didn't look like she was in total agreement with Tyler's plotting plan but she also didn't look like she'd refuse it immediately either.

"I can drive us there," Tyler smirked as he pulled the keys to his Camaro out of the pocket of his shorts.

"You don't even have a driver's license," Becky snorted.

"I have my permit," Tyler said. "Got it a couple of weeks ago."

"That's still not a license," Becky said.

"It's only a little over a mile away," Tyler said. "And I can stay on neighborhood streets for half of that. Then we'd be on Sarah Road for a little bit and we're there. Sarah is never busy, especially during the middle of the day."

Troy looked from one friend to another. Becky was still as a statue as she watched her ex-boyfriend. Troy was sure she was on the verge of yelling a denial at any second.

Clark had stood and was peeking out the window. Troy wasn't sure if he was checking for their guardian angels to run out there and turn himself in before he got into more trouble; or if he was checking to see if another adventure was possible.

Before Troy turned to Angela she spoke up. "Sounds like fun to me," she said which froze Becky who had been forming the words to tell Tyler how dumb and irresponsible he was.

"Sweet," Tyler laughed. "Clark will have to have shotgun. I don't think he'll fit in the backseat."

"Wh… wait," Becky stammered. "What's going on Angela? You can't be serious. We'll get into so much trouble."

"Nobody will even know," Tyler said. "You worry too much. Troy's parents already killed all the demons in the area. There can't be any fallen angels around with all the guardians Troy and Angels have had lately. The boogey man isn't out there waiting for us all the time, Becky."

"What do you think Troy?" Becky questioned Troy ignoring Tyler.

Troy froze with only his eyes moving from Becky then to Tyler then to Angela. "I, uh, I don't know," he said. Angela's cheeks darkened into a touch deeper red as he spoke. He swallowed the tugging sensation of fright at the idea of driving away from the house in Tyler's car. In the end, disappointing Angela won out. "But I think we'll be okay."

Becky sniffed and her eyes narrowed as she looked from him to Angela. "When we are getting killed by Kyle or the devil himself, don't say I didn't warn you!"

"Are you sure you know they're still over by your house?" Tyler's voice squeaked ten minutes later as his garage door rumbled into its rack above them. The harsh brightness of the sun invaded on what had been the relative safeness of the dark garage. Under Troy's feet, the Camaro hummed like a race horse ready to hit the tracks.

"Are you sure you can even back this thing up straight?" Becky called from her scrunched position in the backseat between Troy and Angela. Troy's own legs were jammed at an awkward angle where he'd squeezed in behind Tyler's long frame in the driver's seat. Across from him, Angela looked absolutely squashed to her curved seat with Clark looking like a crammed sardine in the front. If a terrible nagging feeling of being grounded for life wasn't tearing at Troy's insides, he was sure he'd be dying of laughter. As it was, all he could see was his dad's face hovering before him with a frown that made Troy shiver. Their earlier triumph of sneaking unscathed to Tyler's house felt like a stunning and glorious prize that had long ago fizzled.

"Maybe we should go back in," he said hesitantly and barely audible over the radio which was blaring a country song about a man who was going fishing with his hunting dog.

"No way," Tyler said and stepped on the gas. The sports car responded with the slightest squeal of tires which made all of them wince.

"Easy," Angela hissed as the sunlight streamed through the tinted windows. Tyler spun the steering wheel and they careened into the street.

"Close the garage," Tyler pointed to the controller on the passenger side sun visor.

Clark flicked the button and the garage door began to close. They zoomed to the west away from Troy's house. Troy held strong on the Spirit and concentrated as hard as he could on Gabriel's gift of auditome.

"We're good," he sighed as they began to rocket down the street. "Neither of them noticed."

"Your parents might need to look into some better guards," Becky huffed.

"They're both listening to someone talking through their scepters," Troy said as he broke the connection. "Pretty sure they're getting updates on the meeting at the Dome. As long as they don't suspect anything and feel for us in my house, we should be okay. But let's hurry."

"What were they saying?" Angela asked with a grimace as Clark shifted his enormous mass in the front seat.

"I couldn't make any of it out," Troy replied wishing with all his heart that he could have. Not only to know the information himself, but he was sure Angela would have been impressed.

"Who cares!" Tyler whooped as he turned onto Pine Bluff Lane. The house that the tondeo had falsely invaded slid by without a peep. Troy closed his eyes but it was too late not to see a reflecting echo of green eyes from the window.

"Have you ever gone and talked with her mom?" Becky asked knowingly as she watched his face. He shook his head negatively and ducked further into his seat as the memories flashed in his mind.

"What game are you gonna get?" Clark's deep voice rumbled and broke through the budding sadness.

"The new Call of Duty game for sure," Tyler laughed as they pulled to a stop at Sarah Road. Troy, along with all his other friends except for Tyler, looked intently for cars coming down the busier main road. "And probably the new NCAA football one too," Tyler added and stomped on the gas making the back end of the powerful car fishtail with a smell of burning rubber.

Off to Troy's right, he caught the quickest flash of a figure tucked in the shadow of a cedar tree. He did a fast double take but saw only the outline of a head-high sapling.

"What's up?" Angela leaned forward until her face was pressed against the seat in front of her. "I felt the Spirit flare up around you."

"Nothing," Troy said shaking away dark thoughts and kept his gaze locked in the direction he was sure he'd seen a shape hiding in the trees. Or maybe it had been a total figment of his imagination. In the recesses of his mind, he could hear and see his dad's ferocious assault if he ever found out what they were up to. It had to be making him paranoid. He turned to Angela and smiled. "Just nervous a little bit."

"So am I," she mouthed with a tiny, but seemingly unworried giggle.

A few minutes later they piled into Gamestop without a hitch - much to Troy's relief. Ever since he thought he'd seen the figure in the woods, he couldn't shake a feeling of watchfulness hovering over his group of friends. He kept the Spirit swirling outwards in waves praying it was only his imagination running wild.

"Look at this one," Angela murmured from his left. He glanced at the game she'd picked up. On the cover was a valiant hero with a two handed greatsword drawn over his shoulder. Below him with a look of sheer ferociousness was a monster with horned wings.

"That looks just like the selvo demons," Becky whispered. "Almost exactly."

And it was true. If Troy had to guess, he'd lay odds that the creator of the game had seen a selvo at some time in his life. Or had seen a picture of one in a book. But before he could throw in his own opinion about the game, a trembling shockwave shook through his entire body.

"Was that an earthquake?" he asked and steadied himself against the wall with one hand.

"What are you talking about?" Tyler questioned as he perused a section of military games.

Troy looked at his closest friend hoping to see a joking smile. None existed. He searched Becky and Clark's confused faces then turned to Angela. There he found the terror that was gripping him now.

"What was it?" she croaked. "Something just happened. That wasn't an earthquake. It was more like a Spiritquake or something. It almost knocked me down."

Troy nodded in agreement at his own registering of the event. "We need to get out of here," he warned as he pushed outwards with the Spirit. Danger crackled in the air as though a sudden and terrible thunderstorm had surged over the bright blue sky outside.

"We just got here," Tyler griped.

"Check out now," Becky said with the muscles in her cheeks twitching. Tyler backed away from her with his hands in the air.

"Ohhhkay," he said and almost knocked over a Super Mario Bros display in his haste to get to the counter. "Girls suck all the fun out of everything," he groaned when he was out of earshot of everyone except Troy and Clark.

He stepped into the checkout line as Troy reminded himself to breath. Each tick of the clock hung for an eternity as he probed with the Spirit. A raging inferno of darkness swarmed somewhere on the edge of his range. He reached but only the animal-like instinct of a predator ,watching its prey, echoed at him.

Finally, after what felt like an entire school year had ground by, Tyler waltzed from the counter with his bag of new games in tow.

"Come on, come on, come on," Angela hissed. Her normal calm demeanor and smiles had vanished. Fright lived in all of her movements. Her left hand had climbed to her hair and she played skittishly with the band that knotted her ponytail. Troy knew in reality the hair piece was a whip of Michael's making camouflaged by the Spirit. Last summer he'd seen her practice with it countless times at the Hill and, of course, when she'd used it against the selvo demon in their neighborhood.

Troy followed Angela's lead and pulled the tiny sheath from the front pocket of his khaki shorts. In it, the ornate dagger he'd received from his parents on his fourteenth birthday waited. He held the sheath in his right hand and rested his left hand on his scepter where it was strapped to his ribs with a leather pouch.

"What's going on?" Becky asked. Her right hand was already twirling the cross around her neck as though she could feel the same danger lurking that Troy could.

"I think there were demons raised from hell somewhere around us," Angela explained out of the corner of her mouth. The group plunged out the door into the oppressive heat. The air above the concrete parking lot sizzled in shimmering shafts of vapor.

"What?" Clark gasped and immediately began to turn circles. "Where?"

"No idea," Angela said. "I've only ever read about it. I'm not completely sure but that had to be what happened. Don't you think Troy?"

Troy searched his memory for the topic of discussion and saw the statue of David railing about the shock on the world when demons were raised.

"I'd guess the same thing," he offered and pulled his friends faster towards the awaiting Camaro. Above, the clear blue sky roared with the danger of an invisible tornado. The Spirit surged into Troy making all the hair on his arms stand perfectly on end. "It's coming from somewhere over there," he said and pointed behind the building towards a field that bordered the shopping center on the north side. Cedar trees dotted the green grass of the pasture. Huge stacks of empty pallets were lined beside the Wal-Mart Supercenter. The megastore loomed across the lot to the west on a small plateau-like rise of the land. And in the trees behind the store, sliding from shadow to shadow lurked three reidlos. "Oh God," he breathed in disbelief. "Get in the car!"

"Jesus help us," Becky moaned before beginning a rapid succession of Spanish prayers.

"What do we do?" Tyler said. "Where are they? I can't see them."

"On the other side of the dumpsters," Clark's chin was tucked to his chest. His large eyes were glued on the demons and ham-sized fists were balled for action.

"Oh God," Tyler squawked. "Save us."

All Troy could do was agree as he studied the monsters. Paula Tindall's *Dangerous and Deadly Demons* didn't quite do the beasts justice.

The way they slinked and snarled and stalked. It was as if a kid's worst nightmare had been animated straight from the dark recesses of the most frightened consciousness. Their dark, hairless bodies slithered more than walked or ran – sometimes on two feet and sometimes on four. Troy could feel the building panic that encapsulated the reidlos and would make all but those with the stoutest faith freeze in total fear.

"We need to get out of here," Troy shoved his two friends towards the car where Angela was yanking Becky through the passenger side door. Tyler dove for the driver's seat and Clark stuffed himself into the passenger side. With no possible way of making it into the backseat, Troy jammed himself onto Clark's lap as Tyler ignited the powerful engine.

"Wait," Becky called from the backseat. "There are people over there by Wal-Mart. The reidlos are going towards them."

She was right. Four workers looked to be on break at a small round table under a large umbrella. They were laughing over bags of chips and bottles of Coke with no idea of the terror heading their way.

"That's Blake," Tyler hollered into the tight confines of the car.

"From the football team?" Clark asked as he tried desperately to twist around and get a look. All he accomplished was smashing Troy against the windshield and rearview mirror.

"Yeah," Tyler said. "We have to do something."

"Call your parents Troy!" Angela screamed.

Troy reached for his scepter. With a grunt of pain and a popping in his elbow, he managed to tug it free. At once the glow of holy light softened his mood and brought a sense of calm at its touch. "Mom," he hollered.

"Troy," his mom's voice immediately responded. "What's going on? Why are you calling? We're in the middle of a meeting." Behind him, Troy could hear Angela's desperate pleas to her dad.

"We're in trouble," Troy explained. "We snuck out of the house and came up to Gamestop. Me and Angela felt a shockwave we're sure was demons being raised. And now there are reidlos over by Wal-Mart. They're going after some people we know. We have to..."

"Stay right where you're at Troy," his mom ordered. "Y'all don't go near them! Your dad is calling Barbara and Thomas right now. Others will be there in a minute. We're heading-"

"We have to do something," Tyler shouted over Troy's mom. "They're getting close to Blake and the others." And sure enough, Troy saw the four workers freeze and begin to wilt under the fear brought forth by the demons. Tyler hammered the gas without another word. Troy gritted his teeth as he was thrown against the door with half of Clark's mass smashing him.

"Troy, what's going on?" his mom's voice begged for details from his scepter.

"We have to stop the reidlos," he answered without hesitation. "Those people won't last another minute."

"Lord, please protect them," Troy heard his dad's voice as well. "Troy… for God, we fight."

"For God, we fight," Troy hollered letting the words try to build the dying courage in his chest.

The Camaro careened up the asphalt street that separated the two shopping centers. Tyler whipped the steering wheel to the right and barely missed crashing into three parked cars.

When they were a hundred feet away the reidlos turned towards them with wicked grins making jagged lines across their terrible, eyeless faces. Black and gray mottled skin stretched over bodies that didn't contain a single hair. Their hides looked as thick as an elephants and four inch claws flicked and jabbed with every movement. Menacing fangs jutted from both the top and bottom jaws.

"What do we do?" Tyler squeaked.

"Say a prayer," Troy said and rolled out of the passenger side door onto the steaming concrete. He tucked his shoulder and cartwheeled to his feet. Before he took one step, a blasting trumpet of power erupted from his scepter. The reidlos stumbled and rammed into each other but quickly righted themselves with hissing laughter.

"Young ones like he said," the demon in the middle snarled. The terrible face mocked as it turned back and forth with a loud snuffling intake of air through its oversized nose. "Tender and weak. So tasty and sweet. The fear, oh the fear."

"Shut it," Angela yelled as she stepped in front of Tyler. She waved her scepter in a circular arc and holy water poured from the rod in a tidal wave. The demons hurled against each other and dove for cover as the water burned their thick hide and blistered their screeching faces.

"Tyler, Clark, go help Blake and the others," Troy called as he pulled the dagger from its sheath and advanced.

One of the reidlos tore from its hiding place behind a dumpster. It ran on all fours blurring the air like a cheetah closing on a helpless deer.

Troy ducked and produced a shimmering shield from thin air with his scepter. The monster bounced off the shield in a bone crushing avalanche of foul smelling blood and howling pain. Troy jumped forward to stab the beast in the throat but it batted away his attack with a lazy flick of its muscular arm.

"Look out!" Becky screamed from where she stood protectively over Blake and the other stunned Wal-Mart workers.

Troy spun too late and the next demon bowled over him with claws tearing at his chest. He managed to stab a slicing, clawed hand and held on with all his strength. An instant later, Angela's whip wrapped around the reidlos throat. It careened away as she yanked the weapon. Troy wiped at the black blood that stained his shirt but prayed a quick "thank you" as he felt no gashes in his flesh. To his right, Clark and Tyler wrestled in a fight for their lives with the third demon. Troy winced as one of the long claws missed Tyler's stomach by a centimeter.

"Get out of the way," he yelled and ran forward calling the Spirit like he'd never done before. Clark shoved the reidlos with enormous arms and grabbed Tyler then leapt sideways. With all his might, Troy heaved his dagger and watched it spin end over end. At the last second the demon saw the blade but the dagger sunk into its throat before it could make a move. Its fanged jaws snapped convulsively at thin air for one heartbeat before the monster fell silent.

"Troy?" Angela's voice quaked. He turned and saw the two remaining reidlos crouched and ready to attack. Hatred and putrid fear swam in the air over the sizzling concrete. Troy's left hand tightened on his scepter as he looked into Angela's frightened eyes. A true worry of being painfully killed cried in her brown orbs.

Not her.

They couldn't have her. He wouldn't let them. And just as the reidlos darted forward for the kill - so did he.

One of the demons crumpled a foot from Angela as it ran head first into Gabriel's shield which Troy had called in his reckless haste. Angela yelped and flipped sideways over a parked sedan a split second before the other reidlos slashed with its claws.

Three deep lines scraped into the metal with a terrible screech. Troy charged ahead as the monster yanked its paw from the torn car. His shoulder smashed into the bony ribs of the demon and they flew sideways. The side of the car crunched and buckled from the force of the tackle and Troy immediately began punching and kicking every inch of the thick hide he could manage.

Behind his head, Angela's whip cracked. A howl of pain rent the air but Troy could only concentrate on the reidlos that was spinning onto its skeletal knees under his assault. Blood and spit crusted jaws snapped and flashed into an open mouthed smile. Troy did the first thing that came into his mind. He plunged his scepter into the gaping maw.

"Seraphim!" he yelled and a trumpet loud enough to pop his eardrums into temporary deafness blasted the air. The reidlos didn't even have time to squeal as its head rocketed backwards with a sickening snap.

"Troy!" Tyler yelled. "Catch!"

Troy turned and saw his dagger flashing in the sunlight. It careened off course and he jumped and spun with the Spirit. The handle slid into his hand as the remaining demon tore at him. He didn't have time to do anything more than thrust forward with his arm before the reidlos charged full force into him. White spots of pain popped in his eyes as he fell onto his back and slid across the hot parking lot. He gritted his teeth at the taste of blood and prayed that a miracle would come.

"Are you okay?" Angela's voice swam into his head. He opened his eyes and saw her standing over him. With one final convulsion, the reidlos died on top of him. His dagger buried to the hilt in its hard chest.

"I think so," Troy managed a painful breath. "Get this thing off of me."

Tyler and Clark skidded to a halt and dragged the dead demon onto the bloody pavement. Both of them looked ready to puke at any second and they let go of the leathery hide of the beast as quickly as they could. Troy's shirt was covered in black, bubbling blood. His head was ringing and he was sure every inch of his body must be covered in cuts and bruises.

"Help me sit him up," Angela said and began running her hand over his arms. The soft light of the Spirit flowed from her palms and Troy shuddered as the pain eased.

"Thanks," he said with utter sincerity. "I don't think anything's broken. Just banged up a little bit."

"Sit still for a minute," she said with flustered concentration.

"Is that it?" Clark breathed hard as he leaned heavily against the half demolished sedan.

Troy swept the area with the Spirit as Angela's hands hovered over his forehead. He froze as his attention caught a mass of evil in the trees a hundred yards away. The Spirit from Angela's hand shimmered then failed. Wails of eager hatred rolled from the pasture. At least ten reidlos crouched in the shadows.

"Oh God," Tyler moaned after following Troy's horrified gaze. He stumbled backwards and fell over the dead reidlos. "There's more of them. We need to get out of here!"

"Too late," Troy said and rose to a crouch at the sight of the coming onslaught. Tainted and growing fear poured from the horde like a stampede of unwanted emotions.

Nothing could be done to save his friends.

Death approached in the claws and fangs of hell.

Troy glanced at Angela then to Tyler, Becky, and Clark. Hopelessness paled their faces. The end of life was sure to find them soon. Pain and anguish would be their last moments before ascending to heaven. Troy thought he could hear God calling his name in the hot, smoldering air. He shook his head and tried to will away the fear and desperation avalanching from the reidlos.

"Get Blake and the others inside," he yelled. "I'll hold them off as long as I can."

"You won't last more than a few seconds," Angela cried.

"Go!" Troy hollered and bounded towards the catcalling demons. "For God, we fight!" A stunning light shot from his scepter and danced towards the reidlos who rammed into each other dodging the holy beam. Troy tensed as he prepared for the pain about to come.

But before the demons jumped the barbed-wire fence that bordered the field, his parents, grandma, and Angela's parents along with Barbara and Thomas landed beside him. The concrete crunched and flexed as the adult angels streamed forward in the wrath of God. Troy's mom's wings were spread in a towering menace of rage. His dad's broadsword sparkled in the power of the Spirit. Streaking ahead, Angela's dad produced blast after blast of energy from his scepter. Troy could only watch in stunned acknowledgement of how far he had to go before becoming a fully-fledged angel. His puny attacks and tiny, little dagger looked like toddler toys next to the glory of these Godly gifts.

The demons spread into a v-formation that began to disintegrate almost before it was formed. Barbara and Thomas beheaded two of the panicking monsters and Angela's mom dispatched another in a sickening cloud of red and black sludge.

Troy raced forward behind his dad's triumphant attack and formed Seraphim's gift of huspos in his mind. Two reidlos before him fell in a hacking, choking cough as the cloud of fresh smelling mist fogged their hideous faces. They were killed a second later by his dad's flashing sword.

"No!" his mom's voice screamed and Troy saw a blur of motion and felt a gust of wind that ruffled his short hair. He turned and had to hold back a terrified scream. A foot away, the dying, ugly face of a reidlos thrashed in pain. The tip of his mom's sleek sword jutted from its bony back. In its shuddering chest the blade was buried to the hilt. Troy looked into his mom's electrified eyes and wanted to both sing thanks for her saving his life and disintegrate beneath the accusing anger. "Get back with your friends," she said and ripped the sword free in a rush of stomach twisting blood. "Go!"

Troy didn't need to be told twice. He fled from the fight and gathered Tyler and Clark then herded them to Angela and Becky who were consoling Blake.

"Is everything okay?" Angela asked while she poured Raphael's calming shepadia into a young girl who was paralyzed in a mask of sheer fright.

"For now," Troy sucked in a deep breath. "The reidlos are falling fast. But… I'm not sure if I want to be here when our parents come to get us."

"I warned you guys," Becky said. She was lifting a tall, acne pocked boy into a chair at the umbrella covered table. His whole body shook and shuddered and his eyelids fluttered as though they were trying to unsee everything that had happened.

"I'm not sure if they'll remember any of this," Angela said as a delicate light streamed from her hands. "They've all been mumbling but I can't understand any of it. I think the fear got a hold of them right away and froze them. They probably would have died if we hadn't helped."

"They wouldn't have needed our help if we hadn't been here," Troy said knowing it was the truth. "The reidlos were raised from hell because we were here."

Angela nodded sadly.

"Who do you think did it?" Tyler asked.

"Richard Hope," Troy's dad answered as he landed with a thud beside them. "We saw him from a distance before he fled. Your grandma is chasing him but I doubt she'll catch him."

Troy met his dad's gaze and instantly wished he'd mastered the art of turning invisible like Angela had. His mom and Angela's mom landed gracefully a second later.

"We'll go check the security cameras and figure out if we need to hide our presence," Susan said with a shriveling look at her daughter. Troy didn't look up at his mom. He could only imagine the supreme letdown buried on her normally beautiful face.

"What was Richard Hope doing here?" Tyler asked looking as though he wanted to keep the subject off of their own presence in a place they shouldn't be as long as possible.

"Watching you guys," Angela's dad, Paul, said as he walked up at a brisk pace. "Waiting for you to do something stupid. It didn't take long. What possessed you to sneak away from the protection we've set up for you?" He was staring laser beams first at Angela then at Troy and the others.

For a long time all their eyes were locked on their feet. Finally, Tyler cleared his throat. "It was my fault," he said in a calm voice Troy was sure he wouldn't be able to match if he tried to speak. "I talked them into it."

"At gunpoint?" Troy's dad asked. "Because that's about the only reason I can think of that would warrant such a bad decision."

"Not at gunpoint," Troy's voice cracked. "We were all just tired of being watched all the time. We haven't been able to do anything on our own."

"And now you know why," Paul snarled. "You didn't think the protection around you was necessary? We do know what we're doing. We didn't take angels from their normal duties to sit around watching you every night and day. Trust me, it's not what most of them want to be doing. And you pay them back by sneaking out and putting your lives in danger, along with the lives of a hundred innocent people."

Each word struck Troy like a hammer. His lungs burned from holding his breath and he physically had to make his body release the pent up air. A throbbing pain was threatening at the back of his head and he knew he'd be suffering from the injuries of the fight before the day was done. His knees were rubbery but he thought it was more from fear of the punishment his parents were preparing to deliver than from the rapidly receding adrenaline that had been racing through his body.

"We're really sorry," Becky apologized.

"It's not Becky's fault at all," Angela mumbled. "She tried to talk us out of it. It's mainly my fault."

"None of that matters," Troy's dad said holding up a hand to stop Becky and Tyler from talking. "You know all of you will have to be punished. Paul and I aren't your parents," he added looking at Tyler, Clark, and Becky. "But we expect you to do the right thing and tell them you broke some serious rules today."

"What am I supposed to tell my parents?" Tyler asked incredulously. "That I talked my friends into sneaking out and we were attacked by an army of demons? I really doubt they'll believe it."

He quailed immediately when Troy's dad looked at him with his unique version of scary calmness. "Tell them they can call me if they need clarification," he said. "I can get the point across that you need to be in a lot of trouble. If you want to tell them yourself - which I would prefer - I doubt you are allowed to take your car out on your own, right? Especially without permission? Tell them that and that you broke a specific request by Emily and I for you to not leave our house until we returned."

"Okay," Tyler mumbled with his eyes on his twiddling thumbs.

"Good," Paul said. "I shouldn't need to say it but you kids have got to be more careful. There are things going on right now that none of you know."

"Why not just tell us then?" Angela said with her voice rising a tiny bit.

"You'll know when you need to know," her mom answered from their right where she'd just returned from her reconnaissance mission into the store. "And we can't tell you everything because we don't know what's going on ourselves."

Troy built up the courage and looked at his mom. Flushed anger shined from red cheeks. He could tell he'd need to watch his p's and q's as much as possible for the near future.

"All of you get in the car," his mom said with her voice shaking. "And go home. We'll be following above you. Tyler, you made it this far without supervision. I'm trusting that you can drive home without incident?"

Neither, Troy or his friends needed to be told twice. They crammed into the still running Camaro and Tyler began the short drive. "I don't guess that was such a great plan after all," he attempted a soft chuckle.

"Don't even start," Becky warned. "I tried to tell you... but for some stupid reason we always let you talk us into trouble."

To his credit, Tyler didn't argue. Troy trembled at the thought of what was about to meet him at home and at the flashing, painful memory of the fight with the deadly reidlos.

"We're lucky to be alive," he said as they pulled into the neighborhood.

"God was watching over us," Clark spoke for the first time since the fight.

"So was the devil," Angela whispered.

Troy shivered at the thought but knew without a doubt that it was true. He and his friends were being watched. And the fallen angels only needed for them to make the smallest and stupidest mistake. With a look at each friend in turn, he vowed he wouldn't ever let any of them get hurt because of him.

Chapter 7: Back to the Hill

"How bad was it?" Tyler asked over the phone a few hours later.

"Worse than you can imagine," Troy swallowed. "Grounded for the rest of this week and for four weeks when I get back from the Hill. No X-box. I can only use the computer for school work or research… and… they…" he took a deep, steadying breath. "They're talking about not letting me play football next season."

"What?" Tyler boomed causing the phone to static for a split second.

"Yeah, I know," Troy said. Before his parents had said the words, he didn't know how much it would hurt. Football had always taken somewhat of a backseat compared to his mission of becoming an angel, but now that his playing days were at risk; the thought battered against the deep reaches of his stomach. He couldn't imagine not trotting to the practice fields with Tyler and Clark; or not getting to smell the pleasantly familiar (but extremely musty) odors of the locker room.

"They can't do that!" Tyler continued his storming indignation. "Don't they know how important it is?"

"I think they're viewing it as - *not quite as important as us not understanding how dangerous the world is right now.* Those were my mom's exact words at least."

"That's not a punishment only for you though," Tyler argued. "It's a punishment on the whole team."

Troy laughed which felt weird under the circumstances. While his parents railed at him, he had been quite sure he'd never feel a moment of happiness again.

"It's probably not much of a punishment for the team this coming up year," he said. "I wasn't planning on playing much anyway – not with us being sophomores."

"Whatever," Tyler countered with his normal bravado building. "Me, you, and Clark are going to carry the team for the next three years. Three state championships."

"We'll see," Troy said.

"They'll get over it," Tyler mused. "By the time you get back from the Hill, they'll forget all about it."

"Don't count on it," Troy said knowing it was the truth. "What did your parents say about the whole deal?"

"Not much really. My dad was pretty pissed. You know my mom. She just blew it off as kids having some innocent fun. I couldn't really get across to her that there was quite a bit of danger involved. My dad seemed to pick up on it though."

"Did you get grounded?" Troy asked as he stacked and re-stacked a set of books he'd be taking to the Hill in a few days. He'd begun packing that evening to try to get his mind off his parents borderline, insane ranting.

"Uh… no," Tyler said. "He took away my Gamestop gift card."

"But you already spent it," Troy said in confusion.

"Well, yeah… I kind of left out the part about going to Gamestop and what happened in the Wal-Mart parking lot. I didn't know what to tell them," he added quickly before Troy could jump in.

"If my parents find out you aren't getting punished, they're going to be ticked."

"They're free to call my parents," Tyler offered in consolation. "No offense, but my mom doesn't highly value your parent's opinion. Not after she found out how religious they are. You know her. She thinks people who have faith in God are stuck in the middle ages."

"I know," Troy said. "You better pray my dad doesn't find out that you aren't really getting punished though. They'll probably add time to my punishment to make up for it." Tyler laughed but Troy was pretty sure it was a possibility. He sighed as he shuffled around the room then pulled his newly gifted mace out from under his bed. The surface was polished to a high sheen but he went ahead and rubbed some grease he'd bought at *Michael's Angel Fixings* into the wood. "My parents said everyone can come over Friday night to have a small get-together before me and Angela go."

"Okay," Tyler said. "I have something to give you before you leave."

"What is it?"

"You'll find out Friday," Tyler said cryptically.

Troy spent the next two days packing and re-packing his bag. He polished the reidlos blood from his dagger four times and studied his angel text books until his eyes blurred the words together.

"We both spoke to Clark's dad," Troy's mom's voice interrupted a passage on a tumultuous time in the War for Sins during the late 1800's. "He's not going to be able to come over Friday night to see you off. His dad won't allow it."

Troy's stomach twisted a little at the news. "It sucks that everyone is getting punished for something I should have stopped from the start," Troy offered. He'd been trying his best the last few days to accept as much of the blame and responsibility as he could.

His mom watched him in silence for a long time. Finally, the smallest of smiles lifted her lips and brought the first ray of sunshine to Troy since the battle with the demons at Wal-Mart. "I'm glad you seem to be learning your lesson," she said. "But you have to understand how dangerous it is for you to be venturing out right now. For all of you... but you in particular."

"Why though?" Troy asked. "What was the meeting about at the Dome of Windows? What do you know that you aren't telling me?"

"It wasn't anything that you really need to know about," she said and crossed the room to sit on his bed. "Mainly just Luke and the Justice Ministers droning on and on about fights they'd had with demons. And some reports from our spies – if you can call them that. They're still trying to figure out what exactly is going on with Kyle. The only thing they really know is he's forming a group of dedicated fallen angels around him."

"Like the Nightwalker group that Xavier was in when he was young?"

"That's what they think," she sighed. "It wouldn't be good if the fallen angels start building a true network that's dead set on pushing the War to its limits. Kyle is bad enough by himself with a few followers. If he's able to create a large group, it would be difficult to stop him."

"To accomplish what though?" Troy asked. He'd studied that question as much as he could the last couple of days. What was the point in the War for Sins? He knew it had been started by Lucifer but reports and studies differed on the true reasons.

"To steal souls to hell," his mom answered simply.

"I know," Troy breathed being careful not to let the tiniest hint of anger or frustration show. "But what is the real reason? In the textbook, they say that fallen angels believe they can bring an end to the War."

"I think a lot of them do," his mom nodded. "But it's all a deception from Lucifer. He uses them to his ends because he does want an end to the War. It's believed that if the devil finds enough souls, he can escape from hell with all his legions and reign on Earth for eternity. The final hell where all souls will suffer in a burning nightmare. "

"Others believe that he uses the souls to build his power so he can find one uniquely innocent soul who he can then use to defeat God. None of us really know for sure. Even the fallen angels who have re-found their faith couldn't really tell us. They knew what they believed and for the most part, it's the two things I just said."

"Why would any angel want either of those to happen? Why would any of them turn their back on God?"

"Lucifer deceives fallen angels into believing it will actually be a new heaven," his mom stared wistfully at the poster of John Bradford who was frozen in the middle of a touchdown pass. His eyes burned with a passion Troy always prayed he'd be able to capture and maintain in his search for God's gifts. "They think they'll be set up as the kings on Earth forever and that they'll have influence on the pecking order and how things are run. They've been told that all the wrongs done to them will be righted. That they will get back people they've lost..."

"How do they fall for something so stupid?" Troy questioned.

"We're talking about the devil," his mom chuckled softly. "He spawned lies and deception ages ago. Once he gains a foothold on your soul, it's difficult to turn away from him."

"You all packed?" Troy's dad startled him from the doorway. Troy hadn't noticed him standing there and wondered if he'd been listening to the whole conversation.

"Uh... yeah," Troy said. "Just need to throw these books back in my bag. All my clothes and stuff have been packed since yesterday."

"Good," his dad said as he leaned against the oak doorframe. "So, I know you're still under punishment... but this year at the Hill will be your first chance to try out for the Hunters. You going to give it a shot?"

"I'm not sure," Troy said. "I haven't really thought about it. It would be pretty cool."

And, really, it would. He'd heard stories of his dad and his grandpa being on the academy teams when they were going through their angel training days. The Hunters was Passover Hill's team and had held moderate success over the years. Troy's dad had been a captain on the Hunters in his angel training days. As had Kyle, even though those accounts often got hushed.

"Give it some thought," his dad continued. "Butler will really whip you into shape."

"And we're still contemplating your status on the football team next season," his mom added with her smile fading. "It might be good for you to get your competitive juices out in a safer way."

Troy snorted and couldn't stop a wry smile. "Being on the Hunters is safer than football?" he asked. "So angels trying to knock my head off with maces or stab me with swords are less likely to get me hurt than normal guys tackling me when I'm covered in pads?"

"I meant in a safer… environment," his mom sniffed.

"Wait," Troy said as a hidden piece to a puzzle slipped into place. "Not letting me play football doesn't really have to do with my punishment, does it? You just don't want me out there practicing and stuff where the protection might not be as strong."

His mom fidgeted a little bit. The answer came from his dad. "That's part of it. But it definitely is part of your punishment too. You deserve a lot more than a few weeks of being grounded for what you did. I thought you were starting to understand how much danger you put yourself in, as well as your friends and a large group of innocent people."

"I know sneaking away was wrong," Troy said as his teeth gritted without his being able to stop them. It had been the same way for the last two days. Every conversation turned back to his wrong doing. "I don't think it's fair to hold me off the football team if most of your reason for doing it is because of fear. You've said it a bunch of times. We can't live our lives in fear of what Kyle or the fallen angels will do to us."

His parents looked at each other for a long time then his mom got up and walked to the door. "We'll talk about it," she said. "But please don't fight us when we give you the answer."

A rather subdued get-together spluttered by uncomfortably that evening. It was the first time since the reidlos fight that Troy had seen his friends in person.

"I still can't believe you didn't get punished," Becky hissed under her breath where her, Angela, Tyler and Troy were huddled.

"My mom did say something about not letting me to go to church," Tyler shrugged. "But my dad put a stop to it. I think he's starting to like it too."

"Has anyone been able to talk with Clark?" Angela asked. Troy couldn't stop himself from staring at her for minutes at a time. The toughest part of his punishment, so far, had been not being able to see her for the last three days. He'd spoken with her through their scepters; but seeing her in person offered the sweet way she always smelled and the brightness of her pink angel marks.

"His dad won't let me talk to him," Tyler huffed. "He said he wouldn't be available for three more weeks. Not until the summer football camp at OU."

"At least he's not talking about keeping him from playing football," Troy sighed.

"He would if he knew about all the demons and fallen angels lurking around," Becky said with a grim frown. "He should at least let us talk to Clark on the phone though. I miss him."

"So do I," Troy nodded. "And me and Angela won't see him or get to talk to him until August."

"Well, about that," Tyler said and peeked around to make sure no adults were paying close attention. "I got you something, Troy." He reached into the pocket of his shorts and pulled out two identical cell phones. "My dad got a deal with the phone company and bought us a new cell phone package. We got an extra one that is on the service plan and I asked if you could have it for the summer. We can talk to each other as much as we want! It'll be like having our own scepters."

"Troy has his scepter," Angela said but she smiled. "But I think it's a cool idea."

"I doubt I'll be able to get a signal at the Hill though," Troy said taking the smartphone in his hand. It was sleek and thin and would fit easily into his pocket.

"Can't you sneak through the gate every now and then to call us?" Tyler asked.

"Don't even start," Becky growled. "Your schemes only lead to trouble."

"Whatever," Tyler snorted. "He'll be in the Cathedral. Once he's there, he'll have a signal for sure. It's in Mustang."

Troy laughed and nodded. "That's true," he said. "There are a lot of angels at the Cathedral who talk on their cell phones." He glanced at his mom who was having a quiet conversation with his grandma and Angela's dad. "I'll have to tell my parents about it. They might not want me to have one. My dad is kind of old fashioned when it comes to technology."

"Why wouldn't they want you to have one?" Tyler scoffed. "All kids our age do."

"I don't," Becky shook her head making her dark hair dance in long waves. "And Clark doesn't either. And neither do Angela or Troy. You say things all the time without thinking about. The four friends you hang around the most don't have cell phones and you act like everyone does."

"Well, you should," Tyler said not backing down. "And the only reason Troy and Angela don't is because they have scepters and those ferriola things."

"Stop," Troy chuckled and let his hand settle on Becky's shoulder. "Let's not fight on me and Angela's last night here." Becky wriggled her nose but nodded.

They spent two hours eating a dinner of chicken marinara and angel hair pasta. The mood was as light as it had been since the debacle at Wal-Mart and Troy found himself truly smiling for the first time in what felt like an eternity. He'd asked his parents about the cell phone and they'd agreed – although his dad had taken some work. They'd even let him setup times to come through the gate to the Cathedral so he could talk to Tyler, Becky, and Clark.

Overall, Troy thought it had been a rather great night when he said goodbye to his friends. Tyler had given him the customary punch and Becky's tight hug lingered with him as he shut the door to his room and gave his bags one last check. Her final words rung over and over in his head.

"I'll be praying for you and Angela."

It was a simple statement and Troy knew in his heart that it was one hundred percent true. Still, he was sure Becky probably didn't understand exactly how much it meant to him. The Spirit had surged at her words and filled his chest with a deep contentment he couldn't explain.

All the anxiety he used to experience on the nights before he left for Passover Hill were distant memories. His only regret was leaving behind three wonderful friends for the next couple of months; and with the cell phone tucked neatly in his backpack, he'd at least get to talk with them on a few occasions. He went to sleep with his mind running circles on all the cool new angel subjects he'd be learning over the summer. And, of course, his building excitement of spending so much time with Angela.

The following morning was a blur of motion. Troy woke up early. Ate a huge bowl of Cheerios his mom offered him as soon as he stepped in the kitchen. Repacked his backpack for the hundredth time. Polished his dagger and waxed his mace.

At 10:00, Angela and her parents arrived to ride with them to the Cathedral. The car ride was short and Samson's booming voice welcomed them through the giant wood doors.

"Ladies and gentleman," the gigantic statue roared. "Particularly you ladies," he added with a wink to Troy's mom, then to Angela and her mom. "Welcome to the Cathedral in the wonderful city of Mustang, Oklahoma. Well, they say it's wonderful at least. I haven't had the chance to stretch my legs and see it since they saw fit to station me here. But I'm getting away with my myself. It looks a stifling hot day outside, come in and enjoy my charms."

Angela steered Troy around the flailing statue at almost a trot but she giggled when Samson harped on her mom's stunning haircut.

"That will really have her going," she whispered as they moved into the hallway filled with stores. "She was griping this morning about having a bad hair day." A rather subdued atmosphere met them as they walked through the quiet Cathedral. Only one angel hovered in the air playing a harp. The projected screen displaying the Angelic Agenda was droning through a story about an election in Germany that had everyone worried. Down the hallway, Holy Hotcakes was the only store that had more than a one or two customers. Troy peeked into Michael's Angel Fixings at all the deadly looking weapons then stopped for the briefest of seconds at the door of Divine Delights before Angela dragged him along. His heavy suitcases bounced against his legs with the handle of his mace sticking awkwardly out of his gym bag.

"I've been meaning to ask you a favor," Angela said with a quick look around. Their parents were fifty feet behind them where they'd been delayed by Samson.

"What's that?" Troy asked with his interest sparking immediately. Her pink angel marks were stunning this morning. Of course, they were beautiful at all times but the way they danced in a ray of sunlight coming from one of the windows on the east wall of the holy building, made his stomach flip upside down then right side up.

"Well... you probably won't like it," she cleared her throat and Troy's twisting stomach knotted instead. "I want you to try your hardest to be nice to Adam."

"This again?" he shook his head. "I always try-"

"No you don't," she interrupted him. "Neither of you do. He's going through a rough time right now and-"

"How often do you talk to him?" Troy jumped in with his own interruption.

Angela shrugged and popped her neck sideways while she chewed on her lower lip. "Once a week or so, maybe. Not that often. He calls me on the scepter. I can't ignore him. You know his parents were under an investigation with everything that happened last year."

"And they should have been," Troy said. "I still think they might have been involved."

"They were cleared of all suspicion," Angela pressed. "You know that. Your parents and my parents both questioned them. My dad said he doesn't suspect Adam's parents. He thinks Kyle was behind all of it somehow."

"Even if that's the case," Troy conceded not wanting to continue to see the building flush in Angela's cheeks. "It's not usually me that starts the hostilities. Talk to Adam about it. He's the one who starts bullying me and everyone else around."

"Can't you be a bigger man, or angel, and just ignore him?"

Troy snorted and physically had to make his jaw relax. "How is that going to help his attitude?" he asked. "If everyone backs down, he'll think he can walk over anybody."

"I've told you before, he only picks on you so much because he's jealous of you," Angela urged. "And that's only going to be worse after everything that happened last year. And now with the reidlos attack..."

"What do you mean?" Troy questioned.

"Do you pay attention at all when you walk around?" Angela quipped. "For an angel who is so good with Gabriel's abilities, you'd think you know more about the world around you."

Troy thought that was quite unfair. He could instantly recount every bounce and bob of Angela's hair since they stepped from his mom's Tahoe five minutes ago. Or the way her pink angel marks whirled with each word she said. And he knew there were seven people in Holy Hotcakes. Two in Spice of Life but only the shopkeepers in the rest of the stores. She made it sound like he walked around obliviously with his head in the clouds.

"I know what's going on around me," he offered.

"When you try, you do," she almost scolded. "But you seem to have a mental block to listen when people are talking about you."

"Whatever," Troy argued. "I hear everyone at the Hill talking about me behind my back. Last summer, the whispers about my parents being friends with Kyle followed me around the hallways. It's like some people believe we're helping him or something."

Angela studied him for several long seconds. Then she tilted her head and continued. "Let me rephrase… you have a mental block in hearing people around you say anything good about you. All you hear is the negative stuff but most of what everyone talks about is all the cool stuff you've done and how your parents are on the frontlines defending the world against Kyle and the other fallen angels. About how cool the stories are about your grandpa."

"I'd hear them talking about that stuff if they did," Troy countered as they turned into the Burning Bush hallway. As ever, the leaves remained silent and still. Not even the slight stirring of air in the long hallway made the plant make the smallest twitch of movement.

Troy kept his eyes on it until they pushed through the doors of the sanctuary. The lines of wooden pews and the tall arch of the room provided a unique echo of sound but Troy always thought he could feel the grace of God calming him instantly with each visit. He looked up only to be met by the blank wall of white stone at the far end. He fought the resigned sigh with all his strength.

"Still can't see it?" Angela asked quietly.

He shook his head with the tiniest hope that the motion might offer him his first glimpse of the gate to heaven.

It didn't.

"Listen," Angela grabbed his hand sending tingles up his arm. "Please be nice to Adam this summer. You two would probably like each other if you'd sit down and try."

"I highly doubt it," Troy said but forced a small smile. "I'll try though. I promise."

"Thank you," Angela returned his smile and for a brief second Troy felt a thrill as he thought she was going to hug him but then their parents stepped into the sanctuary.

"You two ready?" Paul asked as he lugged Angela's bags into the echoing room. Only the soft sound of a hymn sung in the far corner competed with his voice. He looked up at the gate to heaven and a smile swept over his face making his brown angel marks constrict towards his cheeks.

"Yep," Troy and Angela said together.

"Troy, we have something of a special treat for you," his mom directed her attention at him and away from the marvel of the gate. "Your dad and I decided you can go through the gate on your own."

"Really?" Troy gaped. He hadn't even considered asking this year since he'd been in so much trouble the last few days. The wonder of it hit him instantly like a charging reidlos. He looked at the blank wall and licked his lips. "Let's go," he said and stomped down the aisle with his bags pounding against his legs.

He heard laughter behind him but didn't stop until he was within reach of the rigid white stones. Troy didn't know how old each of the blessed building blocks were; but they looked as old as time. He swallowed and glanced at his mom then his dad.

"Remember to think only of Passover Hill," his dad advised. "Nowhere else."

"If you do wind up somewhere else," his mom added. "Call us immediately with your scepter."

"Okay," Troy answered and swallowed the nervous butterflies that had begun to tug deep in his stomach.

Angela snorted softly and leaned towards him. "It's not hard at all," she whispered. "Even if you can't see the gate."

Troy nodded and with a full intake of air, he stepped forward. Over and over again he repeated *Passover Hill, Passover Hill, Passover Hill...*

"You can open your eyes now," Angela laughed.

Troy did and the antechamber of Passover Hill met his gaze. At once, he joined Angela in laughter and walked across the room buzzing with excited voices of farewell between parents and their children. A trio of tiny angels sculpted of white marble darted at Troy and began pulling the bags from his shoulders. He let them take the heavy luggage and each of them gave him a quick bow and a smile.

"Hey Troy!" a nasally voice shouted. From across the room Ben Lewis flitted towards Troy and Angela.

They looked at each other briefly and both had to hide resigned sighs. Ben had straight angel marks that were bright yellow and constantly wore a smile that matched his wheezy tones. "Hi Angela," he waved. "I just got here too. Must have barely missed you at the Cathedral back home." He looked behind them at the gate and smiled.

"Hey Ben," Troy offered. "Have you had a good winter and stuff?"

"Yeah, I guess," Ben pushed his glasses up his nose from where they'd fallen. "Been kind of busy with everything going on. You know how it is. Dad off helping to fight the War and all." He cleared his throat and looked expectantly at Troy as though some great secret should be coming forth at any second. "How about you? I've heard lots of crazy stories from my dad about - well… they scare my mom to death. She didn't want to let me go to the Hill this summer."

Troy nodded in agreement but glanced at Angela to see if she'd caught Ben's sudden change in direction. He was sure the somewhat nosy boy had been about to say something about him, or his parents, but had quickly moved the discussion to his non-angel mom.

"I bet a lot of parents have been like that this year," Angela said as her bags were flown away in a swaying motion beneath four angel figurines. She looked at her parents who were sweeping by them with a friendly greeting gesture to a big group of adult angels huddled by Solomon's Trap in the Commons area. The fast angel food restaurant was packed with parents and kids alike. Burgers flipped and danced in mid-air as the cook spoke over his shoulder to a pretty teenage girl that had her halo shining brightly over her head. The normal sign reading, *Feed Your Hunger for the Spirit*, shined in welcome.

"With all Downey is up to these days, it's no surprise," said a rather smug voice from Troy's right. He turned and came face to face with Justin Baker who often accompanied Ben around the Hill. His clear angel marks hadn't darkened over the winter and Troy was sure in anything but a bright light, they would be invisible. "You and your parents have been in the news a lot lately, Troy. I read about that reidlos attack in Mustang last week. That's where you're from, right? They said a couple of teenage angels in training were involved along with about a hundred innocent people. It was you two, wasn't it?"

Troy swallowed while Angela worked her mouth in circles. Ben and Justin both stared at them expectantly as other students and parents streamed by from the gate.

"It was us," Angela finally answered in a hush.

"Wow," Ben said and pushed his glasses back up his nose again with a giddy look around the Commons. Beverly Lynch walked by staring unashamed at Troy. She offered the smallest of waves to Angela then hurried down the hallway to the girls' dormitory. "What was it like?" Ben continued. "Reidlos are supposed to be hard to fight."

"It wasn't too bad," Troy shrugged not wanting to continue with the conversation.

"I was terrified," Angela croaked with an anxious giggle. "And don't let Troy tell you he wasn't." She nudged him with her elbow and raised her eyebrows. He laughed but bobbed his head in reluctant confirmation. "We did manage to kill a few of them though."

"Awesome," Ben whooped which made Troy laugh since the normal nasal whine wasn't present in the excited holler.

"Don't let him impress you too much," came a drawling voice that made Troy shudder instantly at the sound. From around the corner of New Eden (Passover Hill's best spot to have teenage fun), strolled Adam Taylor. His long blonde hair curled into his neck and hung with the subtle grace only a movie star would usually be able to pull off. Troy thought for sure he could see a pair of miniature trolls living in the canyon-like cleft chin under the teenage boy's smug smile. "I've heard he causes more trouble than he's ever helped stop."

Troy gritted his teeth and looked at Angela who was watching him and seemed to be waiting for a volcano of anger. "I'm going to go say bye to my parents," Troy said remembering his promise to Angela. He slinked past Adam and didn't even ram him in the shoulder even though every fiber in his body was telling him to.

"Wait up," Angela called. "I'll go with you."

"Yeah, me too," Adam grinned and followed. Troy stifled the urge to turn and yell at him. He found his mom and dad in the same group of adult angels who were having a low conversation near the projected screen which was almost always on the Angelic Agenda news station. The Commons area buzzed with the usual screams of kids being dropped off at the Hill and the delightful smells of the mix of food from the stores.

"Hey," Troy's mom smiled at him as her eyes scanned over the small group trailing in Troy's wake – Ben and Justin had tagged along as well. She stayed locked on Adam for a second longer than the other two and Troy thought for sure he saw her smile flicker. "We're getting ready to head home," she continued. "Make sure to keep your scepter on you all the time. There shouldn't be any trouble here but we want to be able to get a hold of you at a moment's notice."

"I will," Troy said and accepted her offered hug.

"Have a good summer," his dad said. "Let me know how the tryouts go. Don't let everyone scare you away." He patted Troy on the back and gave him a wink. Troy had told him last night that he planned on trying out for the Hunters.

"If you need anything, you call us," Susan said to Angela and looked on the verge of tears. From what Troy had overhead, Angela's mom had been very close to putting her foot down and not letting her daughter out of her sight for the summer training session.

After another minute of good-byes, Troy and Angela's parents walked around the corner into the antechamber towards the gate and home.

"That's a cool scepter," Ben said. "I wish mine was gold like that." He pulled out his own scepter and studied it thoughtfully. A blue backdrop gave way to a tangled rose bush of green and white on the rounded surface. Along the top Ben's name was written in wondrous letters. "I haven't even gotten to use it much for anything other than school work."

"Be thankful for that," Angela said. Over her shoulder Troy saw Adam mingling with his bodyguard looking friend, Danny Mills. The two were never seen apart at the Hill; but for this summer, Troy vowed not to let them bother him. Like Angela had told him on numerous occasions, they were only jealous. He directed his attention at The Lion's Den bookstore and watched in amusement as Daniel artfully dodged a swipe from the huge bronze lion attached to the same statue as himself.

"Beware, for as I told Nebuchadnezzar so long ago," Daniel shouted in triumph. "God is great and will never be beaten. Take this knowledge passed down through the generations and bring the faithless to their rightful place of faith in the Lord God Almighty."

He picked up one of the many books that had been knocked haphazardly across the floor by the raging lion and thrust it into a laughing girl's hands.

Yes… it was another summer at the Hill. But for the second consecutive year, Troy was looking forward to his time learning to become an angel. Not even Adam's leering face could stop a smile from forming.

Chapter 8: Reality of War

It was only a few seconds before he regretted his thought. With a look around the corner of the antechamber, Adam and Danny started towards Troy. "Not all of us will bow down before you just because you have a scepter now," Adam sneered and flipped his hair away from his face. "I mean, what's a scepter when you have your robes." And in that instant, brilliantly white robes popped into view over Adam's body in a flourish. They covered him from neck to feet with the arm lengths matching perfectly to the ends of his wrists.

"Wow," Angela oohed and ahhed as she ran her hand along his shoulder. A monster in Troy's throat yearned to reach out and yank her away but he turned his attention to the cook inside Soloman's Trap instead. "Congratulations," Angela crooned. "They're so pretty."

"Thanks," Adam smirked. "I got them right after Christmas. Rescued a little girl from a school of daimems. I was able to throw her out of the water but the demons almost drowned me. Had my robes on when I finally managed to pull myself out of the cold waves. It was a real shock to be honest." He had a perfect way of telling a story that made Troy's fist want to clench. Adam with his robes... What could be worse? It was a nightmare brought to life. Troy would definitely rather face the putrid water demons from Adam's story than stand there under his gloating presence. He started to leave but hesitated, not wanting to leave Angela alone in Adam's presence.

"They're awesome," Ben sniffed and cleared his throat while nervously pushing his glasses to the bridge of his nose. "Wish I could figure out how to get mine."

"Oh the robes are easy really," Adam boasted with a dramatic pause. "A sword on the other hand, that takes some work." And with that, a gleaming sword, so magnificent it stopped Troy's lungs dead in their tracks, sizzled into view behind Adam's shoulder. Adam reached up and his hand wrapped around a platinum handle. As the sword was drawn he saw that the pommel had a definite cross-like shape. The blade was half as tall as Angela and her stunned expression reflected in its wondrous steel.

"You didn't..." she started but stopped as she watched her ex-boyfriend like he was a celebrity supermodel. "You already have your sword?"

"Yep," Adam grinned and slowly wove the weapon in a slow arc. "I can't really say what I got it for. It's kind of a secret mission that I went on with my dad."

"Did it have to do with reidlos?" Troy managed through constricted throat. Angela shot him a warning look with her eyes scrunched.

"Maybe so," Adam chuckled as though he was some heroic cowboy who saved a dusty old town from a demonic villain. "You have to be a little higher in the angelic order to hear about it. The archangels don't give many of us clearance. They definitely wouldn't even think about letting you know."

Troy snorted which made Danny crack his boulder-ish knuckles like a bull pawing at the ground in warning before it charged.

"So... anyway," Adam's cleft chin lowered. "You really should be proud of that scepter, Decker. Took long enough to earn it. Did you finally find a cow in Oklahoma dumb enough to believe anything you had to say?"

Danny guffawed. Troy gritted his teeth but knew he couldn't stop invisible steam from coming out of his ears. He glanced at Angela who shook her head a fraction with a pleading look in her brown eyes. Ben and Justin hovered with their mouths open as though they were ready to defend Troy but weren't sure exactly what was going on.

"Or maybe it was a pig," Adam continued. "Is that why your scepter's that ugly gold color? Did it come wrapped in greasy bacon and get all stained?" He shook his head and let Danny laugh for several long seconds while Troy tried his best to relax so he wouldn't crack any of his grinding teeth. "It's still a wonder to me that God values the soul of a pig as much as a human. I suppose when that's all you have around to save, it has to count."

"Yeah," Troy fumed not heeding the desperate tug from Angela who was trying to drag him away. "Well, I'm surprised God granted any gift to the son of angels who know how to raise their own horde of reidlos. You and your parents raised any more demons lately?" He stopped for a second and relished Adam's suddenly twitching cheeks. "I know it was your parents who set that trap last year and lured away my parents. Me and Angela and our friends were almost killed by Kyle Downey because of your parents."

"Shut your mouth about my parents," Adam hissed and advanced towards Troy with his sword gleaming in the twinkling light from New Eden's newest video game - which was manned by a stunned teenage boy who was fearfully watching Adam and Troy's building argument. "Just because you think you're above the rules doesn't mean the rest of us have to agree with it. I heard you told your friends about us? Even in a little dump like Oklahoma, the secret is bound to get out with you spouting off about it all the time."

Troy laughed but no humor carried with the sound. "I'll apologize to your parents," he offered. "When they come back to our side and accept their faith in God rather than following Lucifer's heels like little lost puppies."

"Troy!" Angela stepped in between them. Danny lumbered forward with both his gigantic fists raised. Troy bent his knees and gripped his scepter in his right hand. He reached for the Spirit and waited for the attack.

"What's going on here?" blasted a deep voice from the doorway of Sabbath Sundaes. Adam and Danny both froze midstride. Troy didn't turn away from them but his eyes moved to the voice. A deep dread filled his chest as Kevin Butler stepped into the corridor with a raspberry ice cream cone clutched in his left hand. The teacher of the archangel Michael's class appeared as calm as a mountain lake but a fierce determination always blazed in his liquid blue eyes. Troy wanted to step away from the prowling gate of his least favorite instructor. "You guys welcoming each other back to school?"

"Uh... yeah," Adam straightened up and sheathed his sword which disappeared immediately along with his robes. The way his jaw was set under a piercing glare, Troy knew he'd have to watch his back for the foreseeable future.

"Funny way of showing it," Butler licked his ice cream. The muscles under the dark skin of his hands flexed and striated lines ran away up his arms. With each step he took the Spirit sparked in Troy's vision. Even his short, curly beard seemed to shimmer with power. At his feet, a brown hunting dog watched Troy with keen eyes almost as if he was daring him to argue with his beloved master.

"Enoch doesn't think much of your manners," Butler said with his head tilting to the dog. Butler was shorter than both Adam and Troy now; but that didn't stop the extreme intimidation of his presence from rolling over them. "And I think I agree. Twenty laps around the obstacle course would probably help. What do you think?"

"Probably so," Troy groaned not daring to dispute the punishment. He hadn't been to the Hill for ten minutes and he was already getting into trouble.

"I guess," Adam sniffed and held his head high. Danny only nodded and kept his eyes on his toes.

"You two need to get over this little disagreement you've been hanging onto for the last couple years," Butler instructed. "The War is growing. We'll need angels like you to make it through." With that he turned and left. Enoch followed at a trot but watched Troy over his shoulder.

"Come on Troy," Angela cleared her throat and he let her pull him down the hallway towards the girls' dormitories. "Why do you let him bother you so much?" she griped when they were out of sight around a corner.

"You heard what he was saying," Troy started but stopped when he saw her red, scrunched face.

"I asked you twenty minutes ago to not get into a fight with Adam," she growled. "And you almost get into a death match with him before we even get out of the gate. Just ignore him."

"How?" Troy asked and threw his arms over his head in frustration. "Every time I'm around him, he never stops making fun of me. I can only take so much of it."

"You're supposed to be a bigger angel than him," Angela explained. "I saw your face when you found out he'd been granted his robes and his sword. You wanted him to say something to you so you could go off on him. I could tell."

Troy sighed but didn't argue because he knew it was the truth. Such a sudden rage had boiled to the surface when, first the robes - then the sword had appeared. It would have felt so natural and good to punch Adam square in the nose.

"How in the world does someone like him have three gifts from God," Troy sulked and spun his scepter around his hand. "And I only have one."

"Who knows," Angela said with her eyebrows rising which made wrinkles appear on her otherwise flawless forehead. "Maybe it's like your dad always says… faith." She waved before he could formulate a response and traipsed down the hallway into the girls' dorms.

Troy meandered around the Commons and ducked into New Eden's for a few minutes to watch some of the new games. Across the hallway, a group of students had stopped below the enormous projection screen. Mug shot looking pictures of Kyle and Richard Hope flashed along with a few other faces Troy didn't recognize. Each had the headline: *Beware Fallen. Dangerous! Report any sightings to the nearest Justice Minister at once.*

"A friend of my dad's was killed two months ago," an older, brunette girl said in a whisper by the doorway to New Eden. "They think Kyle Downey murdered him all by himself." Troy made sure to look the other way when he slipped out the door and half hid his face by pretending to scratch his nose.

"Did you hear about all the demons they had to fight up in Minnesota?" Troy heard a pocked marked boy say to three younger kids who stood in rapt attention. "It took a group of thirty angels to send them all back to hell. Downey is going to be unstoppable pretty soon."

Troy ducked his head and sped away as several of the angels in training looked ready to flag him down and draw him into their conversations.

It was a constant annoyance at the Hill. The gossiping never strayed far from Kyle and everyone assumed Troy was an expert on the subject.

He hit the hallway leading to the boys' dormitories at almost a run and came face to face with Billy Randell. The boy's mouth flew open and he blinked rapidly. He was several inches shorter than Troy but more muscled through the chest and shoulders. A flashing vision of Troy's mom crying over a picture popped into his mind. The boy in front of him held an unmistakable resemblance to the picture of his murdered mom.

"Hey," Troy said and forced a smile as he searched for a proper greeting.

Billy only produced a stiff nod and darted around Troy without a second glance. Troy turned and watched him speed away then rubbed his face thinking he must have developed a monster pimple to have repulsed the boy so much.

"Troy, over here," Ben called from the doorway into the dorms.

Troy offered a small grin as he continued to feel around on his face for the offending blemish. He made his way through the doorway and was met by ten sets of curious eyes. Boys of all ages, some with no gifts and others with halos already, stared at him. He froze and nearly cantered into Ben in a last minute thought to swerve down the hallway and come back later for a less obvious entry.

"Here he is guys," Ben said triumphantly. "I told you he'd be around before long." He yanked Troy into the living area of the dorm and closed the door. At once a great clamor filled the already buzzing room.

"So where is Kyle now?" asked Brad Thomas who was a sixteen year old with stark red hair and a face full of freckles.

"I heard you fought him and a bunch of fallen angels," hollered Teddy Evanston who had his halo shining merrily over his bobbing head. Troy recognized the Hunter's badge on his shirt which was given to all the team members.

"Don't forget about the selvo," David Moore said. "And my dad said there might have been a tondeo involved too. Is that true, Troy?"

Troy stood flabbergasted with his mouth hanging open. He'd become used to constantly being bombarded with questions, but in the past; there had always been something of accusing aura with each badgering request for information on Downey. This was different. An almost star struck wonder had invaded his classmates' looks.

"Well..." he began but stopped as he gathered his wits. "I have no idea where Downey is. My parents don't really talk to him much these days." Everyone laughed but it halted quickly as they continued staring at him. "We did fight him last year along with a few fallen angels. And there was a pack of selvo demons there too." He left off the tondeo because he knew the innocent eyes would haunt him that night if the subject stayed too long on his mind.

"I heard someone used voxis," Ben jumped into the conversation with a piercing hush in his nasally voice.

Troy nodded and cleared his throat. "Yeah, my grandma. It killed the selvo instantly. Turned them into dust right in front of me. The hair on my arms stands on end every time I think about it. See?" He held up his arm for everyone to inspect the rising blonde hairs.

"Awesome," David said with a low whistle.

"Sweet," Brad yelped. "Wish my parents let me go on demon hunts with them."

"It wasn't really a demon hunt," Troy corrected. "Kyle set up a trap to try to lure me and my friends away from my parents. It was when everyone thought he'd been killed by Richard Hope."

"What's he want with you?" piped in a small boy from the back of the group.

"Don't know," Troy said. "Nothing good, I'm sure." More laughs echoed and Troy took the opportunity to slide a little ways towards the hallway that led to his individual dorm.

"You going to try out for the Hunters?" Teddy asked and moved out of the group. "We need all the help we can get. Megan Veach and Terrell Anderson both got their wings since last summer and Anna Chapman said she's not signing up this year. There should be a few open spots. We haven't had very good finishes the last couple of years. We need guys like you who have dealt with real trouble to sign up and give us a chance."

Troy didn't know what to say and a frog seemed to be trying to climb out of his throat. There had been a few times the previous summer where fellow students had lauded his high scores in Butler's class as well as Moses' class on Gabriel's gifts, but he couldn't remember such a pure compliment as he'd just received from Teddy.

"I was planning on it," he finally managed.

"Great," Danny shouted. "See you at the tryouts. I'm sure you'll make it. Butler knows how much you've handled and I've heard a few people say you've got talent. We need someone who can make the other teams pay!"

With that, Troy turned and escaped down the hallway. He couldn't get Teddy's happy face out of his mind as he unloaded his bags and stacked his angel text books on the small shelves in his tiny room.

He spent an hour thinking about his day and praying for guidance then found his way to the corridor which led to the cafeteria. All around him the wonders of the Cathedral beckoned. From stunning paintings to breathtaking views of the green, river fed valley far below the windows, Troy couldn't help but relax from his confrontation with Adam.

Fifteen minutes to one o'clock, he stepped into the high ceilinged cafeteria with its domed center. Small tables were scattered around the stone laid floor and excited voices bounced off the walls. The pungent smell of fish wrinkled his nose.

"Troy, over here," Angela called from the far wall. A smile instantly sprang onto his face. He bypassed a group of cackling girls and whisked to Angela's side.

"What's up?"

"Look at this," she turned her gaze to the wall where the schedules were posted. "We only have two classes together."

Troy's stomach dropped as he ran his finger down the list of names. She was right, of course. They would only be in Gabriel's and Michael's classes together all summer. "That really sucks," he said feeling a stab of disappointment with each word. "I thought for sure we'd have at least three classes together. Four would have been even better."

"I hate Michael's class," she groaned. "I wish they would let us drop a class. I'd double up on Raphael's if they'd let me. Take one hour with our age and another with the older class. Even though I know I should be practicing with Michael's gifts all I can, I dread having Butler growl at me. Plus, I won't ever be great at fighting reidlos and selvo like you are."

"I doubt they'll let you do that," Troy said feeling a warm bubble build in his chest from Angela's compliment. He took a pen from his pocket and stepped to his right.

"What are you doing?" Angela asked.

"Signing up for the Hunter tryouts," he answered and scribbled his name right below Adam's. There were four other names on the list including Adam's bodyguard, Danny, and Jeremiah Nguyen who was a year older than Troy. He scanned the other two signatures on the list but couldn't match names with faces.

"I can't believe you're really signing up," Angela quivered. "At the competition, the swords and other stuff are made by Michael himself, right? And you actually feel the same pain that would come with any injury they cause?"

"Yeah, but they don't do any real damage," Troy countered. "It's all in your mind. My dad was on the Hunters for three summers when he went through his angel training here. I could tell he wants me to tryout. I saw a picture of him with his uniform on." He stopped as he remembered the picture in the dusty album in his dad's office. "Kyle had his arm over his shoulder-"

"Still," Angela said shrilly in a panic not seeming to hear Troy. "If you get stabbed through the stomach, you'll feel the pain like you're actually getting killed. I can't imagine... It's no wonder they have a tough time getting people to join."

Troy chuckled and looked to the food line where a tilapia dish was being served. His stomach tightened at the smell. "Fish as usual," he said and tried not to inhale.

"Did you expect something else?" Angela joked and punched him in the arm like Tyler would usually do.

They grabbed their trays and moved down the crawling line. Troy snagged a small tilapia filet and loaded the rest of his plate with rice and steamed vegetables. Along the stone wall they found an empty table and sat down.

"I forgot the salt," Troy said as he faced his tray of perfectly cooked food. "And I'm going to need it so I can smother the fish. Do you need anything?"

Angela shook her head while she speared her filet and delicately cut the flaky meat. Troy sped back to the line and grabbed a shaker of salt and a bottle of hot sauce for good measure. He froze when he neared the table. Billy Randell sat uncomfortably beside his chair.

"Look who I found," Angela smiled.

"Hey Billy," Troy offered and hoped this time he didn't have a frightening blemish somewhere on his face to scare away the younger boy.

Again Billy hardly acknowledged his greeting. His eyes darted from his plate then to Angela and back to his plate. What was going on? Troy self-consciously took his seat and wiped a napkin across his nose.

"I was just telling Billy how much I was looking forward to this summer," Angela said. "All of us really need to concentrate on our studies."

"Yeah, for sure," Troy cleared his throat and watched Billy absently push food around his plate with a fork.

"Did you look at your schedule yet, Billy?" Angela asked.

"Uh huh," Billy barely managed a nod.

"It's great you have your scepter already," Angela said starting to look slightly confused and concerned at Billy's reluctance to respond. "It took Troy and me all the way until last fall to get ours. You're a year ahead of us."

Billy's eyes rose and stayed on Troy. A distinct hostility resided in the cool green color. Across his temples, deep blue angel marks twisted and turned until disappearing under his ears. He stared at Troy for a long time before scraping his fork along his plate.

"You okay?" Troy asked hesitantly.

"How could I be?" Billy said each word louder than the last. "My mom was murdered a couple of weeks ago and you're sitting here like it's no big deal."

Troy's insides froze at the increasingly angry words. He looked from Billy to Angela who was looking at him with the same dumbfounded look he was sure had to be on his own face. "I'm sorry," Troy said honestly. "My parents went to her funeral. It's… you know…"

"Terrible," Angela finished for him.

Billy sat fuming for several long seconds then stood with shaking hands carrying his plate. "Yeah, well, if your parents had killed Kyle Downey a long time ago like they should have, my mom would still be alive," he snarled. "She told me it was their fault he ended up like he did. She didn't know why but she said your parents made him fall!" And with that, he stormed off and threw his still full plate into the stone sink near the start of the cafeteria line. Troy and Angela sat in stunned silence while everyone around them whispered and glanced at them.

"I think I'm done," Troy muttered at his barely touched plate.

"Troy, wait," Angela grabbed his arm. "It's not your parents' fault. They can't be held accountable for all the bad stuff Kyle has done just because they used to be friends with him. Nobody really knows what happened except them. All the rest is only rumors."

"I know," Troy said and truly appreciated the words.

An iceberg felt like it was forming in his lungs and making its way slowly towards his chest where it would crush away his life. Billy's words assaulted him over and over.

Was Kyle's fall really his parent's fault? Every summer he'd heard the whispers. All the other students constantly gossiped about his family's relationship with one of the most evil fallen angels in the last century. Should his parents have seen the problems a long time ago and done something about it?

He meandered the hallways for the next two hours with stops in the corner of New Eden and for a few sweaty laps around the obstacle course in Butler's gym-like classroom. Nothing stopped Billy's words from digging deep into his brain.

At sunset he found himself looking over the railing of the observation deck that looked south from the very peak of the mountain. Below him, a thousand foot sheer drop fell into the green valley. To his right, the sun was just beginning to dip behind the tall mountain to the west. On the far side of the valley a herd of elk raced through a grassy meadow surrounded by tall, white aspens.

Troy leaned against the rail and absently held the cellphone Tyler had given him. Ever so slowly he slid the screen sideways. One picture after another flashed from the phone's memory banks. There was Tyler and Clark waving. Becky sitting with the Bible in her lap. And Angela concentrating as she practiced one of the angel abilities from *Touching Grace* by Demetra Davenport.

"It's pretty cool that Tyler did that," Angela's voice carried from the doorway into the Hill. Troy didn't turn but felt her slide up beside him and look tentatively over the ledge.

"He's always kind of known what to get me that would help cheer me up," Troy mused.

"He's a good friend," Angela said. Her left arm came to rest on the railing and pressed against his wrist. The contact sent an electric chill up Troy's spine. It was such a beautiful moment with Angela framed against the sunset that Troy thought for a second he might be dreaming. Her hair rustled slowly in the wind and he could smell a delicate sweetness coming from her soft skin. On her temples her pink angel marks danced in the subtle light.

"He is," Troy swallowed and tried to will himself to lean towards her.

"Almost as good a friend as you," Angela smiled causing another electric current to travel up his back. "I'll never forget seeing you two together after you got your scepter. His face was so… stunned. To finally understand the truth that had been there all along. How he found his faith… it was awesome."

"It was," Troy croaked and began to let his shoulders dip behind Angela but in that moment she stood with a look at the sunset.

"Don't let Billy and the others get you down Troy," she said with a soft pat on his arm. "You'll be a really good angel; you already are."

And she walked across the observation deck and vanished into the school. Troy heaved in a breath of the fresh mountain air and savored the last remnants of the lingering sweet smell left in Angela's wake.

Another summer had begun and it looked like it might be the same as many of the others in the past. He still didn't have the courage to let Angela know how he felt about her. And even if some of the kids at school thought his adventures were cool; many others would keep whispering about him behind his back. Even after the sun had completely set and the valley below had vanished in darkness, Troy stayed sitting on the balcony and wondered if he'd ever have a somewhat normal, angel life.

Chapter 9: Academy of Pain

"Take your seats," the statue of David called in his brash, overly confident voice. His wooden hands were on his wooden hips and he looked ready to expound on the virtues of all Uriel's abilities in a single breath; or perhaps to brag on his defeat of Goliath again.

Troy was already at his desk and studying his schedule for the day. After Uriel's class, he would be under Adam and Eve's tutelage in Seraphim's lesson; then on to Moses' scowling recollections of Gabriel's powers where he'd have Angela with him in class; followed by lunch and the first class of the afternoon with Noah's preachings of the virtues of Raphael's healing gifts; then finally to Butler's sweaty class where he'd learn to fight like the soldier archangel Michael.

"Welcome to another summer at Passover Hill," David said in a somewhat more thoughtful voice than Troy ever remembered him using before. The sculpture's right hand was softly caressing his bearded chin and he gazed at each student in turn. "I'd like to begin with a warning to all of you before we start our lessons. All of you have at least one gift of God and are old enough to hear word of the brewing calamity called the War for Sins. It's strange times when the War rises to peaks of violence and mayhem. Friends fall to the sword or the claws of demons… or even worse to Lucifer's vile promises…"

At this David paused with his eyes searching the ceiling above his wooden head.

"But fear not, for using my teachings you can make it through unscathed and save countless souls along the way! Don't let death and destruction hinder your skills as one of God's great tools. Stand tall like I did and watch the devil's minions flee before your wrath!"

For a second Troy wanted to stand up and clap; and from the awed looks on Hank Dutton and Justin Baker's faces, they were thinking the same thing. On the other hand, Britanny Curry and Beverly Lynch looked positively terrified.

Troy spent the whole class perched on the edge of his seat as David delivered one electrifying story of his brave deeds after another. They never learned anything about Uriel but Troy found his way to Adam and Eve's classroom with a bounce in his step.

"Hey Decker," Adam Taylor's voice welcomed him to the room and deflated the hyped bubble in his chest. "Tell any more of your friends about angels? Or did you decide to go ahead and have an interview with the local evening news out in Oklahoma? Not that that would spread the news much. Cows don't seem to care much about angels and demons."

Troy glanced around the room and found Ben Lewis in the far corner. He ducked his head against the laughter of Adam and Danny, nodded at the dual statues of Adam and Eve who were holding hands as usual, then slid into the desk beside Ben.

"What's up between you and Adam?" Ben asked pushing his glasses onto the bridge of his nose.

"Stupid stuff," Troy answered as he pulled *Singing with Seraphim* from his backpack.

"I thought for sure I was going to get to watch the two best fighters our age go at it right in front of me yesterday," Ben peeked towards Adam. "Have you two always hated each other? And what was with Billy Randell yelling at you in the cafeteria?"

Troy was saved from answering by Eve's sing-song voice.

"Hello young ones and welcome back to Passover Hill," she sang while her age old partner Adam stared longingly at her. "Today we are going to review the Trumpet of Seraphim which could come in handy for all of you as the War for Sins blisters the world with demons and the torture of Lucifer's jealousy. Adam and I will pray to the Lord for mercy and peace for each of you."

For the next hour, Troy's ears were assaulted by a cacophony of trumpets. Surprisingly, Ben produced the loudest blasts of the day.

"Yep, I think I'll be with Seraphim as one of his Singers," Ben said proudly as they walked to Moses' class. Angela was waiting for them at the door.

"How's your morning been?" Troy asked.

"Pretty good," she answered. "A boar and a hound got into a fight in Noah's class. He spent half the time calming them down and asking us to heal their wounds. How about yours?"

"An hour of David bragging about himself," Troy laughed. "Then an hour of Ben blowing us away with his Trumpet of Seraphim."

A huge smile spread on Ben's face and he saluted shyly with his scepter. They stepped into the classroom and were immediately surrounded by a stunning mural of God's chosen people and their exodus from pharaoh's rule.

At the front of the class was the tall, stern statue of Moses who almost always started the hour with his arms crossed. His long wooden staff stuck out way behind the rest of the ornate wooden statue. The wool robes looked freshly shaved from the lamb.

"Come and sit," Moses announced and spread his arms. "For here, thou shalt learn of the blessings and comforts of Gabriel's wealth of love and power. Faith lives and breathes in the stone walls of this classroom. Angels are born and rise to great heights. In this class, the War for Sins cannot harm you for the boundless mercy of the Lord reigns supreme for all eternity. Have faith and thou shall be saved."

Troy, Angela, and Ben sat in the front row of desks and waited as the classroom filled. All around them whispers carried in the air.

"Downey is out there right now," whimpered Beverly a couple of rows to Troy's right. "They say he's after something specific." She glanced at Troy out of the corner of her eye. "Something he thinks can end the War and let Lucifer rise from hell."

"Lucifer needs nothing to cross the dark abyss," boomed Moses. "He has the strength but not the nerve for he knows the Son will come again to strike him into the bottomless pit."

"But I've heard rumors that the fallen angels are looking for a soul that will give him enough power to win the War," Beverly said bravely.

"Baseless gossip," Moses spat. "The deceiver holds no power over the Lord God Almighty, the maker of all things."

"Why do the fallen fight then?" Donna Caswell called.

"Lucifer has deceived them," Moses's wooden features flexed into a grimace. "And himself. He brought sin and found a way to harness its vile touch. He only wants to bring pain and suffering to the innocent souls God has seen fit to create in his image. The War for Sins can only end in Lucifer's demise."

"I wish all the fallen angels knew that," Angela croaked the words then cleared her throat. A nervous titter of laughter crossed the stone walled room.

Moses stared for a brief second at each of them in turn. "It is your job to show them the folly of their ways," he said in a soft but carrying voice. "To show them that faith in God is the only way to eternal paradise. They believe they will be kings of Earth under Lucifer's foul reign but they are only scared sheep with wool pulled over their eyes." He paused and reflected as the words bounced around the room. "Today, in the first class of the summer, we will review Gabriel's fedisome ability to better hear and understand when lies are being spoken in our presence."

Troy tried his hardest to pay attention to Moses' long lecture but thoughts of Kyle and the War for Sins raced through his mind. After the class, he found himself bumping along the hallway beside Angela and Ben.

"What's up Troy?" Angela laughed when he hammered into a trash bin in the hallway outside the cafeteria.

"Nothing really," he lied.

"Don't let all that talk about the War bother you," Angela put her arm around his shoulder. "It is scary and everything but that's why we're here, right?"

"It's just hearing Donna say stuff about Kyle being after someone…" Troy said. "And with Billy yelling at me about my parents last night, it kind of built up on me."

Angela steered them into the cafeteria where they were met by the usual buzz of eating students. "Well, take a whiff of that," she smiled. "Something to be thankful for… hamburgers!"

Troy spent an entirely enjoyable hour at lunch with Angela. They went over the morning lessons, both exasperating on the time spent by the teachers on the War for Sins. Afterward, Troy headed to Noah's class on Raphael where he had to displace a mad porcupine from a desk before taking his seat. Nothing much changed in this lesson as Noah spent half the class going over dire warnings of the plight of the planet then quickly taking them through a review of the azaria ability by flashing small cards of the overfilled Ark.

"How was David's class?" Troy asked Angela when they met outside the gym for their first round of Butler's torturing hour long lesson of the summer.

"Got to hear about Goliath again and about Saul," she sighed. "Then we practiced the lebes ability that controls animals. Kind of useless. It would be nice if they'd coordinate what one class learns to the others. I could hardly concentrate on it."

"You were probably looking forward to your time with Butler too much," Troy joked as he opened the door. They were met by Justin Baker's flailing arms as he spoke candidly with a group of attentive angels in training.

"They say the Taylors had something to do with it too," he whispered in a tone that was loud enough to carry halfway across the cavernous room. "Something to do with reidlos out in California… maybe even some fallen angels. But the big fight was in Oklahoma where Decker lives. I heard my parents say Downey tried to kidnap Decker and his friends but wasn't able to do it. He got away though. Or at least that's the official story. There are rumors that Decker's parents caught Downey and let him go. It's all a big mystery."

A tall, slender boy right in front of Justin bounced on his toes and raised his hand as though asking permission to speak from a teacher. "Did you see that news story today on the Angelic Agenda?" Calvin Lindsey said in an excited squeal. "The fallen angels and their demons knocked down a four story building in Pennsylvania. CNN reported it as a terrorist attack but I heard someone got a video of it on their cell phone."

"If they did, I'm sure an angel has already confiscated the phone," Justin said knowingly with his nose in the air. "Can't let the secret get out like that. They'll monitor the situation and make sure it goes down as some industrial accident. You can put money on that."

"Was anyone killed?" Beverly asked with her hand over her mouth in horror.

"No angels from what I heard-" Calvin answered with a look around. His eyes froze on Troy and Angela. "I, uh, bad thing is… that there were some people killed. It was like fifteen or something."

"God grant them mercy," Beverly prayed then her gaze found Troy and Angela as well and she turned a sudden and distinct shade of green.

"How long have they been standing there?" a short, blonde girl hissed under her breath.

"Long enough," Troy breathed sadly. "Don't worry about it… and my parents didn't catch Kyle when he went after us. He flew out a window of the house where he set the trap and crashed a truck to get away from them. They won't let him go if they ever catch him."

Angela stepped forward with a scowl at Justin then grabbed Troy's hand and led him to the far side of the room where Butler and Enoch had entered.

"How nice of you to join us," Butler smiled and directed his attention at the entire class. "Before we get started, I see there are three people in this class who signed up for the Hunters." He pointed at Adam and Danny, who had been whispering by the wall, then to Troy. "Tryouts will be right after we get done; so save a little energy."

Troy had to stop himself from choking at the announcement. Right after class? How was that fair? He'd be exhausted. He peeked at Adam who was watching him with a hateful glare. Troy gritted his teeth and made a promise to himself to not stop at anything short of a very painful death to make the academy team.

"I won't bore you with stories of how far the War has advanced in the last year," Butler said breaking Troy's resolving pledge. "We all know what's at stake so let's get started."

The whole class spent a painful and sweaty hour swinging across rope bridges, climbing across the ceiling on door knob shaped pegs, and jumping over pits of foul smelling tar. Troy did his best to let the Spirit guide him and fill him to the brim, but he was soaked with sweat and covered in scrapes and bruises by the time 3:00 rolled around.

"Good luck," Angela said around gasping lung-fulls of air.

"Thanks," Troy said with his best attempt at a smile. The butterflies pounding at the inside of his stomach were threatening to escape in a torrent of nerve induced vomit at any second. The only thing giving him any semblance of pleasure at the moment was the worried terror on Adam and Danny's faces as they heaved and puffed on the floor.

After a couple of minutes, which let Troy halfway catch his own racing breath, three other students marched into the gym. A small Asian boy named Jimmy waved at Troy. Behind him were a boy a couple of years older and a girl who had to be seventeen or eighteen. A stunning halo sparkled above her head and lit up whirling golden angel marks that vined down her temples and cheeks. She had a rather tomboyish demeanor in her striding gait.

"Now that we're all here, it's time to get started," Butler said. "We're going to be three members short of the seven member team so you each have a good shot. Make sure you take into account everything you are signing up for before we begin. You'll endure pain like you've never felt before. You'll sweat more than you've ever sweat before. You'll bleed and some of you might even cry. So don't make the decision to tryout for the Hunters lightly."

All six of the angels in training swallowed and shifted nervously but none of them turned and ran screaming from the gym.

"Alright then," Butler smiled and kicked open a wooden crate beside Enoch. Inside were six blunted swords and six banged up shields. "Take a set and let's get started."

It wasn't as bad as Troy thought it would be. They spent the first twenty minutes springing across a maze of ropes and tunnels while following Butler's directions. Then he set them loose on each other within the maze. Troy managed to knock Danny down twice with loud whacks across his wide chest. Then he cornered the older boy he didn't know and banged the shield from his quivering arms.

"Mercy, mercy," the boy cried. Troy nodded and turned his attention across a long rope bridge where Jimmy and the girl were whirling in a flash of swords. Jimmy moved in lightning fast somersaults and flips against the wall while the girl stood her ground and hammered each of his strikes with one of her own. Off to Troy's right he saw Adam staring at him with a wicked grin. At once Troy raced through a tangle of metal barricades but Butler called a halt to the fight before he could make even the smallest offensive move.

"That's good enough," Butler said when they had all climbed from the maze. "Troy, Adam, and Mary; if you want to be on the team, you're in."

Troy's lungs skipped an intake of air and he nearly choked at the quick announcement. Five stunned expressions met his own.

"I'm in," Mary said with a grin that displayed a wide gap between her front teeth.

"Me too," Adam replied next with the quickest of glances at Danny. Troy wondered if there might be a little bit of fear at not having his bodyguard friend with him on the team.

"I'm ready," he supplied feeling a brewing pride starting to churn in his chest.

"Good then," Butler nodded. "Jimmy, you'll be the first alternate if someone backs out... or gets injured too badly."

The short boy looked up at the words with a ray of hope forming over his disappointment. "I'll be ready if you need me," he said confidently.

"First practice is Thursday at 7:00," Butler said while he patted Enoch on the top of the head. "Don't be late."

Troy rushed from the gym not managing to suppress the smile that was exploding from deep within. He reached for his scepter and turned into Adam and Eve's classroom. The dual statues glanced at him before going back to staring into each other's eyes.

"Mom," Troy whispered into his scepter and relished the warmth that spread from God's glorious gift.

"Troy?" his mom answered instantly. "You okay?"

"Yeah," Troy said excitedly. "Is dad around?"

"Right here," his dad's voice said. "What's going on?"

"I just wanted to tell you that I made the academy team," Troy bubbled.

"Really?" his dad nearly hollered. "That's great. It's a big accomplishment. Not many people get the privilege of joining the Hunters."

"I never doubted you'd make it," his mom said and Troy could see the smile carrying with her words. "How is everything else going so far? Classes go good today?"

"Yeah," Troy said breathlessly. "They talked a lot about the War. It was mainly reviewing old stuff but Moses said we'd be studying parimus sometime soon."

"Always good to be able to feel when danger is around you," his dad offered.

"Yeah," Troy said. "I'm going to go tell Angela about making the team. I'll call you later."

"Okay," his mom said. "God has blessed you, Troy. And will continue to do so… We love you."

"Love you too," Troy said and let his scepter drop. The soft glow immediately stopped and he tucked the scepter into the harness.

The next few days were a blur of studying. As promised, Moses' class learned to detect danger around them using Gabriel's parimus ability. Noah taught them how to blind demons on Wednesday afternoon's lesson. Then how to temporarily paralyze people who've been hurt so injuries can be managed.

Thursday morning Adam and Eve showed them a really cool gift from Seraphim called naria that could make people see and hear stuff that wasn't actually there.

"How cool was that?" Ben positively shouted after the class. "That one time, I had Hank turning back and forth trying to catch an imaginary frog." A high pitched, somewhat wheezy laugh lifted from his mouth.

"It was pretty good," Troy said giving him a congratulatory slap on the back. They came across Angela kneeling over her copy of *Touching Grace*.

"Learn anything good in Noah's class today?" Troy interrupted her concentrated studying.

She looked up at him with glossy eyes. "Do what?" she mumbled. "Oh, yeah, I guess. He showed us how to make our hair grow; or recede if we wanted. It could be helpful if we ever need to disguise ourselves. We can also change the color of our hair but I never got the hang of it. You mind if I try it on you?" She brandished her scepter in a hopeful but somewhat distracted manner.

"How about tonight?" Troy chuckled. "After Hunter practice."

"If you survive," she said and reluctantly tucked away the only angel gift from God she'd received so far. "I still can't believe you wanted to be on the team. After you get stabbed a few times, I bet you change your mind."

"Never!" Troy shouted and held up an arm in a mock military salute.

"What did Tyler and Becky say about it when you called them last night?"

"They were all pretty excited," Troy said recalling his first trip through the gate the previous night to talk with his friends on the cell phone. "Becky was kind of like you and sounded worried but Tyler made up for it with a big whoop. He thinks I'll be *ultra ready* for football with the kind of training I'll be going through. No matter how many times I remind him… he always thinks I'll be allowed to use the Spirit on the field."

"Not gonna happen," Angela laughed. "Can you imagine everyone's faces if you jumped thirty feet in the air and caught a ball?"

"How about my dad's?" Troy joined in the laughter. "He'd kill me faster than a reidlos could."

They spent the next two hours studying. That afternoon, to Angela's great pleasure, Butler walked them through sword techniques in class with no practical carnage.

"You care if I come watch your first practice?" Angela asked when they were sitting down to a dinner of lamb chops, baked potatoes with cheese and butter, and long stemmed green beans.

"Not at all," Troy almost choked on his first bite. "I would have asked you but didn't think you'd want to go."

So at ten minutes before 7:00, they marched to the gym. Troy's stomach was doing somersaults and cartwheels as they strolled under the swaying ropes of the maze hanging from the ceiling. Butler was standing in the middle of the room with four tall students huddled around him. Adam stood just behind him with a smirk at Troy.

"I'll sit down over here," Angela whispered. "Good luck."

Troy made his way over to the team and took a spot beside a muscular boy who was three years older than him. On the other side of the huddle, Teddy Evanston winked at him and shot a short wave. For a few minutes the team fidgeted nervously as the remaining members trickled in.

"That's everybody," Butler said. "Let's introduce ourselves so the new guys can feel welcome." He nodded at the muscular boy beside Troy.

"Robert Brown," the boy said and looked each of them in the eye for a brief second. Tannish angel marks in nearly straight lines dove from his widow's peak to his ear lobes. "Team captain. This will be my fourth year on the Hunters. I have all of God's gifts except the wings."

"Teddy Evanston, my third year on the team," Teddy raised his hand merrily. "Only have my wings to get as well."

"Michelle Spears," said an exotic looking black girl who was a year older than Troy. Her brown angel marks were barely visible against the smooth skin on her cheeks. "Second year on the team. I have my scepter, robes, and sword."

"Curtis Kazarooni," said a towering Native American boy who barely moved his mouth when he spoke. A glare looked very comfortable on his long face. Dark red marks danced along the side of his huge jawline like a perfectly drawn tribal tattoo. "Fourth year on the team. I have my scepter and robes."

"That takes care of our returning members," Butler said. "Linda, start us off for the new folks."

Linda shuffled from foot to foot for a second before starting in a bold voice. "Linda Winters. I'm seventeen and have my scepter, robes, sword, and halo. I'm hoping to have my wings before Christmas. I'm looking forward to being a productive member of the Hunters."

"Adam Taylor," Adam jumped in before Troy could open his mouth. "God has seen fit to grant me a scepter, robes, and a sword. Like Linda, I'm looking forward to the chance to make the Hunters a better team and bring the championship to the Hill this summer."

Troy cleared his throat as everyone turned to him. Only Curtis was taller than him in the group but Troy felt tiny in his status of God's gifts. All of them at minimum had their robes (and most had everything but their wings) and here he was standing with only his scepter. "Uh… Troy Decker," he stuttered and drew a deep breath. "I have my scepter but none of the other gifts yet. I'll try my hardest to not let anyone down."

"You'll do fine," Teddy said with an encouraging smile.

"All of us will do good," Robert offered confidently. "We were close last year. With a little more hard work, we'll bring some trophies home with us this summer."

"That's a good start," Butler said and strode towards an enormous set of metal obstacles. Enoch followed at his feet with his intelligent eyes never straying from his master. "Let's do some stretches before we get into the action. Most of you are already proficient with a sword and shield. And a bow and arrow. But if we want to win you'll have to come as close as an angel can come to perfection with all the weapons you have available. And you have to always remember to use the Spirit in all its glory."

They spread out as Butler led them through a series of intricate and difficult stretches. Troy found himself having to let the Spirit bathe over him in order to come close to matching Butler's alarming flexibility and balance.

"Are you two dating or something now?" Adam's snide remark hissed from right behind Troy. He glanced from Angela then again at Troy. "Like she'd have anything to do with a loser like you if she hadn't been forced to move to Oklahoma."

Before Troy could even think of a retort, Butler and Enoch were at Adam's side. Their coach reached out and touched Adam lightly on the arm. Red robes sprang into existence over Adam's long, slender frame. Over Troy and the others, white robes draped slowly onto their shoulders.

"First lesson of the summer..." Butler smiled in a way that made Troy shiver. He pointed to three heavy duty crates fifty feet away in the center of the large gymnasium. Inside were seven pairs of wooden swords and shields. "Beat the other team until they submit; or I tell you to stop. Red against white. Go!"

Troy glanced around then started scrambling across the stone floor to the crates. He caught a split second peek of Adam's stunned and frightened face and broke into a smile. It ended up being the most fun three minutes of his entire life. He managed to slam his sword with a resounding thud against Adam's hamstring and knee while everyone else pelted his squealing nemesis relentlessly.

"That's enough," Butler finally called. Troy met Adam's eyes and relished the budding tears. He couldn't stop a huge grin from forming.

"Hold still," Michelle moved forward and a soft glow pulsed from her hands. Adam sighed as she directed her attention at the many bumps and bruises and cuts across his body.

"Bold move not asking for mercy," Butler praised as he stepped forward with a knowing look at Troy. Troy quickly turned the smile into a grimace but knew Butler had seen his gloating satisfaction. "I like a person who can take their lumps. It shows solid character to keep fighting even when the odds are stacked against you. Let's try that again. Red versus white." Like a lightning bolt, he spun and tagged Troy in the chest with his index finger. Immediately, Troy's robes transformed into the same blood red as Adam's.

"Remember that the other teams are picturing you as a fallen angel," Butler shouted as the five white team members formed a tight v formation. Troy sidestepped until he was right beside Adam. "Mercy can be given... as it should," Butler continued. "But if you are granted mercy; you are out of the match. Work together as a team or you'll come up short. This is the playground of Michael's warriors. There's no room for discontent in the Tournament of Champions. Go!"

"That looked painful," Angela said an hour later. "That one time I thought Curtis had knocked your head off. I can't believe your parents want you to be on the team."

"Eh, it was fun," Troy said somewhat honestly. "Michelle and Robert healed us right after each round."

Angela shook her head. "You had to have gotten like five or six concussions," she said with a frantic tremor carrying in her voice. "Those add up. Remember what Mrs. Barnes told us in Biology last year? Brain damage gets exponentially worse with each concussion."

"I don't see many angels walking around that look like they have brain damage," Troy laughed. "The Spirit cleans up the damage. I have faith in that. This is all designed to get us ready to fight in the War. It will help me in the long run."

Angela studied him for a long time while they walked. Finally, she shook her head and said, "I'll just keep practicing my healing. It looks like you're going to need it."

Chapter 10: Gabriel's Vision

Over the next three weeks, Troy found himself absorbed in huge mounds of homework and Hunter practices. And he wasn't the only student piled behind books or deluged with stacks of paper. Every angel in training at the Hill was working harder than he'd ever seen before. Mostly, he figured, because the Angelic Agenda never stopped its incessant reporting of everything that involved torture, kidnapping, or murder.

"Your mom is definitely right about them," Angela said in the first week of July as she scowled at the TV in the Commons. "They haven't told a single story about someone getting saved in months. It gets old."

Troy nodded while he wolfed down a roast beef sandwich in Solomon's Trap. "You still want to go exploring?" he asked after swallowing the gigantic bite.

"Might as well," Angela shrugged. "It will be nice to find somewhere away from everyone. I'm tired of all the gossip."

"I've been trying to tell you that for a year now," Troy laughed. "I can handle the Agenda reporters going crazy... but all the whispers around the Hill drive me crazy. My dad said I used up most of my visits to the Cathedral in Mustang to call Tyler, Clark and Becky already; so that isn't an option."

"There's a door down the hallway to the girls' dormitory that I've always wanted to try," Angela said with a last sip of sweet tea. "I've heard some girls say stuff about it before. But I've never seen anyone go through it."

"It's not haunted or anything is it?" Troy smiled.

"Nope, only a few demons to keep us company." Angela's eyebrows bounced making her pink angel marks dance and swirl.

Troy cleared his throat to keep himself from staring and looked in the direction of the hallway leading to the girls' dormitory. "I think I'll risk it," he said and hopped from his chair. Angela laughed and followed him down the hallway. They walked past several groups of girls who were all whispering but Troy found himself not caring what they said at the moment. Not with Angela by his side and the promise of an afternoon alone with her in sight. They sped past the girls' dormitory and came to the door. It was taller than most of the other doors at the Hill. The deep, cherry wood gave it a regal stature. Troy reached forward and it opened at the slightest touch. A thin staircase angled deeper into the mountain behind the wooden frame.

Without hesitating Angela grabbed Troy's hand and waltzed down the stone steps. The tight spiral fell and fell with echoing footsteps quickly becoming their only companions. Down they went into ever growing darkness.

"How deep do you think this goes?" Angela asked after a couple minutes of the descent.

"No idea," Troy answered truthfully as he peered around the rounded curve. "Has to come out somewhere, right?"

"Maybe we should go back up and find someplace else to explore," Angela offered peeking at him. "This is starting to feel like one of Tyler's plans."

"Where else is there to explore?" Troy asked with an attempt at a brave chuckle. "Only place would be to go over the balcony and I don't want to end up squashed down in the valley when we slip and fall. Plus, I've heard they punish you pretty bad if you get caught trying it. I doubt anyone would be stupid enough to do it."

"I don't want to try the cliffs," Angela confessed eagerly with a shake of her head. "How about we give it another minute and if we don't come to a door or something, we turn back?"

"Okay," Troy said and this time he took her hand to lead her down the stairway. Before they'd gone another thirty seconds, the stairs ended in a dusty landing. Only the smallest trace of someone's tennis shoes marked the dirt on the stone-flagged floor.

"Nobody has been down here in a long time," Angela said while she gazed down a hallway dotted with four doors. On their left, a series of windows looked out on the distant valley below. The green colors were close enough now for Troy to distinguish individual trees.

"We must have dropped five hundred feet," he whispered. "I wonder if they used to have classes down here?"

"Who knows," Angela said with a huge swallow. "I was joking about demons earlier but this place is totally different than the Hill. Look at all the cobwebs. There's probably giant spiders down here." Her arm bumped into Troy's back as she drew closer to him with a scared look into a dark corner.

"We can practice using parimus," he offered talking about Gabriel's ability to detect danger. Angela nodded and Troy couldn't help but smile at the true concern darkening her face. He breathed deep and called the Spirit. In a rush, the once dark corridor brightened and Troy found his senses touching every stone, spider web, spider, and rat. Even the smallest crack in the stone wall held no surprise for him now. No fear or danger echoed in any of the rooms. "I don't feel anything around. I'm pretty sure nothing alive is down here. Or nothing that can hurt us at least. Watch that rat though."

Angela jumped and her arms wrapped around Troy's neck much to his laughing delight. "Don't do that," she scolded with a swat.

"Hello?"

Troy and Angela both froze at the word.

"I thought you said there wasn't anyone down here?" Angela hissed.

"I didn't feel anyone," Troy answered in a rushing hiss.

"Who's there?" came a voice which Troy recognized this time as a woman's. It was coming from behind the second door of the wide hallway. Thick cobwebs hung in the corners of the frame and Troy counted five spiders creeping along the wooden surface.

"I'm Angela Williams and Troy Decker is with me. Who are you?"

"Have you ever come to visit me before?" the woman asked. "I don't remember the sound of your voice."

"Uh… no," Troy answered.

"Well come in."

Troy and Angela looked at each other. Troy found the Spirit and reached into the room. Nothing echoed at him. "Who are you?" he asked.

"Come in and see," the voice called softly.

"I don't feel anything dangerous," Angela said with the slightest of quake in her voice. "You?"

Troy shook his head with his concentration still locked on the Spirit. He reached for the door and pushed. It creaked and cracked but swept open without resistance. In the middle of a perfectly square, candle lit room was a tall bronze statue. A sculpted woman was staring at them with furtive, longing eyes that made Troy's spine tingle. "No wonder we couldn't feel anybody," he said and felt relief wash through his tense body.

"Hello Angela and Troy," the statue smiled politely. "It's nice to meet you."

"Hi Delilah," Angela said with a knowing but courteous smile of her own. "How are you?"

"Lonely as always," Delilah answered. "Not many of you students come down here anymore. I guess I deserve it...."

"For how you treated Samson?" Troy asked then cleared his throat after Angela rolled her eyes questioningly at him.

"Of course. I betrayed him for gold and silver. I've never lived it down. Not in my life on Earth or in heaven. God forgave me but I don't know if Samson ever did. He won't even look at me in heaven. Regret has been my only friend through all the ages."

"We see him all the time," Angela said. "He's in the Cathedral in Mustang where we're from."

Delilah stared at Angela for a long time in silence then looked over their heads out the open door and into the green valley beyond. "I imagine he likes you," she finally said with a sniff. "He's always had a soft spot for pretty girls."

Troy laughed and Angela slapped him on the stomach. "What?" he said. "She's right. He never misses trying to grab you or flirt with you. Or my mom. Or your mom."

"That's just how he is," Angela waved her hand dismissively.

"And it was his downfall in the end," Delilah said with a sad smile. "To my shame."

For an hour, Delilah treated them with stories of her time in Sorek Valley and of Samson's famous hair. Angela finally interrupted her while she was frothing about the deception of the Philistine's. "We need to get back up to the Hill and study," Angela said. "It was nice talking to you."

"And you," Delilah said with her scowl turning into a sweet smile. "Will you come back to see me?"

"We'll try," Troy waved as they turned and left the room. He closed it behind Angela and guided her to the stairwell. "But not anytime soon. She talked more than Justin. And the way she went on and on about money sometimes… How did Samson ever fall for her?"

Angela giggled as she began climbing the spiraling stone stairs. "I bet she was really pretty when she was alive," she answered. "I never thought about running into a statue of her. She's probably not as cunning and deceptive as she was in real life since the Spirit is guiding her now. If she was like she'd been, she probably would have swept you right off your feet."

"Doubt it," Troy said with a glance at Delilah's door. Their footsteps marred the dusty floor but cobwebs and dirt still reigned further down the hallway. "What else do you think is down here?"

"Who knows," Angela said over her shoulder. "We should come explore some more of the rooms next week."

"Sounds good," Troy answered with a true smile. They spent the rest of the day practicing one angel ability after another. All around them were the sounds of the other students practicing, or gossiping, but Troy only found himself laughing beside Angela.

The next morning flew by with David telling a story of his friend Jonathan who had saved him by warning of a murderous plot by Saul. Adam and Eve took up half of the hour in Seraphim's class bragging on their third son, Seth.

"Be prepared to show us again the proper use of naria," Adam called as Troy collected his bag when the hour was done. "All of you should have a solid understanding of the mechanics behind Seraphim's distractive ability."

"How do they expect us to learn any of Seraphim's abilities when they spend most lessons talking about their kids?" Ben griped when they'd made it to the hallway.

Troy chuckled but wholeheartedly agreed. More than ever, it seemed as though their teachers were harping on the War for Sins, or talking about their past lives, instead of teaching. "At least we can count on Moses," Troy offered. "He usually only spends a few minutes per class not pushing Gabriel's gifts."

"Yeah, him and Noah are definitely the best," Ben wheezed and pushed his glasses up his nose. "I guess you can't say Butler doesn't take Micheal's lessons serious either… but he scares me more than he teaches me."

Troy got another good laugh as Angela came into sight outside Moses' classroom. "We have a guest speaker today," she squealed excitedly.

"Who?" Troy asked trying to peek over her shoulder to get a view of the classroom.

"I don't know who he is," Angela explained. "But I overheard Moses talking to him. He's a Forever."

"Really? I've never met one," Ben said and took a couple of huge steps to peer around the corner of the doorway. He snapped back in a second with a frightful expression. "He saw me looking."

Troy shook his head at Ben and whispered to Angela with a wink. "I'd rather have a Justice Minister."

She gave him a playful withering look as they stepped into the class. Nobody spoke as they took their seats and waited for Moses to begin.

"Welcome again," the regal statue said. "We have a special visitor today as most of you have noticed. Mr. Joshua Carter has agreed to enlighten us with a story of sacrifice. Some of you already have your robes but for those that don't, this might be especially important. Listen carefully for I may quiz you on his tale."

"Thank you Moses," Joshua said as he stepped forward. He was a pale man with whitish, wispy hair. Clear green eyes beckoned from his purely innocent face. A tangle of bright red angel marks danced at the edges of his fading hairline. Troy was sure that if he stood, he'd be at least six inches taller than the grown angel. Ancient wrinkles wrapped around the man's mouth up to his eyes and across his cheeks. "Let me start by telling you that I am a Forever. All of you know of my orders calling in this world. We have been ordained to bring grace and mercy, peace and faith to those who need it. Some angels call us Soul Gazers but that isn't an appropriate term for the lives we lead. We are Forevers because we will forever follow the commandments handed down by our Lord and Father."

Joshua paused for several seconds as he looked at each of them in turn. Troy thought his eyes had stayed locked on his for the slightest bit longer than anyone else's but he imagined everyone probably thought the same thing. "Sacrifice can be a terrible but wonderful thing," Joshua continued. "This noble act is one of God's strongest signs of commitment and love. He gave his only son in sacrifice for all of our sins. And, through sacrifice, he supplies the robes of our kind for the benefit of the world. The story I will tell is from long ago." He paused again and his eyes lifted to the ceiling then closed.

"A boy lived in tiny village outside of Gitta, in what is modern day Israel. This boy was the son of angels and had long sought to follow in the footsteps of his parents. He was only fourteen years old but full of life. In those days, he was almost a man. He lived in a difficult time…"

"The War for Sins was raging and demons spawned from hell in the thousands. Not a year before the story, the boy had been granted his scepter. He loved and cherished his first gift from God but worried over his second. The robes. He found himself watching and waiting for any sign of trouble to speed into danger and save those in peril."

A deep, slow breath escaped Joshua's crinkly nose. He looked around the class with such sadness that Troy wanted to reach out with Raphael's hesdia gift and ease his sorrow. But before anyone could move, Joshua continued.

"When his prayers were answered, he found himself in his village on a busy day for trading furs and crops and animals. Music, song, and dance filled the air as a festival took over the town. The boy's parents had been called away to Nazareth to stop a raging horde of reidlos and had left him begrudgingly alone. But they had scouted the area and weren't worried for his safety. Little did they know that Satan was coming to their home. Lucifer's deceit is always hard to fathom. With his cunning guile, he led away the parents to allow his minions a feast on the village… The boy felt them through the Spirit first. A wave of reidlos stampeding across the desert ground. And in the air a foul band of selvo swarmed. Before the boy could react the fear began taking its toll on the villagers. The songs and music faded and were replaced by the wails and screams of those who see the shadow of death. They tore at their hair or merely froze on the spot. The boy knew he had to act. So he called his parents with his scepter. They implored him to get as many people as he could and flee but the boy knew that wasn't the path God had laid before him. He commanded the people to go and raced to face the demons. One young angel against a hundred monsters of hell."

181

Joshua stopped and took a long drink of water from a golden chalice on Moses' desk. His mouth worked for almost a full minute as though it was building the courage to finish the story.

"I wish I could tell you the story ended happily. But alas, I cannot. The boy fought like a true warrior of the time. The Spirit swept across the desert and blighted the demons. But there were too many... And so ended the life of Ethan son of Amos. He went to heaven a hero with robes as white as snow."

Another long pause followed the end of the story. Joshua breathed deeply and again peered into everyone's eyes in turn.

"What sacrifices have you made?" he asked with such a sudden vigor in his voice that several of Troy's classmates nearly jumped from their chairs. "I see that some of you have your robes but many don't. What will you have to sacrifice to get God's second gift to angels? Your life as Ethan did? Would all of you be willing to give up your life for those around you?"

Troy and everyone else glanced around the classroom. He knew without a moment's doubt that he'd jump in front of a horde of demons to save his friends. In fact, he already had. But the robes of an angel still remained in God's hands.

Why?

With all the self-sacrifices he'd made, he was sure he should have his own set of splendid robes.

"Thank you Mr. Carter," Moses intoned into the silent classroom. "The story of Ethan's bravery has long been one of legend and lore. Would you like to stay as we spend the last half hour going over Gabriel's gift of caemus?"

"I will stay," Joshua said with a small smile. "Then I have to get back to the hospital. There are many lives and souls to save. All of you remember… embrace your faith and the grace of God; and you shall be saved." With that he moved backwards and sat in a chair with his back against the wall. His hands folded in his lap and he tucked his chin against his small chest. Troy wasn't sure if he was praying or taking a nap.

"That was a crazy story," Ben said a half hour later when Moses dismissed the class. "Even crazier than David's stories. Do you think they brought Mr. Carter in just to make all of us think about our robes more?"

"Why would they?" Troy asked. "I'm pretty sure all of us are constantly thinking and praying about ways to get them. I know I do. But it's tough to know where to start. I know I'd do the same thing Ethan did."

"You already have," Angela said echoing Troy's earlier thoughts. "With the reidlos at Wal-Mart and when Kyle was going to kill us in that house. And with the selvo last year. What kind of sacrifice is God looking for?"

Troy didn't answer but the question bounced around his fuzzy brain for the rest of the day. Not even getting his head smashed during a Hunter's training session, later in the evening, pushed it from his thoughts.

"Are you okay?" Angela asked over strawberry ice cream cones at Sabbath Sundaes later in the evening. "I thought Curtis killed you. The sound was awful."

"I'm alright," Troy chuckled bravely. "It hurt but Linda healed me up. Did you notice how much better we're getting?"

"Yeah, I guess. You and Adam do look like you are getting along better anyway," Angela said much to Troy's frustration.

While it was true that somewhat of a peace treaty had been drawn up between the two of them, he still couldn't help but despise Adam's sarcastic remarks and smug grins. Angela seemed to notice his irritation and changed the subject. "How about Mr. Carter in Moses' class? His story reminded me of you."

"What? Really?" Troy asked racking his memory to put the pieces together.

"Just how your first instinct is to push everyone else behind you and run at the danger. It was exactly what you've done every time we've been in a situation like that."

Troy blinked for several seconds to let his beating heart calm. Angela was staring at him with a sparkle of wonder in the corner of her eyes. Almost like a fan would their favorite celebrity. "I don't do it on purpose," he said hoping he didn't sound like he was bragging. A dizzy buzz was going through his head and he reminded himself to breathe – as he often did around Angela. Even after all the time he spent around her; the feeling never left. "Who wouldn't want to save their friends?"

"Well, I do too," Angela mused. "But your very first thoughts are like the boy in the story. Save everyone else and sacrifice yourself in their place. Not to think about it first. Or to make a plan. Just to go straight at the danger. You know you don't have to die to get your robes, right?"

"I know," Troy said. "I wasn't thinking about getting my robes when the reidlos attacked us at Wal-Mart. I just kind of reacted and went with it. I wasn't going to let them hurt you… and the others."

"It probably is a good thing you joined the Hunters," Angela said with a smile. "Every time you see a demon you rush right at it instead of taking the time to be scared. My first thought is how I'm going to get away from it. Then I start thinking about what will happen if I run away… The Hunters will at least get you into fighting shape since you love trying to get yourself killed so much."

"That's for sure," Troy laughed along with Angela. "It'd be nice to have a few Justice Ministers by my side next time a horde or reidlos decides to show up though. A lot better than Mr. Carter and his Soul Gazers, that's for sure."

"You're not supposed to call them that," Angela admonished with a frown instantly darkening her face. "They are the nicest people on the whole planet. And they go around healing people all the time. And helping them find and maintain their faith. It would take a lot of willpower to live strictly by the commandments and try to rein in every sin you have. But they do it without complaint."

"Luke Fischer said they were wacky," Troy said. "And I think I agree with him. What good are they in the war? If a swarm of selvo were attacking a church, they wouldn't use any of the archangel's gifts to fight them-"

"They'd concentrate on saving people," Angela jumped in cutting him off. "Saving them from pain. Or saving their lives. Or more important, saving their souls."

"I'd still rather have a group of Justice Ministers with me."

"I heard you and Tyler talking all the time about how cool Luke was before we came back to the Hill," Angela said with her eyes on her ice cream. "But I think the Justice Ministers need to get their priorities straight."

"Your dad was one of them," Troy said throwing his hands up wildly and getting a reproachful look from the owner of Sabbath Sundaes. He watched Angela and quickly searched for a way to steer the conversation. A patch of red dots had started appearing under her eyes and he knew them to be warning signs that she was getting mad. "I just think I gravitate more towards the Justice Ministers. So maybe I'm a little too hard on the Forevers."

Angela shrugged without comment but looked somewhat appeased. Troy's stomach tightened a little as he tried to think of something to change the subject. "You think we could go exploring down in the lower section again sometime in the next few days?"

"Yeah, if you want," Angela answered as she finished the last bite of her ice cream.

Troy kept watching her and hoped she would keep going but before he could think of anything more to keep the conversation going; a tingle crept up his spine. The slowly crawling prickle made the hairs on his arms begin to stand one by one. The danger he'd looked for with parimus in the lower levels of the Hill slithered into his body like a cold, dark fog. Every shadow darkened and grew. Troy spun around knowing a demon was somewhere in the ice cream shop. A flash of claws flitted before his eyes. But only laughing and smiling students met his gaze.

"You okay?" Angela asked. Her face was scrunched as though she was trying to read a sign from far away. "I felt... it was weird, like something scared you."

"I don't-" Troy began but cut off. For an instant all the lights went out and the world whizzed by in a blur of colors.

Then… in front of him stood his mom. She was standing in the shadows of a house surrounded by ornate trees and manicured bushes. Her long hair fell still as stone in the hot air of the summer night. Troy could smell the sweet, flowery cleanliness that always followed her. He shook his head trying to understand what was happening and why he was here. Just as he opened his mouth to try to talk to his mom, a growl erupted from the dense leaves of a dogwood tree to his left. Before she could produce the tiniest of screams, three selvo demons burst straight at her. From around the corner of the house, two reidlos howled in delight.

"Troy!"

Troy jumped and Sabbath Sundaes dissolved around him. Everyone's eyes were on him where he was sitting as rigid as the statue of Abraham Lincoln. Without thinking, he yanked his scepter from its pouch.

"Mom! Mom! Can you hear me?"

"Troy, what is going on?" Angela asked in pure bewilderment. All around her, the patrons and the owner of the store were gathering.

"Dad!" Troy screamed into his scepter.

"Troy?" his dad's voice answered immediately.

"Mom's in trouble."

"What? What are you talking about? How do you know that?" his dad asked.

"Where is she?" Troy begged remembering the claws and fangs of the raging demons. "There were three selvo and a couple of reidlos going after her. She didn't answer when I called."

"Emily?" his dad's voice barked. "Emily? Paul! Susan!"

"What is it?" Paul's voice responded.

"We have to get to Emily," Troy's dad shouted. At once, the sound of air rushing in the wind whipped from Troy's scepter.

Sweat was streaming down Troy's face and drenching his shirt as he stared at his scepter. Angela was staring at him like he was a maniac in an insane asylum. She began to speak but a terrible, gut wrenching shriek sounded from the scepter.

"For God, we fight!" Troy's dad yelled and the scepter went silent.

"Dad? Dad? Dad?" Troy said over and over again.

"He's busy," the small angel who owned Sabbath Sundaes said. "All we can do is pray for them."

"Let's go," Troy grabbed Angela's hand and began running into the Commons.

"Where are we going?" Angela squawked.

"To the gate. We have to find our parents." Other students dodged them as they streaked across the stone floor. Mutters followed in their wake but Troy didn't pause. Out of the corner of his eye, he saw Mr. Butler striding in their direction with Enoch at his feet. None of it mattered. All he cared about was getting to wherever his mom was getting attacked. He couldn't lose her. The thought sent what felt like a truckload of cement into the pit of his stomach. He raced around the corner and saw the blank wall of stone where the Gate resided.

"Troy?"

Troy froze at the sound. He lifted his scepter with a scared look at Angela. "Yeah?"

"Mom is okay," his dad said softly. "She's hurt but she'll survive."

"Thank you God," Troy breathed and sniffed to hold back the tears threatening to fall. His mom's smile flashed in his eyes and the barrage of punches to the chest, he'd been feeling ever since he saw the demons racing at her, stopped.

"Troy... how did you know she was in trouble?" Paul's voice asked from the scepter. "Where are you?"

"At the Hill," Troy said with a look around. Everyone's eyes were on him. Near the entry to the Lion's Den, Mr. Carter was watching him solemnly. His wrinkled hands were clasped in front of him as if he'd been praying as hard as he could a second before. "Me and Angela were eating ice cream in Sabbath Sundaes," Troy continued. "I saw a vision of my mom. She was standing by herself by some trees. Then the demons attacked her."

"You saved your mom's life," his dad's voice cracked. It was the first time in Troy's life he'd ever heard even a quiver of fear quake from his dad.

"How did you know she was in trouble?" Angela's dad repeated.

"It was parimus," Troy answered knowing it was the truth. "I felt the danger first and then I saw a vision. It was right when it was happening. It was like I was transported to where she was but I couldn't do anything-"

"I've never heard of parimus working from that far away," Susan said. "It usually only works for danger around you."

"Neither have I," Troy's dad said and he cleared his throat. "All we can do is be thankful that Troy is so good with Gabriel's gifts."

Chapter 11: To the Valley

The story of Troy saving his mom spread like wildfire through the Hill. Troy spent the next week fielding question after question about how he was able to use parimus to such great effect. There were even a couple of reports of it on the Angelic Agenda.

"Why does everything have to get blown up like this?" Troy asked Angela after another hour of Moses teaching. He'd been calling his mom every morning with his scepter. Not once did she fail to thank him at least ten times for saving her life. He only wished he could see her smile whenever they spoke.

"It always will with anything to do with you or your family," she sighed. "Because of Kyle."

"Nice job last week," Hank Dutton called as he walked past with Beverly Lynch. As soon as the two of them were five steps down the hallway, their heads came together in a chorus of whispers.

"I'm sick of it," Troy griped. "It's been bad at the Hill before... but nothing like this. Even Robert and the others have been acting differently towards me at the Hunter practices. I can't figure out if they're scared of me or proud of me."

"Why not just ask them?"

"Why should I?" Troy fumed. "I don't go whispering about people behind their back all the time."

"You gripe about Adam and Danny all the time," Angela countered as they rounded into the gymnasium for their daily lesson on Michael's fighting abilities.

"Yeah, but I would do that to their faces," Troy said as his two nemeses came into sight. "Want to see me do it?"

"No, I don't," Angela laughed and guided him away from Adam towards the other side of the crowd of students. "You two have been being a lot better to each other this summer. That's the one thing I've really liked about the Hunters."

Troy couldn't argue with her on that point. While Adam did continue to take shots at Troy, and pretty much anyone else around, the slights didn't hold as much venom as they used to. Either that, or people had finally started to understand ignoring Adam was best since he was such a jerk. "Did you find out if your parents are going to let you go to the tournament to watch us or not?" he asked in a whisper as Butler walked into the gym.

"They're not," Angela answered with a small shake of her head.

"That sucks," Troy breathed. "I was hoping you'd be able to go."

"Even though it's at another angel academy, my mom said she'd worry too much," Angela informed with a deep breath of her own. "Wouldn't it be nice to live in a time when the War for Sins wasn't messing up everything?"

Troy snorted as Butler yelled at them to get a wooden practice sword and take positions for an all against all fight. Angela's shoulders slumped at the news.

"I'll have your back," Troy said.

"And you know what Butler will do if he catches you helping me," Angela warned with a swallow as she retrieved a battered sword from a sturdy crate.

"He won't catch me," Troy winked. "You want to go down and visit Delilah again tonight? It might be the last chance I have before the tournament."

She nodded then went and took up a position with her back to the wall. Troy grabbed a sword of his own and stationed himself in the middle of the gym floor where he'd be able to keep an eye on Angela.

He knew it would be good for her to learn to use a sword better, but couldn't stand the thought of knowing she was getting bludgeoned and battered.

"Go!" Butler shouted. Troy smiled and found Adam's spinning form where he was already attacking Hank.

He jumped and lost himself in the whirling, adrenaline spiking fight.

"You didn't help me much," Angela said still wincing two hours later. She'd been rubbing her shoulder ever since the class.

"Here," Troy moved her hands and concentrated on Raphael's subbia ability. The soft glow of the Spirit gently wrapped itself around Angela's arm then filtered through her shirt.

"Thanks," she breathed while rolling her arm in a circle. "You are getting better at that. I should have had you do it right after class. I can't heal myself as well as I can others."

"Nobody can," Troy smiled and reluctantly let go of her arm. They were on their way down the stone staircase to the room where they'd find Delilah. "Are we going to talk to her again?"

Angela nodded as she sped down the steps. "For a minute," she said over her shoulder. "I'd like to see what else is down here though."

They ended up spending almost a quarter of an hour trapped in Delilah's room before Angela could extricate them with an excuse that she had to use the bathroom.

"Second door down the next hallway if I remember correctly," Delilah purred.

"Let's skip her room next time," Troy whispered. Angela smiled and they moved to the next door leaving footprints in the deep dust. Hundreds of tiny legs skittered in Troy's ears as he concentrated with Gabriel's parimus. Ever since the vision of his mom, he'd had an extra hypersensitive touch with the ability.

"It's weird," he said in the echoing hallway. "I've never had such a… natural feel for any of the other archangel gifts."

"You're that way with all of Gabriel's," Angela said offhandedly as she pushed open a door. Nothing but the empty base of a statue remained in the long, forgotten classroom. "How long do you think this part of the school has been empty?"

"Since 1892," Troy answered immediately which made Angela turn to him with surprise lighting her pretty face. "What?" he grinned sheepishly. "I looked it up. The Hill was the first angel academy in the US west of the Mississippi. There used to be about five times as many students here back in the 1800's. That was before they built Whispering Trees, Faith Forest and the others."

"What are you two doing down here?"

A shudder went up Troy's back at the sound and he had to instantly hold back the anger that surged. He turned and found himself looking at Adam and Danny who were peeking into the dusty hallway from the stairwell.

"Hey Adam," Angela said with a fake smile and a tiny wave. "We found this place last week and wanted to come down for another look. There's a statue of Delilah in that room. You two should say hello. She's really funny."

Troy hid a snort as a cough but kept his eyes warily on Adam.

"We saw you go through that door up there and thought Decker might be getting you into trouble or something," Adam said as he strolled across the stone floor and looked out the window at the darkening valley. "He's good at that. Telling his friends all about angels and trying to get them killed left and right-"

"Yeah, demons do seem to find some way of knowing where I'm at," Troy said not being able to stop his teeth from grinding together. "Especially reidlos…"

Angela shot him a "please don't start" look. She'd heard enough of his ideas about Adam's parents being fallen angels to know where he wanted to steer the conversation. "You guys want to look around with us?" she asked nicely.

"Yeah, maybe so," Adam said. At once his robes and his sword popped into view. "Wouldn't want to get any dirt on my clothes. The robes don't get dirty… but you wouldn't know that would you, Decker?"

"Leave it," Angela whispered at Troy out of the side of her mouth.

Troy looked at Adam for a long time as the boy walked confidently along the hallway. They'd spent hours and hours in the Hunter trainings over the last month. Under Butler's tutelage, Troy knew both had improved at the sword. Adam was fast enough now to rival Robert but Troy wasn't scared of him. Not even with Danny smirking by his side.

"You better stay out of my way at the tournament," Adam sneered. "Everyone on the team thinks you're going to mess us up. No one knows why Butler let a player on the team who only has a scepter."

"Maybe because he can beat you with or without any of God's gifts," Angela snapped.

Troy froze with his mouth open to throw his own insult back into Adam's face. The look on Adam's face was somewhere between unbridled shock and a deep fear as though a pack of selvo had sizzled into the hallway straight from hell.

"Easy there Angela," Adam laughed then cleared his throat. He held his hands up in a placating motion. "I was just having a little fun with Troy. We're teammates now. All of us tease each other a little bit."

"Don't even try to say that," Angela growled. "I asked Troy to treat you better this summer and for the most part, he has. You need to start doing the same to him instead of constantly making fun of him. Why don't you show us why you've already been granted your robes and sword and actually be a decent angel for once. You didn't used to act like such a jerk all the time."

Troy stared at Angela. A bright flush had burst onto her cheeks and stood out against the striating pink angel marks on her temples. She looked ready to physically pounce on the much bigger Adam. If she'd been granted her sword already, he was sure it would have popped into view on her back. A broad smile crept across his lips. Never before had he heard Angela defend him as if his life depended on it. For the first time in his life, he knew he was seeing her truly, and unmistakably, mad. He relished the fact that it was in defense of him.

Adam and Danny had both froze on the spot. Adam's mouth was hanging open and his eyes were scrunched in confused terror. Danny was looking and waiting for instructions from his bully of a leader.

After almost a full minute, of what was wonderful bliss for Troy, Adam finally recovered. "You're probably right," he murmured. "I should make sure to show the reasons why I have more gifts from God than... well, you know, I mean, I should act nicer."

Angela didn't say anything but continued to stare ice bolts at her old boyfriend.

"We'll leave you two here then," Adam said with a slight bow. He grabbed Danny's arm and yanked him around. They sped to the stairs and disappeared.

"Thanks," Troy said into the silence of the dust-filled hallway.

Angela shrugged her shoulders. "I don't know why it set me off so much. You have been better to him this summer – even if you do gripe about him all the time behind his back. Why can't the two of you get along?"

Troy searched for the answer. The immediate response, he'd had to bite his tongue to stop, was that Adam was an idiot. The truth he knew was probably to do with Angela. He thought for sure that the conceited boy still liked her. And from the quantity and quality of glares Troy got whenever Adam saw him with Angela, he was sure that was the correct answer.

"Difference of opinion on most things?" Troy chuckled.

Angela eyed him with her lips pursed. "Your differences of opinions get old," she said. "Come on." She turned and began exploring the lower level which was rapidly becoming dark as the sun set behind the west ridge of the mountain. They both ended up using their scepters to light a path around the spider webbed path. Nothing but empty rooms met the flashlight like glow of the Spirit as they directed their scepters here and there.

"Eww," Angela squawked when they peeked into the long derelict bathrooms. A mass of tangled grass and wood had been erected in the corner stall. A small hiss came from the pile of trash.

"Not sure if we want to see the rat that built that," Troy said and quickly stepped out of the bathroom.

They laughed together as they traipsed down the hallway, ignoring Delilah's call for them to talk to her again, and made their way to the stairs.

"Well, that was a bust," Angela said when they were back in the tidy confines of the Hill's corridors. "I'm going to head to my room and study, then get to bed. When do you leave for the tournament?"

"Saturday," Troy answered. "We'll be gone for three days. The individual competition is on Sunday. Then the teams start Monday with the finals on Tuesday, if we make it that far."

"I'm sure you will," she said. Before he knew she was going to do it, she flitted forward and kissed him softly on the cheek. "Good night."

Troy didn't get a word out in farewell until the door to the girl's dormitory closed behind her. "G-g-good night," he whispered with his hand reaching to touch the spot on his cheek. For what seemed like an eternity he stood as still as a statue. Finally, the strange stares he was getting from all the girls going into and out of the dormitory woke him from his stupor.

He went to bed that night with his mind racing. Sleep didn't find him until the mountains had turned the deepest black.

Angela made no mention of the kiss the rest of the week. Troy had tried several times to bring it up; but the breath always caught in his lungs whenever he thought about mentioning it. Had she expected him to return the kiss? Was she mad at him for standing there like he was frozen in time and space? If she was, she hadn't been acting like it.

"Good luck," she said on Saturday morning where he was lined up with the team in the Commons. His parents were chatting with Butler twenty feet away. They'd come to see him through the gate and wish him luck as well.

"Thanks," he said. "I'll need it. I'm way more nervous for this than I've ever been for a football game."

"Knowing there's a high possibility you are going to get stabbed will make you that way," Angela laughed. She stepped forward and threw her arms around his neck. The hug only lasted three heart beats but Troy was sure he'd almost felt what eternity in heaven was like as her body pressed against his. "See you Tuesday night. Make sure to call me and tell me how you did. And what the Valley of Angels training ground is like."

"I will," Troy stammered as he tried to shake away the paralyzing sensation that coursed through him from her hug.

"Troy?" his dad's voice called.

Troy turned and saw his dad motioning for him to join him by the wall.

"I wanted to make sure you knew how proud of you; your mom and I are," his dad said in his always serious voice. "Not only for getting on the Hunters but for showing how strong your faith is when you saved your mom."

Troy fidgeted under his dad's bright eyes. A feeling, that almost rivaled the elation of having Angela's arms around his neck or her lips kissing his cheek, tore into the upper part of his chest. Here was his dad telling him how proud he was of him. A fully grown angel who had killed thousands of demons and saved as many souls; it made a glow build in his chest he was worried my start shining through skin like the Spirit.

"Also," his dad continued before Troy could think of anything to say. "I wanted to stress the importance of the Hunters. And it's not in the way you are thinking... winning is great but building relationships with your team and with the other players is what the academy tournaments are all about. These are angels who will be your friends and allies in the War for years to come. Make sure to get to know as many of them as you can. Just like you do here at the Hill. You'll need them."

"Okay," Troy said with a swallow to clear the triumphant lump still blocking half his throat. His mom stepped beside them at that moment with one of her bright smiles. She reached out and he leaned into her arms. The soft smell of clean flowers drifted from her skin and clothes. It was probably the tenth hug she'd given him since coming through the gate but he knew he'd stand in the Commons all day and let her hug him, if she wanted. The thought of how close she'd come to getting killed had haunted his dreams several nights in the last two weeks.

"Good luck," she repeated what she'd already said a few times before. "We'll be praying for you. Make sure to hold onto your faith. And remember... for God, we fight."

Troy nodded as Butler began shepherding the team towards the gate. "We're going to the Valley of Angels training camp," he bellowed. "Remember that so you don't get lost." And he disappeared into the blank wall of stone. Behind Troy a large group of the Hill's students cheered and yelled encouragement. A satisfied smile lifted across his face as he walked towards the wall. At the last second he turned and waved to Angela and his parents. Then with his mind repeating "Valley of Angels" over and over again, he jumped forward.

At once, the Commons area of the Hill disappeared and a high ceilinged, modern hallway filled his eyes. Directly in front of him the tall statue of a woman had her arms spread in welcome. Paintings of Bible stories depicted in jagged, darting lines hung on the smooth walls. A crystal chandelier pulsed with a thousand lights over the sculpture's head.

"Hello," the marble statue said in a wonderfully melodic voice. "Welcome to the Valley of Angels training camp." She was looking from Troy to Robert then to Adam who'd come through the gate right after Butler.

"Let's go," Butler growled and stomped around the beautifully chiseled woman.

Troy gazed at the statue trying to figure out who she was. Her long hair was held above her neck in intricate curls. In her eyes was a softness that belied the hardness of the marble of which she was constructed. A small, pearl encrusted crown sat at the very top of her head. Troy searched his memory of all the heroes of the Bible.

"She's Esther," Linda said with a knowing look at Troy's perplexed face. She prodded him in the shoulder to direct him around the smiling statue. A gleaming Hunter badge was pinned to the upper, left side of Linda's chest – just like Troy's. The lone peak insignia trumpeted their home academy as Passover Hill. "You ready for this? I haven't been able to hardly sleep the last couple of nights."

Troy nodded enthusiastically as Esther began telling a story about her days as a queen to a group of awed younger boys. The Valley of Angels held a totally different feel than Passover Hill. No stone was in sight. The arched ceiling was made of deep brown wood that looked like it had soaked in the history of a million angel stories. Clear glass windows dotted the long entry hallway. A forest of tall pine trees swayed on the gentle slopes of a valley in the wind outside.

Teenage angels in training teemed all around the cavernous hallway. Almost all of them had a badge shining from their chests. Troy spotted one for Whispering Trees in California where his grandma trained when she was young.

"Heaven's Falls," grumbled Robert with almost a glare at a pair of tall boys whose badges were designed after a cascading fall of water.

"Granite Ridge," Butler said with his head tilting to a couple of stern looking girls. "Isle of Hibre's Angels from England. St. Sophia in Russia along with Elbrus Peak too. Caverna de los Guardianes from Spain. Desert Flower from Egypt. Gloucester Heights in Australia, Manasco Manor in Italy… and many more. Yep, they're all here. Big turnout this year with the War for Sins ramping up. Everyone wants to be prepared and the academy teams are one of the best ways to do that."

Troy looked around in wonder at all the confident, soon-to-be angels marching through the hallways of the Valley of Angels training camp. Most sported halos shining over their heads. He swallowed and hoped no one asked him how many gifts from God he had.

"We'll be in staying in a dorm on the southwest corner," Butler said and began striding through the crowd. They passed through a gigantic Commons area that made the Hill's seem like a hovel. Stores and shops and restaurants beckoned from every angle. Troy wondered how many angel students trained in the Valley to bring that much business.

"It serves as a Cathedral for the area as well," Linda answered his thoughts with another knowing look at his face. "My aunt went to school here. She's been going on and on about how cool it is ever since she found out I was on the Hunters and would be coming here for the tournament."

Butler continued forward and guided them through a few hallways of classrooms. Troy saw the statues of Peter, Saul, Jonah and Ruth standing solemnly at the front of the empty classes.

Whispers of "Passover Hill" echoed as they swept past doors that looked like they led to dormitories. Hundreds of students of all ages were lingering here and there to watch the entry of teams from around the world.

"Is that Troy Decker?" a boy who couldn't be more than twelve years old squeaked to his staring friend. Both stood on their tiptoes to get a better view and several other passerby whipped around with wide eyes as well. Troy sped past the boys and ducked between Michelle and Robert with his head down.

"The Wall," Curtis said with his humungous head nodding towards a cluster of Asian boys and girls. Troy peeked at the group around Robert's shoulder. "From China. They won two years ago."

"And Heaven's Falls barely beat them last year," Robert said with a tight frown. "Doesn't look like they lost anyone from last year's team. They'll be tough to beat."

"Here we are," Butler called from the front of the pack and motioned for them to go through a door he was holding open. They walked through as a team and found themselves in a forty foot by forty foot room with ten beds stacked almost on top of each other.

"Cozy," Michelle chortled. Adam was looking around with a disdainful look on his chiseled features.

"It will do," Butler offered and tossed his bag onto the nearest bed. "We won't be spending a lot of time in here anyway. Get yourselves settled. Then we're going to have a walkthrough this afternoon. We'll talk about strategies for the individual games tomorrow and go over the positions I'd like you to play for the team events."

The afternoon practice session took place two miles to the south of the school in a small meadow nestled against the walls of the deep valley. All around them the tall pine tries swayed in the calm wind. Above, a striking blue sky was marred by only the thinnest wisps of white clouds.

"For tomorrow," Butler said and held out a piece of paper. "There are twenty two teams in the tournament. There will be 154 participants in the individual competition. They've broken the first round into ten heats. Six of the heats will have fifteen players and the other four will have sixteen. The top two finishers from each heat will qualify for the final round. Robert and Teddy, you are in the third heat with fifteen players. Curtis, you're in the fourth heat also with fifteen. Linda, you are in the sixth heat with sixteen. Michelle and Adam, you are in the seventh heat with fifteen players. Troy, you are in the ninth heat with sixteen players."

Adam sneered at Troy from behind Butler's shoulder. He pointed to his scepter then to Troy then to Michelle's halo which was shining brightly over her head. Troy knew what he meant. What was Troy going to accomplish against the other players who had almost all their gifts from God and who had years of experience on him? His right hand tightened on his mace. He'd brought it along more for comfort than for any practical use. Right now, he wished he could bash it over Adam's head.

"For those of you in a heat together," Butler continued drawing Troy's attention. "Remember that you aren't allowed to help one another. The object is for you to get as many of the soul orbs as you can by the end of the time period; or before you are eliminated by another player."

Troy swallowed at the thought. A whole array of things fell into the "eliminated" category. Getting maimed, cut, sliced, stabbed, whacked, and bludgeoned were all included on the list. Of course, all the weapons were designed, created, and blessed by Michael himself, so no actual damage was done. But the pain was real, nonetheless.

"So how big are the actual soul orbs?" Linda asked. "We've been using the golf balls in training, but nobody has ever said for sure."

"Between a golf ball and a tennis ball," Robert explained. "I was one orb away from qualifying for the final round last year." He said it with a heavy grimace. Troy had heard him gripe about it several times before.

"It's been four years since we've had anyone qualify for the final round," Butler said with a barely perceptible scrunch of his dark face. Enoch whined a little at his feet. "Let's get at least one of you through this year. Two or three would be even better."

"I'm sure we'll get at least one person through," Adam said confidently. Everyone nodded and Adam used the brief distraction to shoot a glare showing what he thought of Troy's chances.

"I like that attitude," Butler said but he gave Adam a piercing glance. "For the team competition, we drew Granite Ridge from up by Atlanta in the first round. They had a decent team last year so let's go over some things we remember about them."

They spent the next two hours going over different plans for the team games. Troy was put as one of the scouts whose primary job was to watch for the other team's players and relay positions back to his own team.

"Don't forget," Butler said to Troy and Michelle. "If you see your chance to attack, don't hesitate. We win by totally eliminating the other team or by having more surviving players after the thirty minute round is over. Try to single them out rather than attacking a large group."

"Those kids from the Wall are masters at that," Michelle said. The brown angel marks on her dark skin flashed in the sunlight. "I still can't believe Heaven's Falls beat them last year."

"Brute force won in the end," Robert said with his mouth working circles around each word as though he was having to force them out. "The Heaven's Falls team will stay in a tight group and force you to attack them in large numbers. That's how their captain, Simon, likes to operate."

"Was he that huge guy we saw when we first walked in?" Adam asked.

Robert nodded and Troy was sure he could hear his teeth grinding together. "He was the one who knocked me out of the individual competition last year right before I was about to grab another orb."

"Well, that won't happen this year," Butler said then looked at Troy. "Simon is in Troy's heat."

Everyone but Adam turned to him with looks of utter caution and worry on their faces. Adam's eyes lit with malicious glee at the thought of what the gigantic angel would do to Troy.

"I'm sure I can handle him," Troy said and tried to smile. All he managed was a half a grimace instead.

"That will be it for the afternoon," Butler said. "Get some rest tonight. Visualize your plans for the individual competition. Don't be afraid to mingle with the other teams. And above all else… say your prayers."

With that, he left them standing in the peaceful pasture of grass. Tall pines towered over the team casting shadows as if in reminder of how insignificant they were. For Troy, the sweet, fresh smell under the canopy reminded him of his mom. He envisioned her bright smile as he followed the others back towards the Valley of Angels.

Chapter 12: Tournament of Champions

"I heard you were in the ninth heat," a voice said bringing Troy from his daydream of the kiss Angela had bestowed on his cheek a couple of weeks before. He was in St. Peter's Pizza Parlor wolfing down a slice of chicken, bacon, and artichoke pizza. He turned and came face to stomach with a giant of a young man. Up he looked until he found himself gazing slack jawed in disbelief at Simon from Heaven's Falls.

"Uh... yeah," Troy stammered. "You too, huh?"

"Yep," Simon said with a tiny grin. "You mind if I sit?"

"Not at all," Troy cleared a thick lump from his throat.

"I'm Simon Birchhead," he said as he sat with three huge slices of pizza loaded with every meat on the menu. He held out a muscled hand and Troy shook it as firmly as he dared. "From Heaven's Falls. A lot of people have been talking about you – wondering if you'll be as good as your dad. My dad has talked about him before. Well, it was about him and Kyle Downey. Said they were unbeatable together when they were playing for Passover Hill."

"I've heard that too," Troy said nervously. "My dad doesn't talk about it a lot but he mentions it every now and then. He'd probably talk about it a lot more if Kyle hadn't been involved."

Simon chuckled while he took a bite of steaming pizza.

"Do you know Robert Brown from my team?" Troy asked hoping to turn the conversation away from Kyle.

"Yeah, a little bit. He's a solid player. It's always tough planning against him. Smart fighter."

"He says the same types of things about you," Troy said with a smile.

"I bet he does," Simon laughed loudly. "And I bet he doesn't too. He wasn't happy when I blindsided him last year in the individual competition. He hasn't talked to me since."

"Were you friends?"

"Not really. But friendly at least."

Troy finished his pizza and talked with Simon for almost an hour. They exchanged stories of what it was like to train at their different camps and how life was in their area with the War for Sins raging.

"I'm sure you get way more involved than I do," Simon said as he rubbed a napkin delicately across his mouth. "Your family is always in our prayers. We've all heard stories of how Downey is after you. Is that all true?"

Troy nodded and glanced around the packed restaurant. All around them angels in training were laughing and joking. Many had stolen glances at his and Simon's table but none seemed to be overly interested. "He's definitely after me," Troy answered carefully. "I'm not sure why... exactly. But it has something to do with getting back at my parents. They were all close when they were my age."

"You don't know what happened to break up their friendship?" Simon questioned.

This time Troy only answered with a shake of his head. Simon studied him for a while then stood with a smile. "Hmm, well... it's getting late. I better go to bed and see if I can get any sleep. I've never been able to sleep much before the tournament games. See you tomorrow."

"See ya," Troy said with a wave and thought briefly to ask the gargantuan angel to take it easy on him. In the end, he stuck with just the wave because he knew the request wouldn't help.

He spent the night trying to get to sleep as Curtis snored loudly from the bunk on his right. And on his left, Michelle was praying and quietly whispering her plans for the next day's individual competition. After two hours of tossing and turning, Troy reached under his pillow and pulled out the sheath that held his dagger. Slowly, he slid it from the small pouch and ran his finger down the blade. Memories of selvo and reidlos crashed through his eyes as he recalled the demons slain by the sleek weapon.

"Rise and shine Hunters," Butler boomed what felt like ten seconds after sleep had finally found Troy. He rubbed his eyes and worked his neck in a circle to get out all the kinks from the fretful half-night of sleep. The dagger was in its sheath still clenched in his right hand. He quickly stowed it in his bag and looked at Butler who was pacing by the door. "Quick breakfast then we need to start getting warmed up. They've made the arena down the valley where we'll be able to sit on the hill to watch."

Breakfast was a gobbled stack of pancakes and four slices of crispy bacon. They'd all changed into red robes with Passover Hill badges gleaming proudly from their chests. Many prayers whispered through the trees as Troy and the rest of the team walked north from the Valley of Angels camp into a forest of pines. Within twenty minutes they emerged into a giant clearing. An arena made from tall wooden walls dominated the scene. Inside were obstacles of spikes, tunnels, tubes, and rope bridges.

"The first heat will be starting in ten minutes," Butler announced as they climbed to a patch of trees almost halfway up the slope of the valley. From their spot, Troy could see the entire tangled arena below. "Robert and Teddy, start getting warmed up. Each round is twenty minutes long so you have about forty five minutes before you're up. Get your minds right and hold onto your faith. It's going to be a wild ride."

If Troy's stomach hadn't been threatening to spew all the pancakes and bacon from the morning's breakfast, the next two hours would have been some of the most enjoyable of his life. The games were like nothing he'd seen before. Fifteen angels in training entered the arena and at the start of the bell raced and fought each other for the small, Spirit filled orbs. The action was both chaotic and breathtakingly artistic. An electric tingle ran through the valley as angels called upon the Spirit to help them in the games.

In the third heat, Robert cut through the other competitors like he was a cheetah chasing down a turtle. Three of them didn't manage to grab a single orb before they were screaming in pain under Robert's blade.

"They're lucky it's not real," Curtis harrumphed when the trainers from their respective schools retrieved them from the field and relieved them of the pain from Robert's blows.

Teddy, who had avoided Robert at all costs during the action, was cut down with five orbs in his sack and missed the finals by three orbs when the whistle sounded to end the round. Robert advanced by being one of the three remaining players and having twelve orbs to his name - the most of anyone so far that day.

"Congrats," Butler boomed as the fourth heat started and Curtis let out an ear popping Trumpet of Seraphim to begin the match.

"Thanks," Robert said with a grin that Troy thought might split his face in two. They turned and were soon lost in the action of the fourth heat.

By the end of the seventh heat, no more players from the Hill had advanced. Troy had stuffed his fist in his mouth to keep from laughing when Adam was slaughtered by one of the girls from the Wall. But he felt truly sorry for the rest of his teammates.

"It's okay," Curtis had said to Butler while wiping blood from his forehead. "I'm built more for the team games." Butler didn't argue as he healed the wound Curtis had gotten from falling off one of the many rope bridges when a boy from Elbrus Peak in Russia attacked him. Michelle and Linda had placed third in their heats. Both were bummed to have missed the final round by such a narrow margin but happy to have performed so well.

"Troy, you're up," Butler growled as the eighth round was winding down.

Troy walked away lightheaded from the nerves. He'd been able to manage the butterflies in his stomach throughout the day because he'd been so enthralled by the action. Now that he was up, a volcano of doubts was threatening to burst from his mouth.

A chorus of "good luck's" barely registered in his ears when he turned for a last look at his teammates. Adam was glaring at him from his seat higher up the side of the valley. His Hunter's badge was splattered with blood and dirt from where he'd fallen after getting cut down by the tiny Asian girl.

"How's it going Troy?"

Troy turned and found the friendly face of Simon smiling down at him.

"Nervous?" Simon asked while he absently sheathed and unsheathed the sword from the belt at his waist. His boulder-like arms and shoulders flexed and twitched as if they were begging to call down pain on those unfortunate enough to get in his way.

"Little bit," Troy gulped at the air and hardly managed a sound. He looked up at Simon's brilliant halo.

"Got it almost two years ago," Simon said with the tiniest of sad smiles as he noticed Troy's gaze. He reached up and ran a sausage-sized finger around the halo. "If I could figure out what God wanted me to forgive someone for… I'd get my wings in a heartbeat and be a fully-fledged angel. My dad has been griping at me for over a year but God hasn't seen fit to grant me my wings yet."

Troy tried to force a laugh but only produced a gargling sound.

"Mr. Decker," a short haired, severe looking angel called. She was floating ten feet in the air beside an arched gate that led through the wooden wall. "You're over here. You'll start on that pedestal there." She pointed through the archway at a carved stump of a tree.

"Good luck," Simon said with a wink as he marched through a gateway thirty feet to Troy's right.

Troy swallowed and pulled the sword from the sheath on his back. Butler had given it to him that morning with words of praise and motivation. It had a purely straight, non-descript blade with a simple grip and barely any guard. It felt like a tiny stick in his hands as he looked around the arena filled with sharply pointed obstacles and fellow angels in training who were ready to strike him down at the sound of the bell.

"Breathe," he whispered to himself. "Breathe." He thought back to all the hours of training and tried to recall every word Butler had screamed at them. His eyes darted around the maze and he began picking out the dots of swirling Spirit encapsulated in the tennis ball sized orbs.

Then, the loud gong of a bell sounded from above. At once, there was a blur of motion as the fifteen other players shot into motion. Troy's heart jumped into his throat as he darted around a tunnel, sidestepped a pair of players whose blades were sparking against each other, then dove for the first orb he'd picked out. The ball fell into his hands with ease and a smile lit his face. He jammed the warm sphere into the sack at his hip and leapt onto a hanging rope.

And his heart almost stopped as his eyes went as wide as dinner plates.

Coming towards him like a freight train was Simon. Troy heaved and somersaulted over the slicing blade from his giant opponent. He spun and blocked the next bone crunching blow then ducked under a third. Simon's face was alight with purely calm concentration. The Spirit shimmered around him like a shield of fuzzy light.

Troy reached for the Spirit himself and almost sighed when it filled him from head to toe. A backwards flip gained distance from Simon who began to follow but was sidetracked as a girl from one of the European camps tried to stab him in the back. Troy used the diversion to slide through a tunnel then run up a long, diagonal barricade. He snagged another orb at the top. It clunked satisfactorily against the other when he dropped it into the sack.

Across the arena Simon was wreaking mayhem and havoc as if the War for Sins depended on his success. Two angels went down in the space of five heartbeats as Troy watched. A third fled from the blisteringly fast sword.

Simon was bashing and banging everything in sight; in what Troy figured was a plan to clear the arena of opponents rather than trying to find any orbs.

Troy circled in hiding near the tall wooden wall as high as he could manage. He flitted from one obstacle to another with his concentration on Gabriel's gifts to warn him of danger. To his surprise, he pocketed another orb before trouble found him again.

This time trouble was in the form of a tall black girl with the castle badge of Manasco Manor flashing on her chest. Troy sped from one obstacle to another but she stayed right on his tail. Blasts of power from the Spirit burst all around him as he rolled and dodged. Finally, he turned and faced her. Over and over their swords met as they stepped and danced into then out of range. After what seemed like a thousand strikes and blocks, Troy sidestepped and stabbed upwards desperately. With a scream the girl fell in a convulsing spasm of pain.

"Sorry," Troy breathed heavily and placed his hand where his sword had looked to pierce her stomach. No wound existed but agony arced across the girl's face. Yellow angel marks throbbed in rhythm with her racing pulse. "Hesdia," Troy whispered and the Spirit glowed under his palm.

"Grazie," the girl sighed. She hopped up and was met by the instructor from her Italian camp. The regal angel regarded Troy thoughtfully for a second before fleeing the arena with his student.

Troy waited patiently and caught his breath as he studied the game. He could only find five other players.

He reached for the Spirit thinking of his dinner with Angela at the Hill when he'd seen the vision of his mom. Gabriel's parimus ability instantly brought focus on a lurking player twenty feet to his right. The boy was hiding in the deep shadows of a long tube waiting for Troy to come into the open.

Troy turned away from him but kept a solid grip on his presence with the Spirit. As soon as he stepped around a corner, the boy pounced. For a full second of brutal fear, Troy waited then dropped and parried the blow that had been intended for his spine. The boy's sword clattered to the dirt floor and he stared agape.

"Mercy," he said with both hands rising into the air and Troy's blade caressing his throat.

"Granted," Troy said and another orb caught his attention. He left the boy who would have to flee the arena in defeat. Two jumps and four steps later Troy won another orb.

"A few more of those and you'll make it to the final round," Simon said making Troy jump since he hadn't felt the large angel who was balancing on a beam ten feet above. "I was going to get that one though…"

Without delaying Troy turned and dove into a long, thin tube. Down he fell at an almost 90 degree drop. He tumbled onto the floor beside a wall of jagged spikes. Simon was still watching from his perch. Troy fled through a tangled mass of wooden beams and nearly ran into a girl from Gloucester Heights in Australia. They exchanged a few blocks and parries before Troy managed to land a glancing blow across her shoulder. She turned and vanished through an archway. Troy let her go and began scanning the maze for any more of the shining orbs.

He found two more without incident before the sharp trill of the whistle blasted into the air. "What?" Troy shouted in surprise. Simon appeared out of the far corner with a broad smile on his face. "Was that twenty minutes?"

"Yep," Simon laughed. "Time flies when you're having fun. How many orbs did you get?"

"Five."

"Eleven for me. And I eliminated six players."

They walked from the arena together to tumultuous applause from the gathered onlookers. The severe angel who had ushered Troy into the battleground moved to each of the five remaining players and counted the orbs in their sacks.

"Simon Birchhead from Heaven's Falls advances in first place," she shouted to the roar of a group on the opposite side of the valley from where Passover Hill's camp was positioned.

"And in second place… from Passover Hill, Troy Decker!"

Troy's mouth fell open as he heard his teammates cheer their approval. "I only got five," he stammered. He let the flow of the crowd push him past the nervous players going into the tenth and final heat of the first round.

"I only got five," he repeated as Butler and Robert stomped through the forest to him.

"It was enough," Robert boomed with a high five in congratulations. "Everyone was so scared of Simon they spent a lot of their time hiding. You did awesome."

"Thanks," Troy said as his stomach settled into its normal place.

"Yes, excellent job to both of you," Butler said. "First time we've had two in the final round in ten years. You both have plans ready? The championship round will start thirty minutes after the tenth heat is over."

Troy had no clue what he'd do for the championship. He hadn't put a single second of thought into it. He stared flabbergasted at Robert as the older boy went over a detailed plan of action against Simon.

"I wish me and Troy could team up against him," Robert fumed with a look across the valley where the Heaven's Falls players were lounging.

"But you can't," Butler said. "Troy, I'd keep your same strategy from the first round. Keep moving and try to avoid the heavy fighting. You're quicker than most of the players so use that to your advantage. You'll both need to watch out for the girl from the Wall. She's the one who took out Adam. She's probably the fastest and smartest player."

"She's tiny though," Robert said with a scrunch to his otherwise determined face.

"That doesn't mean anything when she's got the Spirit to guide her," Butler said and walked away to join the rest of the team. Troy nodded remembering his Grandma Jan who had been killed by a trickel demon over a year before. She'd been one of the smallest adults Troy had known, but her ferocity with the Spirit was legend at his house.

Troy and Robert watched the final heat together. When the bells tolled to signal thirty minutes before the championship round, Troy made his way alone into the woods. There he knelt and prayed about as hard as he'd ever prayed.

"Lord, let me play to the best of my ability. Let everyone escape without injury and continue on the path of your glory. Grant me strength. Amen."

He smiled as he thought of the look on his dad's face when he was able to tell him he made the championship round. He could hear his dad saying, "faith is the key". With a deep breath, Troy walked from the trees and made his way to the arena.

"For God, we fight," he said to himself as the angel who had been announcing the winners, and directing the players to their starting positions, regarded him calmly. His scepter was vibrating in his left hand. The sword gripped in his right was drenched with sweat.

"Same place you started in your earlier heat," she said and pointed once again to the stump. All along the length of the wooden walls, the other heat winners were taking their stations. Robert was directly across the tangled maze from Troy. Simon was on the far wall to his right. Immediately to his left, staring at him with a petite grin, was the small girl from the Wall. Troy swallowed and began searching for the closest orbs. Another whispered prayer slipped through his lips... then the loud ring of the bells made his heartbeat double in an instant.

Not waiting to see what the girl from the Wall was doing, he raced to his right and jumped over a section of the maze. Just as he was about to grab his first orb a sword swung at his head. He ducked but the blade still scalped across his hairline. The pain that erupted made him bite halfway through his tongue and he missed the orb by a foot. His left hand slipped and he fell fifteen feet to the dirt floor with a bone shattering jolt. Every ounce of air in his lungs rushed out in a grunt of agony. Above him was a wiry boy from the Egyptian training camp. The orb Troy had darted for was in his left hand and the Spirit was surging around the sword in his right.

Troy rolled and winced as the boy's sword plunged into the dirt where he'd been laying a second before. He rose quickly and made to deliver a killing strike, while his opponent was trying to wiggle his weapon free; but a tingle of danger sparked from behind. Barely in time, he blocked a mammoth blow from Simon and toppled sideways. The Egyptian boy yanked his sword free and slashed at Simon's legs only to be met with an arm snapping parry. Troy thrust his scepter forward and an iridescent ball of light shot from the end. It slammed into Simon's left shoulder and he buckled to one knee with a predatory glare at Troy.

That was all the signal Troy needed. He scrambled across a rope bridge and slid into a wooden tube at top speed. When he tumbled out, he landed at the feet of Robert and two girls who were fighting as fiercely as lions. Troy flipped over the melee and grabbed a rope hanging from the tallest tower. At the top, he found his first orb and leaned against the wall for a quick and much relieved breath. Below him, the wrath of God seemed to have come to Earth. The Spirit was flashing and angels were speeding in all directions. The top of Troy's head was pounding so bad, he thought he might pass out but instead he peered for the next orb. He found one fifty feet to his right and with a steadying breath, he jumped.

The dizzying battle consumed him for the next twenty minutes. There were hundreds of blocks and parries; along with thousands of jumps, flips, and twists. Through it all, the Spirit kept him company.

"That was unbelievable!" Michelle yelled after they emerged from the arena. She hugged Troy who winced at her touch. His whole body was bruised and bloodied and he was barely managing to stay upright on shaky knees. Sweat drained freely down his face and arms. "Oh, sorry. Let me heal you."

Troy nodded his thanks appreciatively as both Michelle and Linda used the Spirit's healing touch to take away the pains from the game. Nothing had ever felt better in his life. He sighed and for a second all he wanted to do was lie down and take a long nap. But Butler pulled his attention from that pleasant thought.

"They need you over by the winner's circle," the usually brisk teacher said. An unusual smile lit his dark face.

"What place did Robert end up getting?" Troy asked.

"Second," Butler boomed. "Anne, the girl from the Wall won. Simon got third… and you ended up in sixth."

"Really?" Troy asked. "I only got four orbs."

"Simon changes the game for so many people, that four was enough to place pretty high," Butler laughed. "You did good just to avoid him. A perfect plan."

"I thought for sure he was going to kill me when I blasted him that one time," Troy said remembering the fear he'd felt at Simon's glare. It didn't have the same affect, now, as he remembered the intensity in the young man's eyes. Outside the game, Troy could see a sparkle of wary respect as Simon gazed at him. Not the horrifying anger Troy had seen in the heat of battle.

"I'd hate to fight him," Linda said as they walked to where Adam, Curtis and Teddy were watching the winners receive their medals. Robert's face was alight with glee. Troy and the rest of the Passover Hill team cheered raucously as their Captain waved to the crowd.

"Is it okay if I call my parents?" he asked. Butler nodded with a wink.

Troy walked to a clearing and sat down in a patch of tall, soft grass. His scepter hummed when he looked at its golden gleam. "Mom, Dad," he said quietly with a look around the area.

"Troy?" both their voices answered at once.

"Everything okay?" his mom asked.

"How's the tournament going?" his dad said right after.

"Good," Troy answered knowing any second he might burst at the happiness welling in his chest. He spent the next ten minutes going over every detail of his first heat and the championship round. His parent's exclamations and congratulations wrapped around him and made the small grassy knoll seem like a tiny speck of heaven on Earth.

"Do you guys have a good plan for the team games tomorrow?" his dad managed to finally ask when Troy paused for a few seconds to catch his breath after telling a story about almost eliminating Anne ten minutes into the championship round.

"Yeah, we play Granite Ridge first," Troy explained. "I'm going to be a scout so hopefully I don't ruin it. They'll be relying on me to spot the other team."

"You'll do fine," his mom's voice positively beamed. Troy knew her smile was shining from where she was hundreds of miles away. Even without being able to see it, his small clearing warmed as if her arms had pulled him into a gentle hug.

"I'm gonna call Angela and tell her," Troy said after five more minutes.

"Okay, we love you Troy," his mom said.

"For God, we fight," his dad intoned.

"Love you too," Troy said with a huge grin. He waited a few seconds then whispered into his scepter. "Angela."

"Troy?" her voice answered as quickly as his parents had when he'd called them. "I've been waiting for you to call all day. I thought you said you'd call after your heat was done?"

"I would have," Troy said. "But I made the final round."

"Really?" Angela nearly shouted. "That's so great! Wait until Tyler finds out. How was it? Did you get stabbed or anything? Was it painful? What place did you get?"

"Sixth overall," Troy laughed and told her almost the same retelling he had narrated to his parents. Angela's many oohs and ahhs and "wows" added to the happy bubble already ballooning throughout his entire body.

"How did Adam do?" she asked fifteen minutes into the call.

"He got taken out by a girl from the Wall training camp in China," Troy answered trying not to let any glee carry in his voice. "He didn't make it out of his heat."

It apparently didn't work. "Don't sound too happy about it," Angela scolded but very softly.

"I know," Troy sighed. "I can't help myself." At that, she laughed a tinkling sound like the prettiest of fairy tale princesses.

Troy spent over an hour describing the tournament and the Valley of Angels training camp. Michelle and Teddy finally found him and dragged him from the call with a summons from Butler.

"I have to go," he said through his scepter.

"Okay," Angela replied. "Call me tomorrow after you guys win!"

"I will," Troy answered with a genuinely pleased smile.

He spent the evening with the team planning the next day's assault against Granite Ridge. Butler walked them through the plan five times. Then Troy spent another night with his sheathed dagger in his hand running over the next day's event and reveling in his performance in the individual competition. Angela had sounded so impressed and happy. And his parents... Troy wasn't sure anything in the world could make him more ecstatic at that moment.

"Stay low and in the shadows as much as you can," Butler said giving Troy some last minute instructions the following day.

They were on the opposite end of the pine treed valley in front of a huge, covered arena. Three of the enclosed monoliths had been constructed three miles south of the Valley of Angels buildings. Tall, and made from solid wood, they brought a sense of impending doom for Troy. He swallowed the cold nerves clamping his throat and nodded at his teacher.

The day had gone by in the blink of an eye. Heaven's Falls and the Wall had already emerged victorious from their first matchups. Troy and the rest of the Passover Hill Hunter's had drawn the last game of the first round of matchups and had to endure a full morning of anxious jitters.

At the deep gong of a bell, Troy and his teammates streamed into the stadium. The feel was totally different from the open aired arena of the individual competition. Dark shadows danced in the flicker of what had to be a million candles. Hallways and rooms and overlooks dotted the interior. Fluttering spider webs and a haze of dust filled the air. Without trying hard, Troy could picture a horde of reidlos waiting to storm from the darkness of a thousand black corners.

"Troy, go right," Robert whispered. "Michelle, left. The rest of you, stay with me." Troy did as he was told at once. He reached with the Spirit as he entered a narrow hallway of almost pitch blackness. Parimus and auditome both poured from his mind as he searched for any of the Granite Ridge players. He climbed out a thin window and slithered up a beam to the ceiling; where he found a tiny ledge overlooking a large empty space right in the middle of the arena.

For five minutes Troy perched frozen on the spot thirty feet off the ground. Adam came into view on his left at the same time Troy noticed two fighters from Granite Ridge on his right.

They were behind Adam and slowly stalking forward like tigers preparing to pounce on an unsuspecting deer.

Troy squeezed the scepter in his left hand and whispered, "Adam".

The smallest speck of the Spirit brightened Adam's scepter as Troy's message of danger was delivered. Even in the dark confines of the arena, Troy saw Adam sneer. The brazen boy ignored the warning and circled an outpost searching for a player from Granite Ridge so he could get a score.

Troy shook his head in frustration and called Robert.

"Adam's in trouble," he said in the smallest of mousy whispers. "I signaled him but he ignored it. He's on the east side of the outpost in the middle room. Two of them are on his tail and he hasn't seen them."

"Can you take them out?" Robert's nearly inaudible reply. "Wait…I-"

From the far side of the arena the clash of swords erupted. There were yells and screams of pain. Robert's commanding voice bellowed orders while echoing calls of different archangel abilities bounced off the walls and ceiling. Below Troy, the two Granite Ridge players were drawing one cautious step at a time closer to Adam who had stopped and was listening to the melee.

Without thinking, Troy dove from his perch like an eagle. Neither of the opposing players made any notice of him until his sword ran through the chest of the girl on the left. Her scream pierced Troy's ears as he yanked out the blade and sliced through the stunned boy who had been preparing to attack Adam only a second before.

Adam stepped around the corner. For a split second a fearful look of shock masked his face but it instantly turned to disdain.

224

"I had them, Decker," he growled. "I was waiting for them to get closer, you idiot. Now we've lost one of our scouts since you came out of hiding."

"You didn't listen when I tried to warn you," Troy hissed.

"I did too," Adam snapped. "I just didn't want to go shouting about it and let those two know I knew they were there."

Troy snorted his disbelief but the harrying shouts from Robert's direction stopped any retort. "Let's go help," he said and took off in support as the teacher from Granite Ridge came sprinting to help his defeated students.

They found Robert finishing off a fighter from Granite Ridge. Linda and Teddy were on the ground with faces of utter pain. Linda's breath came in ragged gasps and she was clutching her chest. Teddy's grimace reminded Troy of a zombie from a TV show he watched with Tyler and Clark.

"I'll help Linda," he said after sheathing his sword. He knelt beside her with the Spirit streaming from his scepter and right hand. Adam did the same for Teddy.

"Thanks and good luck," Linda called over her shoulder with a sad look as she retreated from the arena. Teddy followed her in a defeated, zombie-like gait.

"Have you two eliminated any of them?" Robert asked after healing the Granite Ridge players of their painful, but actually non-existent wounds.

"Two," Troy answered with a nod. He scanned the dark room but felt no presences in any of the black corners.

"They only have two left then," Robert smiled. "Probably scouts." He pulled his scepter from a pouch on his ribs. A deep blue glow lit the room as he stared at it. "Curtis, Michelle… meet us in the middle room. There are only two of them left."

"We've got this won," Adam clapped with a cocky smirk.

"Don't get overconfident," Curtis said as he appeared from a hallway across the room. "We've all heard stories of a team being down to one player against most of the other team and winning. We don't want that happening to us."

They met up with Michelle a minute later and Robert devised a plan to search the arena as a group. Within three minutes, they found and eliminated a large boy who went down fighting with his halo shining over his head. After the slaughter, Robert helped him from the floor with a respectful handshake and sent him out of the arena.

Two minutes later, they corned a short black girl. "Mercy," she said and threw her sword at Robert's feet.

"Granted," Robert said tilting his head at her in salute for a second before letting out a loud whoop in celebration.

"Good job," Butler said a minute later when the team joined together outside the arena. "But don't celebrate too much yet. We drew the Wall next…"

For a second, Robert looked like he wanted to curse but instead he nodded with a confident sheen flexing on his face. He looked quickly back and forth from Michelle to Troy. "We'll need you two to be more offensive in this game. They generally fight in three pairs with only one scout. If you can manage to ambush one of their paired groups, we can take out the rest together as a team."

"Their scout will be Anne," Butler added. "Be wary of her. Her aptitude with Uriel's tibota ability makes her completely invisible, even when she's moving pretty fast. You'll all need to be at the top of your game. Don't rely on your eyes and ears as much as you do the Spirit."

"Sounds good to me," Michelle said brazenly. "I didn't get to do anything in the first game."

"You won't have to worry about that this time," Butler warned.

The two hour wait leading up to their game in the arena against the Wall's team brought the most nerves Troy had ever felt in his life. Butterflies of all shapes and sizes barraged his insides until every spare millimeter of his body was slick with sweat. None of Robert's constant encouragement to the team helped. All Troy could see was the silent stalking players from the Wall in the dark confines of the playing arena. Prayers lifted from his lips every few seconds and he drew on the Spirit to help push away the doubts.

Finally, after what seemed like a small eternity, Butler directed them at the middle arena. "Keep your heads about you and stick to the plan," he instructed. "For God, we fight."

Troy and the others entered the arena after the bells sounded. With a steadying breath, he took a flight of narrow steps and walked into the darkness. For five minutes, Troy concentrated on Gabriel's gifts of auditome and parimus. Every blur made him think of Anne sneaking up behind him to slit his throat. But nothing stirred in the hallway where he was hiding; or in the room he was looking down upon.

Just as he was about to move to a better overlook, his scepter flashed a spark and hummed in his left hand. "Your four o'clock, thirty feet below you," Adam's voice sounded in a hush.

Troy directed his gaze through the darkness in the proper direction. A pair of wraith-like shadows wavered in a doorway.

Slowly, he leaned out and brought the figures into view. Sure enough, two Asian boys were crouched in waiting.

Troy pulled on the Spirit to blind his approach and slid silently from his hiding place; then tiptoed over a beam to position himself directly over the Wall players. He glanced at Adam who was watching him intently and positioned his sword for an attack.

Before he jumped, a loud crack like a starting pistol popped right beside his head. The two shadows below leapt into action without a fraction of a second's pause. They were on top of Troy with swords blazing a heartbeat later. He parried and slashed and ducked and dodged. His scepter flashed as he sent a warning to Robert. Then with a heart wrenching tear, a bright light burst in his eyes and he fell. Pain engulfed him as he thudded to the ground. He was sure blood must be filling the arena to the brim.

Pain in that instant was all he knew. A shudder ran from his shoulders down the left side of his body and arced around his toes as one of the boys from the Wall came into view.

"Very sorry," the boy whispered in broken English. His left hand ran over the place where a sword had been piercing Troy's chest a second earlier. The pain ceased at once.

Oxygen. Wonderful oxygen brought back the feeling of life. Troy blinked and saw the two boys filter into the darkness. His racing pulse pounded in his throat and he had to physically stop himself from throwing up all over the dirt floor.

Sluggishly, he stood and swallowed the gut wrenching memory of the all-consuming pain. Faltering legs threatened to betray him and he stopped to lean against the wall. His scepter was vibrating with a summons from Butler to leave the arena so he staggered around the corner.

He nearly ran into Adam who was still in the same hiding place he'd been in when he'd signaled Troy. A triumphant and exuberant grin lifted the nemesis' lips. Troy's thoughts snapped to the cracking sound that had alerted the Wall players to his presence. Across Adam's forehead, as if God was putting it there for all to see, Troy could picture Uriel's strates gift written. Without any semblance of doubt, he knew Adam had sabotaged him.

He trudged from the arena as Curtis bellowed and Michelle screamed.

The rest of his team joined him within five minutes. Only Adam had escaped without taking an injury since he'd asked for mercy when he was the only member of their team left.

Troy wanted to shout about his cowardice but rage was holding his tongue prisoner. Of all the terrible things Adam had ever said and done to him, nothing compared to the betrayal of a teammate.

The rest of the team hung their heads but said encouraging words about next year's team. All Troy could see were red spots of anger and brimming hatred.

"What happened to start the trouble?" Butler asked after everyone quieted down.

"Troy got killed," Adam said absently. "I couldn't get over there in time to help him."

"Are you kidding?" Troy growled and everyone looked at him. He shoved his finger in Adam's chest. "You used strates to make those two guys from the Wall look at me. I was getting ready to get them. They didn't know I was there."

"Don't look at me," Adam said holding up his hands innocently as all the eyes turned towards him. "He was getting ready to attack them; but when he bent to jump the beam he was on cracked. Why would I do that?"

"Good question," Butler said. "Troy?"

"I don't know," Troy nearly shouted with his hands going crazy up in the air. "Cause he hates me or something."

"Whatever," Adam snorted. "I care the same I do for you as one of your cows in Oklahoma."

"That's enough," Butler said with a warning glance at Troy. "I have to believe that Adam wouldn't do that. But if I ever find out that it's true, you and me will have words." His glare at Adam was enough to make freshly drawn milk curdle. Adam swallowed but shrugged his shoulders in an unconcerned way.

Everyone left with hollow words of getting closer to see what exactly was happening in the tournament, but Troy stayed glued to the spot. The games continued all afternoon and into the evening. The Wall's team made it to the finals but lost to Faith Forrest from the state of Washington. None of it mattered to Troy. Not the celebrating soon-to-be angels. Not the beautiful pine trees swaying hypnotically in a warm summer breeze. All he saw was Adam's knowing face in the dark confines of the arena. He had betrayed Troy and the team. Of that, Troy had no doubts.

Chapter 13: Tyler's Letdown

"Why would he do that?" Angela voiced her concern for what was at least the thousandth time. In the three weeks since the tournament, Troy had railed on countless occasions about Adam's deceit. Angela had listened patiently and consoled Troy on the loss, but she'd never wholeheartedly agreed Adam was capable of such sabotage.

"He can be a jerk," she repeated much to Troy's irritation. "But he'd never go that far. God wouldn't have granted him his robes and his sword if he did stuff like that."

Troy had tried to hold his frustrations at bay but couldn't stop himself from shooting daggers at Adam every time he saw him. Or from doing his utmost in Butler's classes to break every bone in the conceited boy's body.

"How excited was Tyler when you talked to him this morning?" Angela asked pulling Troy from the shadows of the tournament arena.

"He can't wait to get practices started," Troy answered. "He still thinks I should hit Adam a few more times with my mace before I leave today, though."

Angela rolled her eyes and shook her head as she ate another bite of salmon. "Well, I'm glad today is your last day at the Hill then," she said. "You need a break from Adam. How you've been treating him the last few weeks hasn't been very... angelic."

"We shouldn't have to treat people like him nice," Troy argued. "I don't care if no one else believes me, I know for a one hundred percent fact he used strates to make the Wall guys look at me. I saw his face right after it happened. He was mad about me making the finals of the individual competition and saving him in the game against Granite Ridge. He wanted to get back at me."

His fuming argument only produced a shrug from Angela which added to his approaching volcanic frustration. Perhaps it would be best for him to get away from the angel world at the Hill for a while. He'd enjoyed the summer so much up until the tournament. Ever since then the classes had all seemed to mock his anger at Adam. Moses had even pointed him out in a lecture about Gabriel's detino ability.

"You'll never gain the use of this skill with anger brewing in your eyes," Moses had said in one of the calmest voices Troy had ever heard the statue use. "If you want to bind people with the chains of faith, first you must have the faith yourself. And second you must possess the clarity of thought the gift requires. Wrath will shroud your eyes to the gifts God has granted to angels."

"Maybe your right," Troy sighed and pushed away the memory. "I just… he… you know, why can't he leave me alone?"

"Both of you have to take responsibility for that," Angela said with a knowing look. Her pink angel marks and pretty face made Troy want to let the anger melt, but every time he tried, Adam's sneering grin burst into his vision.

Troy left Passover Hill after their Michael lessons with Butler that afternoon. Angela promised to call him every night and he made the same promise to her.

"We'll see you in a couple of weeks," Troy's mom purred to Angela who answered with a gracious smile and a wave. They went through the Gate and the sanctuary of the Cathedral in Mustang popped into view. Troy took a quick look over his shoulder as his dad materialized through the wall of white stone.

"How was your summer?" his dad asked. "We've heard all about the tournament and everything that happened there, but not much about what you learned in the classes."

Troy shrugged and tried not to sigh. But on the way home, he filled them in on all the angel abilities he remembered studying. "Moses taught us all sorts of stuff about how to counteract attacks from fallen angels. He seemed to concentrate more on that than on fighting demons. We did learn a cool thing from Noah about a way to blind demons. Can't wait to use it."

"It would be nice if you never had to," his mom said with her arm wrapping around his shoulder as they walked into their tidy, suburban home. Troy stowed his bags and made his way to the kitchen where his mom was already preparing a large bowl of grilled chicken, spinach, lettuce, broccoli, and cauliflower.

"Can Tyler, Clark and Becky come over?" he asked as he snagged an olive from a jar his mom pulled from the refrigerator.

"That's fine," she answered. "But remember… you are still on a probationary status from what you did before going to the Hill. We haven't forgotten." She was giving Troy a rather piercing stare. He had only been able to talk his parents into giving him permission to play football this season, two days before. And that took more pleading and begging than Troy remembered doing since he was in kindergarten and wanted a mock battleground toy set from a famous fight in the War for Sins from the late 1800's.

Practices were set to start in the stifling August heat of Oklahoma the very next morning. Troy nodded and smiled to make sure he properly conveyed his intentions to walk on egg shells and stay on red alert for the foreseeable future. They prayed then ate and afterwards Troy called Tyler who showed up with Clark and Becky barely a minute later.

"Long time, no see," Tyler boomed with a typical punch to the arm. He looked at least an inch taller from the last time Troy had seen him. His styled hair and expensive, trendy clothes hadn't changed however.

"Hey Troy," Becky said with a sweet smile and a quick, one armed hug. "I can't wait to hear about everything you learned at the Hill."

Troy returned the smile and the hug before turning to Clark who was looming in the doorway.

"Hi," Clark offered with a tiny wave in acknowledgement. The acne on his dark cheeks had cleared over the hot summer and a few whiskers were poking from his upper lip and chin.

The four of them stayed in Troy's room most of the night since the heat was nearly enough to melt the soles of their shoes to the concrete. Becky and Clark grilled Troy on almost every lesson he had attended, while Tyler stayed primarily on his training with the Hunters.

"I can't believe you felt what it would feel like to get stabbed through the chest," Becky whimpered as she massaged below her throat where a cross necklace was hanging. "What was it like?"

"Not very fun," Troy chuckled. "I might not have had to go through it at all if Adam hadn't tipped the players from the Wall off."

"And you're absolutely sure he did?" she asked. Her expression was innocently interested but Troy caught a subtle hint of something else.

"Have you been talking to Angela?" he questioned raising his eyebrows at her.

Becky's olive skin blushed a little and she cleared her throat. "A few times," she said. "I went over to her house and her mom let me talk to her through her scepter."

Troy shook his head but couldn't help but laugh. Leave it to Becky and Angela to conspire about his bad mood behind his back. "Well, I know without a doubt he did it," he said. "He's a slimy, little…" He broke off as he remembered Angela admonishing him for not being very angelic.

"Idiot," Tyler finished for him. "If I ever see him, I'll punch him for you. Then I'll set Clark on him."

"Leave me out of it," Clark said with a jovial grin but also a seriousness in his bright, brown eyes.

At eight o'clock, Troy's dad reminded all of them about the early start the next morning. He showed them all pictures of the ten angels who would be on guard duty at football practices and when school started. Grandma Denise was one of them. Troy hoped he didn't run into her out in the heat during any of her guard duty sessions.

"Practice tomorrow is gonna suck," Tyler said as the friends were leaving. "Not that I'm dreading it… this heat is liable to kill one of us though."

"Hopefully with practice being from 6:30 to 10:30, it won't be that bad," Troy said.

"I can tell you haven't been around this summer," Tyler griped. "It's gotten to 100 degrees by 9:00 every day. Are there any of your angel abilities to keep us cool in our football pads?"

"None I've learned," Troy laughed and bumped knuckles with the quarterback. He waved goodbye to all three of his friends and closed the door. The rest of the evening was spent polishing his dagger and scepter; then cleaning the blemishes his mace had received in the training hours spent under Butler's watchful eye.

The next morning dawned as hot and miserable as Tyler had predicted. Ten minutes under the rising sun was enough to make every player become soaked in sweat. Troy, Tyler, and Clark hustled and ran and went through tackling drills. Tyler complained about these since he was a quarterback and didn't think he needed to learn.

"If we throw as many interceptions as we did last year, you quarterbacks will need to know how to tackle," Coach Lokey hollered with spit flying in all directions.

"I don't throw interceptions," Tyler whispered to Troy making sure no one else could hear him.

The rest of the practice went by in a haze of yelling, bellowing, whistling, and crunching. Followed by another on Tuesday. And more the rest of the week.

On Saturday, Troy found himself sitting under their favorite shade tree at the park. A deep bruise was proving stubborn to heal on his thigh but he kept at it with the Spirit and it slowly faded.

"Glad you can do that," Tyler said as he stretched. "I bet I threw ten thousand passes this week. My arm would be falling off right now, if you hadn't been healing me every night."

"Is that fair?" Becky asked before Troy could reply.

"What do you mean?" Tyler said with a look of confusion on his handsome face.

"Blake and the other quarterbacks don't get healed," she said regally. "Or the other receivers and lineman. It seems unfair you three get all your stuff healed every day and the others don't. Charlie Cook was in the training room for an hour after practice shivering in an ice bath."

"Well, they should get angels for friends," Tyler replied without a seconds hesitation as if it was the most obvious answer in the world.

Troy laughed but watched Becky. He'd had similar thoughts during the week as he healed his friends but in the end, he'd decided to relieve them of their aches anyway.

"I think we'll be okay," Troy said to her continued look of concern. "I asked my mom about it and she said it was fine. Said it would be good practice for me. I can't wait until Angela gets back though. It's not easy to heal yourself and my shoulder still hurts from when I fell on it Thursday."

Becky looked satisfied enough with Troy's answer and she turned to idly scan the steaming park as she plucked dry grass from the ground. "Has there been much news on Kyle lately?" she asked with a sideways glance.

"Every day pretty much," Troy shrugged. "Nothing exact or anything… just that he's out there causing trouble. There have been stories about him building a big following but it's tough for them to prove anything. For all we know, the reporters could be on his side."

"That would suck," Tyler harrumphed while he examined his grip on a football to make sure he was holding it exactly as Coach Danielson had been telling him to all week.

"God will make it right in the end," Clark chimed in quietly. "He always does."

Troy nodded appreciatively at his often quiet friend. He could always count on Clark to put things in a positive perspective. "I just wish someone would find Kyle and put a stop to this mess," Troy admitted. "It's like he has a radar on my emotions and thoughts. Every time I'm happy he does something terrible to ruin it."

The next week of practices went much the same as the first - with one bad exception.

"I can't believe this," Tyler shouted with enough force to rattle the windows in his dad's Escalade. "After all the work I've put in. All those hours. And I've done way better than Blake at every two-a-day practice. Haven't I?" He looked wildly from Troy to Clark.

"Yeah, I thought so," Troy said and knew it wasn't a lie. Tyler's play had been exemplary at every practice. Troy couldn't recall a single miss-placed pass.

"Me too," Clark added. "But he's a senior. The coaches always put them in the starting positions at first. I bet it will change before the first game."

Tyler looked slightly appeased at the words but an angry muscle remained twitching along his jawline.

"Keep putting in the work and it will turn out for you," his dad offered with a gentle slap on his son's knee. "Don't I hear you saying stuff about God working in your life right now? Have some patience, say your prayers, and see if that's true."

Angela returned the next day. Troy tagged along with her parents to meet her at the Gate. Even being fully prepared for her arrival and being one of her best friends now, the sight of her stepping through a solid wall of stone still managed to steal the breath from Troy's lungs.

"Hey," she called after separating from her mom's loving and overly protective embrace. "Is Tyler still mad about football?"

"Yeah," Troy nodded. "And it won't get any better if he doesn't win the starting spot. It's all he talks about most of the time."

"We need to make sure he keeps going to church," she offered with a thoughtful look on her perfect face. Her hair did its usual graceful swish and the pink angel marks at the edges of her cheeks sparkled in the soft candle light of the Cathedral.

"I'm going to Christ Lutheran with him and his dad tomorrow," Troy said. "Want to go with us?"

Angela looked from her parents to him. "Have you not heard about tomorrow?"

"No," he said trying not to let a spark of fear grow at the fright in her eyes.

"Surely your parents got the call too," she said. "There's a big demon raid in St. Louis planned at dawn."

Troy shook his head and searched his thoughts. His parents had been casually cryptic with him ever since he'd returned from the Hill; but surely they wouldn't keep something this important a secret. "They didn't say anything to me about it," he fidgeted and peeked at Angela's parents. Both were walking determinedly through the hallway to Samson's antechamber, but he caught a flicker of recognition and knew they had been listening to the conversation.

And sure enough, with the single start of a question to his mom when he got home, she headed him off.

"Yes, we're going," she admitted. "Your dad and I don't want to worry you with every demon raid we have to go on now. Over the summer, it became a fairly regular occurrence. You need to concentrate on getting your robes. And football. And school starting. Our angel duties shouldn't even be registering for you. You have a ton of other stuff to worry about."

"Your robes being the most important," his dad suggested from the doorway to the kitchen where he'd been listening. "Then you can start on your sword."

Troy wanted to argue but his mom's smile stopped any griping in its tracks. He merely nodded and went to his room to read a book called, *Sacrifice: What Will You Give Up?* by Alexander Thiessen. Nothing in the many tales of sorrow produced any semblance of a brainwave and he went to bed later with visions of heroically charging an army of demons with his friends tucked safely behind him.

Church was uneventful and peaceful the following morning. Tyler's dad spent most of the sermon reading a document on his phone but he was friendly and respectful to everyone who spoke to him after the service. Troy spent the rest of the day at Angela's house with all his friends. They went over the course schedules they'd all received the day before, then discussed Tyler's favorite subject - football.

"Scrimmage on Tuesday," he reeled off for the fourth time. "At Moore. You going to get to go Angela?"

"I'll try," she said. "But my parents have been really strict with letting me out to do anything. They completely shut me down when I asked to be a trainer for the team like Becky."

"You could probably still ride over there with us," Becky mused. "Mrs. Henderson won't care. If she knew what you could do with hesdia, she'd jump over the water tower to get you on the training staff."

"Wouldn't another angel have to guard the trainer's car, if you go, though?" Clark asked with his huge shoulders turning to look at Angela. "You and Troy were griping about taking them away from their other duties in May."

"There will already be at least one following Mrs. Henderson's car anyway," Troy countered. "All of us have angels following us, pretty much everywhere we go."

"I just thought it wouldn't hurt to try to limit how much we make them watch us," Clark suggested with a shrug.

"Oh, you know they love it," Tyler quipped with a shooing wave as if the conversation was an annoying fly in his thoughts. "And anyway, this scrimmage is important. Coach Danielson told me I'd be in for the second and third series. Then he'd decide who will get to play the last couple. I need to show up Blake as much as I can. I doubt he'll do any good, but I have to be at the top of my game."

"That's not very nice," Angela scolded but a smile was threatening to tug at the corners of her mouth. "You should be rooting and praying for all your teammates to play to the best of their ability."

"Yeah, I am," Tyler sniffed offhandedly and embarked on another long and detailed list of the potential plays they'd be running. Troy couldn't help but laugh and prayed his best friend would make sure to always put the same determination into his faith in God.

The first day of school dawned in a blaze of miserable heat on Wednesday, four days later. Mustang High School students hurried into the buildings waving their hands in front of their faces; or shielding their eyes from the undaunted sun.

The scrimmage against Moore had been played and lost the night before much to Tyler's dismay. "I could have led us to a touchdown on the last drive," he hissed at Troy in the second hour world history class. "I can't believe Coach Danielson put him in there." He glared at the front of the classroom where their coach was sorting through a stack of papers as he prepared for a lecture on a Roman conquest in northern Europe.

"I'm sure the coaches will make the right choice," Troy consoled. "We play Yukon a week from Friday and they said they'd announce all the starters at the film study Saturday afternoon."

"We'll see," Tyler whispered as Coach Danielson stepped up to a podium. "Hey, my birthday is the Sunday after the game. My mom is taking me to get my driver's license the Tuesday after that. You want to go for a ride after practice?"

"I'll have to ask my parents," Troy cleared his throat and motioned at their coach who was looking over the class, and for the moment, waiting patiently for everyone to stop talking. "I wouldn't get my hopes up though." He ended quickly and ducked his head over his history book.

Their sophomore year of school started with many imploring demands from their teachers to study hard since college was right around the corner. They had counseling sessions on Friday to go over the many different avenues they could take after getting their diplomas. For the most part, Troy listened but not a lot of what the counselors hailed as extreme importance, settled into his brain. With one of the most evil fallen angels in a hundred years bombarding the planet with demons and the powers of Lucifer, he figured he had a pass on caring much for what major he'd choose when he started college.

"I'm kind of the same way," Angela admitted when Troy voiced his concern to her on Saturday morning. They were waiting on their parents to finish a conference call in the front room. Troy and Angela had listened to the multitude of voices streaming from the adults' scepters for the first half hour but lost interest when the discussion droned on and on about mundane business at different Cathedrals around the world.

"My parents have been really pushing me to concentrate on school work," Troy said as he flipped idly through *Dangerous and Deadly Demons*. "But it's tough to care about it when angel guards are outside every class door making sure Kyle doesn't come in and kill me. And then, they spend the rest of the time griping at me to find a way to get my robes. Of course, they don't want to help with that at all."

Angela nodded her agreement as the Spirit swirled in a wonderful golden hue down her arms then across her scepter. A soft humming chorus poured into the room and an easy tranquility settled over Troy like a warm blanket.

"Mabido," Troy almost purred under the influence of Seraphim's ability. "Nice one."

"I think I like it better than shepadia," Angela said as she released the power. "It can affect a whole room of people."

"Can't be as sneaky with it though," Troy laughed. "People would hear the humming and wonder where it was coming from."

Angela shrugged with a sheepish smile and turned the page of *Singing with Seraphim*. Ten minutes later, Troy's dad tapped on the door. "You ready to get to the field house?"

"Yep," Troy said jumping from his bed.

"Hopefully you guys all get good news," Angela cheered from her seat at the desk.

"Clark's already pretty much been told he's starting," Troy hesitated. He couldn't quite place his own feelings about the coming news. In the past, he would have been on pins and needles waiting to hear if he was going to get a starting receiver spot. But now, it didn't hold the same pull. He took a breath and glanced at Angela as he was walking from the room. "Pray for Tyler though."

"I will," she said with a serious wave of goodbye.

The football team watched tapes of both of Yukon's scrimmages from the last two weeks. Coaches and players called out assignments, numbers of opposing players, and plays for certain situations. Troy listened as he sat in a pack with the rest of the receivers. His mind, however, was on Kyle and robes and archangel abilities.

After the tapes were watched and the coaches had each made their own rendition of a motivational speech, they began calling players into the office a handful at a time. Troy watched Tyler and Blake march across the locker room together when Coach Danielson called their names. Before they came out, Coach Lewis, the receiver coach, motioned for Troy.

"Troy, you've been doing a great job so far in the practices," Coach Lewis said in his gravelly voice which was used for yelling more than talking. "You made a few nice catches in the scrimmage… but I didn't feel like you outperformed Rich, Darnell, or Josh enough to get a starting spot. They're all seniors and have put in a lot of work over the last three years. You're still going to get a decent amount of snaps though; so I don't want you to get your head down. A little bit of improvement and you'll be starting. And that's a big achievement because you know Coach Lokey likes playing the upper classmen as much as he can."

Troy nodded at the news. "Thanks Coach," he said making sure his voice was strong. "I'll keep doing my best and working as hard as I can."

"That's all we can ask. And I wouldn't ever doubt it from you. Send in Tommy and Chris for me when you go out."

Troy called the two receivers when he made his way back to the locker room then froze. Sadness of what had to be total loss resonated from his right. He turned to the locker where he stored his pads and gear. Sitting with his hands covering his face was Tyler. No tears were falling through the gaps of his fingers but a shout of disappointment echoed through Gabriel's gift of auditome. The Spirit flickered at the raw emotions coming from Troy's best friend.

Clark was taking up most of the rest of the bench beside Tyler with his giant left hand resting on the quarterback's shoulder. He met Troy's eyes as he whispered reassurances to their friend.

"Whatever," Tyler croaked. "I put in a ton more work and outplayed him every practice and scrimmage. I should be the starter. Not him."

Troy glanced around the locker room. The other players were mingling and laughing. None of them seemed to be paying any attention to the sulking backup quarterback.

"Coach Danielson didn't even guarantee I'd be second string at the game," Tyler moaned when Troy stepped beside him. Sorrow masked his normally handsome features.

"He's just trying to keep you motivated," Clark consoled. "Keep practicing hard and you'll get your chance. Randy and Darren both talk about how good you are for a sophomore quarterback. If you keep putting in the work and hold on to your faith; nothing but good can come to you."

"Faith," Tyler growled. "What good has that done me? God didn't do me any favors. I put in the work. It's all I did over the summer. And here I am, a third string quarterback. A lot of good faith did me." He jumped to his feet and began to stalk away but Troy's hand stopped him with a firm, but gentle, grip. The Spirit surged in a glow Troy was sure everyone would see but no one turned. At once, the tightness in Tyler's shoulders sagged.

"Faith is the key," Troy said in a low voice only his raging friend would hear. "Not only faith in God but faith in yourself. Faith in knowing the coaches are doing what's best for the team. And faith in the other players. Show everyone how strong you are. Congratulate Blake and give him 100% of your support. Like Clark said, good things will come."

"We'll see," Tyler said and yanked his arm out of Troy's hand. He left without another word.

Troy joined Clark on the bench and they said silent prayers for their struggling friend.

Chapter 14: The Dark Hearts

A sour fog hung over Tyler for the next few weeks. Homework began to pile up at school for everyone. The football team won the season opener against Yukon and the second game against Choctaw, but lost on the road to Putnam City in week three. Troy had only played a few downs in both of the first two games, but by the third game, he got into the action on eighteen plays. And even made three catches. Clark, on the hand, had played every single snap at right tackle on the offensive side of the ball in each game.

"I hate playing JV," Tyler griped as he sat on a bench between fourth and fifth periods. It was Monday afternoon which meant Becky and Angela were probably avoiding Tyler. Monday's had quickly become a dreaded day of the week since they played "scrub ball" as Tyler called it late in the afternoon.

"I don't mind it," Troy said in the upbeat tone he tried to always maintain around his frustrated friend. "I get to play almost every snap on offense and I have you throwing the ball to me most of the time."

"The line sucks," Tyler complained. "They couldn't block five year old girls."

Clark shook his head in his slow way. "You're completing over seventy percent of your passes and have thrown eight touchdowns in two games. You wouldn't be able to do that if you were running for your life."

"I do run for my life," Tyler exaggerated. "If they blocked better I'd be completing over eighty percent of my passes. And there have been a ton of drops by a couple of the receivers. Jimmy dropped three balls last week. If Troy plays a few more downs with the varsity, he won't be able to play JV. I'll be really screwed then. He's my first check every play."

Clark sighed but didn't want to contend with Tyler's perpetual griping. He left to get to class a couple of minutes later with more words of encouragement.

"When are your parents going to let you guys go for a ride with me?" Tyler asked as they watched their huge friend step nimbly around a group of giggling girls – who kept glancing hopefully where Tyler was lounging.

"Probably never," Troy said with a twist to his mouth. "The Angelic Agenda is scaring everyone to death. Almost every night there's news of someone getting killed. It doesn't help that Luke Fischer, the Justice Minister guy we met, is bugging my dad all the time. It always puts my mom in a bad mood when he calls."

"Angela said her parents have been bad too," Tyler offered. "Speaking of which… homecoming is next week. When are you going to ask her to go with you?"

"I… what?" Troy cleared his throat.

"Come on man," Tyler said with a wicked nudge. "I know you like her. You stare at her all the time with this weird smile on your face."

"No I don't," Troy fidgeted and started gathering his bag.

"Well then don't say I didn't warn you when she goes to homecoming with someone else," Tyler sighed with an exaggerated rise of his eyebrows. "I know Travis Turner asked her out already and I've heard a couple of the seniors talking about her."

Troy's stomach dropped at the thought. He'd tried five times the night before to bring up the subject of the homecoming football game, but no time had ever felt right to ask her out. He looked at Tyler who was watching him with a knowing smile.

"We're just… you know, kind of friends."

Tyler snorted and shook his head as he began walking towards their chemistry class. "If you put as much effort into your angel training and football as you do watching Angela, you'd already have all your gifts from God and be playing receiver in the NFL."

Troy sat on the bench until the tardy bell startled him out of his thoughts. He hurried to class and apologized to Mr. Wilson for being late then took his seat beside Tyler. Could his best friend be right? Would Angela say yes to any of the other guys? A bear seemed to be eating away at his stomach from the inside at the notion. He spent the class in a haze of terrifying daydreams and got into trouble when he forgot to turn off his Bunsen burner at the end of the lesson.

For the rest of the week, Troy poked and prodded and searched for the right time to ask Angela to homecoming. He brought up the game at any opportunity.

"Do you think you'll beat Putnam West?" she asked on Saturday afternoon when he stumbled clumsily onto the subject for the hundreth time. They were studying in Angela's kitchen. A long list of complicated problems from their mutual trigonometry class was baffling him, Angela, and Becky.

"Yeah," Troy nodded. "They've only won one game all season. We're three and one after last night's win."

"Maybe you guys will get way ahead and Tyler can get into the game," Becky said from where she was hunkered over her homework in the corner.

"That would be nice," Angela agreed with a hissing breath. "You think he'd get in a better mood then? I heard him and his mom yelling at each other this morning."

"She's still mad at him for going to church," Troy sighed. "He's been grounded more in the last year than he was the first fifteen years of his life. I'm kind of worried about him…"

"He's lucky you helped him find his faith," Becky said while she nibbled thoughtfully on the end of a pencil. "I can't imagine putting up with him if he was like he used to be. He can be bad at times now, but without his faith, I don't think he would be tolerable."

"Amen," Angela said and smiled at Troy. He swallowed and glanced at Becky who was already consumed in her homework again. Now was as good a time as any…

Heaving in a deep breath, he started to talk but a giant frog seemed to jump into his throat and the words came out in tangled mess. "Youwannagotothegamewithme?"

Becky's eyes snapped from the trig problem she'd been working on. Angela looked at him with a scrunch of confusion. "What?" she asked.

Troy heartily swallowed to force away the blockage sticking behind his tonsils. His brain was scrambled and frazzled as he continued. "I was just wondering if anyone has asked you to go to homecoming with them?" Each word came out in a painfully awkward sounding lurch.

"Oh, not really," Angela said. "A couple of the older boys mentioned it but I told them I probably wasn't going to be able to go to the game."

"Ah," Troy nodded. "Have your parents said no?"

She shrugged and shook her head making her hair bounce and sway like it had come to life as the most wonderful dancer in the world. "Well, they said I could go if they had time to go as well," she mused. "And, Becky and I were talking… if I get to go; to help with Tyler's mood, we thought it might be good to go as a group. You know, us three and Tyler. We know we hang out all the time but thought it might help him get his mind off of not getting to play."

"Yeah, that's, uh, a good idea," Troy said with a humungous, and grotesquely twisted smile. His stomach had plummeted straight from his body and onto the floor at her words. She hadn't exactly declined to go with him, but wasn't this pretty much the same thing? He studied her as she concentrated on her homework.

"You guys will be playing and everything anyway," Becky's voice said into his vibrating ears. "We didn't think you'd have much time to do anything with the homecoming stuff. All it would really be is going to the pep rally together and like Angela said, we'll do that already."

"Yeah, that's true," Troy said and scratched at his forehead while he pretended to start working on his trig problem again. He spent the next thirty minutes trying to find the positives in the situation. At least he'd still be going to homecoming with Angela, kind of. She wouldn't be getting a corsage from anyone and putting her arm in some other boy's arm. The mere suggestion of the hypothetical sight tore at Troy and the Spirit flared involuntarily from his left hand where it had wrapped around his scepter.

Angela looked at him from her homework and opened her mouth but before any words made it out, her dad stepped into the kitchen.

"Hard at it still, I see," he said in his normal, cordial voice. The brown angel marks on his temples gleamed in the bright overhead lights. His slightly crooked-toothed grin greeted them.

"Trigonometry sucks," Angela heaved.

Her dad laughed and stepped to her shoulder where he looked down at the mess of paperwork on the table. "I don't remember much about it myself," he offered.

"Since I'm never going to use it anyway, isn't it kind of a waste of two hours on Saturday?" Angela huffed with a beautiful glare at the thick text book. "Me and Troy could have been out looking for ways to get our robes instead."

"Your school work is important too," her dad said placidly with a pat on her shoulder. "Not as important as getting your gifts from God, but still enough to warrant a few hours here and there. You'll are doing good work. Keep it up." With that he winked and retreated from the kitchen.

"How are we ever supposed to manage getting our robes with no help?" Angela fumed and slammed her trig book closed. "Why won't they tell us what they did to get their robes? It's infuriating."

"I don't know," Troy said. "I've decided that mystery must be part of getting them."

"A personal journey…" Angela said with her eyes appearing to gaze through the kitchen wall. "That's what Noah said when I asked him at the Hill. Like we're on some stupid quest of self-discovery. It would be a lot easier if they'd point us in the right direction like they did when we got our scepters. At least then we had a target. With the robes, it's like we're walking through a cave with no flashlight to guide us."

"It is stupid," Troy offered in agreement. Which was certainly true; but at the moment, the only real thing resonating was another tick on the long and growing failure list within his quest to ask out Angela.

Homecoming week flew by in a chorus of giggles from all the girls in the hallways of Mustang High School; followed by pep rallies where the cheerleaders led them in one chant after another. On Friday night, Troy found himself standing beside Tyler in the first quarter of the game. Their red and white uniforms were unmarked by the green turf as the offense drove down the field with relative ease. Tyler was glowering behind Coach Danielson's back.

"We should be up by a few touchdowns by halftime," Troy offered as he watched Coach Lewis to see if he would be needed for the next play. "Everyone might get some playing time in the second half."

"Oh boy," Tyler grimaced in a quiet voice to Troy. "Mop up duty. That's not what I put all those hours of practice and workouts in for over the summer."

Troy made sure not to roll his eyes as Blake called the signals on the field and ended in a loud, "Go!" The ball snapped into his hands and he faked a hand-off then spun to his left. Charging to meet him was a burly, barrel chested Putnam West defensive end. What happened next made a collective gasp and groan pour from the Mustang Broncos supporters in the stands behind Troy.

"Is he okay?" Jimmy Peakes yelled as he stood on his tiptoes to look over the taller boys standing by the sideline.

Troy sidestepped Coach Lewis and gazed at a mass of huge lineman surrounding the quarterback who was grabbing his knee and rocking back and forth in pain. Troy's immediate thought was to dart onto the field and start administering Raphael's hesdia ability but he stopped at the mere ridiculousness of it. What would the ten thousand people in the stands think if he went out and touched the quarterback's leg and he miraculously jumped to his feet? Instead, he looked at Tyler who was being dragged onto the field by Coach Danielson.

"You've got this Tyler," Coach Danielson boomed in an encouraging shower of spit. "Breathe and relax. It's a job that was almost yours before the season anyway. You've been doing unbelievable in the JV games. This is the same thing – just on a little faster scale. You okay?"

"Yes sir," Tyler said without a second's hesitation. A sparkling grin was visible through his face mask and he met Troy's eyes. Years of anticipation and preparation shined in the glowing bask.

"Alright," the coach said and grabbed Troy as well. "It's going to be 3rd and 9. Let's run twins left, motion right, flood outs. Tyler, look for Troy or Darnell. Only throw it to Josh on the shorter route as the last option. Got it?"

"Yes sir," Tyler said and began trotting onto the field. Troy followed.

"Troy?"

"Yeah," Troy answered.

"Say a prayer for me."

"You got it," Troy said with a smile that vanished when he saw Blake being lifted tenderly to his feet. Him and Tyler clapped as they carted away the starting quarterback then made their way to a huddle forming around, James, the center and leader of the offensive lineman. Clark's eyes were ablaze with intensity under his battered facemask. He bobbed his giant head at Troy.

Tyler called the play with slightly shaking hands and broke the huddle. Troy found his spot and held his breath. When Tyler's shout boomed the cadence, he burst forward. On his fifth step, he gave one quick faint to his left then cut hard to his right. The football was already spiraling in his direction. But he knew the trajectory wasn't carrying it straight into his arms. He dove and with one hand snagged the ball from the air before getting leveled from behind by the Putnam West cornerback.

A loud cheer went up from the Mustang side as Troy got to his feet. The closest referee grabbed the ball from his hands and signaled a first down. Troy looked to the sidelines and saw Rich, one of the starting receivers, running onto the field and waving him off.

"Great catch!" Coach Lewis roared with a bone popping bear hug.

Troy could only nod in reply as he sucked in a deep lungful of oxygen. He turned and saw Tyler take the next snap.

By halftime, the Broncos were up 42-7. Troy never remembered seeing as big a smile on Tyler's face as he did when Coach Lokey called him out for throwing four touchdown passes in the first half. Troy was halfway sure the Spirit was glowing from his best friend's handsomely pleased face.

They finished the game with almost everyone on the team getting some playing time. Even after Troy had sat through a long winded speech from Coach Lokey, changed out of his uniform, and joked around with Tyler and Clark for fifteen minutes, the final score still shined on the scoreboard: Home team 70. Visitors 10.

"That was unbelievable!" Becky shouted and her arms flew around Troy's neck.

He returned the hug but quickly looked for Angela who was standing beside her overly protective mom. Becky took a turn hugging both Tyler and Clark as well; and telling them how good they played. The unbridled enthusiasm in her expression made Troy laugh.

"Tyler, we're so proud of you," his mom said striding forward regally in a three thousand dollar suit as if she was the First Lady of the United States. "We never had any doubts that you'd lead the team to one of the most lopsided wins ever for Mustang. You were made to be great." Her diamond earrings, necklace, watch, and rings all glittered and tantalized in the lights from the field house. She looked like she'd come straight from an expensive jewelry store advertisement.

"Thanks, I hope Blake is okay though," Tyler said with a sheepish grin. "It looked like he got hurt really bad."

"Oh, you're better anyway," his mom said with a shooing gesture at his words. Several of their teammates glanced at her with a frown.

"I'll say a prayer for him," Clark offered quietly.

"That never hurts," Clark's dad boomed jovially from his spot beside Troy's parents.

From the way Tyler's mom's eyes rolled, Troy knew how she felt about the idea of prayer. She didn't say anything but put her arm around her son and began guiding him away as if there was some type of communicable disease floating in the air.

As they passed Angela and her parents, Tyler stopped his mom. He looked from Angela to Troy then to the parents.

"Do you think it would be okay if Angela and Troy went for a car ride with me tomorrow? Kind of a celebration? I haven't gotten to drive them around at all yet... I mean... after I officially got my license and everything." He swallowed at the upraised eyebrows Angela's mom produced in obvious remembrance of their troublesome trip to Wal-Mart.

All the angel parents looked quickly from one to the other. Finally, Troy's dad cleared his throat. "We can probably arrange that," he said with an uncomfortable look at Paul, Angela's dad. "Just one time."

"It will be okay," Tyler's dad supplied in his silken smooth voice. "Tyler's already a great driver. There's nothing to worry about. I'll let them take my Escalade so they have more room. Clark probably wouldn't fit in the Camaro anyway."

"He has before," Troy's mom said in what was surely a warning for the group of friends.

"Tomorrow afternoon after we watch the game tapes?" Tyler asked with a radiant grin.

And so it was that Troy and Angela's parents spent the entire next day making plans to guard their celebratory joy ride.

"Don't forget," Troy's dad commanded. "Peter and Laura will be watching you at all times. Everyone else has somewhere else to be. If you see anything out of the ordinary, Troy, you and Angela call us immediately. We have to meet with Luke but will have our scepters ready. There shouldn't be any trouble but don't let your guard down." A sour look passed on Troy's mom's face at the mention of the Justice Minister but she didn't add anything.

"Got it," Troy repeated the answer he'd already said over twenty times to his parents' different instructions. Angela came into view from the living room where she'd been getting the same warnings and cautionary orders.

They left his house and walked together to Tyler's where the other three friends were waiting. His dad's black Escalade was humming in the driveway in anticipation of their drive.

"Everything set?" Tyler barked.

"Yep," Troy answered.

"Let's get rolling then," Tyler hollered and darted around the SUV and into the driver's seat. Clark piled into the front passenger side while Troy, Angela, and Becky climbed into the leather back seat. Becky sat in the middle barely taking up any of the wide, luxurious captain's chairs.

After they were all seated and buckled, under Angela's mom's watchful eye, Tyler zipped from the driveway and turned down the street.

"Where we going?" Becky asked.

"You'll see," Tyler said with a smile as he cranked up the radio.

"You know it can't be anywhere my parents wouldn't approve, right?" Angela half yelled over a blaring country song.

"I know," Tyler rolled his eyes. "Y'all will like this. I'm sure Troy, Becky and Clark know about it already. But I bet Angela has never seen it."

Troy pondered the words as his friend navigated through traffic ten miles per hour over the speed limit. Tyler and Clark replayed the football game from the night before as they drove but Troy's eyes were glued on the passing city landscape through the darkly tinted windows.

His parent's dire warnings and counsels had set him on edge. And from the way Angela was sitting, he was sure her parents had established the same mood with her.

Tyler turned on SW 59th and headed west into the country. Wheat fields and cow pastures, along with the peaks of houses in upscale neighborhoods, slid by the window. Troy looked for their two angel protectors but couldn't spot them with his eyes. He relaxed into his chair and closed his eyes as the Spirit filled his body. High above and a little to the north, he caught the slightest touch of watchfulness. He knew the two angels were soaring in the sky ready to dive to the rescue if a demon happened to pop out of the ground in front of them.

"What is that?" Angela asked a few minutes later pulling Troy from his concentration.

He looked where she was pointing and saw the feathered tip of a gigantic metal arrow. A smile split his lips. Leave it to Tyler to think of something like this.

"They call it Angel's Arrow," Tyler informed as he slowed to a crawl on the country road and turned off the radio. A thick tangle of cottonwood trees ran along a stream that cut through the flat land in a roughly u-shaped pattern. In the middle was a long meadow of green grass. But tucked at the far end was the remains of the most peculiar structure Troy had ever seen. He'd been by the sight before. Pretty much every kid who grew up in Mustang had.

"But what is it for?" Angela questioned as she gazed at the rickety arrow that had to be thirty feet tall. The aluminum head of the arrow was planted in the ground at an angle making it look like a giant had shot it from across the county and this was where it happened to land.

"Nobody really knows," Tyler said. "My dad said some old, crazy guy built it here like fifty years ago. There used to be a house over there." He pointed to his right at the creek. "But it burned down a long time ago. The guy moved away but nobody has ever torn down Angel's Arrow. Some farmer owns the land now. Probably keeps it to laugh at."

"I've always thought it was really weird," Becky said as she leaned into Troy to get a better look. "It's out here all by itself with no houses around for at least a mile."

"I've heard a lot of high schoolers have parties out here," Tyler mentioned as the arrow started to move out of sight behind the grove of tall trees. "It's outside Mustang city limits so only the sheriff's department would ever come out here to bust them."

"Not something we'll ever have to worry about," Clark said with a nervous chuckle.

Everyone laughed as Tyler sped up. He made a tight u-turn at the four way stop a half mile down the road. They rolled by the arrow again without any of them saying anything.

"So where to now?" Tyler finally asked into the silence.

"How about Braum's or somewhere for some ice cream?" Becky probed.

Troy began to lift his hand in agreement but stopped as a wave of invisible darkness smashed into him. Fear and malevolent distress screamed wordlessly in the air. Troy sat up straight and banged his head on the window as he tried to look around.

"Are you-" Becky started but stopped with a look at his face. On her other side, Angela was as frozen as an ice sculpture.

Troy reached for the pouch under his shirt where he kept his scepter. "Mom! Dad!" he shouted.

"What is it?" his mom's voice came immediately.

"I just felt something," Troy said in a rush. "I can't describe it really. For a second I thought I'd gone blind and deaf... and numb - but it didn't last. Now... I can feel danger. It's not-"

Before he could finish, a black shadow blotted the sun for a second then absorbed the Escalade like a glob of slime. The smell of grotesquely rotted eggs filled the air and made everyone gag. Through the nauseous fumes, Troy saw the console lights go out and felt the smallest of shudders as the engine died.

"The steering wheel will hardly turn," Tyler barked with his teeth gritted. They rolled slowly to a stop with the passenger side tires grinding to a halt in the unkempt grass of the bar ditch.

"Where are you Troy?" his dad's voice boomed into the interior of the car.

"SW 59th," Troy yelled as the sun once again blazed through the tinted windows. "Way out west of Mustang. Where are Peter and Laura?"

"We can't get them on their scepters," his mom said. "What's happening?"

"Some kind of black light hit the car," Angela squealed. Her face was pressed against the window and her scepter was humming in her right hand.

Troy pulled on the Spirit and let the current of peaceful power carry him out of the Escalade. He thought of all the lessons in Moses's class as he searched. It didn't take long for him to find the danger. Up and up, his awareness was carried on the wind. Birds squawked and darted away from a growing menace as giant wings thumped the air.

Black robes filled his vision. Five figures hovered in rage and delight. Three hundred feet almost directly below them was the stalled SUV on the side of the country road. A smile crossed the familiar face of Richard Hope as he pointed a black scepter at the vehicle.

"There are five fallen angels above us," Troy hollered with his heart missing two beats. "Richard Hope is one of them!"

One of Becky's hands shot to her mouth and the other reached for the cross necklace. Clark turned in his seat and looked at Troy with terror alive and thriving in his brown eyes.

Tyler was stomping on the gas and turning the ignition. "Come on, come on, come on!" he yelled and beat on the steering wheel.

"Mom, what do we do?" Troy asked as he felt the black robed angels falling towards them.

"Pray, have faith… and fight," she choked. "We're on our way."

The hair across Troy's body rose at her words. A tingle of pure fright crept across the skin of his ribs. He looked at each of his friends in turn then stayed locked in a meaningful look at Angela. A story echoed in his ears. The tale told by the Forever, Joshua Carter, at the Hill over the summer.

What will you have to sacrifice to get God's second gift to angels?

Troy called on the Spirit as he whispered a short prayer.

Not his friends. They can't have them. He had to keep them safe. Had to save them. He couldn't let anything happen to them.

"Stay here and keep trying to start the car," he shouted. "If it starts, drive towards Mustang as fast as you can." He hammered his way out the door before any of them could stop him.

The fallen angels landed on the asphalt fifty yards away. Richard Hope was in the middle of the group. Black robes swirled unnaturally around his feet. Putrid, decaying wings extended in twitching agitation behind the back of each angel. Halos of deepest red glowed over their heads.

On their chests, an emblem caught Troy's eyes. A heart with bloody entrails, as if it had just been ripped from someone's chest, was smeared in a spattering pattern across the blackness of the robes. Each of the angels smiled at Troy who strode forward alone to meet them.

"What do you want?" he bellowed as he pulled a tiny sheath from the pocket of his khaki shorts. The dagger slid into his right hand. He let the sheath fall to the ground and faced his foes with dagger and scepter ready to fight.

"You and your friends, of course," Richard laughed. "The Dark Hearts need more souls for the war."

Behind Troy, three doors slammed. He glanced over his shoulder and a moan slipped from his throat as his friends walked towards him on rubbery legs. Angela's scepter was now in her left hand and a whip was popping in her right. She stepped up and took position beside Troy. Clark stomped forward with his head held high as bravery dawned on his dark face. He looked ten times bigger than he ever had before.

Hand in hand, Tyler and Becky stopped directly behind Troy.

"Why won't you leave us alone," Angela screeched with a definite wavering in her petite voice.

"Just can't help ourselves, I suppose," Richard said with a deadly smile.

"There are angels guarding us," Troy said trying to buy time. He could feel his parents listening in on the conversation through his scepter. He pictured them flying across the skyline like fighter jets.

The five fallen angels laughed. A short, dark haired woman to Richard's left quivered in giddiness. "Poor Laura and Peter," she cackled. "Don't count on them. They're either dead or dying."

"Where are your demons?" Tyler hollered in his loud quarterback cadence. "Not hiding like cowards behind them this time? Not like you did at Wal-Mart."

"Tired of their mistakes," Richard said nonchalantly and started walking forward. Step by step, the fallen angels drew closer in a shallow v-formation.

"And what about your mistakes?" Troy accused. "You and Kyle couldn't get the job done at that house last year. Your demons aren't the only ones who make mistakes."

A muscle twitched in Richard's unassuming face. "No more delaying," he called with a knowing look at Troy's scepter. "Time to send your friends to an eternity of nothingness and accept you as one of the youngest members of the Dark Hearts."

"At least we'll be in heaven," Becky sobbed with tears streaming down her cheeks.

"You make it sound like some happy place," the angel to Richard's right crooned. "You'll just be a little speck of dust under God's heel. If you knew the truth, you'd know that."

"I know the truth," Becky returned with courage growing in her voice.

The fallen angels were only forty feet away when a gust of wind snapped the trees along the side of the road. Leaves and branches whipped into the air in a frenzy of nature.

Bursting through the tumult flew Laura and Peter. Red spots and splatters of blood darkened Laura's white robes but righteous anger shined on her face. White wings twinkled in glowing sun. A bright light shot from her scepter and boomed against a fog of sheer blackness which erupted around the fallen angels. A snake-like hiss carried in the air at the impact.

"Run!" Troy shouted and pushed Tyler and Becky towards the Escalade. Blinding flashes and Trumpets of Seraphim that made Troy's bones rattle bounced off the asphalt.

"No," Tyler said with a manic look at Richard who was blasting gobs of tar-like energy from his scepter. "We're in this together. We can't keep running."

"We have no chance against them," Angela said with a fearful look at Tyler. "Not for long at least."

A deep, long-noted and hellish horn, so loud it nearly knocked them to the ground, thundered from the dark shadows. Under Troy's feet, the asphalt split and groaned as the Earth shook in terror and fright. A wail, like a thousand tortured souls, split the air in a spine cringing screech.

"We have to help them," Clark said with his brown eyes on the fight where Laura and Peter we being bombarded with darkness and the blurring strikes from the terrible swords of the fallen.

Troy nodded breathing a short, manic prayer. He sent a ball of bright energy into the frenzy of decaying wings. With a look at his friends, he hoped wouldn't be the last time he saw them, he charged.

"For God, we fight!"

All of them shouted the command together and stormed into the battle. Within two seconds, Troy lost himself in a whirring of swords and wings and black fog. He parried a blow with his dagger barely managing to hang onto his tiny weapon. From Angela's scepter, a torrent of fresh water engulfed Tyler and washed away a film of slimy oil that had wrapped around his head.

Richard sped across Troy's vision and stabbed towards Clark. With only a couple of centimeters to spare, Troy deflected the lethal blow using Gabriel's Shield. Clark jumped on the stunned fallen angel but was immediately blasted away in an avalanche of putrid smelling filth.

"No!" Troy yelled and swiped forward with his scepter. Sets of shining, magnificent chains wrapped around Richard's legs. The fallen angel grunted as they squeezed and he toppled. Before Troy could follow him to the ground, the short woman who had cackled at them was on top of him. Her rotting wings battered his head and she swung a short sword at him over and over again.

Screams of anguish, which crawled up Troy's spine like it was a spiral staircase of fear, sounded from somewhere in the chaos. He thought it had to have been Angela or Becky but couldn't chance even the smallest of glances as the woman hacked at him with her sword.

"Look out!"

This time it wasn't a voice Troy recognized. The woman cursed and leapt into the air with her black wings sprouting wide. Troy searched with the Spirit and a smile almost stretched across his face. Six white missiles were shooting over the trees a half mile away. Trumpets blared and the wrath of God came with his parents, Angela's parents, Grandma Denise, and Luke Fischer.

A soft light consumed the road as if bringing peace to an island succumbed in total war. All specks of darkness fled in the undying love of God's pure grace. Troy knew he could bask in it for eternity but pulled himself from the temptation. For out of the light, a tall shadow loomed and darted at him.

The fallen angel's eyes burned with hate and revenge. The man hopped back and forth sideways like a cheetah on the hunt. For the briefest moment he paused as though ready to pounce; then a river of slimy mud shot from his scepter. Troy ducked and rolled but the nasty foulness oozed over his left foot and stuck it in place. He looked up as the fallen angel ran at him and did the first thing that came to his mind. His dagger spun into the air from his right hand and a ball of brilliant light burst from the scepter in his left. The man easily dodged the energy from the Spirit but the hate waxed from his eyes as the dagger buried directly into the bloody heart emblem on his chest. He fell face first onto the unforgiving road with a horrendous, crunching bounce.

Troy yanked his foot free of the muck and cautiously approached the downed man. As he was stilling his resolve to turn over what he thought was most likely already a corpse, a slight movement caught his eye.

Richard had managed to cut the chains binding his legs. With a snarl, the fallen angel dove. Not towards Troy, but at Clark who was still trying to drag himself groggily from the ground.

Troy could only watch in stunned fright. He'd expected the attack to come at him. Why hadn't it?

His eyes locked on the wicked blade of Richard's sword almost as if it was in slow motion. His own arms seemed stuck in super glue as he raised his scepter one slow millimeter at a time. He knew without a doubt he'd be too late. The sword was slicing through the air on a mission of death. He'd have to watch one of his best friends die in a fountain of blood. Another innocent life lost in the War for Sins.

But in the fraction of a second before the Lucifer forged steel buried into Clark's chest, an almost transparent shield appeared in a shimmer of air. Richard's sword clanged off of Gabriel's protective gift for the second time. He hissed through the mist and dust as Troy's mom flew at him.

With the briefest of glares at Troy, the fallen angel shot into the sky.

"Are you two okay?" Troy's mom growled as she landed beside Clark.

"Yeah," Troy answered and looked around. The three remaining fallen angels were all in retreating flight. He saw Grandma Denise and Luke spring into the air after them.

His dad landed beside the fallen angel that had been struck by Troy's dagger. Ever so gently, he rolled the man over. Gasping, struggling breaths made the hilt rise and fall where it was buried in the man's chest.

"Why Doug?" Troy's dad asked. "It's not too late to change your heart and mind. Accept your faith in God and be granted eternal salvation. You have time."

"Can't we heal him?" Troy said with his voice cracking.

"We can't save him," his dad answered with a sad shake of his head. "I'd have to pull the blade out to try and that would kill him instantly." Sympathy softened his normally passive face as he knelt in a brief prayer.

"Save your breath," Doug wheezed with a violent, body shaking cough. His face was a mess of blood and gravel. "I know the truth."

"Who is the spy, Doug?" Troy's mom questioned in a much rougher voice than his dad. "Tell us and be forgiven for all you've done wrong. Like Brian said, you still have a chance."

Doug looked at Troy with a painful smile. "When Lucifer rises," he groaned in ever softer rasps. "What I helped start... forever be... a hero... to... her." The light left his eyes as he said the last word.

Troy swallowed the terrible fact of his actions sending an angel to hell. There was no revelry or jubilation at the thought. Only a cold awareness of knowing another soul was fueling the devil's power. Another angel sent from a world where he was needed.

Soft words brought him from the stupor of the hated knowledge. He turned and saw Angela's dad healing a nasty wound on his wife's leg. She grimaced but her eyes were on the pavement to her left. Troy followed them and the ground fell out from under his feet.

Lying in a pool of blood and oily mud was Laura. If it wasn't for the deadly slash across the white robes of her stomach, Troy might have thought she was resting in a ray of dazzling sunlight. Her eyes were wide and a peaceful smile tugged at the corners of her mouth. Her arms had stretched out and landed on unmoving wings of the purest white feathers. The halo above her head, that had been so bright at the start of the battle, was fading.

One more casualty ascending to heaven.

Tears threatened then slid from Troy's eyes. Death had become a constant companion in the War for Sins but this was the first time he had tasted its cold touch in person. He staggered from the awful sight.

"Troy?"

The beautiful voice brought a glimmer of life into the dark views of the world swirling in Troy's head. He looked up but froze in wonder. Gleaming in the sunlight was Angela. Robes, so white God had to have washed them by hand only a minute before, rustled as if they'd only just draped over her shoulders.

"What? How?" he stammered.

Standing at the edge of the massive battle, with a mask of thorough bewilderment, Angela looked like a hero of long ago in the War for Sins. Someone struggling to find answers after a barbaric fight. Her right hand ran across the material of the robes covering her left arm. She looked desperately at Troy.

"I... don't know," she said and her eyes dropped to her feet where the robes were fluttering.

"Angela?" Her dad jumped from the ground where he'd finished healing the sliced flesh of her mom's leg.

Tears streamed steadily down Angela's cheeks. The pink angel marks on her temples danced but when she looked up, no happiness seemed to exist.

"I don't know," she repeated and turned her back. In the bar ditch where she looked, Becky was hovering over Tyler whose breath came in ragged gulps.

"Tyler?" Troy shouted and ran to his friend.

"I'm okay," Tyler said and waved away a helping hand from Becky. "Angela already healed me."

"I thought you would die for sure," Becky moaned with her own tears streaking the little amount of make-up she wore. "That man was terrible. If Angela, Peter, and Laura hadn't been here..."

Tyler nodded and glanced at Angela. "Thanks," he said but shook his head in confused wonder. "Why did you get your robes?"

"I'm not sure," Angela said in such a quiet voice it barely rose over a soft gust of wind. "Sometime during the battle... I guess... I don't know. I didn't even notice I had them until after those Dark Heart people flew away."

"How did you get them?" Becky asked.

Angela only shook her head and glanced at Troy.

He stared openly at the magnificence of the robes. He'd always thought his parent's robes and wings were the purest white he'd ever seen. But he knew now that wasn't correct. There was a perfect sheen to the cloth of Angela's robes. Nothing marred the flawless gift from God.

"They're unbelievable," Clark said with one of his shy smiles.

"Clark!" Angela said and ran to him with her arms throwing a hug which only went halfway around his gigantic frame. "When I was healing Tyler, I saw you almost get killed. I was so worried for everyone."

Clark shrugged and his left hand landed heavily on Troy's shoulder. "I almost died twice," he heaved without a trace of fright. "But with angels as friends, I think I'm safe."

"Don't be overly thankful for having angels as friends," Troy's dad said as he watched the horizon where the fallen angels had retreated. "Your soul is definitely safe, but your life might be in jeopardy."

Troy understood what his dad had said even though Tyler looked perplexed by the comment. Having angels as friends made faith easy and led to eternal salvation.... But at the cost of dangers not many normal humans see in the War for Sins.

Chapter 15: The Deygon

"How many more people are going to die for me?" Troy asked. It was Sunday morning and he was in the kitchen with his mom. They'd finished a solemn morning service with Grandma Denise and his dad five minutes before. The sparkling cleanliness of the kitchen roared at odds with the black images of the battle rolling through Troy's overloading brain.

"It's not because of you Troy," his mom said and sat down beside him at the mahogany table. "You can't blame yourself for what Kyle and his followers do. The sins are their own."

"Laura would still be alive if we hadn't went on that stupid drive," Troy cried and wiped his eyes. "She'd be at home with her family. She could be hugging her… kids. What if they hold it against me like Billy Randell does?"

His mom peered into the glass of wine she'd brought with her to the table. Troy wondered what she was seeing in the deep redness of the drink. When he looked at it, all he saw was the bloody mess across Laura's chest. "Billy doesn't really hold it against you," she finally said. "He knows his mom is in heaven. He knows who killed her. It's just-"

"He blamed me and you and dad," Troy said slowly as he tried to control his heaving lungs. "He yelled at me at the Hill. It's our fault Kyle is killing so many people."

"Troy," his mom started then stopped and engulfed him in a tender hug. Such softness had never existed in the world until that moment. He relaxed into her arms and breathed the fresh, sweet smell that always followed her. "You aren't to blame for what Kyle has done," she continued. "He's after you for reasons you can't control."

"Why does he want me to fall so bad?" Troy said and stifled any further tears. "He's almost killed all my friends. He *has* killed a lot of your old friends. His Dark Heart people killed Laura. What's it all about?"

"Old wounds," his mom offered but nothing more. She left a few minutes later with a sad attempt at a smile and a gentle pat on his hand.

Troy spent the rest of the day in his room with his friends.

"Let me see them again," Tyler called to Angela who had stayed much quieter than she usually did when the friends were joking around with each other.

She smiled shyly and closed her eyes. The magnificent robes popped into existence a second later.

"They're so beautiful," Becky cooed and softly twisted the sleeve between her thumb and forefinger. "I can't believe I'm touching angel robes. It's so cool!"

Clark grinned so big Troy thought it might permanently stick on his broad face when he leaned forward to lay a hand on Angela's shoulder.

Troy didn't reach out to touch them. Instead he watched Angela who held a look as if she was in a faraway place. Four times during the day, she'd been asked by the friends how she'd been granted the evasive gift from God. Each time she'd blushed, her gaze immediately went to her feet, and she'd blown off any response with a shrug. Troy was sure he caught her peeking at him awkwardly after the noncommittal responses though.

"Did your parents say anything about the Dark Hearts?" Angela asked as Becky and Clark kept touching her robes in a mesmerized daze.

"Not much," Troy answered. "The Angelic Agenda reported they verified it was officially the name of Kyle's followers. Of course, that probably came from our parents - so who really knows. They did mention the Pit Shades. That's what Xavier's group was called."

"Both sound awful," Becky said with a shiver and pulled her hand away from Angela's robes. "I can't believe none of us got killed yesterday."

"Two more of the Dark Hearts are down and out at least," Tyler said smugly.

"But that's not a good thing," Angela murmured.

"What do you mean?" Tyler argued. "Those idiots were trying to kill us. One of them nearly did kill me. And that Richard guy almost killed Clark twice. I don't have any sympathy for them. Let them all die. Then we won't have to worry about them anymore."

"If you kill them when they don't have faith," Troy said with a sad look at his best friend. "They spend eternity in hell."

"They asked for it," Tyler replied and popped his neck nonchalantly. "Oh, I almost forgot," he continued. "James texted me earlier. Blake tore his ACL Friday night. He's out for the season."

Troy didn't need auditome to tell Tyler had meant to change the subject. But he didn't care. The fight had been hashed over and talked about dozens of times. Every detail, except for the main one Troy wanted to know, had been discussed. He glanced once again at Angela's robes.

"That sucks," Clark said. "He's a good guy."

"Yeah," Tyler said with a twist to his lips. "Are you sure one of you couldn't heal him?"

Troy shook his head and Angela responded. "Not after he's already been diagnosed and everything. We can't go around performing miracles for everyone. We'd draw too much attention to angels and that's not how God wants people to find and hold onto their faith."

"Worked for me," Tyler said with a wink. Angela chuckled but didn't continue.

The next week flew by in a tsunami of school homework and upbeat talks from Tyler about football.

"Not even Noah could keep his head above water in Trigonometry," Becky griped on Thursday afternoon. "I won't remember any of it five seconds after we're done with the class."

"I know," Troy agreed wholeheartedly. No matter how hard he tried, the mathematics wouldn't stick in his head. Not with fallen angels and demons crowding for space in his brainwaves.

He looked around and noticed where they were. With football practice cutting short, since it was the day before their next game against the Westmoore Jaguars, they'd decided to go for a bike ride.

"Look who it is," Tyler said motioning with his head down the street.

Troy followed his gaze down Pine Bluff Lane. At the end of a short driveway was the foster mom of the girl he'd wanted to save so badly a year ago. That the girl had turned out to be a tondeo demon, never failed to make a circuit through Troy's mind on a daily basis. The woman was staring at them with a confused twist on her scrunched face. Her normally ragged bath robes had been replaced by tan slacks and an overly tight fitting t-shirt of an old rock band.

"She looks like she's lost a lot of weight," Tyler said offhandedly and shielded his eyes from the setting sun.

Clark waved and the woman returned the gesture with an embarrassed smile.

"Let's go talk to her," Becky said and began biking down the street.

Angela met Troy's eyes warily. Their first meetings with the woman hadn't been exactly pleasant experiences. In fact, she'd generally pretty much yelled at them for approaching her house. Troy swallowed any fear of the memory and followed. As hard as he tried, the ghost of those innocent green eyes beckoned from the window. Nothing was there when he looked. But from on top of the house, he caught the quick fluttering of wings and saw Peter's grave face on guard duty.

"Hey," Becky said brightly as they approached the woman.

Only a nod of acknowledgement returned. Troy held his breath until she looked directly at him.

"Th…th… thank you," she mumbled and took a deep breath. "Been hopin I'd see ya again for a long time. I wanted to tell ya, all that stuff you said… it really helped. I got two more foster kids now. They're good kids. I love 'em more'n anything. We been goin over to First Nazarene every Sunday. Been really good."

Troy closed his mouth and cleared his throat as he tried to pull a gracious smile through his stunned mind. The transformation in her personality was startling; but lovely. Gone were the scowls and growls of the previous year. He called on the Spirit and lightly pressed with auditome. An image of two toddlers laughing and playing on a carpeted floor swam quickly before his eyes.

"You're welcome," he said hoping his voice wouldn't crack. "I'm glad I was able to help."

She bobbed her head and smiled again. Then turned down her driveway.

"See Troy," Becky barked and gave him a punch on the arm that was very much like Tyler's usual method of praise. "You really do help people. She's totally different from how y'all described her."

"She is," Angela said with the first true smile Troy had seen on her face all week. "It's nice to know we've done something right."

All of them laughed as they turned and made their way back to Tyler's house. Their ever present guardian angels hovered high in the distance over a band of evergreen trees. Troy tried not to sigh as he remembered that every time he felt happy, Kyle did something to ruin the mood. He prayed it was different this time.

By the end of October, the Mustang Broncos football team had eight wins with only the one loss early in the season. Tyler's euphoria could hardly be matched. Troy was impressed and surprised by his friend every day. His dad had agreed to start confirmation classes with him at Christ Lutheran; and both were planning on being baptized by Christmas. Every day after practices and before every game, Tyler led the team in prayer. The only negative in his life was his mom who scowled ice bolts at Troy, who she'd come to blame (rightfully) for Tyler's transformation of faith.

For Troy, there were several giant worries on his mind. He still hadn't had anything close to an idea of how to go about getting his robes. Kyle and his Dark Hearts were reeking so much havoc the normal news was beginning to get baffled by the uptick in what they reported as violent crimes and domestic terrorist activity.

And Angela had never approached any type of explanation on how she got her robes. If anyone broached the subject, she tended to smile politely and not say more than two words the rest of the day.

"So the sword," Troy said as he flipped a page of *Touching Grace* and read about Raphael's prendia ability. The hand-drawn depiction showed a woman with a gruesome wound on upper arm. A male angel was hovering over her with a soft glow searching towards the injury.

"Yeah," Angela shrugged. "The next gift on my list. My parents have already started badgering me about it… and prendia is a cool ability." She pointed at the book in his hands. "If someone is hurt really bad, you can paralyze them temporarily while you heal them."

Troy nodded as he scanned the long narrative under the picture. "I wonder if my dad thought about using it on Doug when the Dark Hearts attacked us? Maybe we could have saved him."

"Do you think he wanted to?" Angela asked. She was gazing through her copy of *Singing with Seraphim* but kept peeking at Troy from the corner of her eye.

"Yeah," Troy answered without hesitation. "My dad did. Not sure about my mom though… The war has her on edge more than my dad. She's constantly watching the Angelic Agenda or randomly calling the angels guarding us to check to make sure they're alert. I bet they're starting to get pretty annoyed at her."

"My mom is the same way," Angela sighed. "And the Justice Ministers aren't helping either one of their moods. Luke has been coming over to talk with your dad and my dad every day."

"They're trying to figure out who the spy is," Troy added. "They know someone had to have tipped off the Dark Hearts we were going on that drive. From what I overheard my parents talking about the other day, the list is kind of long."

"That's the worst part about all of this," Angela huffed and slammed her book closed. "Angels have started not trusting each other."

"With a spy in the Cathedral," Troy mused. "Everyone is on high alert."

Angela opened her mouth to respond but an outcry from the living room cut her off. Both of them scrambled from her bedroom and darted through the spacious house. On the large flat screen TV, the Angelic Agenda reporters were in a frenzy.

"…in a panic," the man with orange angel markings barked. "Every angel in the Midwest region of the United States must stay on high alert. The records are being checked as we speak, but estimates are that one hasn't been seen in over 800 years. There have been at least 120 fatalities in the train wreck in Missouri. And countless other innocent people remain unaccounted. CNN, Fox News, and the other stations are reporting the scene as an accident, but an angel who witnessed the event has relayed the truth."

The screen cut away to a rolling hilltop view. Dense trees covered most of the area but a vast scar had been cut along the line of a winding railroad track. Train cars were smashed and stacked in a jumbled mess. A fire was burning in the middle of the wreck and part of the hill was still ablaze. Black smoke lifted to a gray sky above. Through this an angel rose in front of the camera. Her white wings beat slowly in long strokes.

"It was a deygon," she said and trembled from head to toe. "I was in Sedalia, about five miles east of here when it happened. I felt the Spirit tremble and the Earth shake. I knew right away something bad had happened so I flew high. It was raining this morning but to the west I saw the shadow. Fire was torching the ground beneath it and then it crashed into the ground where I knew the tracks ran... Congressman Daniels and his contingent were on the train. They'd been advertising it as a fundraiser for the Democratic Party on their way to Kansas City for a campaign stop. I don't think there will be any survivors. I flew close and that's when I saw the deygon. For a second it looked right at me then flew north into a thunderstorm. It was… terrible."

Troy looked from Angela to her parents. A deygon? He searched his memory of *Dangerous and Deadly Demons* but nothing connected. He knew he'd heard his parents mention the name but had never investigated.

"What is a deygon?" Angela asked echoing the questions swirling in Troy's head.

Her parents looked from the TV to the two angels in training. In answer, her dad pulled an ancient book from the table beside him. The leather spine was wrinkled and the cover looked as if it had gone through a dozen battles in the War for Sins. *Blackest of the Black* was embossed in loopy, golden letters. He turned to a page near the very back of the book and handed it to Angela. Troy read over her shoulder.

At the top of the page was an illustration of a mammoth, lizard looking monster. The beast was in the air over a village of cottages and dwarfed everything in the picture. Fire spewed from its mouth and brewed in red, faceted eyes. Wings that looked wide enough to span a football field were spread in certainty of coming death.

At the start of the War for Sins, Lucifer poured his wrath into the creation of his most powerful demon. None other than God and the archangels can stand before it alone and survive. The deygon of hell. Scales, as hard as the Earth itself, cover the monster forged from brimstone and fire. Teeth and claws and a spiked tail promise instant death. It is known by many as the Soul Reaper for it is drawn to the faithlessness of unbelievers. The beast's sole purpose is to devour the souls of the lost; and power Lucifer's bid to rise against the Lord.

Angels can only attack the deygon in large battalions. Single attack is certain death. The only weakness is a fear of the sun but even that is overcome when the deygon is flying in its fury. The fires of hell pour from its mouth and consume anything touched. Only with the grace and power of God can this king of snakes be defeated. Fight with the faith of many angels; or live in eternal paradise with the Lord our God.

Troy looked from Angela to her parents then back to the picture. All the hairs on his arms were standing on end and a slow tingle was crawling around his body. He shivered involuntarily at the fearful caste on Paul's face.

"Have my parents heard?" Troy asked.

Susan nodded as she watched the reporters on TV flipping rapidly through old scrolls and musty books.

"They're already on their way to the Dome of Windows," Paul informed. "We're going to head there now. You two are going to come with us."

"What?" Angela said suddenly. "To the Dome?"

"No," her mom said. "You'll wait in the sanctuary at the Cathedral. I'm not going to have you anywhere else."

"For how long?" Angela complained. "Y'all could be in a meeting all night."

"As long as it takes," her dad soothed. "We have to get this handled. I can't believe... none of us knew."

"Knew what?" Angela asked.

"That Kyle was strong enough to raise a deygon," her mom answered. Her face was white and clammy. Little of the normal beauty shined at the moment. Now, fear and terror bred a dark stalker. Even the usually vividly blue angel marks seemed dull and weak.

"No fallen angel in living memory has been able to do it," Paul said and roughly rubbed his hand across his forehead. "You heard the reporters. They can't even find the exact date of the last deygon. But it's had to have been almost a thousand years. Probably in the dark ages when the War for Sins was threatening to take over the world. It's not good news."

Of that, Troy had zero doubts. They piled into Susan's car and drove at top speed to the Cathedral. There, Troy and Angela were deposited in pews in the sanctuary as adult angels streamed through the gate to heaven. Troy watched them each step into the solid wall of stone and disappear without so much as a shimmer. Angela's eyes didn't leave the sight either but Troy knew she was seeing the angels step through the breathtaking gate. He wished and prayed for the millionth time in his life God would grant him the sight to see the wonderful arches. But the stones remained.

For five hours, Troy and Angela sat in mostly silence. Troy did step into the corner and have a hurried and whispered conversation with Tyler on his cell phone. He didn't think he'd accurately portrayed the gravity of the situation but had at least made Tyler promise to tell Becky and Clark to stay inside and be wary.

Finally, Troy's parents, Angela's parents, and Grandma Denise materialized out of the wall. It was nearly 9:00pm and they looked haggard.

"What did Gabriel and the other archangels say?" Troy asked.

A buzz had lifted in the sanctuary at the adult's arrival. Several other younger angels had been quietly praying and waiting with Troy and Angela - even Ben Lewis who had remarkably kept to himself the entire time.

"We're going to have to kill it," his dad answered heavily. "We leave tonight. There are Justice Ministers tracking its location. They're pretty sure they know where it went."

"What?" Angela moaned. "The description in that book made them sound unbeatable. Are any of the archangels going to help?"

"No," her mom answered and grabbed Angela by the arm to start directing her from the Cathedral.

"Are all of you going?" Troy asked.

"Your mom is going to stay behind," his dad scowled.

"I'm not leaving them this time," she said with a defensive rise in her normally soft voice. "Me and Susan both agree."

"I still think I should stay too," Susan said and pushed her way around a throng of madly whispering angels.

"Gabriel said all available angels in the United States should go," Paul breathed patiently. "We're already pushing the limits letting one of you stay."

"I just have such a bad feeling about the whole situation," Susan protested as they made their way quickly through the store-lined hallways of the Cathedral. "Kyle used the reidlos attack as a diversion last year to try to get to Troy and Angela. He knew instantly when they snuck out of the house back in the spring. And he was able to put together a party of Dark Hearts on a few hours' notice when they went on the car ride last month. What if this is the same thing?"

"A deygon is a pretty big distraction," Troy's dad answered and gave Samson such a tremendous glare, the usually gaudy flirtations stuck in the statue's mouth.

"That's our point," Troy's mom jumped into the argument for the first time. "Kyle's main goal in everything he's done is to get close to Troy. Is this any different?"

"Who knows," Paul said. "But we can't all go against the archangels' command to find the deygon and destroy it. One of you can stay but not both. We'll need every angel we can get. And for those of you that stay behind." He looked from Angela, to Troy and then Troy's mom. "We'll need all the prayers you can muster."

The next two hours were a flurry of movement in Troy's house. His dad packed knives, axes, bows and arrows, and maces in a bag. Then unpacked them and repacked them with a gold plated shield Troy had never seen before.

"You watch yourselves," Grandma Denise said from the doorway to the garage.

"You too," Troy said with a smile. "You're the one flying into danger against a giant dragon."

"I get to have all the fun then," she said with a salute and left.

"Are they going to be okay?" Troy asked his mom.

"I don't know," she said as she stared out the kitchen window. Her right hand was wrapped around her scepter hard enough to make her knuckles white. Angela was rocking side to side in the recliner in the living room. "All the Justice Ministers are going but nobody is an expert on a deygon so they won't be any more help than a normal angel. I hope your friends are safe as well. Susan and I used every disguising and concealing ability we could think of to hide them, on the drive to Clark's dad's church. Pray for them."

"I will," Troy assured. "And for dad and all the other angels too." He watched his mom as the Spirit flared and faded from her scepter. He'd never seen her as nervous as she was right then. "Was Kyle this strong when he was young?" Slowly, she turned and looked at him but didn't answer. "I mean, everyone is saying that it takes a lot of power to raise a deygon from hell… so does that mean he's stronger than the other leaders of the fallen angels? You know, like Xavier."

"He was very gifted when I knew him," she answered carefully. "One of the best in our year at the Hill. Maybe the best, really - between him or your dad. But he was always more of a fighter. I don't know exactly what it takes to raise demons, but from what I understand it's more of a mental aptitude. Don't get me wrong, he was smart. He just tended to want to launch himself into fights before thinking about it."

"Why did he fall?"

His mom turned and glanced out the window again. Finally, after almost a full minute of silence, she answered. "I don't want to talk about it right now Troy. I know you want to know, but it really isn't important in the grand scheme of things. Like your dad told you last year, Kyle has told himself a lie and believes it."

"What did he tell himself that would cause this much trouble?" Angela asked from the recliner where she was sitting with her arms tucking her knees to her chest.

"Mainly that Lucifer will bring a new heaven on Earth if he rises from hell," Troy's mom answered. "And that all those souls already in hell will be able to rise with him. Kyle thinks he'll be a hero and savior to all of them."

"That's what all fallen angels think though," Troy said with a frustrated twist of his nose and mouth. "There's something more than that with Kyle. Why won't you and dad tell me?"

A heavy sigh left his mom. "Maybe someday... you'll know. Right now, Troy, I want you to concentrate on parimus. With everything you have."

"Okay," he answered her cryptic request. "Why can't you do it?"

"Because you're better at than me," she said. "And something doesn't feel right. I can't place it but I don't feel safe right now."

Troy nodded and an upsurge of pride built in his stomach. His mom thought he was better at an angel ability than she was? He never thought he'd hear something like that. She was so great with every archangel gift he'd ever seen her use. She'd killed hordes of demons and fought toe to toe with some of the worst fallen angels. And now she was asking him to use one of the coolest abilities. He settled into a chair and began praying and concentrating.

Each tick of the digital clock, on the microwave, rolled by under Troy's watchful gaze. Five minutes. Twenty minutes. An hour. Two hours. Three hours. It had to have been one of the longest days in his life.

"Have you felt anything?" his mom asked almost four hours after the departure of the other adult angels.

Troy shook his head. He had sensed what felt like a silhouette of untold danger for the last hour but nothing he thought was *immediate*. He figured it was a foreboding from not getting an update from his dad and the others. Surely by now they should have called with some type of news.

Or maybe it was the exhaustion he felt coming on.

"Nothing at all?" she prodded.

"For the last forty-five minutes or so, its felt like there was a shadow or something," he said. "But its way off in the distance and I never saw or felt anything... exact."

His mom seemed to chew on the words. "Come on," she said after a deep breath. "Make sure you have your scepters. Troy, get your dagger and your mace. Angela, do you have your whip?"

"Yes," Angela answered frightfully with eyes as wide as dinner plates. "Where are we going?"

"I don't want to say it out loud," Troy's mom answered secretively.

Troy and Angela both looked at each other, then Troy raced down the hallway to his room and snagged the mace and its harness from the corner. Angela was in the kitchen with her whip in her right hand and her scepter in the left. Her feet were tapping on the tiled floor.

"Let's go," his mom said and stalked through the door to the garage. They piled into the awaiting Tahoe and his mom pressed the button for the overhead door. The slow grind seemed to take ten times longer than usual. Every dark corner of the garage held threatening, wavering shadows. Phantoms flickered in the overhead street lamp in front of their next door neighbor's house. A moonless night shed nearly complete darkness outside the illumination of the house and street lights. It was as though they were in a dome of dimness with a black creature ready to swallow them whole.

Troy tried to relax and concentrated on all the lessons from Moses' class about parimus. They accelerated backwards and careened into the street. Before he could even get his seat belt on, the tires were spinning and squealing as he mom jammed the gas pedal.

"Where are we going?" he asked.

"The Cathedral," his mom replied with her eyes darting from the rear view mirrors to both side mirrors.

"Why?"

"To go somewhere else," she answered.

"Where?"

"I'll tell you when we get there."

Troy studied the tenseness in his mom's jaw. None of the usual warmth exuded from her eyes. He reached towards her with auditome. Thoughts swirled and mingled; then converged. Worried images of Troy standing alone in the face of Kyle and a legion of demons spun in a tangled mess. A shout of "For God, we fight" left his lips as he charged towards sure death.

The vision broke when she looked at him. "I'm just worried," she said and produced the weakest smile he'd ever seen from her. Barely a single ray of sunshine existed in the attempt.

Troy licked his lips and once again expanded his reach with parimus.

Five minutes later they reached the packed parking lot of the Cathedral without getting attacked. His mom pushed him and Angela through the doors at a hurried pace.

"Dear lady," Samson said wildly and threw a hand buffer into the hallway where Jacob was shaking his head solemnly.

The cleaning tool clattered and banged as it bounced off the wall. His marble skin sparkled with a fresh coat of wax. "I didn't expect you this evening. I was… going to brush off some cobwebs. Help out a little… with everyone gone to fight a demon foul enough to turn even my wonderful hair white, I thought the Cathedral would be empty this evening."

"We won't be staying," she said quickly. "Keep a tight watch tonight Samson. Something bad is happening."

"Nothing will get past me," he grinned and flexed his enormous muscles. "I'll rip anything in half that threatens such beauty."

His mom nodded but her only reply was to grab Troy and Angela by the shoulders and steer them down the hallway and into the sanctuary. She brought all their heads together and whispered in a barely audible tone. "We're going to the Hill. Don't repeat that and don't ask questions."

Troy and Angela's eyes found each other. He was sure the same questions were rolling through her mind. What was going on? And why were they running away so fast and recklessly when nothing seemed wrong?

At breakneck speed they approached the gate. Passover Hill. Passover Hill. Passover Hill. Troy stepped into the stone wall and his foot landed in the empty antechamber of the Hill's Commons area. No laughing or playing voices met his ears. There weren't any angels in training running here or there. As they walked forward, Troy noticed all the stores were closed. New Eden was forlorn in strange silence with none of its games blinking in a bid to get a young angel to play. No tiny angel effigies flew towards them to take their bags for summer training.

"What are we doing here?" Troy asked.

"Waiting for your dad and the others to call us," his mom answered while she peeked into every empty store with her sword at the ready.

"Mom, demons can't get in here, right?"

"No, but fallen angels can," she said with a mad gleam in her eyes. "Keep using parimus. Angela, try auditome to see if you catch any thoughts from someone who might be hiding."

After ten minutes of careful searching, his mom sheathed her sword and walked to the doors to the balcony that overlooked the valley far below. With her scepter, she used some type of angel ability to seal the door then relaxed against it.

"Emily?"

The voice made all of them jump a foot.

"Brian?" Troy's mom said in a thunderous response. "What's going on? Why haven't you called?"

"The Justice Ministers didn't want us to take a chance to give away the plans. We've been on the hunt all night."

"Did you find the deygon?" Troy asked.

"Yes," his dad answered. "It's dead."

Troy and Angela both clapped and cheered and hugged each other.

"But we lost eight angels," his dad continued with a deep breath. "And Luke was hurt really bad. He got burned early in the fight and fell a couple of hundred feet to the ground. We healed him after it was over but he's going to have a lot of scarring."

"Who all died?" Troy's mom asked with a quaver rocking her voice.

"Nobody from Oklahoma. A couple of Justice Ministers from Europe. The rest, we don't know. They'll be missed by many though."

"They are basking in heaven's glory now," Susan's voice said into thin air.

"Mom!" Angela squealed. "Are you and dad okay?"

"Fine," her dad answered.

"What was the deygon like?" Troy asked.

"Terrible," his dad answered. "Had to be two hundred feet long from nose to the end of its tail. And its wingspan was close to that too. It wasn't very fast. That was the only thing that saved us. We had almost three hundred angels on the attack and it still took over an hour to finally bring it down. I imagine nothing will grow in the field where it died for a long time. The ash heap was huge when the Justice Ministers poured holy water over it."

"Thank God y'all are okay," Troy's mom said with a tear leaking from her left eye.

"We'll be home in an hour or so," Paul said.

"We're not at home though," Angela replied.

"What?" Susan's voice snapped.

"I brought them to the Hill," Troy's mom said.

"Why?" Susan asked.

"Something didn't feel right at home. Troy and I both felt it."

Troy opened his mouth then closed it. What his mom said wasn't exactly true but he didn't think right now was a good time to point that out. Instead he gave a noncommittal nod.

"We can talk about it later," Troy's dad said cutting across another protest from Susan. "We'll be there in a little bit. Stay there and we'll go home together."

It took his dad, Grandma Denise, and Angela's parents over a half hour to make it through the gate at the Hill. Troy was happy to go since the oppressive silence of the normally boisterous Commons was more frightening than the shadows he'd seen on the streets outside his house.

"You guys take care," Butler said as he petted Enoch on the head. He'd returned with the other adults. A red scar, Troy had never seen before, ran down the black skin of his left forearm. "Troy, Angela, watch yourselves. We'll see you next summer. Troy, you going to stay on the Hunters?"

"For sure," Troy said with a smile before stepping into the wall of stone.

They streamed through the Cathedral in Mustang. His dad bypassed many questions from other angels who looked like they'd just returned from the fight with the deygon. In the entrance hall, Samson treated them to a short winded tale of his bravery in protecting the sacred grounds.

Ten minutes later they pulled into the driveway of their house. But the Tahoe froze in a squeak of tires. Troy reached at the sensation tugging towards his mind. Danger lurked from the eaves on the roof to the concrete in the foundation. But it wasn't an urgent, threatening danger. More of warning that death had been to visit and had passed unsuccessful.

"What's going on?" Troy asked. His eyes were moving brick by brick around the exterior of their suburban house.

"You feel it too?" his mom asked and turned to him.

"Something was here," he said with a nod. "Or someone."

His dad left the vehicle running as he swung open the door without a trace of fear at the unknown danger. His scepter glowed a soft light and spread over the whole house making a bubble in the darkness. The Spirit hummed and brought peace to everything within the glimmering radiance.

"There's nobody here now," his dad said leaning into the SUV. "Not that I can feel at least. Paul? Susan?"

"Brian, we're here," Paul's voice said from the scepter. "Has your house-"

"Yes," Troy's dad said. "We've had an intruder."

"We'll be right there," Susan said. "I think we should stay together tonight."

They all spent the rest of the night in the living room of Troy's house. He tried to sleep but kept waking at the adults constant pacing and peeking out of the windows. He knew someone had been in his house. The presence lingered in the air like a bad smell that had soaked into the carpet. Whoever it was hadn't stayed long and had tried to hide their visit, but parimus was screaming at Troy about a danger he'd managed to miss in the night.

He watched his mom stare out of a window for a long time. Finally, when the first rays of the sun were filtering into the room, sleep found him. The last thing to go through his mind was how lucky he was to have a mom who was strong and smart enough to save his life.

Chapter 16: Sacrificing Thanksgiving

Uproar was the only way to describe the next few weeks. The deygon battle dominated the air waves of the Angelic Agenda and the print pages of the Holy Herald. There were pictures and videos – which made Angela wince and look away every time they came on TV. Troy had to admit the monster was like nothing he'd ever seen before. Not even the fantasy movies he watched with Tyler compared to the sheer fright of the beast. The scales deflected most attacks from the angels and when it finally fell from the sky in a hellish roar, Troy thought it had to have made a 5.0 earthquake.

The Mustang Broncos football team ended the regular season 9-1 but lost in the second round of the playoffs to a dominant Jenks High School squad.

"Next year," Tyler said the weekend before Thanksgiving. They were lounging in his spacious bedroom and munching on chocolate chip cookies his mom had baked. Troy relished the calmness of the day but could feel the presence of four guardian angels in the immediate area outside. "We'll get them next year and the year after that," Tyler continued from his perch on his king sized bed. "They won't be able to beat us. Our juniors and sophomores are better than theirs. Nobody will be able to stop us from winning Mustang's first state championship."

"If there is a next year," Troy confessed. "For me and football at least."

"What do you mean?" Tyler guffawed. "You did awesome this year."

Troy shrugged and looked at Angela. "Our parents have talked about going into hiding again. A lot of the trouble starts with us so they think the trouble for you guys might die down a little bit if we left. The only reason Kyle is after you is because of me."

"That's stupid," Tyler griped with his hands flying into the air. "We can handle ourselves. They haven't been able to get us yet, right? I can't lose you as a receiver. I'll probably throw thirty touchdown passes to you next year. We had twelve this year in half the season!"

"Football isn't exactly as important as the other stuff going on in Troy and Angela's lives," Becky said simply. "People are dying, Tyler."

"I know," the quarterback returned nonchalantly.

"Even Troy's grandma is scared," Clark offered quietly from his corner where he was texting on his phone. "I overheard her talking to your parents this morning. She said she thought y'all going into hiding might be a good idea."

"Do you want to go into hiding, Angela?" Tyler asked.

"Not really," she said. "But everyone is worried another deygon might get raised. From how much power they said it takes, I don't see how that's possible though. My dad said Kyle probably had to recover for a week from the toll it took on his body."

"I didn't think anyone knew about that kind of stuff?" Becky gaped. Her ever present cross necklace was being massaged by her left hand.

"He's been doing a lot of studying," Angela countered defensively with a glare at the book in her hands.

She'd taken to carrying *Blackest of the Black* around with her and had been forcing herself to look at some of the most rare and dangerous demons known to angels. Troy had taken his turns at the book as well but found it more interesting than scary. Not that he'd ever want to meet any of the demons face to face, but he knew it might help him at some point in his life.

"Who are you texting?" Tyler cut into the conversation. He leaned over Clark and looked over his boulder-like shoulder.

"Just someone from church," Clark said shyly and put down the phone.

"Troy?" his mom's voice announced into the room making Becky and Angela jump in surprise. Clark looked relieved at the distraction and stowed his cell phone in his pocket.

Troy reached for his scepter as he remembered his mom was going to pick him up at 5:00 to go to the store with her. "Hey mom," he said.

"I'll be there in a minute," she said. "Be outside."

"Okay."

"How is everyone over there doing?" she asked as a general question to the group.

Everyone supplied short answers with their version of "good".

"Where are you going?" Tyler asked after Troy put his scepter back in the pouch against his ribs.

"Wal-Mart," Troy answered. "My parents have some people from out of town coming over for Thanksgiving."

"Could she still be listening to us through your scepter?" Tyler asked pointing at Troy's stomach.

Angela laughed and shook her head. "That's not how they work. The connection is only open when we acknowledge someone is calling us. We know when *a line* is open."

"That's good to know," Tyler said thoughtfully. "I was going to say it would be easy for the spy your parents are looking for to figure out what you're doing - if they can listen in on your conversations all the time. Plus, it wouldn't be cool if your parents had been listening to everything we say."

Troy chuckled as he got up and left the room with quick good-byes. He waved to the Henry's who were at the long, ornate table in a kitchen full of expensive appliances and decorations. Mr. Henry boomed a jovial farewell but Mrs. Henry barely acknowledged Troy's departure.

His mom drove them to the store and they shopped for twenty minutes. Two huge turkeys took up most of the space in the shopping cart.

"Who's coming over?" Troy asked as he examined the many Thanksgiving dinner ingredients.

"Just some people to help us try to identify if there is anyone suspicious hanging around the Cathedral here."

"How will they do that?" Troy said and snagged a box of his favorite cereal from the shelf.

"Kind of as a process of elimination," his mom answered. "See if they notice anyone they know and would be out of place. We've been doing it with a lot of people lately. They just happen to be coming on Thanksgiving so we thought it would be nice to spend the holiday with them."

"Do we know them?"

"I'm sure you've probably met them somewhere along the way," she said and turned down the aisle with pie crusts and filings.

Troy watched his mom's back and knew she wasn't telling him something. He reached for auditome but as soon as he did, a worried female voice filled his ears.

Basketball is going to cost $100 with fees and shoes. Thanksgiving, at least $60. Then what are we going to do? Christmas is right around the corner and we barely have the money for the mortgage.

Troy froze and closed his eyes. A different voice poured into his thoughts. This time a man's.

Tired of being broke. Two jobs and we still don't have the money to buy anything decent. If I don't eat lunches for the next few weeks, that will give us a little bit to spend on Christmas.

A vision, of a low thirties couple looking haggardly into each other's eyes over a couch taken up by a squirming toddler and a crying baby, swam in front of Troy. The man and woman smiled sadly at each other as a boy who looked about ten stomped into a tiny living room with a frown. His clothes were frayed and faded but he looked well fed and healthy.

"Am I ever going to get a DS or a Playstation or anything?" the boy asked. "All my friends have them. I don't have anything cool."

"Maybe for Christmas," the woman said with a soft but sad smile.

"Really?" the boy squealed. "Even if it's only a DS, that would be awesome. I can go to Danny's house and connect to the internet on it. That would be so cool!" He left the drabby living area with a bounce and a skip.

"What are we going to do?" the woman asked with a furtive look across the couch.

"I can skip lunches and we can cut back on… something," the man sighed.

"You skip lunches too often. And dinners lots of times too - on the nights you work at Lowes."

"I don't know," the man said with his right hand covering his mouth as if the words were painfully being exhumed. "If I can get that other job in January, it'll help a lot. That would be an extra $300 a month."

"Maybe I should look for another job too," she offered and picked up the baby girl who had started giggling at the rattle toy in her pudgy hands.

"We barely afford the daycare during the day. You'd have a tough time finding a job that would pay enough to cover a babysitter." He looked around the sparse room. Pictures of the kids hung on the wall. A tiny TV sat on a rickety, particle board stand. Brownish carpet was worn and rugged. "When we were younger... did you ever picture this as our lives?"

The woman took her turn glancing around the room. Then her eyes settled on the kids on the couch and towards the back of the small house where the boy was still cheering his possibility at getting a cheap Christmas gift. A true grin lifted on her lips. "There are definitely things I'd change," she said. "But, yes, I've got four things I dreamed of my whole life." She leaned across the laughing baby girl and the bouncing toddler; and kissed her husband.

Troy shook the vision from his head.

"Sad story, huh?" his mom asked. She had grabbed a few pie crusts and several cans of fruit filling; but her eyes were on him.

"Yeah," he answered as he thought about the family. He heard the baby girl coo from the next aisle. A small voice pestered for a box of sweet crackers, only to whine a second later when the box was snatched from his hands. Troy stepped around the end of the aisle and peered around the corner. The parents were fretting over an almost empty shopping cart. The mom finally plucked four generic cans of vegetables and wrote the price on a tiny piece of paper. Down the row, the ten year old boy was standing idly in a patched jacket.

Troy returned to his mom who had continued shopping. "Mom? If I borrow some money from you, could I pay you back with my allowance money when we get home?"

"What do you want to buy?"

"Nothing, really," he said with a shrug.

"How much have you saved?"

"A little over a hundred."

"I have a hundred dollar bill in my purse," she said and rummaged for a second before producing the bill. "You going to go buy a game or something?" A knowing and loving light was shining in her eyes. "All I have left to get is milk. I'll meet you up front by the checkout lines when you're done."

"Okay," he said as he took the money. For a minute, Troy shifted from one foot to another. He'd been saving the money for over six months and been planning to buy himself an iron shield he'd seen at Michael's Angel Fixings. But he knew some things were more important.

The family came into sight around the corner of the aisle where he was waiting. A deep breath lifted his nervous lungs as the dad's eyes landed on him and he offered a polite smile.

"For God, we fight," Troy whispered to himself and stepped forward shyly. "Excuse me."

"Can I help you?" the man asked.

"Yeah, I… just wanted," Troy said and stumbled on the words. He hoped the bill clutched tightly in his hands wasn't getting soaked with sweat. Both the man and the woman were now looking at him with nice smiles and upraised eyebrows. "My family's been fortunate," Troy continued and cleared his throat. "I… well, God knows how good you are." At this both of their faces scrunched slightly. "I'm not saying it right. God is watching you and he loves you." He stuck out the bill and placed it in the man's hand.

"What is this?" the man asked suspiciously. "I can't take this."

"Please do," Troy said and started to retreat.

"Why?" the woman asked.

"To help. You both sacrifice enough. The money isn't anything to me, and it would mean more to me to know that it helped you."

"Wait," the man called as Troy started walking away. "We don't…" But he stopped with a glance at his wife then his kids. "I can't take this from you. Please."

"Have a little bit of a merrier Christmas with it," Troy said. "And have faith. God loves you." He took a left from the aisle at almost a jog and the family disappeared. Troy caught a quiet, "Amen", from the woman as he raced around a couple of displays and slipped into the clothes section. An older couple scurried out of the way of his mad dash.

"How'd it go?" his mom asked a minute later when he found her in the checkout line.

"Good enough, I guess," Troy breathed. "I'm not very good at stuff like that."

His mom produced a radiant smile which took away the rest of the nervous jitters in Troy's stomach. "I'm sure you did fine," she said. "Getting strangers to take gifts can be difficult sometimes."

"That man and woman," Troy started and looked towards the grocery section of the store. "They sacrifice a lot for their kids. I never really thought about sacrifice like that before. All the stories you hear are of people saving someone's life or something heroic."

"Sacrifice comes in many forms," his mom said with a wistful look.

Troy nodded at her mysterious answer and knew it was all he was going to get. The robes had never strayed far from his mind but with everything going on lately, he'd been forgetting to worry and think about them as much. Add on the secretive ways angels always seemed to be granted the gift; and Troy had been hoping and praying he'd accidentally find himself with a wonderful set of the white robes. So far, it hadn't worked.

At noon on Thanksgiving Day, Troy found himself in his kitchen trying to sneak bites of the overly extravagant meal his mom was preparing. Tyler was by his side doing the same thing.

"We're having my grandparents over for dinner," Tyler said as he plopped a chunk of turkey into his mouth. "But I'm cool with two big meals in one day. Aren't Becky and Clark coming over for lunch too?"

"Yes," Troy's mom said. "I spoke with both their parents and they said they'd be happy to let them come over. Clark's dad is going to spend the day with a man from his church who has terminal cancer. Clark's going to get dropped off here after he gets done handing out food at the shelter. Becky should be here in a few minutes."

Troy's dad waltzed into the kitchen in a dress shirt and slacks. He looked overly dressed for the day's festivities but Troy knew he was going to pick up the mystery guests at the Cathedral in a few minutes.

"Troy, you sure you don't want to go?" his dad asked. "Tyler can wait in the car."

"Will I get to see the Cathedral then?" Tyler boomed.

"Uh, no. It will probably look like an empty field to you."

"Why not give me permission to see it?" Tyler requested with his best attempt at a charming, endearing smile.

"Special occasions only," Troy's dad chuckled and grabbed a sweet roll from a pan still hot from the oven.

"When are you going to have them look around the Cathedral?" Troy asked.

"They can start as soon as they get there," his dad said heavily around a bite of the soft bread. "I figure they'll stick around for a few days to try to find anyone suspicious. The Dark Hearts are getting information from someone; so it won't hurt to have an extra set of eyes and ears around."

"I still don't understand it," Tyler mused. "I thought the fallen angels looked different? Those Dark Heart people had those nasty wings and red halos and stuff. Couldn't you have everyone show their wings and halo before you let them into the Cathedral?"

Grandma Denise stepped into the kitchen at his question. "They're pawns of the great deceiver," she said with a characteristic uptick of her right eyebrow. Tyler fidgeted a little under her gaze. "Hiding and camouflaging themselves is something they're good at."

"Just call them all to that Dome place Troy talks about all the time then," Tyler said and didn't flinch from Grandma Denise's penetrating gaze. "Surely God wouldn't let a traitor in there."

"Doesn't really work that way," Troy's dad answered. "I wish it was that easy though. God wants to give fallen angels a chance to find their faith. If they tried to go through the gate to the Dome of Windows, they'd die. The archangels generally send... *requests* for meetings but it's never truly mandatory."

"They'd rather give the opportunity for a fallen angel to find his or her faith, then to send them to their death and eternity in hell. Whoever the spy is knows that and will find ways around it. A lot of angels don't show up for the meetings." With that, he grabbed his keys, kissed Troy's mom tenderly on the cheek, and left.

Clark and Becky both showed up fifteen minutes later. They stayed in Troy's room until they heard the garage door opening. As Troy stepped into the kitchen, he stopped in his tracks. A light conversation was happening in the garage. Pleasantries and welcome were spilling from Troy's dad and met by a gracious voice of thanks and praise. But that's not what had frozen Troy. He reached with the Spirit and his stomach twisted.

"What's wrong Troy?" Tyler said as he bumped into him. "You look like you've seen a ghost."

Troy searched and found his mom's eyes already on him. A sad shrug for an apology was all she offered.

"I found out who our guests are," Troy snarled.

"Who?" Becky asked.

Troy didn't answer but instead stomped through the kitchen and into the living room. His friends followed him and all turned to look at the door leading to the garage with him. A few seconds later, Troy's dad entered followed by a tall man with wavy blonde hair. After the man was a petite and sleek woman who was as pretty as any famous actress in Hollywood.

And following in her wake was Adam Taylor.

A smug little grin lifted the corner of his lips as he looked around the kitchen and found Troy watching him.

"Is that-" Tyler whispered furiously.

"Yes," Troy answered the unfinished question. His hands clenched and he physically held his feet in place rather than storming across the room to punch the arrogant boy.

Adam's robes and sword were glittering in the overhead lights of the kitchen. Both seemed to exude the same baseless pomp as their owner.

Troy sidestepped out of view and grabbed his scepter. "Angela," he hissed.

It took a few seconds but she finally answered in a hushed voice. "Yeah?"

"Did you know Adam and his family were the people coming to try to find the spy at the Cathedral?"

"Not until this morning," she relented in a soft tone. "I know I should have told you but I didn't want you to yell at me."

"Why would I yell at you?"

"You always yell at everyone when Adam's around," she said and Troy could picture her wincing. He remembered her advice from the summer. *Be a better angel than him...*

"You coming over?" he asked.

"Yep, we'll be heading that way in a minute." "See you," he said to Angela and looked at his friend with a heavy sigh. "Come on."

"Troy," his mom said softly. "These are the Taylor's. You know Adam already."

Troy clenched his jaw and produced a tight smile at the tall man who stepped forward and offered his right hand cheerfully.

"Nice to meet you Troy," Mr. Taylor said. He had the same perfectly white teeth as his son but there was an honest *niceness* to his whole demeanor. "Adam has talked about you a little bit before. Mainly that you're on the Hunters together."

"Oklahoma doesn't cross my mind real often," Adam scorched nonchalantly.

"It will be nice to have some time with your friends from the Hill, Adam" Mrs. Taylor said and shook Troy's hand then all his friends. "Looks like Troy has a lot of friends of his own for you to talk with."

Adam gave Troy a blistering smile but it transformed instantly when his mom looked hopefully in his direction.

"Why don't all of you go back to Troy's room," Grandma Denise said with a mischievous glow on her wrinkled face.

"Uh, okay," Troy grumbled giving her a sideways look, that could have started a fire if it had been directed at a dry patch of grass, as he passed.

Troy settled onto his bed uneasily with Tyler sitting on his right and Becky to his left. Clark took up position in the rollie chair at the desk.

"Oklahoma hasn't been too impressive so far, Decker" Adam sneered. "You have Samson as your greeter at the Cathedral… Is he really even considered much of a hero?"

"Who do you have at yours?" Tyler spat which made Troy smile since he'd been meaning to ask the same question in the exact same infliction.

"John the Baptist," Adam answered looking around Troy's room. His eyes settled on the poster of John Bradford - Troy's only non-angel hero - stuck in a football throwing motion over the bed.

"I guess with so many non-angels hanging around, you aren't allowed to have anything cool showing. Of course, in your case – that doesn't seem to mean a whole lot. You've probably told everyone about us in this dusty little town anyway, haven't you?"

"What is wrong with you?" Becky said before any of the boys could yell at Adam.

"Nothing's wrong with me other than being stuck in Oklahoma," Adam chided. "I didn't tell any of my friends in California I was coming here. They think I'm out on another demon hunt with my dad. He's the one who brought the deygon down in the end. He's kind of famous."

"There were over 300 angels on the attack," Troy corrected. "I've seen the videos of when it was finally killed. There's no way anyone would know who actually killed it."

"They all did," Angela said calmly as she walked into the room behind Adam. "And your mom said that everything's ready, Troy."

The way she looked at Adam made him stop the tirade he'd been ready to deliver.

All the kids settled into chairs in the kitchen a minute later. Troy's dad said a long, powerful prayer followed by his mom whisking dishes, of every type of Troy's favorite Thanksgiving food, onto the table. The adults made plates and took them to the living room to watch the Angelic Agenda.

"We'll turn it over to football in a little bit," Troy's dad winked at him, Clark and Tyler.

The meal went as well as can be expected. Adam mainly glowered and ate his food. He kept peeking into the living room and gritting his teeth when his mom raised her eyebrows in his direction.

"Do your parents think they'll find anyone suspicious at the Cathedral?" Angela said after everyone had finished their plates. Clark and Tyler had mostly decimated one of the apple pies already too.

"Who knows," Adam said briskly. "We wouldn't have even been here if the Decker's hadn't called for help."

"My parents have called a lot of people in," Troy said. "We have a spy here." He made sure to say *spy* in a way to let Adam know he didn't trust him or his parents. The reidlos attack from last year still left a bad taste in Troy's mouth. To him, it was a certainty that the Taylors had set the whole thing up to draw away Troy and Angela's parents so Kyle could swoop in for the kill.

Soon, the adults had finished eating and talking. Adam's parents left with Troy's dad. He spent the rest of the afternoon watching football from the couch with Tyler and Angela. Adam didn't say a word until his parents returned at 6:00pm.

"We'll make our rounds the next few days," Mr. Taylor assured as he shook Paul's hand. "If we see anything, we'll let you know."

"Thanks again," Susan called as the couple and their son left with Troy's dad.

"What do you think?" Troy's mom asked a couple of minutes later.

"I'm pretty sure they're telling the truth," Paul said. "I was keeping a close eye on them with auditome all day. I don't think they saw anything out of the ordinary. Joe said he didn't see anyone he recognized… and I believe him."

"I do too," Susan said with a resigned sigh.

"Maybe the spy wasn't at the Cathedral today," Angela jumped in.

But when Adam and his parents took their leave on Sunday, they'd been unsuccessful in spotting anyone, or anything, suspicious.

"I don't believe them," Troy said grumpily to Angela. All the friends had left for home a few minutes before, but as was usually the case these days, Angela stayed at his house with her parents until well into the evening.

"Do what?" she asked with a rapid blink. *Justice and the Spirit* was in her hands but Troy didn't think she'd been reading it. She hadn't turned page 75, on the fedisome ability, in five minutes.

"I'm not sure if Adam's parents are telling the truth," Troy repeated his assertive thought.

"I doubt they could get away with lying to both your parents and my parents."

"There are ways to block fedisome," Troy said motioning to the book with his head. "Some people are really good at covering their lies, especially fallen angels."

"I know. But your dad and my dad were constantly watching them. It's not easy to do it for long periods of time."

"Aren't you worried a little bit about their involvement in that reidlos attack last year?"

She shrugged and closed the book. "Sorry. I've just had… other stuff on my mind."

"Other than a fallen angel spy and a deygon?" Troy laughed but kept a wary eye on her.

"No, I guess not. It's stupid stuff really… you know, I'm… worried about our parents and everything."

"A lot of the trouble goes back to the spy though," Troy said hoping to entice more out of Angela.

"Oh, yeah, I know," she said and shook her head a little as if clearing a distracting thought.

"You okay?"

"Tired," she sighed. "I'm gonna go see if my parents are ready to go home. See ya tomorrow."

"See ya," Troy waved but didn't follow. He watched the door where she'd left for a long time after her departure. Something was definitely wrong with her. It had been ever since she'd gotten her robes. Troy had totally given up on asking her about them but seldom did the mystery leave his mind for longer than a couple of hours.

He resigned himself to *Sacrifice: What Will You Give Up?* for the rest of the evening. Almost all the stories were about angels saving their friends in one fight or another. Troy was beginning to think he'd have more luck trying to sacrifice like the parents he'd met at Wal-Mart. Give up small things for the betterment of family and friends. What those things were, he had no idea.

Chapter 17: No Success

"So when are you going to ask her?" Tyler asked a week after Thanksgiving break.

"Do what?" Troy said as they sat in the field house after a particularly grueling weight room session.

"Angela," Tyler barked with a laugh. "That winter dance thing they're having at the Community Center. We talked about it yesterday. Any of that ring a bell?"

"It won't help," Troy breathed heavily and looked around to make sure none of the other players were in earshot. "She's been a lot more distant since she got her robes. She'd probably barely even register what I said."

Tyler nodded as Clark approached. "I've noticed that too. She still hasn't said anything to you about why she got them?"

"I'm not sure if she knows," Clark said pushing his way into the conversation. "She got them in the middle of that fight, maybe she's not sure what she sacrificed."

Troy pondered Clark's words for a while. Could he be right? Is that why so many angels were mysterious about discussing the reasons for being granted the robes? The more Troy thought about it, the more he doubted. The feeling he'd had when his scepter landed in his hands was one of the most remarkable things he could remember. He'd known that God had touched his life closer than ever before. And he knew instantly and exactly why the scepter had been granted.

"I think she knows," Troy informed.

"Either way," Tyler smiled. "You need to ask her. I'm serious. You two will make a perfect match. You're both angels. You both worry about everything. Both your parents worry about everything. It's a match made in heaven… almost literally."

Troy and Clark both chuckled at Tyler's comments. "I'll think about," Troy said honestly.

"Just do it," Tyler ended in a very macho, commanding voice.

Troy's mom picked them up a few minutes later. So far, the colder weather of the approaching winter had stayed out of Oklahoma. Troy could hear Moses railing about the unseasonal heat being due to deygons and reidlos and untold masses of nylla demons.

They went to Troy's room when they got home and were met by Angela and Becky a few minutes later.

"Do it," Tyler whispered and nudged Troy with his foot. "Hey Becky, could you help me with a history question?"

Becky's face scrunched in bewilderment. "I guess," she answered tentatively. "But you're a lot better at history than I am."

"I can't find in the text book where it says anything about prohibition," Tyler informed. "And I figured you'd be better at finding something on that subject than I would."

"Whatever," Becky rolled her eyes.

"Come on," Tyler said bossily and helped her to her feet. "I left my bag in the kitchen." He shook his head at Clark motioning out of the room.

"Oh yeah," Clark cleared his throat awkwardly. "I need help on that question too."

Troy almost laughed - but the idea of asking Angela to a school sponsored dance stopped much mirth from building.

She didn't seem to notice that Tyler had cleared the room on purpose. She was concentrating on a biological table with the eraser of a pencil pressing softly against the tip of her perfectly pointy nose.

"Angela," Troy said in his bravest voice. She took a second to look up at him when he didn't continue.

"Yeah?"

"There's a winter dance at the Community Center next week," Troy said and was glad not to hear any quivering in the words. He grabbed his knees to stop his hands from shaking nervously. "I was wondering if you'd want to go with me? Tyler, Becky, and Clark are all going."

"Do they have people they are going with?" she asked quickly. Troy figured she was stalling to try to find an easy way to come up with a negative response.

"Tyler and Becky don't really – from what they've said. Tyler, at least. Clark said he invited a girl from his church."

"Would everyone want to go as a group again?" Angela questioned. Troy's stomach began its drop at her words. "Like we did for the homecoming game?"

"That would kind of be okay," he offered and whispered a short prayer under his breath. "But it's also one of those dances where you're supposed to go with a... date."

Troy thought her face fell a fraction. He automatically wanted to reach for auditome but resisted the urge. It didn't feel right to delve into people's private thoughts in many circumstances; and this was a good example of a time when privacy was important. Even if he wanted to know her answer more than anything else in the world.

"Yeah, I mean – if that's how it's supposed to be. I'll go with you."

Troy forced his mouth closed and tried to stop the humungous smile that he knew was erupting across his face. He was worried the smile might stretch his cheeks far enough to make his mouth split straight in two down the middle.

"Okay," he croaked. "Uh, thanks."

At that she chortled and shook her head. "We're best friends. You don't have to thank me for going to a dance with you."

"I know," he laughed and felt his whole face reddening. "I've just wanted to ask you to something like this for a long time."

"Cool," she smiled. "So what am I supposed to wear?"

"Whatever," he said. "You won't look bad in anything. I mean, you know, you'll look… anything will look good."

She giggled a little and her hair danced at the movement. "What are you going to wear?" she asked.

"Probably a suit or something. I have a nice blue one."

"I'll wear a blue dress then." At that, she dove back into her Biology homework leaving Troy breathless and totally relieved.

He waited a minute then nearly ran to the kitchen. In his excitement he bounced off the cherry wood door frame with a wince.

"Are you okay?" Becky asked looking up from a thick history textbook.

"Yeah," Troy said breathlessly. He nodded at Tyler who gave him a happy thumbs up.

"How could you not find this?" Becky quipped moving her gaze to Tyler and Clark. "It was labeled 'Prohibition' in the index."

"Not sure," Tyler chortled. "Guess I was being stupid today."

"Today?" Becky suggested raising her eyebrows with a playful smile. "I'm pretty sure it's been more than today. I could remind you of several times – without thinking about it too much - where you didn't make the best decisions."

"Whatever," Tyler laughed. "Thanks for the help, anyway. Also… there's that winter dance next week at the Community Center. Clark said he's already got a date. And Troy and Angela are going together, want to go with me? Purely as friends, of course. We'll keep our dancing options open."

Becky's eyes had flown to Troy when Tyler made the announcement about him and Angela going together. "That's fine, I guess," she said carefully. "When did you ask Angela?"

"Just a minute ago," Troy boomed joyfully.

"Cool," she said lingering on the word. "If you guys don't need any more help, I'm going to get back to my other homework." She hopped out of the kitchen chair and sped around Troy and down the hall.

"Told you she'd say yes," Tyler cheered and gave Troy a congratulatory punch on the arm. He then turned to Clark. "Who are you taking again?"

"You've met her before," Clark mumbled with his eyes shifting around the room. "At my church. Aleesha."

"Ah, I remember her," Tyler nodded. "Kind of short? Talked about basketball a lot?"

"Yeah, that's her," Clark offered with a small smile.

"You're going to look like Goliath next to her," Tyler quipped.

The Saturday of the dance came as quickly as anything Troy remembered.

He had a nagging sense of dread in the pit of his stomach he couldn't shake. The nerves were worse then he'd felt going into the second round playoff game against Jenks. And they'd ended their football season in that game; so having the same sensation of his impending date with Angela was worrisome to Troy.

"Dude, you're sweating worse than I've ever seen," Tyler admonished as they straightened their ties in the bathroom mirror. "What's going on?"

"Just nervous," Troy relented and looked at himself for the thousandth time. His short, blonde hair was sticking up at an odd angle on the left side of his head. He wetted his hand and smeared the water over the offending cow lick. It ended up sticking out worse.

"You look fine," Tyler huffed. "Let's go. They're all waiting on us."

They made their way through Troy's room and to the living room. Angela was standing by the couch looking as stunning as Troy ever remembered. The blue dress she had on hugged her frame from shoulder to calf. She had a touch more make-up on then usual and would have fit right in at any supermodel convention.

"Don't you two clean up nice," Troy's mom purred from the kitchen entryway. "Almost as good as Clark." She turned and ushered their tall friend into the living area. He was wearing a streamlined three piece suit with a wonderfully red vest. Beside him was a petite black girl in a dress that matched his vest exactly. Her smile lit the room as she looked around.

"Thank you for having me over," she said graciously to Troy's parents. "Clark has talked so much about all of you."

At that Angela and Troy glanced at each other with a secretive smile. Troy had constantly warned his non-angel friends they weren't allowed to mention their secrets.

And he was 100% sure none of them had. Aleesha probably didn't know a tenth of as much as Clark would have liked to tell her.

"You ready to get going?" Troy's dad asked without so much as a trace of a smile.

"I'm sure they are," Grandma Denise clapped; then gave her son a small shooing wave. "And they'll be fine. Let them have some fun."

"I hope so," he mused. "There are a lot of... *resources* being used for a night out on the town."

Troy's mom sighed and nodded. "Brian, we have to let them have some fun," she conceded softly.

"Would you have agreed if you and mom weren't going to be there as chaperones?" Troy's dad questioned cryptically. "Not to mention all the others..."

His mom shrugged and turned to the anxious kids with a brilliant smile. All of them instantly grinned back at the radiance in the gift. "You guys ready?" she asked. When each nodded, she guided them to the garage. Tyler, Becky, Clark, and Aleesha found seats in the awaiting Tahoe. Troy and Angela sat together in the back seat of Grandma Denise's Cadillac.

"I expect a tip," she chided when she got behind the steering wheel. They made the short drive mostly with small talk about Clark and his date. Troy did his best not to stare at Angela but caught himself nearly drooling a couple of times. He wished he could use Raphael's shepadia ability to calm himself.

"Have fun," his mom called from the north set of doorways into the Community Center a few minutes later. They were ushered past the game room filled with air hockey and ping pong tables. The basketball gym had been transformed into a startling white montage of winter themes. Gone were the basketballs which normally bounced off the rubbery floor. The goals themselves were pushed high up against the tall ceiling.

Altogether, it looked barely recognizable. The floor was covered with tables and chairs; except for a huge square at the far end where a make-shift wooden dance floor had been erected. A DJ booth was taking up most of the west wall where friends and family were usually to be found watching the adult basketball league games held in the gym on week nights.

Tyler found them an empty table and they all sat.

"This is great," Aleesha said loudly over the droning music of an 80's hit song.

Nobody was on the dance floor yet. Only half the tables had anyone taking up the seats. Blake waved merrily at Troy when their eyes met. On his arm was a pretty girl Troy knew was on the cheerleading squad, though he'd never talked with her in person.

Almost everyone that walked by called out to Tyler. He returned each with a gracious nod or wave or shout of "hey".

"You want any punch or anything?" Troy asked leaning near Angela's ear to be heard over the two-stepping country song now playing.

"Yeah, that sounds good," she returned with her eyes on the dance floor where several couples were spinning and gliding.

"Anyone else?" Troy asked as he stood.

"I'll go," Tyler said.

"Me too," Clark added and let go of Aleesha's hand then made his way nimbly around a group of girls who were blushing behind Tyler.

"So what do you think my chances are Melanie Thompson will say yes if I ask her to dance?" Tyler questioned as they retrieved plastic cups of punch.

The beverage was being doled out by a steadfast Peter. The angel hardly responded when Troy thanked him.

He hoped he'd been able to convey the *thanks* was meant for way more than the punch, but he thought there was too much alert attention on the angel's face to register his meaning.

"She's a senior," Tyler continued. "But I know she knows I was the quarterback the second half of the season."

"I doubt any girl would say no to you," Clark said as he took a sip of the sweet drink.

"You and Aleesha going to dance?" Tyler asked.

"Sure," Clark smiled shyly. "She's a really good dancer. And singer. She's going to Washington D.C. in March for a singing competition with the church choir. The winners get to sing at the White House for the President."

"That'd be awesome," Troy said and followed Clark through a throng of new arrivals. "What all have you told her about us?"

"Just that you're my best friends," Clark returned knowingly. "It would be really cool to tell her about you and Angela being angels, but I know it's not allowed. Her faith is strong… if anything ever happens in front of her, I'm sure she'll see it. Like me and Becky kind of did when that selvo demon attacked us the first time."

"Let's hope she never has to see anything," Troy laughed.

"Here," Tyler said hurriedly and pushed the glass of punch in his left hand in front of Becky. The music had changed to an upbeat pop song. "I'm gonna go ask Melanie to dance."

"That was kind of rude," Aleesha admonished as he cut through the crowd towards a gaggle of starkly blonde girls.

"Don't worry about it," Becky said rolling her eyes. "We went out for a long time, but we're both over each other. I'm happy to be his friend still."

Troy handed Angela her glass and noticed her looking rather glum. "You okay?" he asked.

"What?" she shook her head. "Oh yeah, trying to make sure to keep a feel for anything dangerous... or suspicious. Lots of people and everything. You never know."

Troy pushed out with the Spirit and searched for any signs of trouble. Nothing echoed at him through the divine power. "I don't feel anything at all," he said.

"Me neither," Angela replied with a small shrug. "I just don't want to be caught by surprise this time."

For the next hour, Troy sat between Angela and Becky. Clark and Aleesha danced together several times and always returned laughing and out of breath. Tyler made frequent visits to the dance floor with several different girls and only returned to their table a couple of times to get a quick drink.

A slow song with a deep voiced lead singer started from the speakers. Troy glanced sideways at Angela who hadn't said much of anything. "You want to dance?" he asked tentatively.

It took her a moment with her eyes blinking rapidly before she smiled. "Sure."

Troy took her hand and led her onto the packed dance floor. His hands went behind her lower back and hers wrapped over his shoulders and around his head. An electric charge surged through his body at her touch.

"Having fun?" Troy asked with his face almost as close as it had ever been to hers. The only other times were when she'd been granted her scepter and the quick peck on the cheek she'd given him at the Hill.

"Yeah... lots," she answered. Over her right shoulder, Tyler was giving Troy a huge, double thumbs up as he treaded across the floor with Melanie Thompson.

"You feeling okay?" Troy said.

320

"Yeah, keeping my concentration up," she sniffed. Troy didn't need fedisome to feel a lie. He thought again of using auditome but dismissed it at once. If she wanted to tell him what was bothering her, she would. He had to assume she had the same nerves as him. Being around each other as "a couple" for the first time was enough to make his knees wobbly. Plus, the constant fear of Kyle doing something to ruin the good time they were having never pushed too far away from his immediate thoughts.

"My mom and Grandma Denise will let us know if anything happens," Troy suggested. "It would be nice to have one night where we don't worry about all the crazy stuff happening."

"It would be," she said with a tiny smile. "Have you had any more ideas on getting your robes?"

He shook his head and brushed away the negative thoughts that instantly formed whenever he thought about his next gift from God. "I figure God will present the sacrifice when it's available," he reflected.

"That is how it seems to happen with the gifts," she mused. "All the planning and pushing our parents do, doesn't help much."

"That's for sure," Troy chuckled as he guided them around a senior couple who were making out ferociously in the middle of the dance floor. Angela spotted them as well and her eyes went wide in embarrassment. "Don't worry," Troy reeled off. "I don't plan on trying to eat your face anytime soon."

She giggled at that and the first true smile of the evening spread across her face. "You think we'll ever be able to come to something like this and enjoy it?" she wondered openly. Troy wasn't sure if she'd asked the question to him or more thought it out loud to herself.

"Yes," he said. Their eyes met and Troy wanted desperately to lean forward and plant a quick kiss on her lips. But she tucked her chin and watched their feet for the rest of the slow song.

They left the dance floor and were met by Becky. "Troy, you want to dance?"

"Uh, sure," he said with a look at Angela. She grinned and motioned with her head towards the dance floor. The music transitioned to another fast paced popular pop song. Becky hooted in glee and dragged Troy onto the floor where Clark and Aleesha were already dancing frantically. With a quick look backward, he caught Angela sitting by herself at the table.

"Come on Troy," Clark hollered. "I know you can dance better than that!"

Troy laughed and turned his concentration to his new dancing partner. He could only shake his head in wonder at Becky's cat-like grace as she swayed from side to side. If she'd been born an angel, she probably would have been as dangerously sly as the girl from the Wall.

The whole song was met with laughter as students all around gyrated and spun. Troy and Becky pointed out the best and by the end of the song, he was sorry to hear it be replaced by a line dance number.

"I don't know it," Becky twittered when Troy tried to get her to stay on the dance floor.

"I don't either," he laughed then allowed himself to be pulled towards their table.

Tyler was sitting beside Angela. He looked out of breath and excited. Angela's face reflected the same glum look as it had most of the evening.

Troy sat and watched her for a while. As the line dance ended and another slow song started, he made ready to ask her to dance again. But a hand on his shoulder stopped him.

"We have to go," his mom said right into his ear. She was close enough for her breath to tickle his hair.

"What's wrong?" he asked as he turned and saw Grandma Denise and Peter standing protectively behind his mom.

"They think they found the spy," his mom whispered and yanked him to his feet.

Angela was up in an instant as well. She grabbed Tyler's hand then Clark's.

"What's up?" Aleesha questioned curiously.

"Nothing," Troy said and tried to produce a smile. "My mom's job is calling her in and she has to go." He reached for the Spirit and calmed any further questions with the smallest touch on her petite shoulder.

"Oh, okay," Aleesha agreed happily. Troy's mom pointed to the doors and they left.

"It was a really fun night," Becky said as they practically jogged across the parking lot.

Troy and Angela piled once again into the back of the Cadillac. Grandma Denise slammed her door then the gas. "Who's the spy?" Troy asked after they were on Mustang Road in a squeal of tires.

"I don't want to say," Grandma Denise said and glanced into the rear view mirror at him. Troy prodded with the Spirit and caught a quick conversation between his grandma and his dad through her scepter. The vision banged close like he'd ran into a brick wall an instant later. "Getting better," she chided but with a smile. "Still too invasive though. I felt it when you tried to dig deeper."

"I couldn't understand what you were saying," Troy cleared his throat. "Sorry."

"Don't be," she said. "I like that you're using your angel abilities more often now. But if you get caught using auditome too much… some people may become wary of you. So use it sparingly… I think being on the Hunters did you some good."

"Maybe so," Troy grinned.

When they got home, they were unceremoniously ushered into Troy's room. Aleesha looked as though she wanted to ask questions but Troy calmed her once again with shepadia.

Five minutes later, his dad entered the room in a hurry. "Grandma Denise is going to stay with you guys," he informed and glanced at Aleesha. "We have to see what's… going on."

"We'll be fine by ourselves," Aleesha assured proudly. "I stay at home alone all the time. My mom has a second job at night and my dad goes up to help Clark's dad at the church."

"Don't leave the house," Susan instructed from the hallway. The adults stormed from the house after her words.

"Whoah," Aleesha chuckled. "Your parents are intense."

"They get that way sometimes," Becky said in quick reply. "But they really are awesome once you get to know them."

"I'm supposed to call my dad when I'm ready to get picked up," Aleesha said. "He's going to meet us at your house Clark. You want to go over there and wait for him?"

Clark's large brown eyes met each of his friend's. "I'd like to," he shuffled and licked his lips. "But Troy's dad told us to stay here."

"Isn't your dad supposed to be home in like thirty minutes anyway?"

This time it was Angela who called on the Spirit's calming nature. The smiling black girl instantly relaxed as she leaned against Clark's gigantic frame where he was sitting on the bed.

"Thanks," he whispered in relief out of the side of his mouth to Angela.

"So… did everyone have fun?" Tyler asked.

"We know you did," Becky complained. "How many different girls did you dance with?"

"Hey," he said putting on his best victimized face. "I know we went together, but I thought it was with the understanding that it was only as friends."

"I don't care that you didn't dance with me," Becky warned truthfully. "But a good Christian guy wouldn't be dancing with ten different girls. You probably hurt all their feelings."

"Whatever," Tyler huffed. "I'm on the lookout for a new girlfriend. Someone of my stature can't stay single for long." He winked at his former girlfriend. "You had your shot, but we both know… we just weren't meant for each other."

"I'm gonna go check to see if your grandma has heard anything," Angela said abruptly before Becky could supply a thunderous response.

"I'll go with you," Troy said.

Angela looked taken aback for a brief second but then nodded and left the room.

"Figured you two would get away from the others so we could have some *angel* talk," Grandma Denise said with a wrinkled grin when they walked into the living room. She was staring out of a window and the Spirit was wrapped around her in a subtle glow. Troy reached as well and let the energy submerse him. It spread and made a bubble of awareness all around the house. No danger lurked in their immediate vicinity.

"I don't feel any danger anywhere close," he said.

"Me neither," Grandma Denise announced and left the window. "But Lucifer's agents can be tricky."

They spent the next half hour in silence. Troy was reaching as far as he could with the Spirit in search of dangers in the dark. He knew Angela and Grandma Denise were doing the same. His grandma never stopped pacing the richly carpeted floor. Troy was sitting on the love seat with Angela. He thought of taking her hand in his but didn't want to break the concentrated look on her pretty face.

Finally, all three of their scepters glowed at the same time.

"We're heading home," Paul said.

"Did you find him?" Angela asked quickly.

"We found who was reported to be the spy," Troy's dad griped. "But he's dead."

Troy and Angela looked at each other in surprise.

"Dead?" Grandma Denise asked searchingly.

"We'll talk about it when we get there," Susan said.

"Kyle beat us to him," Troy's mom added and brought silence to the room.

Another angel lost in the War for Sins. Troy closed his eyes and prayed for an end to the madness. He knew God would hear his pleas, but he also knew it was up to him and the other angels to stop Kyle and his Dark Hearts. He grabbed Angela's hand and relished the squeeze she gave in return.

Chapter 18: Cold Winds Coming

The death of the suspected spy only worsened the paranoia blaring from the Angelic Agenda each morning, noon, and night. Cathedrals all around the world were searching for any suspicious activity.

"It's never going to work like that," Troy's dad griped as they sat watching the 6:00 evening addition of the news. Winter was only a few days away and Christmas break was upon them. The students at Mustang High School had all sat through end of the semester tests a couple of days before. Troy was confident his streak of A's would continue.

"They don't know what else to do," his mom countered. "The fallen are too good at disguising themselves. Kyle isn't letting them make any mistakes."

"The only people that have been able stop any of his plans so far are Troy and his friends," Grandma Denise bragged. "Maybe we should let them deal with it so we can put an end to the madness."

Troy laughed and shook his head. "No thanks," he called from the couch where he was sharpening his dagger.

"We don't even know if Joshua was a fallen angel," Troy's dad said in reference to the man they found dead in his house on the night of the winter dance. "By the time we got there all his angel gifts had faded."

"Why not just go to the Dome of Windows and look for him in heaven?" Troy suggested absently.

A long sigh left his mom's mouth. "I wish it was that easy," she answered. "It doesn't work that way."

"It would be nice if God would help us out every now and then," Troy griped.

"Faith," his dad's voice cut in a growl. "I thought you'd figured that out. You call on the Spirit to help you every day but you question God?"

Troy kept his eyes down and didn't dare look up. He didn't need parimus to know he was bordering on a dangerous line with his dad. But wasn't he right? Where was the help from the archangels? Innocent people were getting killed every day. The Dark Hearts were gaining power and causing havoc. His robes remained resolutely in God's hands in heaven. How much did he and the other angels need to prove their faith?

"Why don't we try to call everyone to the Cathedrals then force them to make a choice to go through the gate to the Dome?" Grandma Denise said into the quiet following Troy's dad. "The fallen won't be able to do it."

"Gabriel and Michael would never agree to it," Troy's mom said.

"Sometimes, I'm not sure if this warrior mentality they have is the best approach," Grandma Denise reeled off. Her jaw set at a glare from Troy's dad. "Don't you try to give me a look. I'm the one who taught you how to do it." She paused for a few seconds until her son looked away. "Raphael, Seraphim, and Uriel constantly preach the importance of controlling the fallen and their demons. But they know that to do that, we might have to use some of the same tricks as Lucifer. Tricking them into coming to a meeting at the Cathedral and trying to force them to make a choice of going to the Dome, isn't bad in my books."

"A sin is a sin," Troy's dad hesitated on the words.

"And we all sin," Troy's mom conceded. "So why would it be different in this case?"

"Go ask Gabriel and Michael." Troy's dad left the window he'd been staring out of for the last minute.

On the way out of the room, he grabbed the golden shield – as well as a long bow and quiver of arrows - he'd been carrying most of the time lately. "I'm going out to do some scouting," he offered and barged out the front door without further comment.

Troy's mom watched the front entryway for a couple of minutes without saying a word. Finally, she shook her head with a frustrated frown. "Maybe Christmas will bring answers."

"A celebration of the Son's birth," Grandma Denise mused. "He who made the greatest sacrifice. It can't hurt."

They both left the room. Troy grinded a sharpening stone across the almost perfectly sharp dagger for another half hour. No matter how hard he tried, doubts and uncertainties blared in his head like they were one of the hellish horns of the fallen angels.

A knock on the front door brought him from the terrible memories of the fight with the Dark Hearts. He opened it to find Tyler and Clark.

"Hey," Tyler said and walked in without hesitation. He went to the kitchen and began making himself a sandwich. "The girls are over at Angela's house watching a chick flick. What are you up to today?"

"Nothing much really," Troy said and slammed the door hoping it would help ease the depressing fears yelling for his attention.

"Clark and I were just talking about Christmas presents," Tyler informed. He plopped down at the table with a stacked turkey sandwich. "You going to get Angela anything?"

"I hadn't planned on it," Troy confessed. "We've never gotten each other stuff for Christmas. Only birthdays."

"I used to get Becky stuff," Tyler said in a garble of spit and small chunks of bread. He wiped away the rest of the sandwich residue with the back of his hand. "I figured since you and Angela were kind of going out now, you might get her something."

"We're not going out," Troy withered. "She went straight back to being quiet and distant after the dance. You've been around her as much as I have, you know how she's been."

"Maybe some flowers or something would cheer her up?" Clark suggested.

"Flowers? For Christmas?" Tyler chortled. "Is that what you're getting Aleesha?"

Clark shuffled his huge feet and his mouth worked for a long time before he answered. "No, I had my dad get her one of those really nice study bibles."

Tyler raised his eyebrows in mock surprise. "Would have never guessed you'd get something like that."

"I think it's a great gift," Troy assured at which Clark smiled in appreciation. "I wouldn't have a clue where to start with Angela," he continued as he pondered the idea. "Maybe something from one of the shops in the Cathedral. She got me a wooden Gabriel statue for my birthday. She's more of a follower of Raphael… maybe I could get something like that?"

"That'd probably work," Tyler said and took his empty plate to the kitchen sink. "What are your plans with your family for Christmas."

"Staying at home," Troy breathed then watched his best friend. "But my parents have talked about taking a trip right after."

"Where?" Tyler asked while he pulled a Gatorade from the refrigerator. He tossed one to both Troy and Clark.

"Not sure," Troy answered. "I don't think they know."

"How long will you be gone?" Clark said with a knowing look on his dark face.

"I don't know," Troy answered truthfully.

"Y'all aren't planning on running away, are you?" Tyler questioned roughly.

"I think they're really starting to think that going into hiding might be the best option," Troy conceded. "For us and for you. They're really worried you're going to get attacked because of me. We all know Kyle is after all of us. And it seems like he wants to make it a point that I witness anything he does… so they think getting away for a while might help calm down the danger you guys are in."

"Whatever," Tyler spat. "I may not be as smart as your parents, but even I can see Kyle won't leave us along because y'all ran off. He'll probably kidnap us and torture us until he finds you, then cut our heads off in front of you."

Troy wanted to yell his friend down for suggesting such a horrid possibility but he couldn't deny the same worries didn't crawl through his mind several times a day. "I wanted to try to take you with us," he admitted. "But even with angel abilities, my parents don't think they could convince your parents of doing something so drastic – without them knowing the truth."

"My mom would definitely never agree to that," Tyler said. "She thinks your parents are whacky." Troy chuckled involuntarily at the statement and Tyler continued. "I bet I could talk them into going wherever you go, though. Both of them have been complaining lately that we haven't had a cool vacation in a long time. Make it somewhere exotic and my mom will say yes for sure."

"I'll mention it to my parents," Troy laughed. They sat in pondering silence for the next minute.

"You want to go out for a bike ride or something?" Clark finally asked. "It's really nice outside."

"Crazy that we're still wearing shorts in December," Tyler added.

"Demons," Troy said and bounced his eyebrows nonchalantly.

"Let's go watch the movie with the girls," Tyler said after Troy's pronouncement.

"That was your plan all along, wasn't it?" Clark harrumphed. Tyler couldn't hide the guilty expression on his face fast enough and Troy laughed all the way to Angela's house.

"I know it's still a few days until Christmas," Troy said. "But I wanted to give you this." He handed Angela a sloppily wrapped box with a huge red and green bow. They were at his house waiting for the rest of the group to arrive. Angela had been dropped off by her parents a couple minutes before.

"I didn't think we were supposed to get anything for each other for Christmas?" she questioned warily. "I thought you and Tyler established birthdays as the only gift giving holiday for all of us?"

Troy had hoped she wouldn't bring up this obvious flaw in his plan but he'd come up with a solution. "I was with my mom at the Cathedral the other day and saw it," he started – which was totally the truth. "I just thought you'd really like it. And it was cheap." This time he hoped she didn't search too hard because he knew she'd spot the lie.

Her eyes stayed on him as her hands tore the wrapping paper and opened the box. When she finally looked, her mouth fell open. "You said it was cheap!"

"It wasn't that much," Troy shrugged. In truth, he'd had to borrow six months of allowance upfront from his mom to buy it. She hadn't asked what the money was for, but like had happened with the couple at Wal-Mart, he was sure she knew.

Angela delicately pulled the bracelet from the box. The gold flickered and made light shine off her stunned face. "Troy, I can't take this," she said and held it towards him.

"Look at it," he said quickly. "It was engraved by Raphael himself. It's supposed to help the person wearing it heal people better when they use hesdia. Kind of helps channel the Spirit for that gift."

"It's too much. We're not even supposed to get each other anything. This is worth like twenty normal presents."

"No, it's not," he implored. "I thought you'd like it and I thought it might actually do some good. We need all the help we can get, right? What if that helps heal someone you might not have been able to heal otherwise?"

For a long time, she looked at the stunning bracelet. Then she wrapped it around her left wrist. "Help me," she said. He fumbled with the clasp for a few seconds but after he got it snapped together, she grabbed his hand. "Thank you... for everything. You've been a really good friend since I moved here. I wish, well, I've prayed a lot the last couple of months to be as good a friend as you are. I haven't helped you at all with your robes. It's, I don't know... it's been-"

She broke off as the doorbell rang and Tyler barged in without delay. A flare of frustration cascaded through Troy's chest at the interruption, but he made sure to keep his face calm as his friends dropped into seats around the living room.

"So how about a bike ride?" Tyler said before anyone else could speak. "It's really nice out right now, but I saw on the weather where it's supposed to get nasty here in a little bit. Cold front blowing in from Canada, or something."

"That would be nice," Angela said with a sad smile. "Since we're going to be gone for a couple of weeks after Christmas, we need to spend as much time together as we can."

"Hawaii…" Becky said with a blissful look on her olive face. "You guys suck." She let out a tinkling laugh and the rest joined in.

"Never been," Troy said. His and Angela's parents had only told them two days before where they'd be going. They'd made them swear to secrecy from everyone except Tyler, Clark, and Becky. And even for them, they'd made them use an ability from Uriel to bind the secret so the friends couldn't talk about it openly in front of someone who didn't know it. It wasn't as absolute as God forbidding (and divinely restricting) talk about angels in front of non-angels, but would hopefully do the trick.

"It's great, Tyler said. "When we went there two years ago, I tried to learn to surf – didn't go so good for me."

"Wow, did the world just stop spinning?" Becky chortled.

"What do you mean?" Tyler said scrunching his eyes as if he was trying to see something a thousand miles away.

"You just admitted you weren't good at something," she continued. "That has to be the first time I've ever heard you not brag about being the best."

"Whatever," Tyler snapped but without any true anger. "Let's go. It's been awhile since we've went around the neighborhood together. Since I have my license now... bikes have kind of lost their fun."

"We were going to go last week," Clark chuckled in his deep way and sounded very much like his minster father. "But you wanted to watch *Eight Dates and Counting*, with that guy from Texas in it, instead."

"You said it was Troy and Clark's idea," Angela said as everyone except Tyler started rolling with laughter.

"Whatever," Tyler repeated and raced out the front door. They followed their huffy friend then mounted their bikes and took off down the street. Clear blue dominated most of the sky. The first day of winter had come and gone without so much as a jacket being needed. Troy looked to the north and could see a distant grayness where clouds were rolling in with the cold front.

They spent an hour riding the well-worn streets of the neighborhood. Angela waved at Mr. Douglas who hollered a joyous response.

"He's still going to church and everything?" Troy asked after they were past the excited, old man.

"Yeah, I try to go talk to him as much as I can," she answered. "But I haven't been over to his house since October. His faith is still strong." Her right hand massaged the scepter strapped under her shirt. "He talks about his wife, Amy, a lot... he knows he'll see her again."

"Troy?" Tyler called from the front of the pack.
"Yeah?"
"Something weird just happened."
"What?" Troy asked and raced to his friend's side.

Tyler looked around and dropped to a mouse-like whisper. "I was about to say something about nagging my parents to take me to Hawaii with you guys. But it stuck in my throat. No matter how hard I tried, I couldn't get it out."

"But you can now?"

"Hawaii," Tyler said experimentally. "You and Angela are going and I want to convince my parents to go too. So yeah, it seems so. I was thinking... didn't you and Angela put that binding thing on us? So we couldn't talk about it around people who didn't know about it?"

"Yeah," Troy said as his head spun. The Spirit surged outward and encompassed the group; then spread like a bomb. The brown grass of the house where they were standing blustered as if hit by a gust of wind.

"Troy?" Angela asked with fear seeping into his name.

He ignored her as he concentrated and expanded the reaches of the parimus ability. A young boy was crying in the house next door. His mom was griping at him for leaving his toys all over the floor. Across the street and up three houses, an old man was frying bacon and humming merrily to himself. On Cedar Hill, two streets over, an early twenties couple were giggling softly as they kissed. High above, three angels circled alertly on guard duty.

Everywhere Troy reached with the Spirit returned a feeling of absolute normalcy.

"Nothing," he said.

"What's going on?" Becky asked.

"If Tyler couldn't talk about us going to Hawaii," Angela explained in a low hiss. "That means that Uriel's binding ability worked... and that someone was listening to our conversation. The Spirit stopped him from saying anything about Hawaii when someone else could hear."

Becky and Clark both looked around frantically.

"Could it have been Mr. Douglas?" Tyler asked. "We were by his house and he was going nuts about Angela when I tried to talk about it. Maybe he was still in earshot?"

"Maybe," Troy said but kept prodding the area with the Spirit. "Let's head back to my house."

They made their way through the neighborhood much faster than they usually would. No shadows or darkness loomed behind any of the ornate bushes or expensive cars. All five bikes skidded to a halt safely in Troy's garage a minute later.

"Should we tell our parents?" Angela asked as she peeked around the corner of the garage.

"Probably," Troy said. "But I don't think it was anything. Like Tyler said, it was most likely Mr. Douglas still being able to hear – or maybe someone had their window open before the cold front gets here."

As he finished, a cold blast of wind gusted into their faces from the north. Leaves and small bits of trash tumbled in the air with the front.

"Oh, wow," Becky complained and wrapped her arms around herself. "That's freezing."

"Only because you're not used to it," Tyler said bravely. He guided her into the house where they were met by Troy's parents and Grandma Denise.

Over dinner, an hour later, Troy and his parents rehashed the afternoon's odd happening. His dad called the angels who had been guarding them. All three said that nothing had felt out of the ordinary during the whole bike adventure.

"Thanks for telling us," Troy's mom winked and shot him a wonderful smile. She then turned to his friends. "So what's everyone doing for Christmas?"

"Me and my dad are going to Aleesha's," Clark supplied. Troy loved hearing the excitement in his usually subdued friend. Seeing Clark happy was one of the best tonics in the world.

"You and her getting serious?" Tyler asked.

At that, Clark shrugged but a secretive grin tugged at the corners of his mouth.

"How about you Becky?" Troy's dad said over the Holy Herald. He'd already read the paper all the way through twice but tended to read it three or four times a day. Troy wasn't sure if he was looking for some secret code in the columns and articles; or if he used it to keep his mind focused on Kyle's atrocities.

"My parents were going to go to my grandma's," she said slowly. "But I talked them out of it. I thought it would be easier on our angel guards to stay close."

"You shouldn't worry about stuff like that," Troy's mom assured. "All of you need to live your lives as normally as possible. Troy and Angela will start having more duties once they get their swords, halos, and wings; but that won't be for a couple of years, or so."

"It's tough not to worry when we're around angels all the time and see all the trouble," Becky pressed but with pride over any hint of accusation.

"I'll be staying at home," Tyler cut into the flow of the conversation with a wistful look on his face. "My grandparents are coming over Christmas day. I wish – and I've prayed for it too – my mom and dad would find their faith. I think my dad is close but my mom is hopeless."

Becky and Angela both let out collective "aww's" at the sweetness in Tyler's statement.

"We can all help," Troy's mom supplied with a soft, supportive touch on Tyler's shoulder. "With some people, it takes a little more time. Don't give up. And hold on to your own faith."

"For God, we fight," Tyler said.

"That we do," Troy's dad sang with a smile. "And Angela, you and your parents will be spending the day over here."

She nodded but didn't respond.

Troy said his good-byes to his friends two hours later. They'd sat together overpowered by the news accounts of heroism and bravery on the Angelic Agenda. Unfortunately, heroic tales often led to tragedy and angels were being killed at an alarming rate around the world.

"I'll keep praying for all of you," Becky whispered to Troy when she gave him what had become a customary hug of farewell. "My own, personal, guardian angels."

Troy closed the door behind her with the Spirit flaring. He searched the darkening streets as he heard the engine of Grandma Denise's Cadillac rev. With the cold winds blasting, none of the friends except Tyler had wanted to walk home. Grandma Denise had offered to drive them - much to Troy's relief. He couldn't shake the feeling someone dangerous had been trying to listen to their conversation on the bike ride. But without proof of any sort, he had to admit that the troubled mood was probably brought on more by the Angelic Agenda's terrible news; and not an actual, immediate threat.

He walked into the kitchen and stopped. In the corner of the living room, he saw his mom sitting in his dad's lap. The recliner looked as comfy as it ever had. Troy remembered snuggling in the chair with both of them when he'd been much smaller. Right now, it looked as though they didn't want any company. Soft whispers carried in the air but Troy made no attempt to hear them. When he turned to quietly sneak from the kitchen, he saw his dad start a loving kiss with his arms engulfing his mom in a tight hug.

Troy went to bed wondering how his parents had met. He knew it had been at the Hill, but they'd never told him the exact circumstances of how they started dating. For a long time, he tossed and turned with thoughts swirling from Angela, then to his parents and on to Kyle. Many prayers of a safe and happy Christmas passed from his lips before sleep finally found him.

Chapter 19: Angel's Arrow

A fire crackled in the grate. Troy's parents rarely used the brick fireplace on the western wall of the living room. Mostly it was there for decorative plants and vases. Family pictures sat on the mantel running above it and a round clock with the hands pointing to ornate Roman numerals hung over it all.

Today, a hearty fire burned huge cedar logs. Troy had been sitting by it and occasionally stirring it for over an hour. It was the morning of Christmas Eve and all he could see for the near future was fun in the sun – with Angela by his side. He'd packed his bags for Hawaii the night before. The normal swimming trunks and sun tan lotion had been met by an axe and a round shield his dad added right before Troy zipped his suitcase.

"What time is everyone coming over?" his mom said into his peaceful thoughts.

"Around noon," he supplied lazily and stretched.

"Dad doesn't light a fire very often, does he?" she asked as more of a fact.

"Nope, it's nice. Even though it's not really that cold out."

"I think it's more for comfort than anything else," she said with a smile lighting up the room. She sat beside him and put her arm around his shoulders. They sat together without saying a word for ten minutes. A hypnotic allure of tranquility flourished in the flickering fire.

Just as Troy was about to say this was the most peaceful he'd felt in the last two years, his mom's scepter glowed to life. Strangled shouts immediately jumped into the air. His dad and Grandma Denise flashed into the living room from the back of the house. Both their scepters were alight with the same manic cries for help.

"Turn on the TV," his dad shouted and a spark of energy shot to the screen. The reporters on the Angelic Agenda were panting and raving. Every angel gift they'd been granted from God was shining from the TV.

".... towards Austin, Texas," the woman hollered with barely any semblance of calm. "All available angels are required to report to the Cathedral in Cedar Park. The deygon was spotted hovering over Lake Travis five minutes ago. Angels are already on the scene trying to distract the demon before it can move into heavily populated areas."

"Brian? Emily?" Angela's parent's voices split the air and took over the medley of panic streaming through the scepters.

"What do you think?" Paul continued.

"We have to go," Troy's dad said without hesitation.

"Can we leave the kids at the Cathedral again?" Susan questioned. From the bangs and clatters in the background, it sounded as though she was jamming weapons into a bag.

"I'm not leaving them alone anywhere," Troy's mom cried. "Absolutely not. We all know someone tried to do something the last time a deygon was raised. What if Kyle is waiting for us to leave them somewhere? His spy has known almost everything we've been doing."

"It can't be Kyle himself though," Paul countered. "From all the research I've done, he'll be exhausted for at least the next week. Raising a deygon is a nasty job. It takes a toll on the soul who brings such a monster from hell."

"I don't care," Troy's mom persisted. "I'm not leaving them. Kyle's Dark Hearts are just as bad as he is."

"We don't have time to argue," Grandma Denise snapped. Her teeth clattered after she was done. With barely a nudge using auditome, Troy caught a vision of her flying like the tiniest of bugs beside the mammoth deygon from months before. In the melting flames from its mouth, he saw fear caste in his grandma's eyes.

She looked at him with the same fear from across the living room. He swallowed then nearly choked at the idea of anything that could make his normally stout grandmother scared.

"Mom is right," Troy's dad said. "Bring Angela over here. Emily can take them to the Cathedral and then decide from there where to take them through the gate. Only she will know until after we've killed the deygon."

"What about Tyler, Becky, and Clark?" Troy shouted. "We can't leave them behind."

"We have to get going," Paul commanded through the scepter. "Brian and Denise, be ready. We'll be there in a minute. Peter, Luke, and Sara have swept the area and didn't feel anything dangerous. They're already heading to the Cathedral. The other kids should be okay."

"I hate not having anyone here guarding us," Troy's mom said stubbornly. "Even for a few minutes."

"There's nothing we can do about," his dad said from the hallway. Now in his hands were the gold plated shield and a huge battle axe. Troy had never seen his dad with a weapon that looked half as wicked. The angel sword granted by God had always looked lethal, but there was also a beauty surrounding it. This weapon held none of that luster. Only a butcher would think it pretty.

With his wings spread wide, his halo shining above his head, and robes white as snow covering him from shoulder to feet; Troy's dad looked as heroic as Samson portrayed himself in his boisterous tales.

His mom's hands reached out and fell into his dad's. They embraced and after one swift kiss, his dad turned to the front door with Grandma Denise.

"I love you," his mom called.

"Love you too," his dad returned. "Take care of your mom, Troy."

"Okay," Troy quaked. "Love you dad. Be careful."

His dad nodded and reached for the front door at the same time Angela barged through it from outside. A cold gust of wind poured in with her feverish entry. She looked absolutely terrified as Troy's dad and grandma streamed past her in full battle attire.

"I can't believe it," Angela moaned as she looked at the TV. The Agenda was tracking the deygon on a map. It still hovered over the thin lake northwest of the Austin, Texas city limits. "My dad is freaking out," she continued. "He keeps saying he didn't think it should be possible. Not so soon after the other one was raised. He thought it would be years before Kyle would have the strength to raise another, if he ever could again."

"We won't be staying long," his mom said. "Call your friends and tell them what's going on. Tell them to stay home and stay inside."

Her eyes were now glued to the TV but Troy felt the Spirit wrapping around the house as she called upon the divine power. Troy joined her in searching for anything out of the ordinary.

"What if it goes into the city?" Angela asked with her voice quivering. "Angels will never be able to hide it from the regular news. Think of all the people with cell phone cameras. Someone will get video of it and post it online. So many people will get killed…"

"If Kyle makes an attack out in the open like this," Troy started as he pulled his concentration back to the room around him. "Isn't that a bad sign? I mean, we're always talking about how Lucifer doesn't want people to really see demons – unless they're unbelievers and they're killed before they have faith. If people see demons, they'll know God is real as well. It will make faith easier… so – could it mean he finally has enough power to raise himself from hell? To come out into open war?"

"If he does," his mom said confidently. "God will strike him down and the last battle of the War for Sins will be fought."

Troy searched her face and hoped to draw some of the confidence brewing there. He heard one word in his dad's even voice: *Faith*.

"We need to get going," his mom said five minutes later. Angela had spoken to Tyler and Clark. Both said they would stay inside even though Tyler balked at the idea of hiding. Becky had immediately agreed and began praying before Troy hung up.

"I can't feel demons or fallen angels anywhere around," his mom continued. "What about you two?"

"I haven't felt anything," Troy admitted.

Angela shook her head negatively as well.

"We're going to the Cathedral," his mom said. "If we're attacked on the way, there are weapons in the back of the Tahoe. There won't be anyone to help us. We'll have to fight our way there." She lowered her voice conspiratorially. "Go through the gate to the Valley of Angels training ground. We'll re-group there and go somewhere else."

Troy and Angela nodded then made their way to the Tahoe. As before, the slow grind of the automated garage door rambled for an eternity and more. Troy expected the shadows of a dozen Dark Hearts to be waiting on the cold driveway, but only the empty street met his gaze.

"Stay alert," his mom breathed and the Tahoe's tires spun.

The neighborhood flew by in a blur of houses as Troy prodded everywhere with the Spirit. Parimus repeated on his lips over and over between silent prayers. His mom darted the huge SUV through traffic down HWY 152 at break neck speed.

"Troy, call Tyler and reiterate to him to stay inside," his mom said as the Cathedral rose into view in the distance. "And have him get a hold of Clark and Becky. Once you two are safe, I'll come get them and find somewhere to take them."

As if in response to her request, the cell phone - Tyler had given Troy eight months before - buzzed in the pocket of Troy's OU Sooners hoodie jacket. Tyler's name popped onto the caller id screen.

"Hey Tyler-"

"Troy!" Tyler yelled. "Where are you?"

"At the Cathedral," Troy said in a rush.

"Are your angel guards with you?" Tyler questioned roughly. Troy heard the wooden blinds in his friends living room slide open.

"No, Angela told you earlier, they're fighting the deygon. Pretty much every angel in the United States has been called to help."

Tyler didn't say anything for a few seconds and dread began filling Troy's stomach. "I just saw five or six angels fly over your house then towards Angela's street," Tyler growled. "But I think… I didn't get a great look at them, but I thought their wings might have been black like those Dark Heart angels."

"What?" Troy's mom cried out and snatched the phone from his hand. "Tell me exactly what happened!"

Her eyes grew wider and wider as she pulled into the packed parking lot of the Cathedral then jammed the brakes. "Stay here," she barked as she exited the still running vehicle.

"Where are you going?" Troy yelled.

"I'll call you on your scepter in a few minutes," she said. "Get into the Cathedral and stay there until I get back." Her wings sprouted instantly behind her and she took off like a rocket ship. A whirlwind of the Spirit funneled around her mad flight.

"What's going on?" Angela squalled from the rear driver side seat.

"Tyler thinks he saw a group of fallen angels check my house then fly towards yours," Troy said with his mind racing.

"Should we call my parents and your dad?"

"I don't know," Troy said feeling totally lost. "What if they're attacking the deygon? We can't bother them. Last time, they didn't call us until it was over. And no matter what my dad says… I know it's because he knew he'd need to concentrate and not be thinking about two things at once. I'm not going to be responsible for getting my dad, or grandma, or your parents killed."

"We can't let your mom go fight a bunch of Dark Hearts by herself though," Angela swallowed.

Troy looked at the expectant wood of the front doors leading into the Cathedral. "Get buckled in," he said.

"You can't drive," Angela cowered in her seat as Troy climbed over the console. "You're not going to get your permit until we get back from Hawaii. I have mine but my parents have hardly let me drive at all."

"I can today," he said and yanked the shifter into reverse. It was both an exhilarating and terrifying five minute drive home. Troy didn't go near as fast as his mom had on the rapid journey to the holy ground but managed to barely miss two cars and the tall, concrete curb of HWY 152.

"Slow down now," Angela begged. "We need to look around with the Spirit first. If there are fallen angels, we can't speed right at them. What if it's a trap?"

"I'll try to call my mom," Troy said. "She should have called by now anyway."

He grabbed his scepter and let the warmth flow up his arm. "Mom," he whispered and waited. The digital clock mocked him as if flipped to a new minute. "Mom, mom, mom!"

Nothing echoed into the silent Tahoe except his and Angela's rapid breathing. "Something's wrong," he said and winced at the meaning behind the words. Very little would keep his mom from answering his call. And none of the reasons were good. He hammered the gas and ignored Angela's squeal of despair. They made it to his house less than a minute later.

Tyler and Clark came rushing at them as soon as they pulled into the driveway. "I'm sure we saw something over by Becky's house," Tyler panted in the cold air.

"Get in," Troy hollered. As soon as their feet hit the floor of the SUV, Troy smashed the gas and they sped around the turn towards Becky's street.

Troy's heart froze when her house came into view. On her knees in the driveway was Becky's mom. She was reaching for the clouded sky with tears cascading down her face.

Troy nearly forgot to put the Tahoe in park before he was jumping out of the driver seat. "Mrs. Lopez," he screamed. "What happened?"

In answer, she plowed a rapid shower of Spanish words. Troy had no idea what she was saying but could feel the sheer terror in every word. He reached for the Spirit and saw the crusty wings of six fallen angels flapping wildly in the air. Terrible laughter cackled in the vision as slimy, black ropes oozed from Richard Hope's scepter and wrapped around Troy's mom and Becky. Neither could resist as the Dark Hearts lifted them and swooped into the air.

"They have my mom and Becky," Troy said with a hollow ball of pain starting to rip at his stomach. Mrs. Lopez tore at her hair as she continued to wail with her left hand stretched to the west. Troy's palm caressed her face and the Spirit glowed with the peace of the Lord. Ever so slowly, Mrs. Lopez calmed and rose to a kneeling position. "Pray for them," Troy whispered into her ear. He turned to Angela, Tyler and Clark. Three sets of humungous eyes greeted him.

"Angela," Troy said. "We have to find them."

"I'm calling my mom and dad," she said frightfully.

Troy nodded. "I'll call my dad and grandma too."

He slipped into the driver's seat and squeezed his scepter. "Dad."

From both his scepter and Angela's scepter a tremendous, skull pounding roar of pure horror made all of them cover their ears. The howl of rage went on and on, never breaking the deafening rage of the deygon.

"Troy!" his dad's voice hardly carried over the drowning noise.

"Dad!" Troy yelled at the same time Angela was screaming into her scepter. "Mom has been kidnapped! And Becky! By Dark Hearts!"

"... - can't.... – what... – on..."

"We need your help!" Troy hollered at the top of his lungs. Clark was leaning away from him in the passenger seat with his face scrunched against the wailing roar.

"Troy, I can't understand anything they're saying," Angela said and shook his shoulder. Her scepter wasn't glowing now and Troy cut the connection to his.

"They can't hear us," he said and started driving west out of the neighborhood. "Becky's mom was pointing this way. We have to search for them, Angela."

She nodded and closed her eyes. "Tyler, can you drive?" Troy said. His ears were still ringing and the request boomed much louder than he expected.

"Yeah," Tyler said. "Pull over." They exchanged seats and Troy took up position beside Angela. His eyes fell shut and he focused with all the strength in his body. Out and up the Spirit ventured. An invisible cloud of divinity. Over houses, across the school parking lot, through a shopping center on Mustang Road. Cars full of talking and laughing and griping people passed under his vision. The Spirit carried his consciousness west.

Ever west – as if a mosquito drawn to a bug zapper.

Brown cow pastures blurred past. A line of trees drew his attention along SW 59th street. Before his eyes climbed the tall shaft of a metal arrow. The head was buried into the hibernating grass of a small meadow. And strapped, in black ropes to the nock of the arrow protruding from the ground, were Troy's mom and Becky.

"They're at Angel's Arrow," Troy choked.

"By themselves?" Angela bellowed.

"They're tied to it," Troy added. "We have to go help them."

"You know it's a trap," Clark said with his brown eyes boring holes into Troy.

"We can't leave them," Troy said holding his head high. "Tyler, pull over and y'all get out. Angela, you can keep trying to reach your parents to tell them. Then follow when they get here."

"No!" Angela hissed. "We're not letting you go alone."

"They don't want to kill me, remember?" Troy countered. "They want to kill all of you and try to make me fall."

"We're not going to sit around and let you get yourself captured," Tyler said heartily. "And let Becky and your mom get killed in front of you. We're going." His foot punched the gas and all of them were slammed into their seats.

Troy poured his thoughts into his scepter once again. "Dad!"

The roar immediately blared into the Tahoe and Tyler almost careened off the road in surprise.

"Troy… - you… - I… - can't-"

With all his might, Troy pictured the Angel Arrow from his vision and yelled, "Angel's Arrow!" Then he silenced the screaming wail of the dragon demon.

"Hold on to your horses," Tyler shouted and the Tahoe began racing down the road.

Troy scrambled into the back of the weaving SUV. He lugged a duffel bag into the seat between him and Angela and unzipped it. Inside were short swords, axes, and several wooden maces.

"I've got my whip," Angela stuttered with a fearful look at the stash. "I'm better with it than I am with any of those."

"Take the bow and arrow at least," Troy said and yanked the weapon free. He unsheathed a short sword and ran his hand down the foot and half long blade. Satisfied, he strapped it around his waist then chunked two maces into the front seat.

"What?" Tyler gaped. "Give me a sword."

"You'll cut your hand off before doing any good with it," Troy said shaking his head. "It takes a lot of practice. You can swing those like baseball bats." He reached over the seat and produced two shields. "Both of you can have a shield too. Me and Angela have our scepters."

"Fine," Tyler griped as he cut through a parking lot to skip the light at HWY 152 and Mustang Road.

"What good is any of this going to do?" Angela cried. Her mouth was open and she was looking at the roof of the Tahoe. Troy wasn't sure if she was pleading to God or trying not to let tears roll down her face like a waterfall.

Troy didn't respond for a long time as he watched Mustang flash by in a series of blurs. He called upon the Spirit and let it wash over him. Then he reached for Angela's hand. The warmth and grace of God's grace flowed between them. At once, she nodded and sniffed away the fear. "Faith," Troy said in his best ever imitation of his dad. "For God, we fight."

"For God, we fight," she whispered the age old command in return.

"There it is," Clark said fervently from the front seat. His beefy hand was pointing to the west. A half mile down the road, Troy saw the u-shaped bend of trees and the top of the odd structure sticking up at an angle. The wheels of the Tahoe skidded to a stop a minute later. At the base of the arrow, Troy saw his mom and Becky strapped. Both were slumped in unconscious heaps.

"You know it's a trap," Angela said softly repeating Clark's earlier statement. Her hands were clenched in the stunning white robes covering her petite frame.

Troy nodded. Unseen shadows waited in wicked anticipation within the grove of cottonwood trees. There was none of Lucifer's black fog yet, but terrible, excited whispers crept in the air through the Spirit.

"I know," Troy said without any waver in his voice. "But I have to go. Y'all don't. You should stay here and see what happens. Then go for help. Maybe I can free my mom and Becky. Wake them up and get out of there."

Angela stared at him with a sad tilt to her pretty face. "Troy, something horrible is in those trees. I can't feel exactly what it is, but I know there are fallen angels here."

"We're not letting you go alone," Tyler snorted. There was an earnest, honest shine on his handsome face. "That's final. We knew what we were getting into when we came with you. Since we found out you were angels and had monsters and demons and the devil after you, we've known being your friends would be dangerous. But we accepted it. Troy... have faith."

The hairs across Troy's legs and arms stood on end. He looked at each of his friends and dipped his head in acknowledgement of their sacrifice. One by one, they opened their doors, crossed the bar ditch, and slipped through the barbed wire fence enclosing the pasture. Every step brought screaming warnings of danger from the Spirit. Troy called upon the power and let it soak every square inch of his body.

His mom and Becky consumed his sight. Step by step they grew larger. Tall, brown grass was rising around their prone figures. His mom's face was peaceful and quiet as she slumbered.

Slowly, her chest rose and fell bringing the first pulse of hope Troy had felt in the last half hour. Becky's head was lying on his mom's shoulder. Her quiet, innocent beauty resonated in the air like a guitar chord that had just been strummed.

Behind all the tranquility of his loved ones, a storm raged in the cold wind. Black death trembled in the trees. And from the very center, of the most tangled mess of underbrush, stepped Kyle Downey.

Northerly winds fluttered the sandy hair on top of the fallen angels head. His cheeks were even more hollowed than the last time Troy had seen him. Blue eyes burned a maniacal electricity. His green angel marks looked almost black under the overcast sky. A mocking smile was lifting his lips. Barely any of the old handsomeness, Troy had seen in pictures from the man's youth, remained. Here was a soul clawed too often by Lucifer's will.

"Troy," Kyle said and spread his hands. Six fallen angels in the robes of Dark Hearts stepped from the trees. Decaying wings and halos; and the smell of sulfur came with them. Richard Hope was in their midst as well as another angel Troy recognized. He'd seen the man at the Cathedral a hundred times. Hanging in the air while playing a harp. Singing hymns in the sanctuary. Laughing with Samson. The Spirit pressed and the name floated into Troy's mind. Jim Hutchins. The spy. "You are proving much more trouble than I ever imagined," Kyle continued. "I, honestly, must applaud you. I never thought it would be this difficult to get you. But this time I have a deygon on my side to keep your protectors occupied. Raising it was hard enough," he shivered and his teeth clattered together like a chain saw. "Making it lay low and be quiet for the last couple of weeks has been even more difficult. I guess it was worth it now. You'll soon be another Dark Heart for-"

"I don't know why you keep trying," Troy cut him off. "I'll never fall. Lucifer will never sway me to his side. I have faith like my mom and dad."

"That's because you don't know the truth… yet," Kyle said and a pained look crossed his tortured face.

"The truth about what?" Troy laughed. He looked from his mom to Becky then to the three friends standing by his side. "You think I want to be standing beside you and the idiots on your side? With decayed wings and rotted faces."

"Don't forget the constant smell of crap," Tyler added.

"No matter what happens," Troy continued with a frightful grin of appreciation at his best friend. "I'll never fall."

Kyle shook his head and looked into the sky. "So much deceit in the world," he mused as he leaned casually against the gigantic arrow. At his feet, Troy's mom and Becky remained unaware of the danger right above them. "God has long said Lucifer brought the lies and treachery, but that's not true. Lucifer saw the flaws in God's plan. He moved to help solve those problems and God cast him out. He removed Lucifer from the light and left him to wallow in the mud and fires. All Lucifer wanted was for the souls God created to keep their own identity. Not this eternal loaning service God put into place. You think you'll spend eternity in blissful paradise… but once you die with faith, he chuckles to himself and snatches your soul into his bloated *love*. You no longer have a conscious. You are no longer you. When Lucifer wins the war, he'll let people hold on to their souls forever. To remain themselves and not get absorbed into nothingness. He said he may be able to bring back those lost…"

Troy breathed deeply and said a prayer for strength. The short sword pulled slowly from its blessed sheath. He looked at the shining blade. At the way the pommel, ribbed handle, and guard made it look like a cross. The symbol of Jesus' ultimate sacrifice.

"Lucifer wants to create a paradise where we get to keep our souls when we pass from this life," Kyle boomed much more loudly than he had been speaking. "All those who died without the *grace of God* will rise up and win back their spirits. They'll dine forever at the new lord's table."

"You believe what you want," Troy said with his chin held high. "I could care less at this point. My parents pray and hope you'll find your faith again." At this all the Dark Hearts hooted in laughter. "I'd like for you to see what you've become and beg for forgiveness; but I don't think it's going to happen. Leave my mom and Becky out of it. Let all my friends go and I'll stay with you."

"Very brave," Kyle said with a sardonic salute. "But I do admit, you would probably be hard to make fall with the hope of seeing your friends and family in the back of your mind. Watching them get ripped apart limb by limb would do you some good. Then I'll start making you understand the truth. You'll know you'll never see them again. But you'll come to understand you can be a hero to billions of other souls."

A tremble shook Troy when the leader of the fallen angel's finished. Every shadow in the trees flickered and flexed. Clawed arms and feet tore at bark and grass. Fangs snapped. Curses of a terrible, hellish language lifted into the wind. Dread pounded deep in Troy's chest as demons of every shape and size slunk from the darkness.

A horde of reidlos battered against each other fifty yards away. At least a hundred strong, they churned the grass into mud with hideous chuckles of amusement.

A pack of fifty selvo watched from dark perches in the cottonwood behind Kyle.

Buzzing and blistering, a circular mass of nylla popped from the highest reaches of the tallest trees. The tiny, flying horses glared and hissed.

The lionish heads of two, massive sinna demons cantered through the underbrush. Muscular tails prodded the closest trees leaving behind thick quills oozing poison that would instantly rot flesh and bone. Foot long claws thrust forward from their human feet. Knotted muscles flexed on their shoulders. The sight of them alive was nothing like *Dangerous and Deadly Demons*. A strange, mesmerizing gait carried the half lion, half humans forward.

And lumbering from the deepest shadow came a horror Troy had hoped he'd never see in person. It looked as though the devil had crashed together four huge boulders and turned them into rugged, charcoal gray hide. Blue, static electric bolts sizzled over the gigantic, ten feet tall frame. The face – if it could be called such – of the trickel sneered in apparent delight. Troy stifled a shout of fear and disgust. He'd seen the quickest of visions from his dad of this very demon. He could feel the presence like it was the familiar dreading of his worst nightmare. Here was the menacing monster that had killed his grandparent's a year and half before. Troy remembered their sad funeral like it was yesterday. The beast roared and a lightning bolt scorched the grass at its trunk-like feet.

"Oh God," Angela squealed as the demons advanced. "Please help us. Raphael, save us. Gabriel, please."

Clark was muttering frantic prayers. His knuckles were flexing on both the mace and the shield.

Tyler's eyes were wide. He stood with his mace and shield helplessly at his side as if hypnotized by the sheer, overwhelming evil of the approaching army.

"I need you Troy," Kyle said with a sad look down at Troy's mom. "I want you to feel the pain I felt. You need to feel the suffering of forever losing someone you love. To watch them die and have God suck up their soul like they're the smallest ant. To know you'll never see them again."

"Get my mom and Becky and go," Troy said with the quickest but most meaningful glance he'd ever given to the three friends standing by his side. The Spirit touched him. A deep understanding pressed at its touch. Paradise awaited. Calls of love whispered in his ears. A wave of confidence travelled up his spine and goose bumps tingled down the skin of his legs.
"For God, we fight," Troy prayed and looked straight at the band of Dark Hearts. "Gabriel!"

He charged with blasts of light arcing from his scepter. Kyle looked stunned for a heartbeat but easily deflected the only threatening burst of power. Troy's feet hammered the grass as he closed the distance. His mom's face filled his eyes and he thought of her wonderful smile as he leapt.

With his arching flight boomed a Trumpet of Seraphim. But it hadn't come from his scepter. Nor, he knew, had it come from Angela's. He landed in front of Kyle and an involuntary smile split his face. The Spirit softly caressed his name and brought news of those at his back. He didn't need to turn to feel the wrath and power coming with his dad and a multitude of angels. Fifteen in all - flying in glory and the lust for battle.

God had answered his prayers.

Chapter 20: A Choice of Sacrifice

The short sword sliced and banged off a black shield that erupted out of nowhere from thigh to shoulder in front of Kyle. Troy spun and somersaulted as the Dark Hearts hissed and shot black oil and shadowy darts of energy.

Pure rage twisted Kyle's face as he attacked. Troy circled and planted his feet in front of his mom and Becky. From his scepter popped a vibrating, luminescent shield. It grew in circles until covering from chin to knees. Kyle's two-handed great sword smashed into it making Troy's shoulder crack in protest. All around demons were howling and charging. Grass, branches, and dirt were flying in the wake of their terrible claws. The trickel loosed a thundering bellow which split a tree; and a zap of lightning arced straight at Angela. She dove to the side and the bolt gouged a five foot scar into the Earth.

"No," Troy growled. He sprung into the face of two reidlos. The short sword sang praise as if Michael was swinging the blade himself. Neither demon survived the onslaught of the archangel's great fury. The remains of their twitching bodies tumbled into bloody messes in the dormant grass.

The Spirit beckoned and Troy flipped backwards. Slicing down with all his might, the rubbery, black ropes, wrapped around his mom and Becky, snapped. At once their eyes opened.

"Troy?" his mom squinted at the inky darkness swarming the pasture like a horrific, living fog.

Black filth sparked over and over from the Dark Hearts scepters. Butler and Enoch cut through the chaos in a blinding tornado of the Spirit. A woman screamed in the distance as bubbling brimstone swallowed her arm. Jim Hutchins swarmed in his black robes and struck a killing blow with a katana-like sword.

"What happened?" Becky coughed at the acrid smell. She winced from the ugly chorus of snarls and howls.

"Can you stand?" Troy hollered and deflected the clawed hand of a reidlos.

"Kyle?" his mom growled and all her angel gifts instantly flared. Her wings brought the promise of safety and comfort to Troy. A handful of nylla demons squalled and tried to divert their attack. With two quick strokes, they were dead.

"Brian! No!" his mom yelled.

Troy stabbed at the hind leg of one of the sinna demons and ducked behind Gabriel's shield when two quills shot from its tail. He forced his eyes to follow his mom's advance. There was Kyle striking and slaying. Two angels fell in blood at his feet. But still standing was Troy's dad. Their swords met in sparks as the two old friends danced and wove through the tumultuous fight.

"Becky," Troy said funneling her under the bend of the huge, caricatured arrow sticking out of the ground. "See if you can get Tyler, Clark, and Angela; and get out of here."

"Okay," she squeaked and darted from the relative safety. Clark and Tyler were standing back to back. Repeatedly, they whacked at the cloud of nylla flying in zig-zags over their heads. Angela was firing arrows in all directions. Troy shot a blast of energy from his scepter and nearly took the head off of a reidlos sneaking up behind her. Her eyes found his through the haze of battle and she bobbed her head in thanks.

Across the field, the trickel was slamming a man side to side between two trees. The awful crunches made Troy shiver in disgust. He jumped into the fray as the sinna attacked a pair of angels who'd swooped forward to guard his mom's back. The Spirit glowed from his skin as it engulfed the sword in his hand.

Such love had never existed. It was as if God's own hands were squeezing with comfort and care.

The pure beauty of the Lord's divine grace absorbed through Troy's skin. He seemed to barely move as the short sword pulled his hand with it and slammed into the base of the beast's neck. A roar of death rattled from its throat as black blood sprayed over Troy's clothes. He left the blade in the demon and yanked his dagger from its sheath then flicked his wrist. It sailed end over end and planted directly between the burnt wings of a fallen angel. The woman shrieked and reached over her shoulder before falling to the ground in a heap of black robes.

Troy searched the fight for his parents and friends. Becky had successfully made it to the group and was ducking behind Clark. Angela had dropped the bow but her whip was cracking the air in front of two reidlos.

In the middle of a pack of angels, Troy saw his mom blasting into a threesome of Dark Hearts. Richard Hope's crazy laugh lifted through the mayhem. He cackled as he blocked and dodged the attacks from Troy's mom and the other angels.

To Troy's right, he caught the blurring motion of his dad and Kyle's continued struggle. The trickel was stomping towards his dad's flank. The brutal promise of death haunted its wart-encrusted face. Troy ran at the giant demon. He kicked aside two nylla and rolled under the poisonous quills from where the remaining sinna had taken refuge in the trees.

361

"Here!" Troy bellowed before the trickel could attack his dad from behind. An amused sounding harrumph - like dry gravel in a cement mixer – cascaded from the monster's jagged mouth ten feet off the ground. Troy dodged a massive fist and blasted a gash into the giant's knee with a silver flash of the Spirit. The howl that issued next was nothing compared to the explosion of electricity. Troy was sure a cloud of pain and death must have mushroomed into the atmosphere and all the way to the sun. The shockwave carried him in a cacophony of bouncing, branch-breaking barrel rolls far into the grove of cottonwood trees.

Bruises and cuts dotted his body. He spit blood and tried to shake the pain from his groggy brain. The sickly smell of scorched hair hung in his nose.

In haphazard, blurry ellipses, Troy caught peeks of the clustered trees then the continuing chaos in the pasture. But a smashing foot cleared his befuzzled mind. The grunting trickel plowed through the cottonwoods in a wood splintering frenzy. Troy was sure it was the end. He raised his scepter, shot a burst of energy, and dove as an anvil-sized fist planted where he'd crashed from the electric explosion.

"No," a voice shouted. Over the trees came two angels. Troy blinked and tried to wipe the blood and mud from his eyes. Without any semblance of fear, Joe Taylor was standing in front of the monster. At his side was a man in square glasses. Wispy, thin hair waved beneath the fuming torrent of the trickel's breath. Skinny, but powerful wings pumped the air from the angel's back. Troy knew he'd seen the man somewhere before. He pulled on the Spirit and the memory tumbled from the corners of his mind.

He saw Ben Lewis trailing behind his mom while this man chuckled and told Ben to make sure she didn't fall into the gate to heaven.

The trickel swiped but Joe Taylor slipped through its grasp and buried his blade into its rocky wrist. A piercing howl ripped from the monster's jaws.

"Troy, get back to your friends!" Luke Fischer hollered as he landed in a gust of wings. Jagged scars bubbled the left side of his face. The tall Justice Minister was smiling as he attacked. Machine gun looking bolts of light left his scepter and pounded into the roaring demon.

Troy didn't need to be told twice. He darted around a tree and began making his way as fast as he could to the sounds of carnage in the fighting field.

"I told you a long time ago that I'd kill you," Kyle Downey's voice froze Troy in his tracks. He spun and saw his dad wrapped in crispy, smoking black chains. The two men were in a small clearing in the middle of a dense thicket of trees. Kyle's two handed greatsword rose slowly over his head.

"No!" Troy screamed and the Spirit slammed into Kyle's chest. The fallen angel tumbled backwards with a snarl.

"You interfere way too much for a fifteen year old," Kyle snapped as he climbed to his feet.

Troy dodged the putrid smelling oil the fallen angel shot at him. He flitted forward and scooped up his dad's sword. He hadn't held it in a couple of years. The texture and shape of the grip brought images of holding the perfect weapon, in the living room of their house, when he was nine years old. He heard his dad preaching of the benefits of faith and forgiveness.

"For God, we fight," his dad grimaced against the tightening chains. Confidence beckoned from his eyes. Not confidence in himself, but confidence Troy would save him.

Troy nodded and attacked. He could tell right away from the lazy parries and easy dodges, Kyle would have no problems winning the fight. But something was holding his attack. "Why don't you want to kill me?" Troy questioned and sidestepped a half-hearted stab from his deadly enemy.

"Watching you fall will give me much greater pleasure," Kyle said. "Then we can work together to win the war and help Lucifer bring eternal paradise to the world. I can get back those lost to me. And perhaps you can get the thing you most desire." His eyes flashed towards the chaos of the meadow. "If she doesn't die first. It could get much more complicated if she does."

"Good luck," Troy spat. Instead of attacking the fallen angel, he spun and hacked at the chains holding his dad. The Spirit sparked when it met the crafting of Lucifer. For a second Troy thought his attack had done no good, then the chains disintegrated in a puff of smoke.

His dad grabbed the sword and faced his old friend. God's wrath darkened his normally stoic face. "Your trap has failed again, Kyle. All your demons will die today. And your Dark Hearts will either join them or be captured. When are you going to realize you've picked the wrong side? Your dad-"

"Don't you dare mention my dad!" Kyle snapped. Black, inky power surged from his zombie-like wings. "You have no right. Not after you left him to die."

"You don't know the whole story," Troy's dad returned with a begging plea in the words. "You would never listen to what we had-"

"Nothing you can say will change it," Kyle said and fire brewed in his blue eyes. Satan was alive and well in the heat of his stare. He swung his scepter and wriggling, venomous snakes scattered over the ground. Ten of them hissed and struck.

Troy's dad yelped, snatched him by the hand, and jumped into the air. Kyle followed with a tremendous scream of anger. "I'm going to have to let you go," his dad called to Troy after barely dodging two jets of slime. "That tree," he pointed far below. "Go help your mom."

Before Troy had contemplated the size of the drop, his dad released his grip. Gravity kicked his stomach into his throat and a startled screech left his throat. Branches lunged at him as the ground loomed. Wrapping himself in the Spirit, Troy reached out with the divine power and grabbed the thickest limb of the closest cottonwood tree. It yanked him sideways and he slammed into the bark with a shudder of pain.

Looking up, he saw his dad and Kyle fighting ferociously like two crazed eagles. Not daring to take a shot with his scepter, Troy judged there was at least a forty foot drop to the ground. He dove away from the branches below and flipped in one long arc before landing lightly on his feet in the crunchy grass.

His dad and Kyle disappeared a hundred yards away behind two of the tall, thin trees. Troy prayed for his dad's safety as he raced to the Angel Arrow clearing. When he got there, he stopped to weigh the carnage.

Demon bodies were scattered all around. Putrid smoke rose from their slowly disintegrating bodies. Three of the Dark Hearts were dead, including Jim Hutchins who had a long sword protruding from his stomach. A couple of hundred feet to Troy's left, he saw Angela's whip flash and crack. The nylla she'd targeted pinwheeled from the air, but a host more buzzed over the heads of all his friends. Tyler and Clark were both gasping for air as they swung wildly with their maces. A nasty, red welt rose from Tyler's cheek where he'd already been stung.

And rushing towards them were two of the remaining reidlos. Their hairless bodies grinded over the ground in a promise of the killing machines they'd been forged to become by Lucifer.

Troy started to dart for his friends but a bone shattering roar halted him. Fifty yards to his right, his mom was backing away from the trickel demon. Ben Lewis' father and Luke Fischer were by her side. Grandma Denise was racing into the sky after a fleeing Dark Heart.

Richard Hope and one of the remaining Dark Hearts were flanking the gigantic demon. Hiding in the trees was the sinna demon. Its lethal quills were poised and ready to dart almost instant death with a twitch of its tail.

The trickel bellowed and charged. Joe Taylor's sword was still sticking from its forearm but the beast didn't seem to notice. Currents of electricity blasted from its rough hide. Troy's mom was zapped in the leg by one of them and she stumbled.

He made to run to her aid, but Becky's wail of despair drew him left. Angela was on the ground with four nylla stabbing her with their barbed tails.

Back and forth Troy was torn. Richard Hope was hacking at his mom as she fought from her knees. Desperate parries were only just keeping her alive. Clark cried out as he saw the attacking reidlos rushing at the group of friends. Tyler was screaming in rage and horror. Angela cried from the pain of Lucifer's fire being delivered in the venom of the nylla.

Troy's heart pounded in his chest hard enough to make his whole body shake. His mom's smile filled his eyes and his breath caught in his throat as he raced left.

Left, towards his frantic friends.

Forty feet away he jumped into the air. The horrible flock of nylla scattered when he battered them with the Spirit.

He landed and yanked the long sword from Jim Hutchins corpse. "Look out!" he screamed as the first of the reidlos bowled into Tyler. Claws and fangs ripped at his best friend's throat. A gargle of terror yelped from Tyler's mouth as he fell. Troy slid across a dirty scar in the ground, where the trickel had wounded the Earth with a bolt of lightning, and sliced horizontally. The demon's head split down the middle from the blow. Nasty blood splattered Tyler's face and he retched.

Troy spiraled to his feet and ducked under the claws of the second reidlos. With one stroke, he cleaved the beast's leg from its body; then plunged the sword straight through its ugly face.

Holy water rained from his scepter as he directed it at Angela. The nylla shrieked and zipped into the air. They were met by the furious long sword in Troy's hand. One by one, they snapped into bloody pieces of twitching leftover demons. Chopped, horse-like flesh only a hell hound could eat.

"Are you okay?" Troy said helping Angela from the ground. She was wincing and twitching from a score of pulsing red bumps.

She didn't look at him, but nodded. "Is Tyler..?"

Troy turned and knelt beside his friend. Clark was picking up Becky in his peripheral vision. He heard her whine but knew she wasn't seriously injured.

"Tyler?" Troy asked softly. The soft powers of hesdia glowed from his hands as he gently turned over his downed friend.

"I'm… okay," Tyler breathed with a pained face. Deep cuts just below the carotid arteries in his throat were mending from the touch of the Spirit.

Red blood gushed from the puncture wounds and mixed with the black foulness that had sprayed from the reidlos. Troy pushed all his thoughts into the Spirit and worked to knit the strands of flesh. "Troy," Tyler breathed easier a minute later. "But… how did you get your robes?"

"What?" Troy said and almost dropped his friend in bewilderment. He looked down and saw stunning white robes engulfing his body. A sheer softness touched his arms and ran warmly over his chest. From the fabric drifted a sweet smell of flowers and fresh cleanliness.

Troy froze at the scent. Fear raced from his toes all the way up his body. Every cell in his lungs locked together in choking fright. He looked across the field. Angela's parents had joined Ben Lewis' father. The trickel was on its rocky knees and crumbling under their furious strikes. Troy's eyes were drawn to the ground at their feet.

There was his mom. One of her wonderful smiles graced him and her perfectly blue eyes shined with love and hope. Her blonde hair was tousled and the halo above her head was shining but also shimmering.

From her neck, two sinna quills stuck in piercing horror.

"No!" Troy yelled and stormed across the blood soaked grass. His eyes were locked on his mom's and he saw them flicker and dull. The sinna demon cut across his path. A growl left Troy's mouth. More terrible than any demon he'd ever heard, the growl seemed to shake the ground and the Spirit battered the cottonwood trees where the assassin had hidden. Quills splintered against a shield Troy called to life in an instant. Surprise haunted it's now fearful specks of eyes as he twisted and slashed. The demon's tail twitched once then cartwheeled into the whipping branches of a tree. It fell with its mane covered head burying in the brown grass.

Troy stabbed into the sinna's dead torso until Luke Fischer grabbed him from behind. "It's dead," the scarred Justice Minister shouted. "Leave it."

Throwing the smoking sword aside, Troy raced to his mom. Her halo had vanished and her wings were disappearing one wonderful feather at a time. The ghost of a smile still danced across her lips. Troy collapsed to his knees as the world stopped its perpetual spinning. An anguished cry filled his ears as his dad landed and scooped his mom into shaky arms. Tears blurred the sight as his dad wept and cradled his dead wife. Grandma Denise was bawling as she gripped her son's shuddering shoulder.

Moon sized comets of anguish slammed into Troy's chest. His choice had led to this. He could have ran to his mom's aid. Could have killed the sinna demon before it shot its poison into her bloodstream. Could have sacrificed his own body to stop the quills. He could have… stopped this from happening. Kept his mom alive.

Pictures flashed from memory. Her smiling at him as she gave him a description of the gate to heaven in the sanctuary. The sweet lullaby she sang to him at night until he turned ten years old and said he was too old for that kind of stuff. Her laughing as she went through one of her never ending escapes from Samson's grasp at the Cathedral. The fury as she sliced down the selvo demon attacking Troy and his friends.

She'd always been there to help him. To love him. To laugh and smile.

Now, it was gone forever. Only dust inside his raging mind. Cut down by one of Lucifer's foulest demons. Delivered to paradise, but never again to wrap him in a warm hug. Troy reached and brought the cloth of his robes to his running nose. The fresh smell of flowers made him shudder.

His mom was gone.

Soft arms wrapped around his shoulders. From both sides, Angela and Becky hugged him. He melted into their mutual embrace.

"I'm so sorry," Becky whispered. He felt tears run from her cheeks to mingle with his own.

A racking breath heaved at his stomach and threatened to buckle him from the pain. Angela's hands were glowing where they were touching him, but the pain of loss was doing its best to hold back the calming nature of the Spirit.

He looked towards his dad and through the tears saw a figure standing on the highest branch of a tree in the distance. Hatred lined Kyle Downey's face, but Troy also saw pain in the hollowed eyes. Love, long forgotten. The fallen angel bent and vanished into the clouds a moment later.

Angels formed a half circle around the spot where his mom had ascended to heaven. Angela's parents were crying in each other's arms. Luke's nightmarish face was twisted in grief. Butler was slowly petting a whining Enoch. And behind all of them, Troy saw Linda Taylor cradling her husband much the same way as his dad was holding his mom. Joe Taylor's face was smeared with blood. His lifeless arms hung in the dry grass. Other angels were singing comforts and breathing prayers. Adam had lost his dad in the War for Sins.

All around the field, angels were mourning their losses. Troy didn't care to count the dead. None of it mattered in his heart. Not now. Not with his mom's body being lifted into his dad's arms. Her feet and arms dangled. Her face was pulled close under his chin.

Troy rose with him and their eyes met. "How did it happen, Troy?" his dad choked. "I told you to help her. You should have... what happened?"

Troy couldn't produce any words as his throat tightened and threatened to leave him in a crumpled, gasping mess. His head shook side to side as he searched for a way to tell his dad it was his fault. All his fault. He'd let his mom die. He'd chosen... Angela's life over hers. The pain erupted and overwhelmed him. Only with help from Angela and Becky did he manage to stay on his feet.

His dad's bleary eyes were on him waiting for a response. "Angela... and Tyler and Becky and Clark were in trouble," he stumbled upon the wheezing words. "I thought they were in more-"

He didn't want to finish the sentence because he knew it wasn't the total truth. He'd known his mom was in deadly peril. He'd seen the Dark Hearts and the trickel looming over her. With a terrifying picture, he remembered the sinna lurking in the trees - waiting to shoot its deadly, venomous quills.

For several heart ripping seconds, his dad looked at the robes covering Troy's frame. His nose twitched and Troy wondered if he smelled the loving fragrance of the most perfect mom in the world.

But then he turned without another word and his wings thrust him into the air.

Chapter 21: God's Grove

"I could have helped her," Troy repeated his plea. He was sitting in a haze of pain in the recliner in his living room. A picture of his mom haunted from the mantel above the fireplace. She'd been alive here only a few short hours before. Hugging and comforting him. Talking excitedly about their trip to Hawaii.

"You did what she would have wanted," Grandma Denise urged. She was standing over him protectively. More warmth than Troy ever remembered seeing shined from her wrinkled face. "She's proud of what you did today. You sacrificed yourself to save your friends."

"I didn't sacrifice myself," Troy moaned. "I... sacrificed her."

"Stop," she said kneeling and wrapping him in an overly tight embrace. "If you'd helped your mom, none of your friends would be alive."

Troy searched his memory of that moment when he'd come from the trees. He could see his mom scrambling and swinging with a determined look on her angelic face. From his left, he heard the snarls of the reidlos as they closed on Tyler and Clark. His grandma was right. They would have died. It didn't change the fact that he chose them... chose Angela – over her.

The fresh smell drifted from his robes once again. He closed his eyes and prayed for them to go away. When he opened them, his prayer had been answered. The clothes he'd worn to the fight now covered him in tattered glory. Burns and cuts and rips ruined the material in fifty different places.

"You'll want to have those on for the funeral," Grandma Denise sniffed. Tears raced down her wrinkled cheeks. The rigid, orange angel marks were spider webbing into the white hair of her temples.

"A funeral?" Troy squeaked through massive tears of his own. "Already?"

"Your dad says it's what she wanted. You'll go through the gate with him. Only he knows where she wanted to be buried."

"He blames me," Troy said and melted under the horrific knowledge behind the words. "He knows I could have saved her but-"

"Hush," Grandma Denise chided. "Your dad would never blame you. He knows you did what an angel should do. God granted you your robes for doing the right thing. He knows it. And so should you."

"Mom getting killed was the right thing?" Troy growled through his grief.

She shook her head softly. "You did the right thing."

All Troy could do was re-live the smile she had shined his way at the very end. His grandma scrambled him up at 4:00 and pretty much carried him to her cold Cadillac. Waiting in the cold wind were Tyler, Becky, and Clark. A huge, red welt burned on Tyler's cheek. His left eye was nearly swollen shut from the pressure of the nylla sting

"Sorry about your mom," Tyler huffed. "We all loved her." He didn't offer one of his usual punches, but instead ducked his head.

"Praying for you," Clark mumbled and wiped a runny nose.

Becky didn't say anything. Her slender arms folded around his neck and for a long time she held him.

Troy knew she didn't have any powers of the Spirit, but thought she might have somehow used it to comfort him. When she finally broke free, a quick, tear soaked kiss landed on his cheek. Before Troy could think of anything to say or do in response, she retreated into Tyler and Clark's arms.

The drive to the Cathedral was cold and silent. Standing tall against the north wind in the parking lot, they met Troy's dad. Wrapped in linens of purest white, his mom was held in his dad's quivering arms.

"Troy," his dad leaned and whispered in his ear. "Follow me to the sanctuary. Then through the gate. We're going to the Hill. Put on your robes."

Troy met his dad's eyes warily and nodded understanding. He searched the brown orbs for forgiveness. For traces of sympathy. But only stony sternness reflected.

Without saying a word, his robes popped into existence. At once, the sweet, clean smell bombarded his nose with sadness. His dad turned and walked towards the huge, wooden doors leading into the holy building. They opened at his approach. Samson came into immediate view.

The gigantic statue was wiping invisible tears from his marble skin. Wails lifted from his normally gregarious mouth. It sounded like a mortally wounded lion from one of the hero's tales in the Bible. He didn't call out or say a word, but the sound of his grief echoed in the tall antechamber.

Angels lined the hallways of the Cathedral. All were somber as Troy and his dad passed. Many had wounds from the fight with the deygon or the battle at Angel's Arrow.

Troy had overhead his grandma say the deygon had been defeated at the cost of twenty-one angels. It's giant body was still disintegrating into the banks of the lake near Austin, Texas.

Hoarse whispers filtered from the bowed head of the clerk from Michael's Angel Fixings when Troy and his dad walked passed. The owners of Spice of Life quietly hummed their favorite hymn. One lone harp played from the air. Luke Fischer's grotesquely disfigured face hung above the music. His fingers danced over the chords. The sound carried Troy onward. Down the Burning Bush hallway and into the sanctuary.

Angela and her parents stood near the altar. Their red, blotchy faces paid tribute to the loss of the most perfect angel in the entire world. None of them moved as Troy approached with his dad and mom. Angela peeked up when they climbed the couple of steps, but no words came from her mouth. Even her pink angel marks looked subdued in the dreariness of the day.

Images flashed from the fight hours before. Angela in trouble. Getting stung over and over again by the pesky nylla demons. Her cries of anguish. He'd promised himself a thousand times he'd never let anything happen to her. He'd saved her, but the cost was tearing him apart. Her wonderfully brown eyes dropped to his mom's body. Tears flourished and fell.

Troy took one step and hugged her. It was almost involuntary – as if the Spirit had prodded him in the middle of the back. She melted into his arms in sobs of sorrow.

"I'm so sorry," she pleaded in a hissing hush. "Your robes… I, my robes, they-"

She hiccupped and sucked in a long breath as though hoping her stalled sentence could take back the atrocities of the day.

"Come on Troy," his dad said in a shaky voice after a few seconds. He nodded at Paul and Susan then disappeared into the blank wall of stone.

Troy concentrated on the wall. He hadn't even put a second's thought into the gate to heaven on the trip. Somehow, he knew God wouldn't have granted him this particular gift. And really, Troy was thankful. If the gate had appeared in all its glory at that moment, he knew it would be forever tarnished with the blood of his mom.

Like his robes were.

His thoughts turned to the Hill and he walked ahead without a backwards glance.

The lonely Commons met his gaze. His dad was already halfway down the empty hallways. Above his head, five of the tiny angel statues bowed their heads as their wings fluttered. Troy trotted to catch up and managed it right when his dad stopped at the doorway leading to the deck looking out over the valley below. Normally, when Troy exited these doors it was to the sight of a green valley cut by a winding river. But now, peaks that usually loomed rocky in the distance were covered in snow. Wind swirled snowflakes into the Commons as his dad kicked the doors open. A valley of ice met them.

"When we were about your age," his dad said slowly with his breath fogging. "Me and your mom… and Kyle, found a grove on the other side of the bend down there." He motioned with his head indicating a glacier-like mass of stone.

Troy wondered how they ever thought they had the right to blast him with lectures of staying safe when they'd broken Passover Hill rules and scaled the sheer cliffs.

He remembered Angela teasing about it during their time last summer, but they'd both dismissed it instantly in gales of nervous laughter. Troy didn't think this was the right time to make a point though so he kept his mouth shut as his dad continued. "We called it God's Grove and came here together often – even after getting all our gifts and becoming fully fledged angels. Your mom made me promise to bury her there if she was ever... taken."

His dad swallowed as all his gifts from God glowed against the swirling snow. "Grab my foot when I take off," his dad called against a gale of wind.

Troy didn't even have time to nod as his dad lifted into the air with his mom carried easily in his arms. He snagged both rising feet and let the Spirit help carry him over the balcony. Below, the world dropped away into a dizzying gulf of air.

They soared around the ledge of snow packed rock. Troy forced his eyes to stay open against the onslaught of freezing cold and terrifying heights. For a full minute, his dad's wings worked against gravity as Troy partially shielded his face from the freezing blast behind his fluttering robes. Then in an alcove of stone, Troy saw a glitch in the mountain. The smallest of deformities in the rugged terrain.

His feet landed in a patch of brown grass protected from the snow by the looming cliff above. The clearing faced east and would be warmed by the rising sun in the spring and summer months. A lone spruce tree rose from the frozen dirt. The slanted mountain formed a cave into its depths forty feet from the sheer ledge. Troy pictured the small meadow green and lush in the warmer times of the year.

"It's not the same right now," his dad reflected Troy's thoughts. "When we found it, it was the darkest green. This spruce tree drew our attention. Your mom loved it here." He walked into the tightening crevice then gently laid Troy's mom at his feet. With a small swipe from his scepter, a boulder jumped to life and rolled from the far wall. In the dark confines of a perfectly rounded cave, three crosses beckoned - each white and pure.

A sob left his dad's mouth. The sound clenched Troy's diaphragm and squeezed every particle of oxygen from his lungs. The cold outside was nothing compared to the creeping chill invading his heart. Troy wanted to let his arms fall over his dad's heaving shoulders. He needed the support to stay his shaking legs. But the memory of the accusation in the steady eyes at the Cathedral froze him in place.

"I always hoped it wasn't true," his dad muttered and his glassy eyes looked at the cross on the left. Dangling from it was the silver necklace Troy remembered seeing at the Cathedral when his dad returned from Jessica Randell's murder. The sparkling white opal in the middle was twinkling merrily in the light intruding from the boulder's removal. At its side were the green amethyst and blue sapphire. "Now, he's lost forever," his dad finished. He knelt and raised Troy's mom then carried her as if she was made of the most delicate glass. As soft as a feather falling on a pillow, he placed her body in front of the middle cross.

For long minutes, they stood silent. Memories washed over Troy.

His times as a toddler holding his mom's tender hand. Her stories about her parents in Maine.

378

He almost chuckled remembering her shrill voice yelling at him for trying to darken his light green angel marks. But mostly, he thought of all the times in the last two years where she'd helped him. Not only saving his life, and his friend's lives, as she'd done numerous times; but also of the good advice she always supplied. The gentle nudge in the right direction.

His dad prayed and cried with his knees buried on the cold stone in the shallow cave. Troy wondered if there was a limitless supply of tears in his own body because he was sure enough had fallen to leave him dry. But they kept building then sliding down his puffy cheeks.

After an hour, Troy's dad stood and swished with his scepter. Rocks from the corner of the cave began piling softly over her body. One by one they closed her from view. Troy watched with a heaving breath as the final sight of his mom's face, under the shroud, was covered by the smooth stones.

He turned with his dad. But his eyes lingered for a heartbeat on the necklace. Kyle's necklace. The man who was responsible for raising the demons that killed his mom. Who kidnapped her and took her to the Angel's Arrow. Who sent her prematurely to heaven - forever stolen from Troy's mortal life. He wanted to spit on the necklace. To drown it in blood and hate.

A whispered promise blared in his head but never made it from his throat. His sword beckoned as the next gift from God. Given for an act of love.

Unbidden, Angela's face floated in front of Troy's vision. He'd have to search for the right time to express his feelings. Tell her how much he cared for her. What sacrifices he'd made for her.

His sword awaited.

But all Troy really wanted - more than anything in the world at that moment - was revenge. Revenge on Kyle Downey. He watched as the boulder rolled back into place at the mouth of the cave. His eyes moved over the mound where his mom was buried and stayed locked on the necklace. For the first time in his life, hatred burned in his heart.

Kyle would pay for the death of his mom.

Watch for Book 3 of the series, *Love's Sweet Sword*, to be released in early 2014. Check our Facebook page or website for details.

www.facebook.com/angelswithoutwingsseries

www.angelswithoutwingsseries.com